Also by Nisha Minhas

Bindis & Brides
Passion & Poppadoms
Sari & Sins
Chapatti or Chips?

Nisha Minhas lives in Milton Keynes with
her partner and two cats. *The Marriage Market*
is her fifth novel.

Visit www.nishaminhas.co.uk

The
Marriage
Market

NISHA MINHAS

POCKET
BOOKS

LONDON • SYDNEY • NEW YORK • TORONTO

First published in Great Britain by Simon & Schuster, 2006
This edition first published by Pocket Books, 2006
An imprint of Simon & Schuster UK
A CBS COMPANY

Copyright © Nisha Minhas, 2006

3 5 7 9 10 8 6 4 2

Simon & Schuster UK Ltd
Africa House
64–78 Kingsway
London WC2B 6AH

www.simonsays.co.uk

Simon & Schuster Australia
Sydney

A CIP catalogue record for this book
is available from the British Library.

ISBN 14165 2256 5
EAN 9781416522560

Typeset in Sabon by M Rules
Printed and bound in Great Britain
by Cox & Wyman Ltd, Reading, Berks

For the love of my life, Dave
∞ OX9!

$$F = \frac{G \times M_1 \times M_2}{r^2}$$

India's Footprints

Why do I miss a place where I've never truly been
or crave acceptance from a people I've hardly ever
*   seen*
or dream of landscapes that still my beating heart
or imagine long lost relatives had never truly part.

Why do I . . .
When will I travel across that dark blue sea
and follow my ancient footprints, and find my inner
*   me*
and touch the earth that grew my world, and
*   handed me my path*
and accept unless I remember India, my life will be
*   but half.*

By Dave Bell Carney

Acknowledgements

A special Thank You to my partner, Dave – If I were to tell you how much you have helped me, I would have another 125,000-word book on my hands. Then again, words cannot describe. You are one in infinity. Where would I be without you? U + I = Delta Cephei. Thank you for each and every day.

My family – With all my love.

Lorella Belli – It's always hard to find the words to thank you, Lorella, for being my agent and friend, for all the extras you do that go way beyond being an agent. You truly are a gem, one of a kind and irreplaceable. Thank you to the power of ten.

Kate Lyall Grant – Thank you for your continuous faith in my writing. For always putting me out of my misery with your supersonic editing. For your constant support, help and advice. Basically for being one hell of an editor. You truly are top-of-the-range. And an extra thank you for coming up with such an excellent title for this book.

Aislinn Casey – Thank you for everything you have

done to help promote my books. It's been a pleasure working with you.

Kari Brownlie – Thank you for coming up with such fantastic Bollywood-look covers. They truly are amazing.

All at Simon & Schuster whom I don't get to meet but I know do such a marvellous job behind the scenes. Thank you so much.

My readers – Thank you for buying my books. Without you, they would be collecting dust somewhere, or pulped and turned into the 10,000th reprint of *The Da Vinci Code*.

Barnardo's Phoenix Project offers confidential support to Asian women, children, and young people experiencing domestic violence. If you would like to contact them, visit their website www.barnardos.org.uk or call 08457 697 697.

Chapter One

Sometime in the not too distant future, instead of relying on a man's honesty regarding the amount of women he has slept with, a woman will be able to check his bedroom history by scanning in the barcode printed on his willy.

Those clever scientists will have developed a way that will link his barcode up to a database where his list of partners, sexual diseases, fetishes and sexual fantasies will be displayed on the computer screen. Only then will the woman be sure that the man she is thinking of sleeping with hasn't lied his way into her knickers. Only then will she be sure her man is not a liar.

Jeena watched as Aaron set the aluminium stepladder down in the hallway before following her into the kitchen. It wasn't so long ago that Aaron had promised her that he would never lie. He wasn't like most men, he'd told her, where lies were an everyday occurrence, he believed that porky pies were a sign of weakness – he was only discussing this very issue on the phone with

1

Kylie Minogue the other day. Jeena had smiled to herself, 'He should be so lucky!' But she liked the novelty value of a man who didn't lie. She just kept her fingers crossed that if he ever saw her elderly gran his first honest words to her weren't, 'Shouldn't you be dead?'

'How long have we got?' Aaron asked, searching for the kettle. 'Time for a quick cuppa?'

Jeena checked the microwave clock, 10.57 a.m., at least one and a half hours before her family were due back from the *gurdwara* – temple. Her mum, dad, eighteen-year-old brother Jugjinder, aka JJ, and gran all paying homage to the Sikh gurus, all praying for happy times. Jeena sighed; her prayers were of a different kind. She just hoped that the gurus would forgive her for being deceitful to her parents this morning. Feigning sickness to get out of chores was bad enough in her father, Papaji's, eyes, but to get out of prayers was a definite no, no.

'I'm one step ahead of you kids,' Papaji had once said with a smug voice. 'I've bought a book on medical conditions and will find it easy to check your ailments.' But the kids were one step ahead of Papaji and used his medical book against him; coming up with fake symptoms for illnesses with only one remedy: rest. It all worked extremely well until Jeena's brother, JJ, attempting to skive a biology test at school, explained to his father that he thought his ovaries were hurting. 'Honestly, Papaji, my stomach has been cramping all night. Damn these ovaries.' Suffice to say JJ took the test that day and failed miserably. And he never felt pain in his ovaries again.

After a cup of tea and two slices of jam on toast, Aaron asked for a quick tour of the house.

'I've never been in an Indian household before,' he said, staring in fascination at all the plastic-covered furniture in the spare living room. 'And this is normal behaviour, is it?' He paused. 'I mean, do all Indian houses have a polythene room?'

'I think so, yes,' Jeena replied, giggling, slightly embarrassed. 'As far as I know.'

She led him upstairs and explained the reasoning behind keeping one room covered in plastic. How, when Indians have visitors, they remove all the polythene and invite the guests to sit in the 'best' room. It's a mark of respect and also a way of showing off the posh furniture. Some families will obviously take things too far when kitting out their best room, leaving so little cash for the rest of the house that the family resorts to sitting on homemade beanbags filled with lentils and eating off wallpaper pasting tables in the 'less than best' living room.

The house was enormous, as were many of the older houses built in Primpton, with high ceilings, sash windows and open fireplaces in most of the rooms. Aaron seemed impressed as Jeena showed him bedroom after bedroom, all fitted and decorated in a modern style, with bright happy colours, expensive wooden furniture and thick, squashy carpet. Subtle reminders that you were in an Indian household eyed you from the pictures of gurus on the walls, and jostled your senses with the fragrant smell of joss sticks. The only things missing, thought Aaron, were the mystical thumping sounds of the *bhangra* drums and some strategically placed bowls of Bombay mix.

'And this,' Jeena pushed open the door, 'is my room.'

And that, drooled Aaron, staring at her huge king-sized bed, is heaven. Without thinking too much about what he was doing, Aaron began to undress. Beds had that effect on him. As did naked women. As did semi-naked women. As did women merely talking about being semi-naked. As did ad infinitum. He was just about to remove his boxers, when Jeena protested.

'We didn't come here for that, Aaron.' She stood admiring his fabulously succulent body with its deeply-carved six-pack. Hours and hours of hard training had honed his physique to the perfection that it was. Only a mad woman would tell this man to put his clothes back on. 'I'm going to count to four thousand and if you haven't put your clothes back on by then, I'm going to be *so* annoyed.' She smiled, entwining the red highlights of her hair around her index finger. 'One . . . Two . . .' The boxer shorts shot past her face. 'Three . . . Four . . .'

He lay back on her bed without a stitch. He'd lost count of the number of dreams he'd had of making love with Jeena in her bedroom. Although, Aaron looked at his surroundings, in his dreams the décor wasn't pink and the walls were certainly not covered with pictures of Bollywood stars. In fact, if he remembered rightly, in his dreams, Jeena's walls were coated with pictures of him. A selection of photos from all angles with the headed caption: AARON.

'Two hundred and eighty-three . . . Two hundred and eighty-four . . .'

Aaron laughed at Jeena while she counted. He had to admit that this was the strangest relationship he'd ever had. Normally his women couldn't wait to introduce him to their parents. It was usually when they mentioned the idea that he dumped them. But this one, Jeena, the beautiful Indian princess, was confusing – why didn't she want her parents to meet him? She was a *Countdown* conundrum if ever there was one: ECSDIVEUT. Six letters, he would love to SEDUCE her. Four letters, she was extremely CUTE. But Aaron could think of a nine-letter word, no conundrum this time, just an adjective to sum her up: SEDUCTIVE.

And you don't just leave seductive things standing around, counting away their lives. Aaron jumped out of bed, grabbed her gently and wrestled her back on to the mattress.

'Can I order a quick Indian, please?' he asked, kissing her neck.

'Old joke,' she replied, feebly pushing him away. 'And haven't we got something to do? The reason why you're here? The reason you brought the stepladder.'

Aaron had clearly forgotten. While Jeena had been counting, he'd been doing a little bit of counting himself. He'd worked out that the parents were due back within the hour, leaving him plenty of time to give Jeena four orgasms. Or at a push five. Six would be just plain greedy. But now the reality of his visit had hit. The loft. The blasted good-for-nothing romance-wrecker loft. Why did lofts always have to get in the way?

Both relaxed their heads on the comfy pillows, staring up at the Bollywood stars mobile. The faces of Aishwarya Rai, Hrithik Roshan, Shah Rukh Khan and Karan Johar, all twirling with the heat rising from below. It was nice to see the Bollywood stars spinning themselves for a change, thought Jeena, for it was a well-known fact that some Bollywood stars presumed the world spun around them. It's even rumoured that written on the doors of the stars' changing rooms, before their names, are the letters: DoyouknowwhoIam?

Jeena turned her head to face Aaron who had his eyes closed – God he was so damn dishy. A bit rough and ready but that was just how she liked her men. It was moments like this where she questioned her freedom. Maji and Papaji had always told her and JJ how lucky they were to have such liberal Indian parents with such modern views on bringing up their children. 'You are more or less free to do what you want,' Maji had often told them. Jeena snuggled up to Aaron's warm body. So why did this moment feel so stolen? Why had she felt it necessary to keep her eight-month relationship with Aaron a secret? Why? Because he was white and her parents' idea of being liberal parents didn't match up to her idea of what liberal parents should be. Oh, sure, she was allowed out (as long as she gave a detailed account of her whereabouts), and sure, she was allowed a job (she really enjoyed working as a columnist and Agony Aunt for an Asian news-paper), and sure, she didn't feel tied down like many Indian girls of her age (her parents had even bought her a car, her pride and joy Clio.) But when it came to pick-ing her own man, the only thing she was sure of was she wasn't allowed to. That decision would be Maji and Papaji's. Aaron began to snore loudly and Jeena prodded him awake. Maybe it was time for him to do what he came here for.

With the stepladder in place below the loft hatch,

Aaron waited for Jeena to return from the kitchen with what she had said was 'essential' for the mission. She arrived with a torch and a pair of yellow Marigolds.

'Here,' she said, handing him the items. 'Wear the gloves. I'm not having you touch me afterwards if your hands have been infected with fibreglass. Just the thought of it is making me itchy.'

Two rungs up and Aaron spoke, 'If I don't return within ten minutes, hide the ladder and set fire to the house. The mission has failed. Understood Number Two?'

'Just hurry up and bring it down.' She slapped his bottom. 'Chop chop.'

Aaron heaved himself into the loft and kneeled on a plank of wood. He shone the torch from left to right, breathing in the musty damp, impressed at how uncluttered the huge attic was. Almost a whole floor of wasted space with just the odd box here and there and a few rolls of old carpet. He focused the beam on the water-tank and with deliberate, tentative move-ments, slowly edged himself towards it, careful to spread his weight on the flimsy boards that were pre-tending to be a floor. Jeena's directions were clear: pull up the small square of blue carpet directly in front of the tank and underneath the loft insulation he would find the books hidden in a dustbin bag. Remove one book and return the carpet and insulation exactly how he found it.

It's amazing, thought Aaron, just a few feet away from his destination, amazing what lengths a man will go to to feed his sordid mind. It had been about a month ago, when playing a game of truth or dare, Jeena had confessed to having had a book published. Aaron had appeared to be impressed. 'An erotic book,' she had stated. Aaron had appeared to be impressed and now sporting a hard-on. His demands over the next four weeks were simple and very repetitive: when can I read it? When can I read it? When can I read it? Aaron pulled back the square of carpet, joy spreading across his face. He couldn't wait to find out exactly how filthy Jeena's imagination was. He shifted aside the fibreglass and lifted out the black bin bag. Oh please let her mind be as depraved as mine, Aaron prayed. PLEASE!

Aaron held the novel in his hands and a proud lump formed in his throat: my lover wrote this. A blonde slutty-looking woman in suspenders and a black red-laced corset straddled a Harley Davidson motorbike. The title of the book was *Naked Riders* by Daniella Quinn. Breaking his promise to Jeena, Aaron opened the book to page one and excitedly read a few lines.

My name is Nikita and I have slept my way through the Hells Angel clan of the north. It is time to ride to my next town to feast on more men. But first I must say goodbye to the head of the Hells Angels Donny the Death Machine McDoogle. My passion for him is written in the tattoo on my round, juicy buttocks . . .

Aaron's laughter echoed in the loft, this was priceless. Carefully restoring the carpet and insulation to how he'd found it, Aaron began to crawl back towards the loft hatch.

After swearing on the lives of a hundred people, Aaron convinced Jeena that he hadn't taken a sneaky read of her book while up in the attic. 'I don't lie, Jeena, it goes against all I live for, but if you don't mind could we skip page one when we read it?' A thump landed on his arm. 'My beautiful, Nikita.'

The stepladder was put back in the boot of Aaron's spanking new red BMW Sport and he returned to the kitchen for a quick goodbye cuddle. Which soon turned into a quick goodbye snog. Which, if Aaron had had his way, would have turned into a quick goodbye shag on the kitchen table.

'I am not having sex with you on the same surface as the one my mother makes *chapattis* on. NO!'

'What about the living room?' he panted, unclipping her lacy bra. 'I'll even do it in the polythene room if you like; at least there I don't have to worry about any spillage.'

'I am not having sex with you in either of the living rooms, where paintings of Guru Nanak look down upon me. NO!' *Spillage?* she thought. *God, he really does believe his own hype.*

Aaron dropped his jeans to the floor. 'I suppose we're left with the bedroom then?'

One minute later the two of them were rolling about naked on Jeena's bed. The Bollywood mobile above them spinning wildly. The noise of their passion verging on animalistic. The lust in their eyes out-of-control.

'Don't move a muscle,' Aaron ordered, hopping out of the bed and rushing out of the room. Ten seconds later he was back. This time wearing a bright yellow turban on his head which, coincidentally, matched the bright yellow condom on his willy. 'I'm Ali Baba and you are my Princess of Persia,' Aaron said, balancing on a pretend magic carpet. 'Would you like to rub my magic lamp?'

Jeena's shrieks of laughter only encouraged him more. She loved it when their romantic endeavours were different. Theme sex was becoming an important part of their bedroom antics of late. Julius Caesar and Cleopatra. Tarzan and Jane. Homer and Marge Simpson. Even Ann Widdecombe and . . . Aaron had told Jeena she was on her own with this one, there was no way he was shagging Ann Widdecombe, role play or not. Unless he played David Blunkett – then it didn't matter who he shagged.

He jumped on the duvet and stared into Jeena's dark-brown eyes, almost the colour of soy sauce, trying to raid her mind for what position she wanted. Before he had time to wonder too long, she'd pushed him over and wriggled herself on top. They both rocked to and fro, enjoying each moment, lost within their own cocoon of pleasure. Aaron smiled at Jeena, while adjusting his turban. There was nothing more personal than when two people were making love.

Until the door opens and a set of four Indian faces stare in with their jaws on the floor.

'Deeper, Aaron, harder!' Jeena yelled. 'Why have you stopped?'

Aaron directed his piercing blue eyes to Jeena's father who appeared to be in a state of shock. 'This is not what it looks like, Mr Gill.' He winced, trying to think of a reasonable excuse as to why it might 'appear' that he was rogering his daughter (apart from the obvious 'we were playing hide the *mooli*'). Staring into eyes which were rapidly losing patience, Aaron blurted out, 'Actually, I'm sorry, I don't want to insult your intelligence. It's *exactly* what it looks like. You don't need to make an appointment with Specsavers.' He tried a weak placating smile. 'And please tell your wife that she doesn't have to cry.'

With her body so hot with embarrassment she was likely to spontaneously combust, and her mind so filled with shame she was likely to burst into tears, Jeena stayed facing Aaron. She could feel the eyes of her family all glaring into her naked back. For some reason the yellow turban didn't seem so funny anymore. From where her parents were standing it might appear that the two of them were making a mockery of the Sikh headgear. When in actual fact it was just a private joke. Which at the moment didn't seem so hilarious and, more importantly, didn't seem so private. The real joke, if there was a joke, was on Aaron and Jeena. And the punch line was this: they were fucked (in both senses of the word). The uncontrollable sobbing of Jeena's mother was getting louder and louder.

'I want you out of my house,' Papaji shouted at Aaron, then turned his attention to his daughter. 'And I want you bathed and dressed and downstairs in half an hour. And tell your man to take off my turban. It's an insult.'

With that comment the four heads at the door disappeared and walked down the stairs as though in mourning. Five minutes ago they had pulled up onto their drive only to find a gleaming red BMW parked in front of Jeena's Clio. Strange. In the house they found items of clothing scattered on the stairs. Very strange. And upstairs, coming from inside Jeena's bedroom, were painful-sounding noises. Strangest of all!

'Do you want me to hang around and smooth this over with your dad?' Aaron asked, tugging on his T-shirt.

Jeena was tearful. 'You don't understand at all, do you? Indian girls don't have sex before wedlock. They definitely don't have sex with white men. Smooth it over? You'll be lucky if he doesn't shoot you.'

'Look, I'll go downstairs and speak to him man-to-man. I'll tell him that . . .'

She interrupted, 'What? You'll tell him that you love me? Is that what you'd say? Or will you tell the truth and explain to him I'm just one of an endless list of women who you shag whenever it takes your fancy?' Jeena sat on the mattress, tucked her face in her hands and began to cry heavily. 'I knew I would regret ever meeting you. I was warned against it by so many people. Even your own friends told me to steer clear. "Don't let him sweet talk you," they all said. "Don't let him within a hundred yards of your bed." "You'll never be his 'only' girl. Men like Aaron don't have 'only' girls."' She sniffed. 'The thing is, I can see what is bad about you but for some reason I can't keep away. What does that make me? A slut! A slut who shares you with God knows how many women. It makes me feel dirty. It makes me feel sick.'

Aaron placed his arm around her. 'I promise you that we'll sort this one out. What beer does your dad drink?'

She looked into his eyes. 'Just go, Aaron, before I really lose it with you.'

'I'll put him down for Kingfisher then.' He kissed her

on the cheek and stood up. 'I'll call you in the next few days. Try not to worry. These things happen all the time.'

As he closed the door behind him she muttered, 'Not to Indian girls they don't. *Definitely* not to Indian girls.'

Chapter Two

Pulling away from Jeena's house, Aaron noticed Jeena's gran at the window staring menacingly at him. And Aaron sympathized wholly. She probably felt as disgusted at seeing a young couple having sex as he would be if he saw an old couple at it. She had every right to be holding that knife up to the window and waving it in a threatening manner, every right indeed.

Slipping the gear into fifth, Aaron took the dual-carriageway which would take him to his home on the outskirts of Primpton. Primpton, just twenty-five minutes north of Coventry in the Midlands, was much like any large town, with its fair share of pubs, clubs, shops and leisure activities. To a southerner the Primpton accent sounded northern. To a northerner, the accent sounded southern. And to people who lived in Primpton, they thought they didn't have an accent at all, it was all the other people who spoke funny.

A huge picnic park took centre stage in the middle of town, with its wealth of trees, greens and bridle paths. The pride and joy of the park was the enormous Lake

Charlotte, which, rumour has it, was formed from the tears of the men whose heart was broken by Charlotte many centuries ago.

Aaron popped in a CD, The Flaming Lips, and drummed his fingers on the steering wheel to 'Yoshimi Battles the Pink Robots' while waiting at a set of traffic lights. He loved his town Primpton, and even though he'd only been living here for six years, he owed it everything. He owed it his prosperous business, the Paper Lantern Martial Arts Centre, that he'd been running since his return from Japan six years before. He owed it the wonderful converted factory which he lived in. He owed it the beautiful women whom he shagged here. But most of all he owed it his virtually worry-free peace-of-mind. Which, at only twenty-eight years of age, was quite a blessing. One of his martial arts instructors in Japan, his *sensei*, had once told him that if you have peace of mind before you are thirty then either you are kind and care a lot, or, you're not so kind and couldn't give a shit. 'Or I could be both, *Sensei*,' Aaron had joked to the ancient leather-faced teacher. 'I could care a lot about myself and I could be very kind to myself but I could also not give a shit about anyone else.' He was forced to do another thousand sit-ups while *Sensei* threw medicine balls at his stomach. The moral was: never joke with someone who could beat the living crap out of you – even if they are nearly eighty-five years old.

And what was the moral or lesson of today's little escapade? wondered Aaron. Maybe learn how to be a contortionist then next time a girlfriend's parents storm the bedroom, one could hide in the bedside drawers.

As long as the drawers weren't full of knickers and tampons, Aaron thought laughing to himself, imagine getting found hiding amongst Jeena's panties and bits. How embarrassing.

He rewound his mind back to Jeena's mum, dad, gran and brother all watching from the doorway. PEEPSHOW at no. 56. It was only the sound of Jeena's mother's tears that had prevented him from trying to lighten the situation with, 'Please, *please,* no flash photography, it destroys my rhythm.' And, selfish as it sounds, he was quite happy in the knowledge that if anything was thrown his way by a heckling spectator then he had the turban as protection. Hardly something he would consider teaching in his martial arts classes, The Turban Defence, but not to be sniffed at either.

He remembered the heavy weight of guilt pressing down on him as he saw the sadness in Jeena's mum's face. The only thing that had stopped him from jumping out of bed and giving her a cuddle was that her daughter was still straddling him. Instead, just before leaving, after collecting his jeans from the kitchen table, he'd popped his head around the door of the living room and casually said to Jeena's mum the words that always kept the mother on side, 'You look young enough to be Jeena's sister. Are you sure you're not her twin?' He doubted that Jeena's father had meant to lob the fire poker at him like that. But not one to outstay his welcome, he'd legged it down the hall, shouted 'Good luck' to Jeena up the stairs, and then charged out of the front door.

Aaron drove into the car park beside his home and

17

martial arts centre. The 6000-foot ground floor was home to the Paper Lantern Martial Arts Centre and the second floor, another 6000 feet of it was home to Aaron's home. The converted old cotton mill backed onto the River Wes, which was useful when Aaron had had the building gutted, as he could send the rubbish by old-fashioned barge boat down river instead of paying for expensive skips. Situated in the old industrial area of town, it used to be a post-code which house buyers would shy away from. But since many of the factories had now closed down and turned their warehouses into expensive penthouse suites, the area was now in demand. Having his own business was a dream come true for Aaron, made even sweeter because no one had ever thought he'd pull it off.

He pressed the fob on his key ring and watched, with his usual pleasure, as the double doors to his garage smoothly opened. A surfboard, a small dinghy and a canoe sat to one side in a state of dehydration. Buying the boats had seemed a good idea at the time; he'd visualized taking out a stunning babe on the water, paddling to a romantic location and seducing her on the banks of the Wes. As it happened, the last time he'd taken out the dinghy, he was nearly mowed down by a speedboat. It wouldn't have mattered so much but there was only one life jacket on board, and, without thinking, his selfish side made a grab for it, leaving poor stunning babe with only one solution: to swim for her life.

After climbing the outside metal stairs up to his abode, Aaron keyed in the alarm code and entered. The huge, open-plan space was awash with light from the multitude of windows. Wooden flooring, white walls, white sofas and chairs, and a luxury fitted chrome kitchen. Energy flowed through all spaces, with musical wind chimes tinkling, an aquarium bubbling and various Japanese artefacts giving off a Zen-like feel to the place. Amongst the plain whites and wooden floor there was the splash of red, which to followers of Feng Shui was a very auspicious colour. Red cushions, red blinds and red rugs with tiny Japanese symbols. And on the walls there hung dynamic pictures of *samurai*, *ninja* and other warrior fighters.

Learning about the way of the warrior meant learning about the spiritual side of a warrior's mind. Keen to exploit any advantage that he'd garnered from his Japanese counterparts, Aaron had introduced Feng Shui into his home. Anyone who happened to step foot in his place, always commented on the mystical aura that surrounded it. From the open-plan living area to the three bedrooms and bathroom area, it was hard to feel too downcast in a house like this.

However, it was pretty easy to feel lonely. He'd once discussed loneliness with himself before and he'd got into a bitter argument. But it was either having a place to himself or sharing a place with someone. And sharing sounded too much like commitment to his ears. Having to think not just about yourself but about your partner. None of this coming home when you feel like it, sleeping with who you feel like, or even watching what you want on TV when you feel like it. He wondered about the relationship he shared with Jeena. Her demands were simple, she never stayed over, never insisted he phone every day, and not once had she refused to give him a blow job. From a pair of short-sighted eyes one might consider the relationship to be perfect. But, deeper down, with clearer vision, after listening to the various hints that Jeena gave out, one might come to the conclusion that she was hiding something. That maybe, when all was said and done, what Jeena really wanted from Aaron was some sort of commitment.

He had two words for that; NO and WAY. After the watershed it might sound a little different. More like NO FUCKING WAY. At the moment his relationships were all fun. Nothing too heavy. Nothing too like listening to a woman explain how she can't wait for the day she does the school run. Just fun, sex, and relationship lawlessness. In fact, just normal behaviour for the modern man of the new millennium where men didn't settle down until they were in their thirties. Typically, as Aaron and his mates were approaching their thirties, they were thinking about changing the settling down period to their forties.

Aaron pondered further. Today things had become more serious with Jeena, and, like pulling the wrong straw in a game of Ker-plunk, all Aaron's thoughts had dropped down together like marbles. Things were clear now: Jeena was a nice girl, extremely pretty, stunning body, full of life and he was sure she would find someone else, but it was nigh time she was dumped.

He brewed himself a Gunpowder tea and sat in his office area which looked down upon the River Wes. The June sunshine reflected off the choppy water adding more colour to an already beautiful scene. It was dead easy to work with a view like this. Aaron tapped into his business files on the computer and surveyed his activities for the coming week. Eight jujitsu classes as usual, Mondays to Thursdays twice nightly. He operated a strict code of practice when it came to cancellations. Three strikes and you were out, unless there were extreme circumstances (and, as one of Jeena's friends, Kitty, soon found out, washing her hair was not considered an extreme circumstance). There was a huge list of people eager to join his establishment and he didn't have time for slackers. Not surprisingly there were no cancellations this week. With just the eight classes a week, it seemed a waste of space to have his business empty on days without a jujitsu session, so Aaron hired out the floor space on Fridays and Saturdays to a karate club and for the remainder of the time he would take one-on-one classes for advanced students.

With money coming in left, right and centre, it had been a long time since Aaron had worried about bills. Which left his mind with plenty of room to worry about other things. Silly things. Almost pointless things. Like: if Ronald McDonald had a fight with the KFC Colonel, who would win? Or if a black belt kebab took on a sumo chicken burger, who would fare the best? Even a wrestling match between ketchup and mayo kept him up half a night. It was difficult sometimes for Aaron to think about anything else but fighting.

Down on the River Wes, a small, neglected boat called *Medusa's Head*, not that much more modern in design than the *Kon-Tiki*, chugged past, with the captain waving up to Aaron like he normally did on a Sunday. Aaron was sure that one day he would hear the

21

disastrous news that *Medusa's Head* had been capsized by a swan or a batch of frogspawn. He waved back and the boat chugged from view.

Next up were a few diet plans for overweight pupils. It was normally a matter of checking over their day-to-day food consumption and removing just a few items. Aaron used to call it 'The Vowel Diet' and it meant discarding any items of food with a vowel in it. Until the clever bastards worked out that KFC and XXXX (lager) had no vowels. Aaron looked over the details of his latest project. Mr Sinclair, *Weight*: twenty-two stone, *Idol*: Bruce Lee. Surprise, surprise, thought Aaron, smiling, Mr Sinclair probably shat bigger things than Bruce Lee, but he was a paying customer and Aaron liked nothing more than a good challenge. Aaron was just about to calculate how many millions of calories Mr Sinclair would have to drop from his diet to look good in a pair of Speedos when his mind was thrust backwards to Jeena's house.

A vision of Jeena popped into his mind. Her face full of trauma when they were caught doing the dirty by her family. Ever since leaving her house earlier today, this vision, like a screen saver, kept returning. Aaron shoved Mr Sinclair's file to one side, leant back in his cushioned swivel chair, ran his fingers through his dark-brown hair – the colour of Kellogg's Bran Flakes and the designer messed-up look of Shredded Wheat (which took two hours of grooming to achieve) – and asked himself, was dumping Jeena really what he wanted to do? Aaron cast his brain back eight months. From the beginning he'd been crystal clear about how he conducted his life. He'd explained to Jeena that he slept around, that one woman was never enough and that he would never, ever settle down. Honest, clean sentences that sounded pretty grimy when he said them. But Jeena responded in kind. She wanted nothing more than a bit of fun, even to be one of his many women, to keep the relationship simple. Not once, in the beginning, did Jeena hint that she wanted anything more than a good time.

Aaron stood up and walked out to the living area. Jeena had been to his place on many occasions, checking out every nook and cranny, passing comment on the books he read, the music he listened to and the DVDs he watched. 'Even though we have fantastic sex, Aaron, I still feel it is my duty as a friend to mention that this apartment feels like it needs a good woman: it's too boyish. And before you say it, I'm not hinting that the good woman should be me.' But was she? Aaron now wondered. Had Jeena's heart been set on the two of them as one all along? Her comments today, after they were caught, appeared to corroborate this. In her anger her mask had fallen off. Her true feelings had shown their face. 'I can see what is bad about you but for some reason I can't keep away.' That didn't sound like a woman who only wanted fun in a relationship. 'What does that make me? A slut! A slut who shares you with god knows how many women. It makes me feel dirty. It makes me feel sick.' Stark, honest, venomous words which seemed to betray Jeena's façade. Most women would have left a man who made her feel so terrible about herself, who made her feel like a prime slut. Friend or no friend. Most women would have run a mile.

A crease worthy of Botox jumped onto Aaron's forehead. And what was all that gibberish about Indian girls not having sex before wedlock? Especially not with a white man. She'd never mentioned that one before when her legs had been up in the air and she was gasping for air. Christ, if he had known that he would have been insulting an entire nation of Indian people by having sex with one of their women out of wedlock then he would have thought twice about mounting her. Aaron checked that idea over for a minute. Actually, he realized, that was a lie. The fact that one billion people would have been in uproar would have turned him on even more.

But the problem remained. It was obvious, now that the truth of Jeena's feelings were out in the open, that the relationship between them would become way too heavy. Demands which he wouldn't be able to live up to would creep into his life. Expectations would weigh him down. He would become a mere shadow of himself.

'No way,' Aaron said, checking his watch. 'It's before the watershed but what the heck. NO FUCKING WAY! I'm far too young to be bogged down with a deep relationship.'

Before he had time to gather his thoughts, Aaron was flicking through *Yellow Pages* for florists. He never knew how much to spend on a 'dumping' bouquet. Weddings normally cost him £100.00. Funerals £200.00. Birthdays £50.00. Births £25.00. And for the 'sorry I broke your ribs in my jujitsu class', he'd normally grab a few weeds down by the river and drop them off at the hospital in visiting hours.

It took Aaron ten patient minutes on the phone, with no one picking up from any of the florist shops, to remember that it was still Sunday. The day of rest for some and for others, he sighed, the day of family get-togethers. Aaron walked to his bedroom and flopped on the gigantic bed. It had been many-a-year since he'd had a true 'family get-together'. And the only one he could envisage in the foreseeable future was when he died. Where he would meet up with his parents in heaven.

When Aaron was only eight years old, his mum and dad had been killed in a car accident. He could remember, as if it were yesterday, when the policewoman came to his school in Northampton and plucked him out of assembly to tell him the devastating news. He wondered why a policewoman would be crying. He wondered why she gave him such a tight hug. And then he wondered no more as, with a quivering mouth, she softly broke the news. His mum and dad were dead and Jesus was looking after them now. School was finished for the day and Aaron was driven to stay with his gran, his father's mother, his only surviving relative. For the next eleven years he lived with his loving grandmother in Northampton until the day came for him to up sticks and head to Japan for three years under the tuition of a top martial arts school for the gifted. The Paper Lantern became his home and family for the next three years, presenting him with his 8th-dan belt, the *hachidan*, for jujitsu on his departure.

In tribute to his adopted family in Japan, Aaron named his own martial arts school after it. He sent photos of his school to his *sensei* who replied in a short letter, written in Japanese, explaining how seeing the photos had been the proudest moment of his life. The letter was framed and placed above Aaron's bed, giving him the most positive of feelings every time he awoke.

But getting to sleep was sometimes impossible. This was where his peace of mind became noisy. Wondering what if, what if, what if. Thoughts of his parents and his childhood would sometimes sneak around his mind, whispering questions he couldn't answer, opening his wounds deeper. His mother was always a forward thinker, Gran had often mentioned, forever planning ahead. And it came as no surprise to anyone who knew her that even at the young age of thirty-three she had kept a will. After the funeral, when things had calmed down a little, Gran had called Aaron down from his new bedroom in her house and presented him with a package which his mother had left for him. The instructions printed on it were clear: *Dear my beautiful boy, you must only open this when you are ready. Love Mummy x*.

Aaron jumped off the bed and swung back the doors to his fitted wardrobe. Standing at the bottom was a big, heavy, fire-proof safe. Aaron keyed in the electronic numbers on the pad and heaved back the door. Amongst his martial arts medals and a briefcase filled with photographs, a bundle of money and a velvet box encasing his parents' jewellery, there sat the package his mother had left. For nearly twenty years the parcel from his mum had waited to be opened. Twenty long years. As usual, Aaron took out the wrapped bundle, placed it on his bed and stared at it for the next few minutes. There was no power on earth right now which would give him the courage to open it. He knew that as soon as he'd ripped it open, then the last of his mother's spirit would die. Any words in there were still alive as far as Aaron was concerned, until he read them. Any gifts were alive with the last touch from his mother until he touched them. Any sight was still alive until he'd seen it. There was no way that he was ready to finally say goodbye to his mum. He replaced the parcel back in the safe, closed the metal door and lay back on his bed.

Would he ever be brave enough to see what was inside?

Chapter Three

What was the point of women keeping their handbags full of make-up when really what they needed most was a rock? Then, when things got too embarrassing, they could crawl under it. And if that didn't solve the problem, they could just bash themselves over the head with it.

Up until the point of being caught having sexual intercourse by her family, the most embarrassing moment in Jeena's life had been the day she was spotted by her aunt, at the age of ten, eating a Big Mac outside McDonald's. 'Since when did Sikhs eat beef?' her aunt had lectured, snatching the burger and tossing it in the bin. Jeena's reply, 'Since when did aunts have moustaches?' did not go down too well. Now Jeena was at ground zero when it came to embarrassment and her shame was somewhere in the rubble.

Washed, dried and dressed in a pink and white Pineapple tracksuit, Jeena descended the thirteen stairs, took a huge nervous gulp of oxygen then walked into the living room. A melancholy atmosphere stifled the air; the choking presence of bad news awaited. Papaji pointed to a sofa chair for his daughter to sit, and told JJ to leave the room while they discussed what to do with this traitor of the Indian way. Maji and Nanaji sat with their eyes glued to the floor. Two generations of women who couldn't work out why the next generation was finding it so difficult to follow in their footsteps. The room was uncomfortably quiet until Papaji finally spoke in Punjabi.

'We sacrificed everything to come to this country, Jeena, and our biggest fear has always been that one day we would regret it.' Papaji's voice was calm and cold. 'Alas, I think that day has now come. You have failed us and shamed us.'

Jeena lowered her head. This very same room with its pictures of Sikh gurus, photos of family occasions, Indian artefacts and Bollywood DVDs had been the venue of many father speeches. The proud day when Jeena had graduated from the University of Birmingham; the momentous occasion when Papaji had opened his own accountancy firm, Gills & Bills; the day when JJ was born; and even the time when Papaji had bought his first Mercedes. All happy events worth celebrating. Not once had Jeena, or any of the family for that matter, thought a day would come when Papaji would be making a speech about his only daughter sticking a knife in the family's heart. Jeena hated herself right now. And she wouldn't have blamed her family for hating her either.

Maji stared at her daughter, shaking her head in disgust. 'We were very lenient on you. We gave you much more freedom than most Indian parents would have allowed. These days it's very hard to know how much leeway to allow. We hear stories all the time of girls running away from home because the parents are too strict.' Maji looked across to her husband then back to Jeena. 'Many people told us to marry you off quickly and by doing so you would not stray from the Indian path. Your father and I argued that by giving our children freedom, you would repay us with loyalty.' Sadness swept across her face. 'Not in this case, Jeena, you have repaid us with treachery.' And she began to sob into a tissue.

Jeena felt the clammy hands of guilt molesting her entire body. Maji was right: they had given her a huge amount of freedom. Even down to letting her dye her black shoulder-length hair with red streaks. And she knew of Asian girls who didn't even know what it felt like to go out without a chaperone. Nightclubs, pubs and bars were pure fantasy for most Indian girls. But Jeena's parents would permit her these freedoms on one condition: she didn't talk to men. It was a trust thing – and that was something Jeena might never have with her parents again.

With the slow delivery of a police inspector Papaji worked his way through a list of embarrassing questions. When did she lose her virginity? Who did she lose it to? How many men had she slept with? How long had this latest relationship been going on? Why was he wearing Papaji's turban? And on and on and . . .

In a shaky voice, Jeena explained that Aaron was the only man she'd had a relationship with END OF STORY. Now was not the time to go into Pete, Andy, Simon and Jeff or the university flings, not to mention the school days which were pretty raunchy too. Maji and Papaji didn't need to know about the shopping sprees to Soho with her best friends, Kitty and Flora. Or the sex-toy parties she attended. They'd probably choke if they knew that she'd run up a five-hundred pound debt with Ann Summers. And that's not even mentioning the twenty-five pounds she'd spent on batteries. It was a trust thing.

Jeena coughed. 'And the reason he was wearing the turban,' she continued, 'is simply because,' and she whispered the next bit, 'he had cold ears.'

Papaji appeared nonplussed at Jeena's explanation. 'So, who is he? This man who gets cold ears in the middle of summer. Is he married? Has he got children?'

'HA!' she said without thinking. *As if* Aaron would ever be married. 'Erm, I mean no, he is single and childless. He loves me.' *HA!* she thought without saying. *As if Aaron would ever love anyone.* 'And I love him.'

Maji eyed Papaji who eyed Nanaji who remained staring at her slippers. Love, in the way Jeena had meant it, was a word that didn't sit too well in an Indian household. They saw it as a parasite feeding off Respect, Honour and Trust. Interfering in true family values. More a Western word than Eastern. Love meant lust; it meant sex at all costs. Families split because of love. Unwanted babies were born because of love. Sexual diseases were transmitted because of love. Love was an own goal as far as Indian families were concerned. It was a sure-fire way of being relegated to the bottom of life's premiership.

'It's just sex, Jeena, nothing more,' Papaji stated. 'Ask yourself whether he would still be hanging around if you didn't give him what he wanted.' He sighed. 'What all white men want.'

Papaji was probably right, she decided, Aaron only wanted her for bonks. With a slim size ten figure and illegally long legs, most women would have been happy with that. But God had gone further with Jeena, adding an enormous bust, gorgeous face and annoyingly slim hips into the bargain. Aaron's first words to her were, 'Are you from the future?' But she wasn't perfect. Oh, no, not by a long shot. If one looked really close one could spot a tiny, tiny almost insignificant mole just beside her left eyebrow. No wonder Aaron enjoyed her company in the bedroom. No wonder Papaji knew what he was talking about with men and their wanton ways.

Jeena viewed her father. A towering man with broad shoulders. Relatives called him GodSikhy because he was so huge. He always looked immaculately smart with his suit and turban and his thick beard finished off the article. A true Sikh. It was at times like this that Jeena wished she had grown a matching beard behind which she could hide her embarrassed face: no one wants to listen to their dad discuss sex – especially an Indian dad. Jeena dropped her eyes to the floor.

'We're not prepared to let you wreck your life with this man, Jeena.' Papaji stood up and began to pace the room, continuing the lecture, but this time in English. 'You've made your bed and now you will lie in it.'

Bed of nails, thought Jeena. 'I know. Sorry, Papaji, I'm truly sorry.'

Nanaji made a huffing noise, then went back to playing dead.

'And so,' Papaji carried on, 'and so, you must respect our wishes and never see this man again. And because we can no longer trust you, we have no option but to make arrangements for your wedding as soon as possible. It's about time we started looking for a husband anyway; you're twenty-seven, time's running out.' Papaji stopped by a wooden cabinet and picked up Jeena's graduation photo. 'We had such high dreams for you, Jeena.' He placed the frame back carefully. 'My only dream now is that I can find a man who is still willing to marry you even though you have already lost your virginity to a white man. No one in *this* country will want to marry you, which leaves the only other option. You must marry a man from India.'

'India?'

'India! You will live with him in India. There will be no temptation from white men there.'

Jeena felt as though every cell in her body had picked up a banner, 'Say No To Arranged Marriages' and was marching through her veins. INDIA! The country she used to speak of with pride had suddenly turned into the place of her worst nightmare. She'd known all along that an arranged marriage was on the cards – she had held out little hope that Aaron would save her from one – it was expected, it was almost foretold. It was and is the Indian way. But she'd presumed the Indian man would be like her, a British-born Asian, someone who spoke English, someone with things in common with her.

She'd heard horrific stories of women from Britain marrying men from India. It's so hard to check on the legitimacy of a man's criteria when he lives ten thousand miles away. Women had travelled to India to find the man only wanted a slave, or a passport into Britain. She'd heard tales of men who had lied and were already married. Even men who just wanted to make money from a good dowry. Everything she'd heard so far about marrying a man from India had been negative. It was very hard to be a Brian here and always look on the bright side of life.

Tears began to fall down Jeena's cheeks. She'd never thought of her parents as muggers before, but now they had just mugged her of her life. She would complete the full circle of her family. Her parents had begun their life in India and were planning on finishing it in England while she had begun her life in England and she would be finishing it in India. It was time to up the volume on her crying.

'What about my job? My friends?' she sobbed. 'What about seeing you lot? If you send me to India I'll hardly see you all again.'

Maji couldn't hold it together and joined in the sobs. Even Papaji's eyes watered over. But Nanaji, she just stared at her slippers. Rooms did not get much sadder than this. (Apart from deaths in the family). (And when the mango pickle jar is empty).

While Jeena cried her way through a box of tissues, Papaji went on to explain how this would all work. Tomorrow, Monday morning, she would go into her office and hand in her month's notice. Then she would work out the month. No contact with Aaron. Arrangements would be made with Papaji's elder brother, Gurjinder, in New Delhi to begin looking for a potential man for Jeena. Next month the whole family would travel to India where Jeena would be married off to the best man his brother could find. No buts.

Her life would begin anew out there.

'And if I decide not to go,' Jeena said, knowing what comment Papaji would respond with. 'What then?'

'Then you are no longer my daughter and you will never see any of us again.' He knelt down in front of Jeena and handed her another tissue. 'This is all your own fault, Jeena, no one but yourself is to blame here, you know that, don't you?'

She looked into his distraught face and knew he was right. 'Please don't send me to India, Papaji, I promise I will never shame you again.'

He shook his head. 'It's too late.'

Jeena pleaded with her eyes to her mother. 'Please, Maji, say something, I'm your daughter.'

But Maji just turned away.

Chapter Four

After falling out of bed at five a.m., a typical weekday morning for Aaron would involve plenty of noise. First he would switch on his cinema-sized TV to *News 24* at full volume. Next he would turn his radio on, full volume. Then, he would load his cassette tape titled: *Industrial Drill Noise*, full volume. Finally his CD player would be blasted with Metallica at full volume. He was now ready to meditate.

It was 5.15 a.m., Monday morning, and Aaron was in a state of peaceful oblivion meditating on his meditation mat in front of his giant, big-bellied, dimple-cheeked Buddha in the living area. His *sensei* had helped teach him the art of shutting out noise, a technique which came in quite handy at a Westlife concert, and he loved to push his abilities to the limit by adding decibels of different varieties. Just the other day he had managed to slip into his trance with the sound of babies crying and jumbo jets taking off. The only sound so far which had thwarted his meditation attempts had been the recording of Ian Duncan Smith's

Conservative party speech a few years back when IDS had famously said, 'The quiet man is turning up the volume'. Aaron had found it piss-pants laughable (along with most of the nation).

Half an hour later, and with a cleaner, freer mind, Aaron threw on his shorts, T-shirt and trainers, collected his iPod, then left his apartment for a refreshing seven mile jog along the River Wes. As if by magic other joggers would appear from nowhere en route, boasting about their latest job promotion, bragging about their new wage increase, almost challenging Aaron to race them. Their jogging get-up would be the latest fashion, their jogging shorts would be the tightest their circulation could handle and the sock they put down their pants would be the biggest that money could buy. The only time that Aaron could bring himself to talk to them was when he could see dog shit up ahead. Just at the last moment he would point to the sky and say, 'Look at that lovely weather, hey' and then listen to the satisfying sound of squelch as their top-of-the-range Air Nike trainers hit the bottom-of-the-range stinky dog turd.

After the jog, next up was stomach exercises. Crunches, leg raises, sit-ups and side bends. A strenuous abdominal programme which gave new meaning to the word, 'burn'. Finally it was time for a relaxing shower. Relaxing? Try standing under an ice-cold shower for fifteen minutes until the skin turned blue and the nerves went numb. Shivering like a newly-born penguin, Aaron towelled himself down with a fluffy blue towel.

'I'm fucked,' Aaron said, talking to his fish as he ate

his breakfast. A bath-sized aquarium stood in the southeast corner of his living space – the wealth area – and imperative to the Feng Shui rules was that the fish tank must contain nine goldfish. One of the nine fish must be a black goldfish. This fish is supposed to absorb any bad luck. Aaron flicked the glass and eyed the black fish named Tyson, which was obviously absorbing something other than just bad luck right now. 'You're getting fat, Tysee. You'll get a double chin if you're not careful. You should take a leaf out of my book and keep a strict diet.'

Diets were an intrinsic part of martial arts. High protein, medium carbohydrates, low fats were the rules which governed most top fighters. A fit fighter was rarely a fat fighter. Anyone who knew Aaron would have seen his attention to what entered his mouth. Chicken breasts, tuna steaks, lots of vegetables, plenty of water and at least four of his famous smoothy protein shakes each and every day.

Wearing black shorts and a red T-shirt with the words SILVER BULLET, Aaron flopped onto the monster white suede sofa with a protein smoothy, pleased in the knowledge that he still had most of the day to himself before his first jujitsu class at six p.m. was due. Down in the Paper Lantern's reception checking through the e-mails was Mary. Mary was middle-aged, extremely neat and tidy, and a real bonus for Aaron's business. She worked four evenings a week and a couple of hours in the mornings while the cleaner was cleaning. Nothing was too much trouble for her, whether it be dealing with the clerical side of things or the personal side. Aaron had often told her that if she were only forty years younger then he would marry her himself. Without her he was sure he would have no free time.

And his free time was normally spent pleasuring women or chewing the cud with his mates. He'd explained to his buddies that his life was becoming more hectic by the day and in future, if they wanted to spend some quality hours with him, would they be so kind as to book it way in advance. His friends had told him sarcastically, 'Sure, mate, it would be our *absolute* pleasure to book you in advance. How does ten years from now grab you?'

Taking a sip of his strawberry protein shake, Aaron sat glued to the plasma-screen TV attached to the wall. The disadvantage of having such a massive TV, he thought – while watching a couple of toothless inbreeds arguing over who had been the first to sleep with the family goat – was when viewing the American daytime talk shows, the misfits of society that appear on them are magnified horrendously. The bleating goat was walked out onto the stage and one of the inbreeds got down on one knee and produced a bunch of flowers.

'I've had a fucking 'nough of this,' Aaron said, switching the TV off, ignoring the fact that he was swearing before the watershed. 'What next?'

Next? Next up, when in doubt next up was always a Bruce Lee film or a *No Holds Barred Cage Fighting* DVD. He thumbed his way through his martial arts DVD collection, plucking out a classic, *Enter the Dragon* starring Bruce Lee. It was hard to believe that such a tough guy had been killed by a simple aspirin tablet. Aaron only hoped for the family's sake that the tablet had been a 500mg dose and not one of these piddley 50mg tablets. Aaron pressed play on the DVD player and settled back in the sofa floating on a cloud of nostalgia.

Two hundred karate chops later, the doorbell rang. Aaron checked his watch, 9.25 a.m., it was a bit early for post – that normally arrived at four p.m., these days – so who could it be? Aaron tried to think who might be outside the door. He ran to his office area and quickly flicked through his diary. No women were pencilled in for today, he sighed with relief, some days he just couldn't be arsed to entertain. Then he checked the phone, it was flashing sixteen messages; now why hadn't he listened to them last night? Before he had time to call up his e-mails, the doorbell was ringing again with fist knocking as backing vocals. Someone was dead keen on Aaron answering the door.

So he did.

And he couldn't believe his eyes.

Standing before him, dishevelled and pitiful, was Jeena. Normally Jeena's appearance was impossible to fault. Make-up perfectly applied, hair glossy, clothes, sexy short skirts and daringly low tops – overall awesome. Right now, with her hair tied back, not a scrap of make-up to be seen and wearing jeans, T-shirt and trainers, she looked about as fashion conscious as someone who lived on the streets. Aaron had to bolt his mouth shut with his *Big Issue* jokes. It was plainly obvious that Jeena had been crying, and crying hard. He pulled her in and hugged her tight, holding her this way while she let the tears roll free again. He whispered in her ear that everything was going to be all right. Even though he didn't have a sodding clue what was wrong. He told her every cloud had a silver lining. When every door closes another one opens. He explained that nothing is as bad as it seems. And that if she thinks life is awful here, think about the impoverished destitute people suffering in Africa. He asked her if she'd seen the film *My Left Foot*, and how bad it must have been for that poor bugger. He was in the middle of mentioning how lucky they were in this country not to have rabies and other foaming-at-the-mouth diseases, when Jeena finally pulled away from him, feeling slightly better.

'I'm in big trouble, Aaron, I need to talk something through with you,' she said, as Aaron ushered her inside. They both sat on the sofa; Bruce Lee was still fighting in the background. 'Is that Jackie Chan?' she asked, a smile fluttering about her lips. 'The greatest fighter who ever lived.'

Aaron switched the TV off, gave her a slim smile in return then stared at this woman who appeared a little lost right now. Her eyes flicked to his and then to the floor. There was a childlike frailty about her which tore at his heart. Not because he loved her – for God's sake he was thinking about dumping her only yesterday. And not because he was a sucker for tears. The reason he felt this way was because he knew that she was in a state today because of his doings yesterday. Ultimately, if it hadn't been for him begging to see her dirty novel, then they wouldn't have been caught in a compromising position. Scientists call this the Butterfly Effect; Aaron just called it, One Thing Led to Another.

Jeena called it, The End of Her Life. Her mother had often warned her that the Gurus could listen into people's minds. 'Avoid impure thoughts at all times, Jeena,' she would say. 'Or your punishment will be severe.' But did Jeena listen? Oh no. Impure thoughts, impure acts, at one point in her life she couldn't even pass a banana without imagining some disgusting act. No wonder the Gurus had retaliated. No wonder they wanted her to avoid men like Aaron Myles. Jeena stole a glance at his thoughtful face. Even in repose he was gorgeous. Each of his cells filled with the 'hunk' gene. Was it any wonder she'd nearly had an orgasm the first time he'd spoken to her? God, it seemed like only eight months ago.

Because it was. Jeena had been asked by her editor on *Asian Delight* to fill in for the sports writer who had been injured by an out-of-control javelin. Normally her writing entailed a weekly column devoted to Asian topics and her 'Ask Jeena' agony auntiji problem page. Sports were alien to her, but not wanting to let her boss, Mr Akhtar, down, she had agreed to visit the Paper Lantern Martial Arts Centre to interview the instructor about his attempts to bring Indian and Pakistani lads together. Aaron likened it to a mini Kashmir crisis and called it his Fight to Unite class.

Inside the airy centre, Jeena, in horrendously high heels, had clomped her way across the wooden perimeter, avoiding the matted area, also known as the *tatami*, which was filled with angry-looking Asian youths, dressed in white jujitsu (*gi*) suits, beating the crap out of each other. Marching up to the instructor, who was far too busy strangling someone to notice her, Jeena observed that from a fashion point of view, the instructor's dark-blue *gi* top seemed far more impressive than the white. She coughed to gain his attention.

Still choking the youth, Aaron looked up and was instantly knocked back by her beauty. *Thank god these trousers are baggy*, he thought, releasing the gasping youth and then covering his groin area with a tug on his top. Wow! He checked for a wedding band, no band. Double wow! And apart from a tiny, tiny, almost insignificant mole just by her left eyebrow, she was perfect. Obviously not of this world.

'Are you from the future?' he asked, not realizing how ridiculous that line sounded, until after he'd said it. 'Erm.' He pointed to her red-streaked hair, cringing. 'Your hair looks pretty futuristic to me. I bet you get loads of jokes about having matching hair down below?'

She appeared shocked. 'NO! Actually, no one has ever said that before.'

'Oh, sorry.'

They both laughed. Looking back now, this would have been the optimum moment to walk away from Aaron. Forget the interview. Forget the *Asian Delight* newspaper. Forget HIM! But love never plays fair and already, even after just a few minutes spent with him, Jeena had succumbed to his spell. She'd half listened to him explain about how getting Indian and Pakistani youths off the street to solve their disputes under the watchful guidance of an instructor was a step in the right direction. It was about trying to diffuse the tension that had bubbled up within the Asian community of Primpton lately. Jeena jotted down notes: how wonderfully blue Aaron's eyes were, how healthy his tanned skin appeared, how sexy and fit his body was, how adorable his face was. She even wrote what positions she would most like to screw him in. She was quite sure that this was not the article her boss had wanted. It was certainly not the article she had wanted Aaron to see as it fell to the floor in front of him. Quicker than Bruce Lee's One Inch Punch, the pad was back in Jeena's hands. And before Aaron had time to ask what the doodle was, the one which looked suspiciously like a man on top of a woman, Satman, the photographer from *Asian Delight*, had arrived. Jeena instructed Satman to use half a roll of film on the Asian youths in various poses and at least four films on Aaron. 'Close-ups, and ask him to remove his top. It's *deadly* important,' was the order.

Just before departing Jeena thought it was worth putting Aaron in his place a little. He was far too confident for her liking and needed to be taken down a peg or two.

'I was just wondering, Mr Myles,' she began, chewing her pen thoughtfully, 'how you can possibly call yourself a fully-fledged ju ju instructor, when everybody knows that the top belt is a black belt, and you have the audacity to walk around with a red and white striped one. Any good reason why this might be so?'

A spray of chuckles came from the Asian youths who were waiting in line to be dismissed from the lesson.

Aaron spoke in a condescending voice, 'A good reason as to why I might be wearing a red and white belt as opposed to the famous black belt? Well, in the sport of *ju ju*.' More chuckles from the lads. 'In the sport of *ju ju*, the red and white belt is king. The black belt is just a stepping stone towards this belt. Clearer now?'

'Completely,' she replied.

But when Aaron gave her his phone number – everything was a complete haze. Instinct warned her away from him, throw his number in the bin, forget you ever saw him. Inquisitiveness tucked the number safely in her purse. What harm could a piece of paper do? It's not like a few digits on a sheet of A4 could get someone pregnant, is it? It was an old dilemma for a British-born Asian rearing its ugly head again: what happens when a white man, whom you feel some attraction to, begins a process which could, in some cases, lead to the bedroom? Do you fight it, ignore it or go with the flow?

This wasn't the first time that Jeena had been forced to make decisions about the opposite sex. Four previous boyfriends and plenty of action with other men had given rise to the very same puzzle on many occasions: fight it, ignore it or go with the flow? But in all cases up until now, never had she been worried that lust might turn to love. Now however there was something in the sinews of Aaron's body that seemed to warn her that love was on the cards. And falling in love with someone when your parents were expecting you to have an arranged marriage was the jujitsu's version of a knock-out. At all costs it was expected of an Indian woman not to get herself in a situation which could lead her down the wrong path. *At all costs.*

And now, eight months later, Jeena closed her eyes as she slumped back on Aaron's sofa. Why, oh, why, did she have to love Aaron so badly? With all his faults anyone would think it would be an easy matter to just forget a man like that. Until one had experienced his sexual passion. Until one had seen his kindness. Until one had watched him sleep. Until one had seen how funny he was.

Until one had fallen in love with him. Jeena was sure a directory as long as the Hollywood Botox waiting list existed of women who'd succumbed to Aaron's charm. She was aware that on many occasions she'd shared him with others. Hoping against hope that one day he'd realize that she was The One. He'd once told her that as soon as a woman declared her love for him, she was dumped. It was a survival mechanism. Hence Jeena never confessed to him how much she loved him, even how much she cared: it was her own survival mechanism. Her friends told her she was mad, a slut, a bad example of womankind. How could she share a man with anyone, they lectured, how could she stoop so low? So how does one explain to eager ears that the reason you have lowered your standards is because the day will come soon, when your standards will hit rock bottom anyway. The day you are forced into an arranged marriage. Surely living with a man whom you haven't chosen, who doesn't care about you, but only cares about his dinner being on the table, and that his wife is able to produce boys, and her cleaning is up to scratch, and ... surely having to sleep with a man whom you don't know, who has never whispered the words, 'I love you', who will never whisper the words, 'I love you', surely sleeping with that man is far worse than the man whom you choose yourself – even if he does do the rounds with a netball team's worth of females.

Anyway, what law exists that excludes Indian women from having fun before they settle down to a life of dreary, domestic, hardship? Who can really blame young Asian girls from straying a little when they know the future is bleak and bare of fun? Surely the glue of the Indian way isn't strong enough to keep all the feet stuck to the righteous path. Life is so short at the best of times so why not fill that life with excitement and joy? Why give it all up for four kitchen walls in the day and four bedroom walls in the night? Especially when those bedroom walls feel more like a cage if the Indian woman is unlucky enough to be married to an ogre of a man. What's more, Aaron made Jeena feel so alive and free when she was with him, surely no one had the right to begrudge her that bit of happiness.

After waiting for her heart to calm a little, Jeena sat up and tapped Aaron on the knee. 'I'm ready to tell you my problem now,' she said.

'Okay, fire away.'

'How would you feel about getting married? I've been thinking . . .'

Aaron was out of his seat and down the other end of the apartment as if he were being chased by a hornet. To him, the word 'marriage' had a larger sting than a hornet anyway. Jeena watched him adjusting ornaments as he angrily talked to himself. She listened hard.

'Oh, great idea, let's all get married. Let's completely fuck up our lives.' He slammed down an ornament of Fu Shinn, the God of Luck. 'Excellent idea, Jeena, let's join ourselves together in matrimonial HELL!'

Jeena shouted, 'It's your bloody fault, Aaron, none of this would have happened if you hadn't pressurized me.' She glared with crazed anger. 'Blow jobs, bondage, bonking, that's all you ever think about.' She stared at the DVD case of Bruce Lee discarded on the floor. 'Sex and sodding fighting. What about your responsibilities in life, Aaron, what about paying for the wrong you've done. Do you know that my parents are sending me to India to marry a man next month? A man whom I have never even met before. I'll be gone from this country and I won't ever come back. I'll have to say goodbye to my friends, my job, I won't even get to see my family unless they happen to take a trip to India. My life is down the toilet and it's all because you wanted a fucking shag! I told you it was too risky, but oh, no, you knew best.' Jeena punched the red cushion pretending it was Aaron's head. 'So, don't give me this "let's completely fuck up our lives" because, Aaron, you already have fucked up my life. And unless you marry me, I don't see any way that I can get out of it.'

He returned to the sofa, tail between his legs. Jesus H. Christ, *Mamma Mia*. Hell's Bells. Numby Nunchuckas. H.E.L.P. And Aaron had presumed she was here because she felt bad for not putting him in the acknowledgments for her dirty book – even though she didn't know him at the time – it was either that or she was upset about getting caught in bed by her parents. One of the two. Never had it crossed his mind that her parents would punish her so drastically for such a trivial matter. God forbid what the punishment might have been if they had been caught doing it doggy style. Aaron quickly excused himself to swallow a few Nurofen Plus tablets, explaining to Jeena on his return that marriage talk would most certainly bring about a knifing headache.

'Can't you marry someone else?' Aaron suggested. 'What about Ryan, he said you were "well fit"? Hang on I've got his number somewhere.' Aaron rose from his seat. 'I think he left it on his wedding invite.'

Jeena could feel her blood pressure rising. 'You mean the very same Ryan who is engaged to Vicky, whose wedding is only next month? *That* Ryan?' Aaron nodded sheepishly. 'You mean the Ryan who looks nothing like you? Don't you think that my dad might notice the difference between you and him? It's not like he's ever going to forget your face. The vision of you shagging his daughter in his yellow turban will haunt him until the day he dies. Ryan? No, I don't think so.'

'Look, Jeena, I'm only trying to help sort out *your* problem. There's no fucking way I'm marrying you so get that notion right out of your head.' He walked to a window and peered down upon the river. 'Besides, I was going to dump you last night anyway. Our relationship has run out of steam.' He paused dramatically. 'It just fizzled out, Jeena.'

She angrily picked up his Bruce Lee DVD case and threw it, hitting him in the chest. 'So, you're quite happy for me to be raped then, are you? You don't mind that I might be lying scared in some dingy grotto in Moradabad while my husband gropes and molests my body covering my mouth with his hand so I can't scream?' Her words were stark and pruned of any hope. 'Could you honestly sit back while my life is wrecked, knowing that you might have been able to help me? Is that the sort of man you are? A bastard.' She watched Aaron's jaw tense as he soaked up all the information. Jeena carried on, 'And it's true, I was going to have an arranged marriage anyway, to a strange man . . .'

Jeena went on to explain how the arranged marriage system was supposed to work in this country. How her parents would have taken it upon themselves to find a worthy match for her. A man who they thought she would most likely have the most successful marriage with. Under supervision to begin with Jeena would be allowed to meet with the man and with a bit of luck get to know him better. Small bonds would hopefully form between the couple in this period and if all went well, after a few meetings both sets of parents would agree on a date to marry. Aaron listened with interest, he'd known of the arranged marriage system from his time in Japan, but he'd assumed that in this day and age it was only extremely strict parents who still practiced it. He'd assumed wrong and he continued to listen with fascination as Jeena described what happens to a girl who goes against the family's wishes. A girl who sleeps with a man before wedlock. A girl like her.

'In their eyes, Aaron, I'm not that much better than a whore. And whores get punished.' She spoke sullenly, holding back tears, praying that Aaron would find it in himself to put aside his fear of commitment and let his compassion come through. 'One month is all I have got left in this country until they whisk me off to my nightmare. They want a quick wedding and that means they'll accept the first man who comes along. He could be sixty-years-old, he could be a wife-beater, he could be a bit slow, there's even a slim chance that he could be nice. But, it's not the way I want my life to be.' She paused. 'My parents think that you are only after me

51

for sex so if we could prove them wrong then they might change their thinking. If we could convince them that we love each other, that we are made for each other and that we would rather die than be apart. If they could tell by the look in our eyes that we belong together, then they might back down. But it's only got a hope of working if we get married secretly first.'

Aaron could feel that Jeena had him by the moral balls and her grip was tightening. Since day one he'd been on a quest to shag Jeena in her own bed. A relentless, won't-take-no-for-an-answer quest. Time-after-time Jeena had put up the blockades, refusing to give in to what she considered a rather childish whim. And then knowledge of her dirty book, *Naked Riders*, had come to light, a novel that she was so ashamed of she had hidden it under the loft insulation in the attic. She agreed that Aaron could read the novel once she'd managed to fetch it from the loft. And this was where Aaron's devious plan had come to fruition. If he could convince Jeena that she must stay away from the attic then she would have to ask him into the house to retrieve it for her, but how? Then one day, while in a state of meditation, the solution had risen to the top of his brain. Aaron recalled how easy it was to dupe Jeena with a small amount of fear; he'd phoned her and asked, 'Jeena, I was thinking, this might sound like a daft question but have you had your asbestos jabs? It's only that if you were to go into your attic without the antidote in your bloodstream then you might never be able to have children. You'll get "Asbestositis" a horrible, *horrible* disease. If you like I could go up into the attic. I had my asbestos jabs done years ago while in Tokyo. I'll be safe.'

And so it was settled. Aaron would go into the loft to retrieve the dirty book and, by killing two birds with one stone, he would get to shag her in her bed as well. Flawless!

Risking a migraine, Aaron dived into wedding talk, as they both sat together on the sofa drinking espresso coffee. 'Okay, let's say we get married and we manage to convince your parents that everything is kosher, what happens if you or I actually meet someone who we *really* want to marry? What then?'

'We divorce!'

'Just like that?'

'Just like that, Aaron. We're only talking being married for a few years here, you know. A few years to get my parents off my back. Then we divorce. And then no Indian man would ever want to marry me, and that goes for men who live here or from men who live in India, because I will be a divorcee who has been soiled by a white man. I'll be no better than a garden slug in their opinion.'

'Soiled? Slug? Charming.'

Marrying the Indian way wasn't about love – never about love. Its rules were more closely based around commerce. Selling a product and that product being the bride. How good was she at cooking, how light was her skin tone, how tall was she, how well off were her family, how educated was she. All these attributes would be collectively added together and in not so many words a price would be attached to her. She would then go on sale to what some people call the arranged marriage system, but others might well refer to it as The Marriage Market. She wasn't a person anymore just a product waiting to be bought. And who would want to marry off their son to a divorcee who had once been intimate with a white man? No one.

A thoughtful Aaron walked to the far end of the room and stared down at the engraved sign above the aquarium: WATER, WATER EVERYWHERE BUT NOT A DROP TO DRINK. Jeena was a sinking ship and she was sending up her flares. Could he really ignore her and let her drown? To him, Jeena would just be a mildly inconvenient burden until they divorced; it was hardly the end of the world. To her, it meant that she might escape having to live a dreadful life in India – which would most certainly be the end of her world. On numerous occasions women had referred to him as a perfect example of a perfect man in the looks department but also a perfect example of a bastard in the compassion department (or words to that effect). Maybe it was about time to set the record straight. Maybe what Jeena was asking of him wasn't such a big deal after all. It was just a favour. Nothing more than that. He owed her that much. And if one really thought about it there was a high possibility that he might receive the prestigious Esther Rantzen's 'Heart of Gold' Award for his decency. Which was way better than the 'Jim Fixed it for Me' medal he never got for asking Jimmy Savile if he could fix it for him, with one hand tied behind his back, to beat up the wrestler, Giant Haystacks.

'One year,' Aaron shouted across the room. 'I'll marry you for one year and we divorce on our anniversary.' He joined her on the sofa. 'A few rules though.'

Her smile said, 'Name them.'

'You will sleep in one of the spare bedrooms which you can decorate as you please in accordance with the strict Feng Shui rules. I will continue with my lifestyle which obviously means plenty of women sleeping over. I'll explain to them that you're my lesbian roommate to keep them happy. We will tell our friends the truth. I would like you to chip in with the bills but I will not expect you to pay any rent as you'll be my wife, but I will expect you to treat this place with the respect it deserves.' He lifted his leg and farted and then pondered, searching for anymore rules. 'Oh, and please don't leave the toilet seat up.'

After agreeing to his rules, Jeena received the answers to a few of her own questions. Yes, she was allowed friends around. And yes, he would accompany her to a few Indian dos, weddings etc., to keep up the pretence with her parents. But, no, he would not be opening a joint bank account with her. Absolutely not. Bit of a shame really.

'What about sex?' Jeena asked, forcing her hand down the back of the suede sofa and pulling out a dead bonsai tree then quickly tossing it on the wooden coffee table. 'Does sex play a part in our marriage? Or should I get myself a vibrator?'

'You can get yourself a suitcase full of dildos for all I care, just don't disturb me when I'm meditating. And to your question: does sex play a part in our fake marriage? I think not. Now that I know that you're going to be my wife I'm quite turned off you if you must know.' He shivered. 'Yuck.'

'Just as well, a vibrator gives me a much deeper orgasm than you could ever dream of.'

'Don't back-chat your future husband.'

Chapter Five

D ay after day Jeena listened in to her parents as they discussed the destruction of her future. And night after night she prayed that Aaron was working on her salvation. He'd promised to 'take care of everything'. From the booking of the wedding in Gretna Green to the buying of the rings in Argos. No detail would go unchecked, he'd boasted, it would be the most organized sham marriage in history. Aaron explained to Jeena that these days Gretna Green needed fifteen days notice before permission for a marriage could be granted. The romantic notions of eloping couples turning up in the middle of the night were long gone. Which was just as well in some cases when, come morning, after the alcohol has worn off, the attraction to each other has worn off also.

After fourteen worrying days, Jeena left for work as usual, but on this hot, sunny June day her route was to take her to Kitty's flat on the edge of town. The joy of driving her own car was something that she'd never quite got used to. She smiled to herself half-heartedly. If this plan to marry Aaron in two days time did fail then the chances of her ever driving again would be slim-to-none. Unless her new husband owned an elephant. God, the thought of trying to park one of those beasts would be a nightmare; it was hard enough parking her Clio.

From the top flat, Kitty opened the window and shouted, 'Mind my Mini, you silly cow. Use the bloody side mirrors. They're not just for decoration you know.'

Plenty of vrooooming and cursing later, the Clio was safely tucked in behind the Mini and Jeena was safely parked on Kitty's sofa. This flat had been the girlie meeting place for years. Three school mates, Jeena, Kitty and Flora had discussed no end of topics between these walls. Periods, pregnancy scares, men, drugs, sex, men, reputations, venereal diseases, men. Considering the amount of embarrassing situations that had been talked about in here, the walls really should have been crimson, instead of the peachy orange they were. Flora once even admitted that she had the hots for that geezer the Archbishop of Canterbury. Now you don't go telling people stuff like that – unless you completely trust them.

And boy did these girls trust each other. Kitty, the hairdresser, with her long, blonde hair extensions, and Pamela Anderson body (complete with authentic implants); and Flora, the fitness instructor, with her short, chestnut hair, model pretty face and ultra slim body (diet freak), two of a threesome capable of walking down any shopping centre and completely curing all forms of erectile dysfunction (possibly excluding Bobbitt erectile dysfunction) with a triple wiggle of

58

their hips. Kitty, who was forever involved in a 'he's definitely the one this time' relationship until she dumped them, was single at the moment. As was Flora, whose last boyfriend was frightened off when she refused to give him a blow job stating that if she were to accidentally swallow the calorie-rich sperm it might blow her diet. But she would spit it back in his face if he so desired. She never saw him again after that.

After removing the Beyoncé CD because it was making Flora paranoid about the size of her backside, Kitty popped in Coldplay instead. Three large glasses were filled with white wine. An ashtray was perched on the sofa arm filled with pre-loaded spliffs. The time was 9.35 a.m., and Jeena's hen night had officially begun. As far as the girls were concerned, drugs and drink were the legitimate way to celebrate an illegitimate wedding. After swigging a little and spliffing a little the friends congregated in the tiny kitchen as Kitty prepared the red-dye mixture she would be colouring Jeena's roots with. A direct contradiction to what Jeena's parents had demanded she do with her hair. 'You will not be turning up in India with red hair. Make sure that by the time we leave it is dyed back to its original black.'

Jeena thought about those words while watching Kitty snap on her plastic gloves. Over the last two weeks she'd lied to her parents more than she had in her whole previous lifetime. She'd told them that she'd handed in her notice at work. She'd explained that she'd not seen or heard from Aaron since that awful day. She'd promised that she would be the best-behaved daughter from now on. All lies. All lies delivered with the silky smoothness of a second-hand car dealer. And now she had her comeuppance. Now, guilt, the unwelcome guest, was back.

They say that to kill someone you lose part of your soul. Well, Jeena was discovering, the same holds true for lying to your loved ones. Her soul was in tatters, held together by the smallest of threads. There was a very high possibility that she could lose her whole family by marrying Aaron in just two days' time. She would become bad fruit from the family tree left to rot with her conscience.

Jeena closed her eyes as the cold, smelly dye began to sting its way into her scalp. Her parents seemed to believe that their children should think like them. Should agree with them. Should never question them. What good is a mind like that? In fact what *use* is a mind like that? It's as if any disagreement with the parents is considered a direct act against them. Jeena remembered her parents pointing out photos of other rotten fruit over the years. Distant relatives who had gone against the Indian way. Their family ties had been cut and they had been tossed out to face the world alone. Jeena had often wondered what the girls were up to now. Whether they regretted going against the Indian way or whether they had ended up happy.

After listening to Flora lecture Kitty on the vitamin deficiency of her fridge contents the conversation turned to Aaron.

'I'm in a bit of a dilemma,' Flora began, rearranging the fridge magnets, spelling out the word CASTRATE. 'I want to continue with my hate campaign against Aaron, but since he's agreed to help you out,

Jeena, I find myself almost . . . *almost* liking him. It's so weird.'

Through a mouthful of chocolate, Kitty agreed. 'Mmm, mmm, I know, it's like he's been given a halo or something. For a man who is scared of nothing, and I mean nothing, Jeena, except marriage, to agree to marry you as a favour, well, he's gone up in my books.' She placed a plastic cap over Jeena's head. 'It's so noble.'

Kings were noble. Lords were noble. Aristocrats were noble. But philanderers . . . were they noble? Jeena was about to agree, 'Yes, I think Aaron is noble', when Flora sparked up.

'Noble or not, he'll still leave you standing at the altar, Jeena. I'm giving odds of three to one against him turning up at all.' She lit a spliff and dragged deeply. 'But fuck it; let's enjoy this hen day and night anyway.'

There was now room for improvement in Jeena's mood. Tomorrow, on the eve of the wedding, five of them were supposed to hurtle up the motorway to Gretna Green in Aaron's BMW. 'I want my bride to arrive in style,' he'd told Jeena. 'But if you think I'm having a sign on the back saying JUST MARRIED and cans rattling behind, you can think again, I fucking hate that sort of crap. It's so tacky.' Another rule he imposed, 'No talking in the car. I can't bear the thought of a four-hour car journey with you, Kitty and Flora nattering away. I'd probably just crash on purpose.' But it was all right for him to talk to his mate, Tyler, oh, no problem there. Because Tyler, his best man, quote, 'Didn't talk shit'.

The girls slumped themselves on the sofa, already the worse for wear, and it was only midday. The hen night was planned for ten p.m., at the aptly named Roosters nightclub. At the speed the three were gulping the booze, it was quite doubtful that the girls would be arriving at the nightclub with the same stomach contents they had at the moment. Very doubtful.

'We must pace ourselves, people,' Jeena shouted, after banging her foot on Kitty's PlayStation. 'Or one of us is going to hurt themselves. First Aid box please.'

After seeing to Jeena's cut foot, Flora, who loved the sight of blood, as long as it wasn't her own, sat crossed-legged on the floor. There was something of extreme importance that she had to say, but first she had to think of it. It was in her brain somewhere, she'd only filed it last night.

'Oh, oh, I remember it now, Jeena,' Flora said, passing the ashtray and spliff across to Kitty. 'He thinks he's only marrying you for one year, but what about forcing him to marry you for life. Refuse the divorce *or* alternatively you could take him for all he's got. That martial arts centre must be worth a cool half million at least. Think about it, you could cream him for half.'

They all laughed. And laughed. And laughed.

Kitty simmered down first. 'There is another way to keep him married to you, which is slightly kinder. Why not make him dependent on you. There's no way a man will get rid of a woman on whom he's become totally reliant. That's why men love gadgets so much. Anything that saves them time or has flashing lights is a winner.'

'So, if I become a gadget, I keep my husband?' Jeena responded, confused.

'An all-cooking, all-cleaning, all-sexual, all-listening, all-ego-boosting gadget who is prepared to wear slutty lingerie on demand, damp his throbbing head down with a flannel when he's got a headache and even hand-wash his underwear when the washing machine is broken.' Kitty grimaced at the thought, possibly remembering an old flame of hers called Darren, who had saved a fortune on toilet roll over the years. 'Oh, yeah, and if you're a really good gadget you'll fix that broken washing machine to save him the bother.'

Flora joined in. 'No, Jeena, you'll fix that washing machine so *you* don't have to hand-wash his skids. Basically, what Kitty is saying here is that you must become Aaron's slave. Bring him coffee in bed in the morning, make sure he's got three square meals on the table each day – and I don't mean "square" shaped meals – and when the day of the divorce arrives he'll weigh up the pros and cons of keeping you on for another year, because he's a selfish bastard like that, and decide whether or not you're worth keeping. Before you know it, Jeena, he'll be eating out of your hand and head-over-heels in love with you. Mission accomplished.'

The theory wasn't as far-fetched as one might think. As soon as an Indian girl marries an Indian man she automatically becomes his slave. And not only his slave but also the slave to the extended family. Washing, cleaning, cooking, ironing, chores, chores and chores. Ask most Indian women to sum up their marriage in one word and most would say, 'graft'. Of course, the words 'used' 'bored' 'unappreciated' and 'wasted' wouldn't be too far away from their lips either. Words that Jeena doubted would be used to describe time spent with Aaron.

God, the thought of living with him in the next few days was beginning to sink in. Under the same roof, within the same walls, the same air, even the same toilet – ouch – and together under the same name. Mrs Jeena Myles, wife to Aaron Bruce Lee Myles (Deed Poll had a lot to answer for letting men like Aaron pick names like Bruce Lee). She'd practised the signature until the pen ran out. In front of the bathroom mirror, she'd practised introducing her husband, Aaron Myles, to a group of people. She'd even practised her 'shy' face when people said 'My, you make a lovely couple, you really do.' And once, when in a real state of self-denial, she'd practised the look of surprise when Aaron asked her to be the mother of his children. Two boys, three girls.

And one doctor to lock her in a straitjacket.

The fact of the matter was that Aaron didn't love her at the moment, it was the sad truth. But, and it was a very big but, if she could make him fall for her, using everything in her power, including stooping real low, then after twelve months, there was a chance that he might, just might, nearly admit, sort of say, in not so many words, without beating around the bush too much, after ten pints of Special Brew lager, finally agree, after much deliberating that he had feelings for Jeena which were similar to love. Either that or he would hand her the divorce papers with a huge, relieved smile, proving once and for all that Jeena had her head in the clouds and it was filled with cuckoos.

Part of Jeena's plan today had been to phone her parents and explain that she would be AWOL for four days. That she needed time to think. And not to worry.

The conversation would be short and sweet without time for any emotional blackmail from her dad or a sobbing frenzy from her mum ordering Jeena to come back home this instant. That had been the plan. But even with enough Dutch courage in her veins to burst a dam in Holland, Jeena couldn't bring herself to pick up the phone to speak.

So she took the cowardly route instead. TEXT messaging. The best invention in the world (excluding the Rabbitron XXX deluxe G-force explosion vibrator, of course) for people too timid or too ashamed to use their voice.

Or too scared. Jeena asked the girls to be quiet as she worked on her text message. One drunken slip and a sentence like 'love yer loads' could end up as 'love yer lobes'.

After composing her message and sending it to her mother's mobile, Jeena began to cry. The next time she saw her family she would be a married woman. Not quite the wedding her parents had dreamed about. Not too many mothers dream about being absent from their daughter's big day. But then again, not too many Indian mothers dream about their daughter marrying a white man.

Especially a white man who appeared to make most of his decisions, not with his heart, but according to how much testosterone was in his bloodstream at the time. A man who could turn a daughter against the family's traditions, who would sweep her off her feet until all she could think about was the next time they made love. And it didn't help that this man was a man who refused to let a woman leave his bed until she was completely fulfilled (he couldn't bear the thought of the finger being pointed at him with the words, 'Useless in the sack'). How could the Indian way possibly survive with men like Aaron Myles about? Lust and Tradition have had some battles over the years. But when the bugle sounds and the back-up army of love joins the attack, it's game over guys, tradition is defeated. How could an Indian woman possibly believe that an arranged marriage is the best way after experiencing the power of love?

And how could a Western man marry a woman when he knows he doesn't love her? This was the question posed to Aaron by three of his mates as they sat drinking and chatting in the Apple & Maggot pub, overlooking Lake Charlotte, in the centre of Primpton. He'd phoned Tyler, Charlie and Sean explaining he needed help on a life-changing decision. Although he didn't expect to receive too much worldly advice from ex-army Charlie once he was tipsy, as an inebriated Charlie talked of nothing but Gulf War Syndrome. Which was enough to make Aaron want to shoot him with a uranium-tipped shell sometimes.

It was 8.07 p.m., and the Apple & Maggot was chock-a-block, the thick stone walls encasing an already lively Monday-evening crowd. A few months back a new pub, The Pirates Inn, opened in this part of town, with the management from Apple & Maggot fearful of an exodus. But they needn't have worried, as nothing beat the old feel of this ancient holding. Low crooked beams, comfy worn stools, wooden tables complete with woodworm, a roaring log fire to keep the winter chill away and the finest home-cooked traditional meals in the Midlands. A pubber's paradise.

Normally Aaron only drank on three occasions in the year: Christmas, birthday celebrations and the anniversary of Bruce Lee's death. His *sensei* had told him, 'You take control of the drink or it will take control of you.' Wise words to a sober mind, but complete nonsense to a drunkard. Today, Aaron decided, would require a stiff drink or five. In only two days time he was to be married. M.A.R.R.I.E.D.

'FUCK IT,' Aaron said, in an unexpectedly loud voice, causing a few punters to jump. 'What the hell have I agreed to?'

'Do you want me to play REM "Everybody Hurts" on the jukebox, again?' Tyler asked, grinning at his pathetic-looking mate. "Everybody hurts . . . sometimes."'

Aaron wasn't listening. 'You're right, I can't marry her, I don't know who I was trying to kid but there's no way I'm going to be a husband.'

Charlie burst out laughing. 'You, a husband? I'd pay anything to see you take your vows,' he hinted. 'How about you stick Kitty in the boot and that way I could come along? I'm serious, Aaron, I really want to be there for you, I don't want you making a fool of yourself alone. And before you say, "I won't be alone, Tyler will be there", that's all well and good, but will Tyler crack up laughing when you make a mistake? I don't think so. Or will Tyler rub salt in your wounds when you've got that wedding ring on your finger? NO, he's not that type of guy.' He stared with his begging look. 'I won't let you down, mate; I'll make it the worst day of your life for sure. Guaranteed.'

Despite Charlie's efforts to be invited, for some reason Aaron refused him a BMW ticket to Gretna Green. After waiting for Charlie to cease his bachelor jokes, Aaron withdrew a piece of paper from his pocket and flung it on Sean's lap.

'It's my wedding gift list.'

Sean scanned the list while Aaron disappeared to make a quick call to his martial arts centre. For the next four days his stand-in, Rick, would be taking his classes. But to make sure that the teaching standard was kept high, Aaron would be checking over the CCTV footage of the lessons on his return. Any slackers, whether they be pupil or instructor, would be given a strike. Three strikes and you were out. Aaron returned to his friends, satisfied that his business was in safe hands.

'Odd wedding presents, Aaron,' Tyler pointed out, laying the list out on the damp wooden table:

I would be very appreciative of any of the following gifts:
The 'Which' Guide to Divorce by Imogen Clout
Making Divorce Work: In 9 Easy Steps by Keith Barret
She Wasn't For You by Dr L. Onely
A Painless Divorce by N. U. Rofen
How to Mend a Broken Heart by Christine Webber

Aaron picked up his pint and sipped it. 'I'll be such an expert on divorce after reading a selection of those books that women will be afraid to marry me. It will be perfect! Besides, I need something positive to read in the year that I'm ma—'

'Go on, Aaron, you can say it,' Charlie coaxed, rubbing Aaron's hand. 'Take a deep breath.'

'Ma-rid. Married. I'm okay. I'm okay now. It's just a word. It's only a . . .'

'No it's fucking not,' interrupted Sean. 'It's a prison sentence and you know it. Don't marry her; she'll screw you for all you've got. I, as your trusted friend, boycott this disgraceful act. I, as your loyal follower, veto this shameful wedding.'

Charlie sneered at Sean like he was an idiot then turned to Aaron. 'Think about it: how could you say "no" to twenty-four hour sex? Sex on tap is to be welcomed with open arms. Don't listen to this imbecile and his pathetic veto.' Charlie stared into space. 'You know how difficult it is for me to hold down a relationship with my Gulf War Syndrome. I'm snooping through girlfriends' purses, following them in my car, paranoid they are having an affair – and that's only after the first night.' He paused, ruffling his gelled-up hair. 'I suppose you're all wondering what my point is?' He banged the table angrily. 'I don't fucking know what my point is, I've got Gulf War Syndrome, haven't I? It makes me forgetful.' Silence from the table. 'Oh yeah, I remember now, you've got sex on tap when you marry Jeena.'

'If I marry her, then she becomes my wife and if she becomes my wife she then becomes a turn-off, so, in reference to this twenty-four hour sex I'm supposed to be having, I won't. In fact, even on the wedding night it will be separate beds. There can't be anything more disgusting in this world than having sexual intercourse with your wife. It's unnatural.'

The lads erupted with laughter.

Aaron looked around, thankful for having mates like these. All of them were martial arts fanatics – possibly not the best table to start a fight with – and all of them were keen bachelors. Happy in their single lifestyles. But all of them seemed to be missing a few marbles. Maybe those kicks in the head by overzealous martial arts students tallied up over the years. But they were loyal and they'd made Aaron feel welcome when he'd first arrived in Primpton six years ago. Which was quite the opposite of the people he'd left behind in his hometown of Northampton. Not one single person could he count on from that town, except his gran. Not one single person could he honestly call a friend. Not one person with whom he still kept in contact. As far as he was concerned he filed them all under the 'B' category. Backstabbers, Bullies and Bastards. And one day, possibly soon, he promised to file them under the category 'R'. Revenge, Retaliation and Retribution. Soon could not come soon enough sometimes.

But now was always here.

And right here and now the last straw dropped, and the camel walking around in Aaron's desert mind felt its back break. It suddenly dawned on Aaron that by marrying Jeena in two days' time he would be doing someone an injustice. How, in who knows how many years, would Aaron explain to the woman he fell in love with, that once upon a time he had married another woman, called Jeena, not out of love, but as a favour? How would he sit her down and tell her that he married a woman just so she didn't have to go to India? Aaron had always assumed that marriage was a one trip pony. For life. You only did it the once. If he married Jeena all his ideas would be washed away in a guilty promise and he would have to marry twice. It was not how he wanted his life to be.

'I've decided not to marry her,' Aaron began, breaking the concentration of his three mates, whose eyes were glued to a stunning babe who'd just sashayed her way in. 'It would be wrong.'

'Wrong?' Tyler said, raising his voice above the rowdy pub crowd. 'And what the hell have we been telling you for the last two weeks? Of course it's wrong. If you don't love her, then you can't marry her. It's the right decision.'

Sean piped up. 'Thank God for that, I thought we'd lost you to the Couples Club, I really did. I hate to say it, Aaron, but this would have been the worst decision of your life. Your biggest mistake. Forget Chernobyl; this would have been your meltdown. Forget the sinking of the *Titanic*; this would have been your iceberg. Forget Hiroshima; this would have been . . .'

'My Atom Bomb. I get the picture, Sean, my worst mistake.'

'You betcha.'

But it wouldn't have been Aaron's worst mistake, not by a long shot; only he didn't know it yet. That would be something which would be revealed when he finally decided to open that package that his mother had left him nearly twenty years ago. For now, though, he could only wallow in guilt. Reflect on the sad truth that he was about to commit Jeena, a woman whom he cared for very much, to a life of misery in India. After promising her one thing, he'd stab her in the back and deliver something else. She'd pressurized him into agreeing to a wedding, which in his heart he knew was wrong. Anything else to help her out of a predicament he would have done with pleasure. But this? Marriage. It was way too much. Way, way, way too much.

A troubled Aaron stumbled to the pub toilet and splashed his face with water. His reflection in the mirror should have shown a man with an executioner's cloth over his head, he thought, for in many ways he was about to put an end to Jeena's life.

'You complete, bastard, Aaron,' he said to himself, then walked out.

Chapter Six

Jeena's parents had been studying her text message for so long now, that the battery on the mobile was nearly drained. The message had arrived at 1.04 p.m., and it was now 9.22 p.m. Any expectations that another text was following with the words: *I was only joking*, had been ruled out. Jeena's mother read through it yet again:

> *Dear Maji & Papaji, please do not panic.*
> *I have left home for four days and will*
> *be back on Thursday. I need time to think.*
> *Love Jeena XXX*

'Oh, *Babaji*, please bring me back my daughter,' Maji uttered to the painting of Guru Nanak on the wall as she clasped her hands together in prayer. 'Please keep her from harm.'

A string of urgent messages on Jeena's mobile answering service and text messages had not been replied to as yet, and frantic efforts to phone Jeena's friends, Kitty and Flora, to see if they might know of her whereabouts had drawn a blank; no answers on either of their mobiles. Her workplace had informed them that she had taken the rest of the week off. This disappearance had all the hallmarks of love sickness or, worse, the stamp of 24-carat lust. And as time ticked by the thermometer of suspicion rose dramatically. This was looking ominously as if a white man might be involved. The same white man who had chosen to corrupt their daughter under this very roof.

The strain of the family crisis was showing on everyone's face except for Nanaji who hadn't uttered a single word since witnessing that awful bedroom scene between Jeena and Aaron over two weeks ago. Wrapped in a shawl, she sat engrossed watching a Bollywood movie on the giant TV. Maybe she felt safer in a fantasy world of cinema than the real world where white men wore turbans while making love. Whatever the reason for her muteness, it was becoming quite a concern for everyone.

'You okay there, Nanaji?' asked JJ, slumping next to her on the sofa, dressed as a typical eighteen-year-old in baggy jeans, baggy T-shirt and chunky trainers. 'Would you like me to turn the sound on? You'd like that, wouldn't you?'

No answer.

'What about a nice cup of *lychee chai* and some shortbread biscuits? You like those don't you?' He held one under her nose. 'Yes you do, yes you do, yummy, yum, *yum*.'

Papaji shook his head. 'JJ, just because your gran is having a quiet moment, it doesn't mean you have to talk to her like she is five years old.' He placed his hand on his wife's shoulder. 'I don't want to do this, but I think that we have to search Jeena's bedroom. There might be a clue in there as to who this man is and where he lives. I've got a sneaky feeling she's staying with him.'

Suddenly there was hope in the room. A small tea-light amongst the gloom, and, without wasting any more time, both parents and JJ bounded up the stairs, opened Jeena's bedroom door and began their tooth-pick search. Immediately JJ was scolded for tipping the contents of Jeena's drawers on the carpet.

'We are not the police, JJ, please do this with respect,' hollered Papaji. 'This room has to be put back exactly as we found it.'

JJ huffed. He couldn't believe the fuss they were kicking up over his sister's disappearance anyway, and he had every sympathy for Jeena. Christ, if his parents knew what he got up to in his free time they'd book themselves into the nearest mental home and ask the warden to throw away the key. Boozing, spliffing, whizzing, joyriding, shoplifting, anything with an 'ing' except for shagging, but he was planning very hard for that one. He was quite aware that Indian women and girls got the bad deal in an Indian household. It was a historical trend which had survived to the modern day. And he was more than aware of what extremes an Indian girl would go to so that she might live a life with some enjoyment. On more than one occasion he'd suspected Jeena of having boyfriends – finding rubber Johnnies in her handbag when he was stealing fag money had been quite a clue. Another time he'd seen her kissing a white man outside a nightclub.

Not to mention it was a different man to that Aaron bloke.

In many ways he admired his sister for taking the risks she did, it was just a shame that his parents had caught her out in the end. He thought back to that hilarious moment when they'd walked into Jeena's bedroom and seen a live porn show. All he could think about at the time was, 'Where's my digital camera? I wish my mates were here to witness this, they're never going to believe me.' But still he couldn't get over the naiveté of his parents when they had climbed the stairs saying, 'What on earth is going on up there?' Nothing could have been clearer; his sister was having sex. Wake up to yourselves Indian parents! Hadn't Jeena's moaning words, 'Fill me up, big boy' rung any bells?

Looking for something when you don't know what you're looking for takes time. Especially when the room you are searching belongs to someone who hoards. Jeena would have hoarded her used air if she had had a place to store it. Endless cards, letters, photos, drawings, postcards and take-away menus was jammed into every spare drawer. Files and files of photocopies of the articles she'd written for *Asian Delight*. Folders of receipts, bills and invoices. Not to mention shoe boxes, handbags, hat boxes, and boxes with boxes in them. Was it any wonder that the house was sinking?

Like huge mice they rustled away, desperately searching for anything that might lead to the home address of the white man. The clock passed ten p.m. then eleven p.m. then suddenly Papaji shouted, 'I think this is it.' He held aloft a large box with the word

AARON scribbled on the top in marker pen. Either Aaron was a hobbit and was hiding inside the box or there were items relating to him in there. Papaji tipped the contents onto the bed and three sets of pupils doubled in size. A pile of lingerie so sluttish that whores around the world would shake their head in embarrassment. A pair of pink, fluffy handcuffs. A small photo album containing photographs of Aaron and Jeena together at parties, barbecues and even a trip to the coast. There were newspaper clippings of Aaron and his martial arts school, the Paper Lantern. A few X-rated drawings (sexual suggestions) from Aaron and some ditty notelets (normally apologizing for turning up late and wrecking the date). Also a notepad filled with diary-like entries of special days spent with Aaron. On the very last page Papaji and Maji saw the words which confirmed their worst fears:

I love him
and I dream of being with him.
I would do anything for him and
I know he is the only man who I
could be happy with.
No other man on this earth
comes even a little bit close.

While Maji was sobbing, Papaji scanned his eyes over the newspaper cuttings for clues. It was only a matter of seconds before he knew where this dirtbag called Aaron Myles, the man his daughter loved, lived. A photograph of Aaron smashing his head on a pile of bricks had the title: THIS LOOKS PAINFUL. With a caption explaining how

8th-dan Aaron had bought the run-down cotton mill and converted it into a martial arts school on the bottom floor with a luxury apartment on the first floor. 'Living on top of my dream business is a dream come true,' Aaron was quoted as saying. 'I dare any burglars to try my gaff. I'm ready and waiting 24/7.'

'You had better be ready,' Papaji stated, with all the righteous indignation of the head of the household. 'For I am coming to take my daughter back.'

JJ tried not to laugh at his dad's cute bravery. Had his father learnt nothing over the years? The man, Aaron, was a freaking 8th-dan. Which means in plain English 'RUN FOR YOUR LIFE.'

'Papaji, he's a killing machine,' JJ said, stuffing the newspaper clipping of Aaron winning some jujitsu title under his father's nose. 'Please don't go alone to Aaron's. I'm begging you. And if he demands to wear your turban you just take it off and *you* give it to him. No questions asked. None of this throwing pokers this time. Honestly, Papaji, you'd be a fool to mess with a martial arts expert. He's one of the best.'

Papaji nodded knowingly. 'And what am I, chopped liver? Don't you remember me telling you how me and my brother, your uncle Gurjinder, won the inter-village wrestling match in India? I haven't forgotten my skills. I can take good care of myself thank you very much, you'll see.' He smiled, hiding the worry that was now jabbing at his insides. 'But if it will make you all feel better I'll bring a dozen people along as back up.'

Maji and JJ both sighed with relief. A dozen should do it.

*

Forty minutes later and thirteen Indian men were waiting in the car park of the Paper Lantern. Except for the security spot lights, the building was devoid of light. It was obvious that no one was home . . . yet.

This 'yet' business was troubling Papaji. Why weren't Aaron and his daughter home? What could they be doing at such a late hour? His anger burned like flaming coals. This was one of the many reasons why the Western way of life was so incompatible with the Eastern way. Only muggers, murderers, burglars, drunks, homeless and freaks walk free in the middle of the night. He checked his watch: 1.30 a.m., and ordered one of his nephews to go and try the doorbell again (just in case).

'This time, leave it ringing for ten minutes. They could be in deep sleep,' Papaji demanded. The vision of his daughter lying next to this white fiend was causing his stomach ulcer to flare up. 'Make it fifteen minutes. No make it . . .'

He was interrupted by a set of car headlights lighting up the car park. A taxi pulled in and a slightly drunk Aaron wobbled out. Papaji felt panic was not too far away. But he'd already promised himself that no matter what, he would be bringing Jeena home tonight. From that moment on he wouldn't let her out of his sight until he had married her off in India. He'd keep her locked up in her bedroom with only a bucket for a toilet until the day they left for the airport. That would teach her what happens to Indian girls when they stray; when they try to turn their back on their parents' wishes and traditions. Papaji waited for another door of the taxi to open, but it just drove off.

So where was Jeena?

Aaron's immediate impression of the group of people walking across the car park towards him was that he was late for one of his jujitsu classes. By the time the crowd had arrived to within just a few feet it had occurred to Aaron that one, he was never late for a jujitsu class (the three strikes and you're out rule applied to him too), and two, he never held lessons at 1.30 in the morning.

And three, he didn't recognize any of the men – all of whom were Asian – except for one: Jeena's father. With a semi-drunk brain sobering rapidly it didn't take Aaron more than a couple of seconds to realize that this scene meant trouble. Trouble for him. Aaron looked over the faces of the men, their brown, angry features eerily distorted by the shine from the quarter moon. He hadn't felt fear like this for a long time, so long ago, in fact, that his alcohol-drenched mind was having a hard job remembering when. Instinct took over as Aaron quickly tried to establish who out of this group was the stronger. The golden rule, when out-numbered, is to attack the foundations and the rest would crumble. And the rule of rules is 'Never strike first!' Only now was he regretting those extra pints with his mates and the visit to Northern Lights night-club in celebration of his final decision *not* to marry Jeena. For one, he needed to be alert. For two, the whole cab journey back from Northern Lights he'd been telling the taxi driver, 'I'm bursting for a pee; as soon as you drop me off I'm running to the first bush I can find.' Aaron doubted that these severe-looking men, half with turbans on and half without, would appreciate him pulling down his trousers and hosing down the car park while they waited. They probably wouldn't think it very gentlemanly.

'What's all this about?' Aaron asked, directing his comment to Jeena's dad.

'We don't want any trouble, we just want Jeena. Where is she?' Papaji replied, his loud voice successfully disguising his nerves. 'She doesn't belong to you. She's not your property.'

'You mean she's gone missing?' Aaron faked concern. 'Have you tried her mobile? I've got her number here somewhere.'

One of the lads spoke, 'Don't fuck us around. Do you think that Asians are just going to let you white scum steal our women while we sit back and do nothing? You've got another thing coming if you do. Now, like her father kindly asked, tell him where his daughter is and then we'll leave you alone. We're not going anywhere until Jeena walks out of that building.'

Well, you've got a bloody long wait, thought Aaron. 'You're wasting your time, I don't know where she is and even if I did, I wouldn't tell you. Now, please, fuck off my property.'

As if pre-planned, the Asians stepped in and surrounded Aaron in a circle. Instantly he was sober. Fear squirted adrenalin into his bloodstream, clearing his mind and sharpening his reflexes. It was only now that Aaron recalled where he'd felt this fear before. From a period in his life which he'd tried hard to forget. He could honestly say, hand on heart, that after the day his parents had died, his childhood had been one, *painful* nightmare. Made worse by the fact that his gran, who suffered terribly with arthritis, was trying her utmost to be a replacement for both his mum and his dad.

Gran had tried her best to look after him with what money she had, clothing him and feeding him on a budget which most kids in his class had as pocket money. 'Aaron is a pauper and his nanna buys his clothes from jumble sales.' 'His parents didn't really die; they just wanted an excuse to get away from pauper Aaron.' 'Fifty pence to kick him or three kicks for a pound.' The children would surround a scrawny Aaron in a circle and take it in turns to kick and punch him. His gran would ask where all the bruises and cuts had come from and his reply was always, 'Football'. Which wasn't that far from the truth if one thought of Aaron as the ball.

The teachers, when investigating the rumours of the bullying, were presented with a wall of blank faces from the culprits and a young boy called Aaron, with a lost expression on his tear-streaked face, putting on a brave front but really too damn scared to grass anyone up. It left the teachers with no option but to pity him. But at night, when it was silent, Aaron promised himself that one day, he would get his revenge on each and every one of those nasty bullies from the Fletcher Gang. They would pay the price for calling his family losers. For ripping up his school books. For spitting in his packed lunch. For making his life a misery.

After six long years of bullying, at the age of fourteen, a fed-up Aaron had walked into his local martial arts centre. 'I want to be better than Bruce Lee,' Aaron had told his first instructor, who had laughed. Who had continued to laugh. Until, as Aaron trained harder and harder, and increased his body weight, everyone was in agreement: Aaron had champion in his bones and England was too backwards to nourish the marrow. There really was only one decision to make: send him to train with the best in the world, send him to Japan. Looking back, it was funny how the bullying had stopped the moment Aaron had got his yellow belt in jujitsu.

Now, he was an 8th-dan, and for the first time in years, Aaron was faced with what appeared to be a bunch of bullies. His heart rate was up and his reactions were on red alert. One side of him wanted to give the group a quick demonstration of some strangleholds and kicks, the other side wanted to resolve this amicably.

'Look, Mr Gill,' Aaron began, stepping towards Jeena's father, amazed at the size of this colossal man. 'I can see that you're very concerned about your daughter's whereabouts, but, sometimes you've got to let go of the apron strings and let her be. I'm sure that she'll turn up safe and sound before you know it.'

Not only was there a huge gap in years here but also a huge gap in cultures. Indian girls only had their apron strings cut when they were married. And even then, they weren't truly cut, only partially frayed. Papaji fumed with internal anger. Lectures from the younger generation never sat well with the older Indian men.

'I stand here facing the man who has corrupted my daughter's mind and used her body for his pleasure. I want to spit on him. I want to show you my great country of India and ask you whether you think you have the audacity to change the way Indians live. Do you honestly believe that our culture is so weak that it needs someone like you to improve it? Jeena is my daughter, I own her. Like you own this building.' Papaji pointed to the high brick walls. 'It is my job to protect her and keep her safe. I won't have people like you wrecking my plans for her. So, I suggest you listen to me very carefully. Jeena is getting married in a few weeks time. I have found a good man for her in India and she *will* be his bride. All your corruption will mean nothing to her out there amongst her own people. You won't be able to touch her when she's thousands of miles away.' Papaji dipped his head in closer. 'The longer Jeena stays away from us, the worse will be her punishment. So, if you do know where she is, then, for Jeena's sake, take me to her. My patience is already running out.'

'And, does she love this man you are forcing her to marry in India?' Aaron asked, ignoring the sneers and jeers from the crowd. 'Are you sure that this man will treat her right? Imagine if he turns out to be a wife-beater. Imagine if you marry your daughter off to a man who doesn't care for her well-being in the slightest. Could you sleep knowing that your daughter, the one you watched grow from a baby to a teenager to a woman, is unhappy and she is unhappy because *you*, yes, *you*, Mr Gill, forced her into something she was against?' Aaron watched Papaji's eyes drop. 'How can you marry your daughter to a complete stranger knowing that this stranger will take her to bed and have sex with her? You talk about me using your daughter for pleasure; at least Jeena knows who I am. And, more importantly, at least she wanted to go to bed with me; with your man in India she will get no choice. It's almost rape!'

Papaji had heard enough. How could he even begin to explain the Indian way to a white man? What, indeed, was the point? Papaji ushered his followers out of earshot for a quick meeting, then returned.

'If you see Jeena, then tell her that she is expected back home. Her poor mother is crying her eyes out at her disappearance. Remember what I said, the longer she stays out the worse will be her punishment.' And with that comment the Asian men got into their cars and sped away.

Sped away to leave Aaron in a huge dilemma. What was he going to do now? Listening to Jeena's father explain how he 'owned' his daughter was enough to send shivers down Aaron's spine. Owned? Children aren't cars, or houses, or Rolex watches, you can't own a twenty-seven year old woman. Was this the way all Indian men thought? Was ownership of Jeena transferred to her husband in India after the wedding? Would she then become her husband's property? What would happen to the Jeena he knew? The crazy, beautiful, fun, loving woman he knew wasn't capable of being owned unless you were willing to take away her personality. But what use is a woman without one of those? Jeena would become just an empty shell.

A vision so clear it could have been real popped into Aaron's head. Jeena, dressed in a sari, sitting on a bed on her wedding night. Her face sad and her eyes filled with tears. A man bursts into the room, her new husband, half drunk on booze, half drunk on power. He orders Jeena to strip, he wants sex and he wants it now. A frightened Jeena removes her sari while his semi-blurred eyes watch her become naked. She lies back on the bed and she cries as this virtual stranger forces himself on her. After the deed is done, the man turns his back on her and falls asleep. While he snores, Jeena thinks to herself, 'Why couldn't bastard Aaron have saved me from this hell? It was only for one year and now my whole life is a prison.'

Without time for doubt to creep back in, Aaron fished out his mobile and dialled Jeena's number. As he expected her phone was switched off.

'Hi, it's me,' Aaron spoke into the answer service, 'just ringing to remind you that we're getting married on Wednesday. Don't be late. We'll pick you and the girls up at twelve noon as planned. Cheers, wife. Aaron.'

After switching off the phone, Aaron smiled to himself. Thursday was going to be a great day. He couldn't wait for the morning after the wedding when, after driving back to Primpton, Jeena and he would turn up at her parents' house with fantastic news. 'Hi, Mr Gill, guess what? You don't "own" your daughter anymore. You see, Jeena and I are now husband and wife. We are officially married and there is nothing that you can do about it. I am your new son-in-law; fancy some wedding cake?'

It would be a major relief to know that he had done right by Jeena.

There was no way he was going to let the path to Jeena's happiness become obstructed by the ancient traditions of India. He was not going to stand by while Jeena's father wrecked his daughter's life. And if, for one moment, her father thought that he could punish

Jeena for her wrongs, then he'd be making the biggest mistake of his life.

After all, wasn't it a husband's duty to protect his wife? Even if it was from her own father.

Chapter Seven

With a hangover so severe that Aaron had to threaten his nine goldfish with his George Foreman Lean Mean Fat Reducing Grilling Machine for making too much gill noise, he arrived, after picking up his best man, Tyler, at Kitty's flat and threatened the girls also. 'My single status is about to die, ladies, so as far as this journey goes, it's a funeral. And funerals mean silence. Plus the fact that I've got a stinking hangover. So, please, no giggling, chattering or even whispering. Or I'll just have to kill you all.'

Tyler laughed.

'Same goes for you, mate,' Aaron said, slouched back on the sofa, sipping strong black coffee and closing his eyes.

'Miserable fuck!' Tyler responded.

All three girls nodded in agreement. This was supposed to be a happy day. The sun was shining, the girls had enjoyed a fantastic hen night, it was the eve of Jeena's wedding, the friends were all feeling the buzz dressed in their bright, slinky summer dresses and sandals, and Mr

Grouchy Head waltzes in with a face like off-milk and a mood which most storm clouds would be ashamed of. People on Death Row were more cheery than this.

Kitty, who had been introduced to dishy, blond, blue-eyed Tyler on a few occasions before but had paid him little attention (due to the fact that he was bastard Aaron's mate), was now paying him lots. A hot feeling inside and a warm flushing outside could mean only one thing: she was highly attracted to him. She was only thankful that she wasn't ovulating at the moment otherwise she'd most likely have mounted him already. She smiled across to him and he smiled back. It was sorted then, Kitty told herself: he was up for it if she was. She had two nights in Gretna Green to seduce him or to be seduced. He could definitely be The One. At least one couple might return from this trip to Scotland with a happy expression.

Coffees all drunk and last minute make-up in place, Aaron demanded that the girls reduce the luggage that they were thinking of bringing from three cases and bags each to just the one bag each.

'I don't know what you think I'm driving, but it's not a bus.' Aaron pointed to a stuffed bin liner. 'And what's in that?'

'Electric blankets,' replied Flora, staring at him like he was an idiot for asking. 'It gets cold up in Scotland.'

'One hot-water bottle between you, I might agree to, but no electric blanket.'

'I'll just have to use you then, won't I?' Kitty nudged Tyler. 'You'll keep me warm, won't you?'

Half an hour later the girls had dwindled their luggage down to a respectable amount and the five descended the stairs of Kitty's flat to set off for their four-hour journey to Dumfriesshire in Scotland. With Kitty and Flora asleep on the back seat and Tyler and Aaron chatting away at the front, Jeena admired the passing scenery as her mind wandered. She used to play a game with her brother when they were growing up called 'Brave or Stupid'. They would think up scenarios and judge them either 'brave' or 'stupid'. For example, Gran is asleep on the couch and you creep up and steal her false teeth, then return them to her mouth coated in spinach. Brave or Stupid? Or Papaji has just finished doing a number two in the toilet. You enter the bathroom after him. Brave or Stupid? You fill Papaji's turban with itching powder. Brave or Stupid? She wondered what her brother would make of her speeding up the motorway to marry a white womanizer whom she would be divorcing in exactly one year's time. Brave or Stupid?

Jeena watched her two friends sleep. Their lives were so much simpler than hers. They never worried too much what their parents thought of their lovers. Kitty and Flora didn't walk through life worrying whether or not they would be able to make round *chapattis* for their future husband. Or worrying whether or not they would be able to produce baby boys for him. You never heard them worrying about not being a virgin anymore. They certainly never had to worry about coming home from work one day to find that their parents had fixed up a meeting with a total stranger on the assumption that this would lead to marriage. Jeena smiled as Flora snored. Yeah, their lives were a whole lot simpler than hers. Simpler and filled with less worry. She pinched Flora's nose until the snoring ceased. And as far as Jeena could recall, their lives had always been that way.

At school, those wonderful days at Applebrook Comprehensive, she remembered Kitty dribbling at the sight of Mr Barlow, a stand-in P.E. instructor with thighs like trees. 'He's definitely The One for me,' she'd said, warning the rest of the girls in the year to steer clear, he was hers. And Flora, dear Flora, was always inundated with offers from boys, kissing them at lunch time and ending the relationship by the last bell. Flora and Kitty even updated the rules of Kiss Chase to a far superior game called simply 'Kiss'. No chasing, no wasting of energy, no breaking stiletto heels, the girls just stood still with the top buttons of their shirts open and their lacy bras on show while a line of hormone-filled boys queued up to kiss them. Kiss, soon became Snog which after a year or so became Shag.

Jeena had explained to her two school friends about her arranged marriage commitments and how having boyfriends was a definite no no. Although they found it hard to understand, the girls did sympathize, making an effort not to talk about boyfriends in front of her. Before long, however, Jeena's own hormones had kicked in, her breasts began to grow (and grow and . . .) and by the time you could say, 'Fuck me, is that Jeena? Look what happened to her tits and arse over the summer holidays', she was being pursued by rampant boys with filthy motives. It wasn't long before she was swapping her Indian traditions for a quick grope in Peter Nixon's pants. Pete, the captain of Applebrook's Scrabble Team, soon became her secret boyfriend. Her secret thrill. Her own Triple-Word Scoring HUNK. She now felt an equal to Kitty and Flora, as her experiences with the opposite sex began to match theirs. Jeena became two different people. Eastern Indian girl Jeena at home and at the temple. And Westernized Indian girl at school but especially in the bike sheds.

Teenage dreams of the past were brought to a halt as Aaron broke her concentration with a weird question, 'Did you bring a quilt?' he asked Jeena quietly, his eyes watching her through the rear-view mirror. 'It's just that Tyler wants to wear one as well as me. We want to make this Scottish wedding as traditional as possible.'

Jeena sat with a puzzled expression. 'He wants to wear a quilt?' Then it dawned on her what he meant by 'quilt'. 'Ho, ho very funny. A kilt. Very funny.'

Aaron and Tyler laughed which woke the other girls.

'Oh, at least Mr-Bear-with-a-Sore-Head is feeling better,' groaned Kitty, yawning like a guppy fish. 'Are we allowed to speak now, your Royal Highness?'

Indeed they were. Having been starved of natter chatter, the girls went into gabbing overdrive. Aaron rolled his eyes at Tyler, then drowned them out with a Greenday CD 'American Idiot' on full volume. Gretna Green was getting closer all the time; nerves that he normally saved for special occasions like jujitsu fights were having a ball in his belly. He just hoped that this all turned out well for Jeena in the end. He'd decided not to mention to her that her father and his twelve goonies had paid him a visit last night. She didn't need to know about any of that right now – and maybe she never would. Each mile further away from her family, he was sure, was tugging at her heart and ripping at her conscience.

Through the rear-view mirror he'd noticed her eyes become watery at times, obviously feeling the pain in her decisions, wondering what her future might bring. She'd mentioned that there was a good chance that she might be disowned by her parents the moment they returned from Gretna Green as husband and wife and still she wished to pursue this route. Brave or Stupid? Well, in his eyes, what Jeena was doing could only be described as brave, and for that he would make it his duty to fulfil his obligation to her and make this wedding day a special day to remember.

Even if that meant he had to sleep with her. Even if that meant he had to go back on the words he'd said to her: 'Now that I know you're going to be my wife, I'm quite turned off you ... Yuck!' Even if that meant he had to fake his orgasms. Besides, he didn't want a rumour going around that Aaron, the beast in bed, couldn't perform on his own wedding night. Not on your Nelly.

A few miles later, it began to become apparent to Tyler that Aaron was going through another one of his doubtful 'I hope I'm not making the biggest mistake of my life' patches when he noticed that they were driving up the motorway at only twenty m.p.h. Someone was obviously not in a rush to reach Gretna Green all of a sudden. Either that or, Tyler noticed Aaron's eyelids were nearly closed, either that or Aaron needed a coffee BIG TIME. He offered to swap seats and take over the driving once they had reached the obligatory motorway service station break just a couple of miles up the road.

As soon as the car came to a halt in one of the service station parking bays, the girls shot off to check out the shops. This was the perfect opportunity, and possibly the only opportunity, that Tyler would get to saddle Aaron with his moral point of view before they reached bonny Scotland. McDonald's seemed like the ideal place to give Aaron a super-sized portion of his philosophy. Their bums soon filled two plastic seats by the window; ready to knock on the glass if the girls happened to pass by. Aaron had already accepted that he would have to wreck his diet with a McDonald's, but it sort of paled into insignificance when you were about to wreck your life with an unwanted marriage.

'Have you seen the film *Green Card*?' Tyler asked, biting into his Big Mac, as Aaron shook his head. 'It's about a woman marrying a man in America so that he will get his green card. They live a fake life. Is that what you want, your life to be a fake?'

Aaron eyed Tyler over the top of his soggy Quarter Pounder. Here was a man with his head screwed on correctly (most of the time) and he could smell bullshit from a mile away. In fact, he'd smelt bullshit on the first day he'd met Aaron, about six years ago. Tyler was a carpenter by trade and was two years into a successful business designing, making and decorating fibreglass surfboards, when Aaron had turned up at his unit, Heavenly Waves, explaining that he needed a top-of-the-range surfboard ASAP because he was entering the World Surfing championships in Hawaii the following week. Some of the top surfers were names on Tyler's client list and he'd never heard any of them use words like 'It's got to be shark proof' or 'Will I get splinters in my feet?'

After some gentle probing from Tyler, Aaron had

eventually admitted that he'd never surfed in his life before and the real reason why he wanted the board was to do with sex. How he'd picked up a stunning Australian babe who was now under the impression that he was a 'World Champion Surfer' in the 'heavy-weight division'. How she was coming over in a few days to check out his nonexistent surfboard. How 'a shag depends on that board,' Aaron had begged. Soon, the two of them had reached an agreement after Tyler discovered that Aaron might not have been a great surfer but he was one of Britain's finest martial arts experts. Tyler *would* build a board worthy of a world champion in time for Aaron's date if, as a return favour, Aaron would agree to teach Tyler how to defend himself against crazy psychos. As Tyler worked his way through his belts, white to black, himself becoming quite an expert in jujitsu, the two of them became good, solid mates. A bit like the advice that Tyler dished out when he thought it wholly necessary: good and solid.

'I'd rather live one year in a fake marriage than live my whole life knowing that I've fucked up Jeena's,' Aaron explained. 'And if you're worried that my life will be ruined because I won't be allowed to sleep with other women, then don't! I've made it perfectly clear to Jeena that I won't sacrifice my sex life for her. In fact, I'm pretty sure that it will turn most women on know-ing that we're shagging in one room while my wife is next door in the other.'

Tyler laughed. 'I think you're missing a huge point here, Aaron. Has it not occurred to you that Jeena might already be in love with you? You've been together for, what, eight months now? I'm sure her feelings must run a little deeper than lust. I've got a horrible feeling that she might just be using this "arranged marriage" situation to trap you.' He sipped on his Sprite. 'You said yourself that you're saving her from a loveless marriage, and yet the irony here is that by saving her from one, you're prepared to have one yourself. It's got to be wrong.'

Tyler spotted the girls walking past, weighed down with cuddly toys and books, and knocked on the window to grab their attention. His concentration returned to Aaron. 'I think she's a great girl and all that, but, mark my words, once you marry her, divorcing her won't be so easy. You should have got that prenuptial agreement like I said.'

Aaron swallowed hard wondering whether the chat he'd just had with Tyler would be harder to digest than the Quarter Pounder his stomach was rebelling against. Prenuptial agreements sounded so cold, so American, so business-like and robotic. Yet, wasn't this wedding tomorrow just the same. Cold, robotic and business-like. When Aaron said the famous words, 'I do' wouldn't Cupid be jumping up and down with anger, screaming, 'Yeah, he does, but only for a bloody year and only for a bloody favour.' When Jeena and he stood on the same spot where thousands of other couples had stood and swapped their wedding rings, wouldn't the air echo with the ghostly sound of, 'It's a farce.' When the Minister said, 'You may kiss the bride', would Aaron put him in a headlock and tell him not to be so perverted: he can't kiss her, he doesn't even love the woman. And when the organist played the first tune for the newly-wed couple, would it be the sentimental classic, 'D I V O R C E' by Tammy Wynette?

The three girls joined the lads at the table – Aaron and Tyler were in the midst of arguing whether a curry sauce from McDonald's would beat up a BBQ sauce in a fight – grabbing a quick bite to eat themselves. Jeena had a non-beef Sikh-friendly Fillet of Fish, Kitty had two Big Macs and diet-freak Flora had the leftover gherkins. Munching away, Jeena noticed that Aaron kept darting her brief glances and then turning away. A few minutes of this and it was plain to see that his thoughts were revolving around her. He'd hardly spoken a word to her all day and yet his eyes were talking volumes. If she could have opened up his mind she was sure she would find a vision of the pair of them handcuffed together. 'Marriage devours a man's soul,' Aaron had often said. 'For a piece of bedtime pudding men become weak and fall into the grasp of an all-controlling, all-demanding, all-moaning, I've-got-you-under-the-thumb-now-my-lad-your-life-is-all-over woman,' Aaron had announced once while giving a best man's speech. 'As soon as the ring hits his finger his life hits the shit fan.' The last thing Jeena wanted was for Aaron to go through with the wedding with a head full of doubts. Or, as the Scottish would say, a heed full of doots. Besides, she couldn't bear the thought of living with him for a whole year while he sulked his way through life with a face so miserable anyone would think he was married to Anne Robinson.

As they got up to leave the McDonald's restaurant, Jeena pulled Aaron to one side before he strode off ahead. She needed to talk to him and it had nothing to do with his stealing a huge, huge handful of serviettes.

Jeena quickly assured him that Scottish people had ceased wiping their arses on tree bark years ago; they were not as backwards as he must have thought – they did in fact have toilet roll nowadays.

'I got them for Tyler. If he eats a Big Mac too quickly, he sometimes regurgitates tiny fragments of masticated mince. I'm not having bits of burger on my car's leather seats. Thank you very much.'

'Oh, lovely,' Jeena replied, trying to wash away the picture in her mind. 'So, how are you?'

Aaron smiled. 'What's this? I'm fine, and yourself?'

'Who me? Oh, I'm okay.' Jeena felt awkward and embarrassed but she had to address the situation. 'Sleep okay, did you?'

'Just tell me what's on your mind, will you?' he asked gently, kicking his trainers on the bleach-washed floor.

She took a deep breath. 'Right. I'm going to tell you straight, so if this sounds like I've gone all cold on you then it's because I have to be this way to say what I have to say.' Jeena looked around the virtually deserted diner, thankful there was no audience. 'If you don't want to marry me then say so now or forever hold your peace. I know you are doing me a huge favour but there is no way I can go through with this marriage if I know that every day, for a whole year, I'm going to be reminded by you what a great sacrifice you had to make. So, Aaron, this is your perfect chance to get out of it. If you have any doubts then say so now.'

After a quick think, with Jeena's father's words 'Jeena is my daughter, I own her' reverberating in his mind, Aaron took her hand and stared hard into her eyes. 'One year, I'm sure I can handle it. What could possibly go wrong? Come here, you look so worried.'

Jeena closed her eyes as Aaron held her tight. Moments like these were priceless to her. Moments when Aaron's entire being was concentrated on her and only her. Relief warmed her frosty thoughts as they stood in the middle of the burger bar and the pair of them enjoyed a long, meaningful, satisfying McHug.

Which, unfortunately for Jeena, did not lead to a McFlurry of kisses.

Chapter Eight

It was the morning of the wedding, with Jeena and Aaron resting peacefully in their hotel beds. Over 200 miles south, and resting just as peacefully in Aaron's gigantic bed, was a naked woman called Stacy. She'd been rolling around the bed half of the night pretending Aaron was making love to her. Breathing in his XS aftershave scent, rubbing herself against his sheets, wallowing in her own private fantasy. She'd lost Aaron for the time being – he'd dumped her only three days ago for mentioning that she might be falling in love with him – but she was sure she could win him back somehow. Although his last words to her wouldn't have left most women with much hope: 'Would you prefer to give me a goodbye kiss or a goodbye blow job? Your choice!'

What about the goodbye slap! Neatly followed by the goodbye insult, 'Bruce Lee was gay.' But 'goodbye' was something Stacy never wanted with Aaron. She'd imagined a great future with him, even though she'd heard about his track record with women. Like most

women who met Aaron over the years, she'd presumed
that she would be the one to change him. To mend his
ways. To make him loyal to her. It never occurred to
her that she would fail. Stacy Carter never failed at
anything; from being the prettiest girl in her school
(not to mention the most popular) Stacy breezed
through life, with the help of Daddy's flush wallet,
melting men's hearts, and dissolving their confidence. It
was always *Stacy* who dumped the men. It was always
Stacy who told men to back off. It was always *Stacy*
who stole other women's boyfriends. And, like
Goldilocks, but with brown hair, it was always *Stacy*
who was used to sleeping in any bed she wanted to.

Most men, given the chance, would have had trouble
keeping their minds clean when she was about. Always
dressed provocatively, showing off as much of her perfect body as was legal. Spending a ridiculous amount of
money on facials, manicures, pedicures, hair stylists
and tanning lotions. If looking good was art, then she
was the Monet of fashion. How dare Aaron dump
someone like her. Five whole months and twenty-two
days and sixteen hours and twelve minutes they had
been together. After meeting at a New Year party where
she had danced suggestively in front of him for half
the night, Aaron had asked her back to his apartment
for sex. She'd never come across someone so up front
before. The sex was magical but she'd had rather a
shock when she awoke the next morning to the sound
of aeroplanes taking off in the living room. Which
turned out to be Aaron meditating in front of his
Buddha with a tape of Heathrow Airport's runways
in the background. It was at that moment, just as a

Boeing 747 was taking off, that it dawned on Stacy that Aaron was not your typical guy. Beside the fact that in the looks department he was as hot as a steam pudding. Beside the fact that his tight, muscular, fit body with his scrummy six-pack could kick-start the lowest sex drive, and beside the fact that when he'd made love to her last night he reached parts that other desserts couldn't reach. Beside all that, Aaron had hidden depths and she couldn't wait to dive down to discover them.

But now she was dumped. After putting up with his womanizing ways for five months, twenty-two days, sixteen hours and twelve minutes, and without her managing to change him one iota, it was over as far as Aaron was concerned. He had warned her though; he'd made it extremely clear from the very beginning that his life would never revolve around just the one woman. His very words, if she remembered rightly were, 'I sleep around and if you want to be included in my circle of "special" women, then jump aboard. I only want a bit of fun without heavy commitments.' So Stacy had jumped aboard and nearly drowned when she'd realized that she'd fallen for him big style.

Stacy looked through the open curtains in Aaron's room while she lay on his bed. There was nothing but bright blue sky out there; June should be very proud of itself, thought Stacy. Nearly as proud as she was of herself. What great initiative she had shown to have made a secret copy of Aaron's front door key that day she'd popped out to buy the ingredients for a romantic Valentine dinner she was cooking him while he was taking a class in the martial arts centre downstairs. 'Let yourself in, Stacy. Please no offal though.' With a copy of the front door key and the number to his home alarm, she could more or less come and go as she pleased when Aaron was out and Aaron would be none the wiser.

Which was why she had stayed the night and why she was here today: Aaron was definitely out. During a conversation she'd had with him about three days before he'd dumped her, he'd explained how he was taking a business trip to Scotland for a few days. It was his reason why he couldn't see her this week. 'Let me come with you,' she'd pleaded, but was met with, 'Don't crowd me, Stacy.' She certainly wasn't crowding him today.

Stacy loved bedrooms, it was where sex normally took place. She also liked bus stops but that was another story. Taking a good look around Aaron's large, airy bedroom her mind did wonderful things with his body. Imagining it in all kinds of positions as she played his dark mistress. She sat on the bed, bouncing up and down, feeling the obvious quality of its tightly packed springs. Her bare feet tapped a tune on the deeply varnished wooden floor. From one wall to another there stood a hand-crafted fitted wardrobe. Just beside the bed was a small chest-of-drawers. And the windows were dressed with a beige and cream set of curtains matching the décor of the room throughout. There was a simplicity to this bedroom which was extremely pleasing to Stacy. A bedroom in which she felt at home already – and she hadn't even moved in *yet*.

Pulling out her red leather suitcase from under Aaron's bed, she grabbed her neatly ironed clothes and placed them on the now made-up duvet. A tiny excuse of a pink designer skirt, a white cropped T-shirt, G-string, bra and her kitten-heeled sandals. The last time she'd been here she'd showered with Aaron; today she would have to shower alone. Then after the shower, it was time to get to work and begin what she was really here for.

She'd seen many films where women seek revenge. *Fatal Attraction* being the most famous. Bunny boilers reaping hellfire on men who've cheated on them. This was not about revenge; it wasn't about cooking cute cuddly pets on the stove with a sprig of rosemary and thyme, then serving them up with new potatoes and steamed asparagus topped with a light melt-in-the-mouth buttery sauce. Mmm. It was about none of that. It was about winning back Aaron. Rekindling the embers of a once wonderful partnership. Retying the knot.

After showering and dressing and nosing through Aaron's appointment diary, Stacy wandered casually around the spacious apartment assessing the situation. Aaron was extremely keen on living his life by the principles of Feng Shui. His whole structured existence was dependant on the rules that Feng Shui provided. No clutter. No sharp corners. No overhead beams. Right down to which direction his bed faced. Stacy had been reading up on this philosophy, gathering information which she might be able to use to her own benefit. For starters, in each house, flat, apartment whatever, there is a Romance Corner. The southwest area. It is this space which, if not correctly set up, will have negative vibes on your romance.

With a compass in her hand, Stacy walked to the

southwest part of Aaron's living area. In his case it was his dining room. Already hanging from the ceiling was a beautiful crystal chandelier which encouraged happiness in his love life. All Stacy needed to do was to add an item which would destroy the energy flow of the apartment and by doing so destroy the energy flow of Aaron's love life. She flicked through the pages of her Lillian Too Feng Shui guide and smiled. To destroy Aaron's current romance – whoever that might be with – it was necessary to place a piece of wood near the crystals, which was an earth element, and the wood would wipe out the auspicious vibes. Within minutes, Stacy had removed her sandals, stood on the glass dining-room table and hidden a couple of matchsticks amongst the crystal stalactites. The book stated that bad Feng Shui in this area would lead to divorce, loneliness and a total absence of marriage opportunities. What a result! It was now only a matter of time before she'd be comforting Aaron in her arms. He would soon be all hers.

And only hers.

Chapter Nine

The oldest inhabitant of Gretna Green had lived there for over 250 years. Where he lived, nobody knew, but come any wedding service, he would always arrive on time and bless the couple with his arrow. His name was Cupid and his purpose was to ensure love flourished. What he would make of Jeena's and Aaron's wedding was his business, but it is doubtful that he would approve of Aaron sleeping with another woman on the eve of his wedding.

For sleep with another woman Aaron did.

The previous evening, after arriving in Gretna Green and checking into the four-star Golden Arch Hotel, a beautiful converted Victorian mansion, the group settled themselves down for a night of drinking and chatting in a homely pub called the Cat & Whiskers, just a stone's throw away from their hotel. Rickety wooden chairs (covered in red tartan cloth) and tables, a radio as a jukebox and a home-cooked food menu which boasted locally caught salmon and organic garden vegetables. On a blackboard behind the bar, written in chalk were the words:

For That Wedding-Night Passion
Try the Cat-o'-nine-tails cocktail
and whip up some action in the bedroom.

Within minutes of Aaron downing his second Cat-o'-nine-tails he was already on the lookout for potential sexual partners. Much to the disgust of Jeena, Kitty and Flora. Aaron tried to explain that it was not uncommon, in certain tribes, for the man about to get married to go and have sex with as many women as he could on the night before wedlock.

'The Buga Buga Tribe, if you must know,' Aaron had said, trying hard not to laugh, winking at the listening landlord. 'Don't you watch the Discovery Channel?'

It was the first time anyone had heard of The Buga Buga Tribe and before they had a chance to interrogate him further, he was across the busy pub and chatting up a pretty blonde, or in the words of Jeena, a 'treacherous tart'.

Even Tyler, who'd seen Aaron stoop extremely low in his life, was embarrassed at Aaron's lack of respect towards Jeena. And if Aaron thought he could blame his awful behaviour on the two cocktails he'd drunk, then Tyler would quickly remind him that he, himself, had already downed three Cat-o'-nine-tails, and you didn't see him trying to mount the first skirt that walked into the pub. After being jollied by the girls to go and fetch him before he did something he regretted,

Tyler stood up to find that Aaron had already left the pub with the blonde. Over the next hour or so, as he listened to the three girls describe Aaron, Tyler was surprised to hear that there was so many varieties of pig out there.

In some ways, both Kitty and Flora were not so shocked. Hearing of Aaron's new-found kindness, when he'd agreed to sacrifice his single status to help out a woman in distress, that woman being their best friend Jeena, had been not only hard to believe, but also somewhat creepy. The Aaron whom they had grown to hate, the *real* Aaron, the man who broke women's hearts as soon as they opened them to him, was the Aaron who had just left the pub with the blonde. His actions tonight simply validated what they already really thought of him. A bastard.

Running out of breeds of pig, the girls were about to rip into Aaron with different species of snakes, when, waltzing into the pub, with a broad smile on his now-sweaty face, was Aaron himself. He narrowly escaped getting caught up with a highland fling dance being performed by four pant-less kilted men, who kept shouting, 'Hoy' every time they lifted up their kilts to show off their own home-grown vegetables.

With a self-satisfied expression on his face that made all three women want to whack him with their hand-bags, Aaron sat down and greeted them all a good evening.

'One question, Aaron,' Jeena asked, eyeing his rum-pled Red Lizard T-shirt. 'Did you screw her?'

'Twice! Once against a wall and once on a bit of grass.'

All three girls stood up in disgust and left Tyler and Aaron to their own company. Just before leaving, Jeena turned her head and noticed that the blackboard had been updated. It now read:

For That Wedding-Night Passion
Try the Cat-o'-nine-tails cocktail
and whip up some action in the bedroom.
As used by The Buga Buga Tribe.

She sneered at the landlord. Men! Sex was just a big joke for them. Then focused her attention on Aaron who appeared to be receiving a hefty bollocking from Tyler. She closed the pub door behind her and joined her friends underneath the star-pricked night. That was the last she saw of Aaron until the next day.

The next day!
Even though the wedding was a duff wedding, the three girls still approached it as they would have if it had been a meaningful wedding. This meant certain tools and special brushes. Expensive make-up and an eye for detail. Hours and hours of refining and adjusting until what stands before you is the perfect bride.

Jeena closed her eyes while Kitty guided her to the huge antique mirror in their hotel room. Even the girls were gobsmacked at how beautiful Jeena had become. An Indian queen stood amongst them. For Jeena was not only graceful and beautiful but she was also sexy, exotic-looking and exciting. It was such a shame that she happened to be marrying a complete and utter rattlesnake; it almost seemed like a waste of effort.

'I'd marry you myself,' Flora said, playing with a loose curl in Jeena's hair. 'Go on then, have a look at yourself, and try not to cry.'

Warily, Jeena opened her heavily made-up eyes and stared sadly at the reflection of a woman she hardly recognized. Her mother should have been here today and so should her family. The Indian lifestyle is so geared to the wedding day that hardly a week will go by in any Indian household without a wedding being mentioned. Her house was just the same. Maji and Nanaji were constantly preaching about how special the wedding is for an Indian bride. It is supposed to be *the* day when she makes her entire family proud. Jeena wiped her tears, scared to think too deeply. There was not a chance on this earth that her parents would be happy about what she was doing today, no matter how beautiful she might have looked in her wedding sari, especially as that sari was a gift from an aunt who lived in India, for Jeena to wear on her wedding day. No doubt her aunt would have taken a negative view of the way in which Jeena had 'stolen' it from her mother's trunk to use in her secret marriage to a white man.

The red and gold silk bridal sari could only be described as breathtaking. Each stitch, each square-inch of fabric shone with historical meaning. On her hands, Kitty had painted, in painstaking detail, henna designs worthy of an art gallery. Her black hair, with its red highlights, had been left loose with just a few curls. On her *mehndi*-coated feet decorated with a few elegant toe rings, she wore red high-heeled strappy sandals. To add a little sexiness to the picture, she wore a low-cut sari blouse showing off her ample cleavage; and

111

her slim tummy, complete with a circle of jewel-like bindis around her navel, was left on view. Indian women have been marrying in saris since the year dot. Fashions change over the decades; some saris are more sequinned and sometimes even the colour changes to pink. But, when all is said and done, putting history to one side, putting arranged marriages to the other, when one sees an Indian bride in all her glory one can not help but gasp.

Trying to show gratitude with a weak smile, Jeena could tell that her two friends knew what she was thinking. They both stood by her, themselves dressed in royal-blue silk saris, bangles and bindis, and gave her their special hug. Heartfelt hugs they usually gave each other when one of them had been dumped. If the girls were to have cried now, so much mascara would have run that, from the black puddle on the floor, people might think they had struck oil.

This special moment was wrecked by the sound of Aaron shouting through the door that he wanted to apologize. Jeena asked Kitty to let him in and after aiming looks of severe distaste in his direction, both Kitty and Flora made themselves scarce and joined Tyler in the room opposite. Aaron was sure he heard the words, 'You poisonous African viper snake' followed by a loud hiss, as Kitty slammed the door behind her, leaving him and Jeena alone in the luxurious, thick-carpeted, double-bedded room. Named the Phoenix Suite possibly because of the huge open fire.

Dressed in a slept-in T-shirt, tartan shorts (don't ask), unshaven and a hairstyle so unkempt it would make a tramp laugh, Aaron stared at Jeena standing by the large, open window. His first thought was that President Bush had a lot to answer for, for not signing up to the Kyoto Agreement, and causing the climate changes. Either that or the room suddenly felt so warm because he was now staring at the most beautiful woman he'd ever set eyes on in his entire life and the term 'hot under the collar' could now be reclassified as 'hot in the boxers.' Jeepers Creepers he was momentarily lost for words. Muzzled by beauty was a new one for him.

Finally the silence ended. 'That's a mighty fine dress you've got on there, lady,' he said, in his best John Wayne voice. Then realized by the harsh expression on her face that he had better start acting his age. 'I mean, you look amazing. Totally stunning. Awesome. It must have taken at least an hour to get ready.'

It took a fucking hour just to henna her feet.

She replied: 'About ten minutes actually. I don't go in for all that trying to look special for a man . . . unless he *is* a special man. Honestly, these are the same clothes I used to do the gardening in.'

'Really?' Aaron appeared amazed. 'And to think I went out and bought a brand new Armani suit. Gardening?' Suddenly it clicked. 'You're having me on, aren't you?'

So what if she was. A few jokes at his expense was chicken feed compared to how he'd made her feel when he shot off in the dark last night to pin some broad up against the wall. She watched and listened to an obviously nervous Aaron jabber on about this and that until it was time for him to knuckle down to his apology. It was totally clear that Aaron was having pre-wedding nerves. He was a caricature of a man hen-pecked into a marriage.

'I'm feeling pretty lousy about myself right now, Jeena, as though I've let you down.' His dark-blue eyes swam with remorse, as he sat down on the bed next to Mr Piggles, Jeena's two foot high teddy-pig. How the fuck she'd managed to smuggle this in his car he'd never know. 'What I did yesterday was unforgivable. I know we're not having a real marriage but that's no excuse for how I behaved. People out there don't know we're not getting married for real and for them to see me, your groom, messing around with another bride; what will they think? They'll pity you.'

The last time Jeena's mouth grew this wide was at the dentist. She was shocked beyond belief. 'Please tell me that the woman you shagged "twice" last night wasn't someone else's bride. *Please*, Aaron. No one goes this low.'

'It's not my fault. I told her it was wrong but she refused to say stop. If it makes you feel any better, she's only marrying the man for his money anyway.'

Her face twisted to a snarl. 'What sort of people do you mix with? I can't believe that you've come to this wonderful, romantic place and turned it into a red-light district. Only *you* could do that.'

After listening to Aaron repeat his apology over and over, varying his tactics each time, Jeena finally agreed to forgive him. What choice did she have anyway? It was either call it all off and face the wrath of her parents or see the plan through and face the wrath of her parents. At least by marrying Aaron, she could officially say that she had a future to look forward to in England;

114

the country where she was born. Besides, even with all Aaron's faults, there was this small matter she had to deal with. This matter of her loving him.

And also this more important matter she had to deal with: *why* did she love him? To people looking in he would seem like the oddest of choices. He was a fiend, a womanizer, an adulterer. His willy had been through more tunnels than an underground train. What was worse: as soon as a woman declared her love for him, all of a sudden her tunnel was out of use and their relationship had come off the rails. Any form of commitment had him yanking at the emergency stop cord as if there was a body on the line. And in a parallel universe it was *his* body on the line. The train of love was about to end his life.

But why was he like this? The question had been on repeat in Jeena's mind ever since she'd found out about his phobia. Kids who had had a bad experience with spiders, would sometimes grow up with arachnophobia. Or a nasty experience in a small space might have them grow up with claustrophobia. So what in God's name had frightened Aaron so much as a kid to have him grow up with commitmentphobia? Or, as it is more scientifically known, gametophobia. Maybe his parents were divorced and he'd gone through hell when they split up. Or perhaps he'd been hurt deeply by an ex-girlfriend. The truth of the matter was she didn't know. In fact, there was much about Aaron that she didn't know. He kept the past closer to his chest than a poker player. No peeping for even his closest of friends. He'd show his hand when the time was right and until then Jeena instinctively knew not to delve too deeply with him. He was originally from Northampton, he'd lived in Japan for a few years, he'd opened a martial arts centre in Primpton and that . . . was all she wrote. Sisters? Brothers? Family? Had he even been to prison? She knew nothing.

Except she loved him. BUT WHY? Jeena had wrestled round after round with this. He was fantastic to look at, fantastic in bed, fantastically funny and fantastically good company. Mr Fantastic. But none of this was enough to bring the scales down in favour of love, especially when 'womanizing bastard' sat on the other side of the scales. So what gives? It had definitely gone beyond the infatuation stage – that happened on the first day she slept with him when, following a short after-sex snooze, she awoke to find another woman's knickers under her pillow. Infatuation flew across the room along with the knickers. She didn't even want to ask him if the sheets were clean after that. Her mouth certainly wasn't with the amount of expletives pouring out of it. So it was *not* infatuation.

He hadn't saved her from a murderer, so it was *not* hero-worship either. She was not in to materialism, so it was *not* his money. It wasn't his stylish clothes, or his total self-confidence. It wasn't even that he had once told her that if she needed to let one go in public he would quite happily take the blame. A real gentleman for sure. All she could pinpoint it to – the reason she was in love with Aaron – was a situation which had occurred on their very first date.

They had arranged to meet at seven p.m. outside Dr Herbs alternative medicine shop on Primpton High Street. It was November and the Christmas lights, draped from lamppost to lamppost, seemed to shiver in the cold wind. People were wrapped in thick coats, scarves and hats to keep out the chill. It was hard to believe on such a bitterly cold and dark night that Jeena's heart would soon be filled with the warm glow of love.

Aaron had arrived on time, which was a good start in Jeena's eyes who was far more used to men turning up with a lame traffic-jam excuse. Immediately he'd grabbed her and given her an Eskimo kiss on the nose, claiming that at temperatures reaching below one degree, it was a pure act of survival.

'When it gets below minus ten degrees, Jeena, then obviously a kiss isn't good enough,' he'd said, taking her gloved hand and walking up the street. 'Shagging is a great way to prevent hypothermia.'

Jeena had had to remind herself that this was only the second time she'd seen him, the first being the *Asian Delight* magazine interview at the Paper Lantern Martial Arts Centre, and already his initial topic of conversation was bonking. Not that she should have been too shocked. The phone chat she'd had with him the other day to organize this date was enough warning for anyone, when he'd opened the conversation with questions such as: are you on the pill? To which she'd replied sarcastically, 'Oh yes, I take my vitamins every day.' Aaron had followed this, just as sarcastically, with, 'Good job I didn't ask you if you wear a cap, you'd probably have replied "No, I have a bobble hat".'

The two ambled onwards, nattering about food, restaurants, eat-all-you-like buffets and eating. Even a bad detective would surmise that the pair of them were getting hungry. They were just about to cross the road and head for a trendy Indian Michelin Star restaurant called The Spice Cave, when raised voices emanating from an alleyway between two shops caught the pair's attention. The unmistakable sound of someone being punched had Aaron's body on fight or flight mode.

Halfway down the dark and smelly alley, amongst the skips and wheelie bins, a group of three teenage youths, all of about nineteen years in age, appeared to be laying into another teenager. Jeena tugged hard on Aaron's arm.

'Keep out of it, Aaron, you never know these days. One of them might have a knife.'

He was about to reply when one of the youths shouted, 'Fuck off, scumbag, none of your business. Go on, fuck off!'

Aaron looked into Jeena's worried eyes, shrugged and jogged down the alley towards the trouble. As far as he was concerned there was no justifiable reason in this whole world for bullying. Big countries did it to smaller countries (for oil). Big armies with bigger weapons did it to smaller armies with smaller weapons. And big groups of lads would do it to smaller groups of lads. Aaron could recall the faces of his own bullies smiling as they kicked him down the science block stairs. He could hear the laughter as they tried to force dog shit into his mouth. And he could feel the pain when the punches rained down on him as he cowered away from their hard, bony fists.

Before Aaron even knew what was occurring he'd knocked all three of the teenage bullies to the pavement. He saw the fear in their eyes match the fear in the lad they had been punching. Without blocking their way, he watched as they ran off, hoping that their mothers knew how to wash dirty stains out of their now-soiled tracksuit bottoms.

Refusing to make a song and dance about it, Aaron pulled the bruised and bloody-nosed youth to his feet; checked to see if he was okay then handed him his business card stating that he was welcome to use the martial arts centre for free. He quickly explained how he would give him a crash course in the art of self-defence. Aaron saw hope in the boy's eyes and it felt good to bolster his confidence.

Just before Aaron left, he asked, 'What was all that about anyway?'

'They wanted my mobile phone.'

Aaron shook his head. Muggers these days really had dropped their standards. It used to be jewels, watches and wallets they were after, now it was phones, trainers and sunglasses. He wondered how long it would be before muggers were mugging you for your hair gel. (Although, at some of the prices of hair gel in the shops nowadays, we were being mugged already).

From a doorway, Jeena had watched the whole event unfold. So Aaron had a kind side to him. A protective side which was hidden deep within. He had reversed the situation perfectly, breaking the bullies' morale and helping someone who needed help. When he'd rejoined her, she'd expected his heartbeat to be racing away, instead, he was as calm and collected as someone who had just returned their library books (without a fine). This moment, this defining moment, was the moment when she fell in love with him. It was as simple as that.

*

Now, eight months later, she was about to marry him. In some ways she wasn't that much better than the youths beating up that teenager. Because in some ways she was a bully herself. Would Aaron have really gone through with all this marriage business if she hadn't virtually bullied him into it? She doubted it.

Jeena was alone with Aaron in a hotel room. She wondered how many other couples in Gretna Green's history had broken the 'groom should not see the bride in her dress before the wedding' rule. She prayed bad luck would not come their way.

She walked towards Aaron in her sari and sat next to him on the bed. In just over an hour, they would be heading for the Marriage Room at the Blacksmith's Shop to become man and wife. She gazed at his ragged appearance and hoped that an hour would be enough to expose the gorgeous hunk she knew was hiding under that grime. She put her head on his shoulder and he placed his arm around her. It was a magic moment to be savoured.

After a few minutes, Aaron stood up. 'I've booked us the honeymoon suite. It's your choice if you want to join me or else I'll have to wallow in champagne all by myself.'

'Please ask me properly.'

He shrugged. 'Okay. Shag in honeymoon suite later. Multi-orgasms guaranteed. Deal?'

It was difficult to refuse such a beautifully put offer. 'Deal.'

They smiled at each other, then Aaron sauntered off. Before the door, he turned. 'Did you mean deal as in "deal" or deal as in "no thanks I'll use a dildo"?' He ducked as she threw a pillow at him. 'Well, I suppose I'll catch you later then. For our wedding, Mrs Myles.'

Mrs Myles? Jeena thought. Something was telling her she should be miles away.

From him.

Chapter Ten

After keeping the girls on tenterhooks as to what form of transport the five of them would be travelling in – A Rolls Royce? Horse and Carriage? A vintage Bentley? – Tyler emerged from the hotel entrance with news that their chauffeur awaited them.

'We are going in a stretched,' Tyler began as the girls all screamed in glee. 'A stretch-TAXI.'

All eyes turned to Aaron: stingy bastard.

With the taxi windows open all the way, because Tyler couldn't resist the Kipper Special pre-wedding breakfast, their transport soon arrived at the Blacksmith's Courtyard in the grounds of Gretna Hall. The afternoon sun was out in force with a few wispy clouds decorating the blue sky. On the short journey up here, they had passed other wedding parties celebrating on the lush green landscaped lawns. So many brides and so many grooms, with so many wedding vows just waiting to be broken.

After paying the cab fare, all five stood on the cobblestone of the courtyard. The air tingled with hope and good fortune. This was a small wedding party for sure, but a well dressed one at that. Both Aaron and Tyler had scrubbed up remarkably well in their black-designer suits. Bridesmaids Flora and Kitty looked exquisite in their blue saris, and as they walked in their heels it was obvious that the two of them had put in the practice required if one wanted to wear a sari without it unravelling and exposing one's underwear to all and sundry. And the best flower in the bunch, Jeena, looked every inch a goddess.

With only ten minutes to go until the wedding was due to begin, Kitty passed around a small bottle of rum for the nerves; each of them swigging a tipple, each of them pulling a gurn face as the foul-tasting liquor hit their taste buds. They were about to walk the final thirty yards or so to the Blacksmith's entrance when rowdy male voices from another wedding party behind them stopped them in their tracks.

'Don't marry him, he's got VD,' one voice shouted.

'He's had a sex change!' another voice. 'He wears women's panties when he's having a jujitsu fight. He owns the *Queer* Lantern Martial Arts Fighting School. Don't marry him!'

Aaron turned round and smiled. Well, well, well. What a surprise! Sean and Charlie, dressed in designer suits, greeted him with a manly shake of the hand. Aaron, with some alarm, noticed the camcorder hanging around Charlie's thick neck. It was a well-known fact to all of Charlie's friends that he was desperate to get a home movie played on *You've Been Framed*. Even if that entailed fucking someone's life up: like pushing the bride into the wedding cake or greasing the local swimming pool's diving board with lard.

'We wouldn't have missed this for the world; our best mate tying the knot and us not being there, are you mad?' Charlie said to Aaron, giving Jeena a kiss on the cheek. 'Nice dress, darling. Going somewhere nice?' He cracked up at his own non-funny joke then turned his attention to Kitty and Flora. 'My, my, what have we got here?' He raised his hand, still the joker. 'No, don't tell me. Two Turkish belly dancers?'

The general response was, 'ho, ho.' What a result, they had a comedian aboard.

With Charlie's mouth on overdrive, Sean decided to take Aaron to one side.

'I'm still dead against this wedding, mate,' Sean began, in almost a whisper. 'I'm here to show support but I disagree with what you're doing.' He leant in real close. 'But, I can't wait to see you sweat when you take those marriage vows. It will be well worth that sodding four-hour journey up here.' He glanced over to Charlie who was busy showing off in front of the girls. 'That fucker talked about Gulf War Syndrome the whole shitting way. I nearly drove into a lorry just for some peace.'

Aaron and Sean laughed, which made Charlie suddenly paranoid, which, he told everyone, was a sure sign of GWS.

'Were you laughing about me, Aaron?' Charlie asked. 'It may be your wedding day but carry on like that and it will be your funeral as well. Got it?' He glared at Sean – his so-called best friend. 'And don't think I didn't catch *you* laughing either.'

'Stop trying to turn your life into a conspiracy theory, Charlie,' replied Sean, who, like most people, was used to Charlie's petty squabbles. He then focused his attention back on Aaron. 'Did I tell you that this plonker phoned me up a couple of days back at five in the morning? He said, and I quote, "I'm done for, Sean, there's a man outside my house in a dark suit". It only turned out to be his fucking milkman.' And they both laughed again.

At that moment the elderly usher opened the door to the Blacksmith's Shop and called them all inside, paying little heed to the argument in full swing between Sean and Charlie regarding who could break the most bones with a roundhouse kick. The usher was used to arguments of any kind – he was a Scot after all.

Trying to soak up as much of the atmosphere as possible, Jeena admired her surroundings. The wonderful flagstone floor, the pure whitewashed walls and the heavy blacksmith's anvil standing on top of a raised platform. Jeena wondered at the variety of wedding dresses which must have been worn over the years in this most traditional of non-traditional wedding venues. From jeans and T-shirts to fully flowing gowns. From cowgirl suits to Superwoman costumes. Even Shirley Temple dresses (for the extra short women) to Marilyn Monroe outfits (for the extra busty women).

And now, today, Indian.

After some kerfuffling around, Jeena and Aaron took their places before the Minister who, in a soft, Scottish accent, read out some lines from his leatherbound tattered book. Aaron tried hard not to look at the thread veins covering the Minister's bulbous nose; it was quite obvious that he'd been taking quite a few liberties when drinking from the body of Christ. Either that or someone had attempted to draw a map on his hooter.

It wasn't long before it was time for the pair of them to take their vows. Vows that each of them had written for the other to repeat. Vows that each of them thought would make for a more interesting wedding if they were to go against tradition and write each other's. Jeena handed Aaron his vows which had been typed out on a fancy bit of card. Many hours of deliberations and deep questioning had gone into the make-up of those words and she hoped that Aaron would not take offence at some of them. It had obviously slipped her mind when writing them that their wedding wasn't even a real one. And more importantly that Aaron didn't even love her.

With the Minister shuffling his feet impatiently, Aaron took hold of Jeena's hennaed hand, tried to block out the vision of his mates standing behind him with smug looks on their faces and began to read the words.

'I, Aaron Michael . . .' He paused, so wishing now that he'd never changed his name when he was a teenager. 'I, Aaron Michael . . . Bruce Lee . . . Myles take –'

His voice was interrupted by the most boisterous laughter this Minister had ever borne witness to. Even he, the Minister allowed himself a quiet chuckle. Bruce Lee? Of all the names. After a good five minutes the room had settled down enough for Aaron to continue.

'I, Aaron Michael Bruce Lee Myles take you, Jeena Kaur Gill to be my hope and my dreams, to be my pathway to a future of total happiness. To give me strength when I need it the most and to hold me tight when I feel weak.' He paused again and gave Jeena a 'What the fuck is this?' look, then carried on. 'To love you until my heart beats no more and to burn with passion when you are near. To . . .' He stared up to the Minister, pleading with his eyes. 'I can't say this next bit.'

But the Minister was having none of it and urged him on with a nod of his red bloated head.

'To say "I love you" at least *thirty* times a day and to mean it. To never stray with other women. To dream only of you. To wake up thinking about you and to go to sleep thinking about you.' Through gritted teeth he said, 'Yes, I'll take Jeena to be my lawful wedded wife. And I agree it's the best decision I have ever made.' He placed the wedding band on Jeena's finger.

The tittering behind had reached maximum accompanied by snaps from cameras shooting off and the gentle hum of Charlie's camcorder as each finger-licking detail was captured in pure pixel purity. The lads' night in from now on was bound to include Aaron's wedding video.

Onwards, and it was now Jeena's turn to read out Aaron's vows. He handed her the crumpled-up piece of paper. Hidden amongst the doodles and crossed-out sentences was a small paragraph with the heading: EMPTY PROMISES.

'I, Jeena Kaur Gill, take Aaron Michael Bruce Lee Myles to be my wedded husband. I promise never to argue with him. I promise never to ask him who the woman in his bed is. I promise to give . . .' Jeena stumbled, then shook her head. 'I can't read this, Aaron, it's too crude.'

The Minister, who obviously liked a bit of pre-wedding friction, told Jeena she *must* read on. 'Please lend Aaron the same courtesy that he lent you, Jeena. Okay?'

She begrudgingly agreed and continued with her courtesy. 'I promise to give you a blow job on your command. I will drop all I am doing to see to your blow job needs. I will not become a moaning wife. And if this loving relationship does prematurely end then I will not take half of your martial arts centre or anything else for that matter.' She placed the wedding band on Aaron's finger.

And even though Jeena's family was absent, and the room was barely filled with people, and it was all so rushed, and most of the glitz and glamour was missing, and the rings were from Argos, still, it was a heart-stirring moment for Jeena and one which would live with her forever.

'I now pronounce you man and wife. Congratulations, Mr and Mrs Myles. You may now kiss the bride.'

Their eyes met and they kissed each other. Wolf whistles were not the norm at a wedding but then again Charlie wasn't your normal wedding guest. Aaron and Jeena were not your normal married couple. And this was not your normal wedding.

How could it be when in exactly one year's time the two of them had already agreed on a divorce?

Party poppers ripped high into the wooden beams, Tyler let loose with his gas siren, Flora and Kitty cried with smiles on their faces, Charlie and Sean cheered as if they were at a football match, Jeena apologized to the Minister for her guests' behaviour and Aaron . . .

. . . Aaron looked green with sickness as the words, 'Mr and Mrs Myles' reverberated through his now non-bachelor mind. He glanced at his watch, just another 364 days, twenty-three hours and fifty-three minutes to go. He fiddled with the gold band on his finger. The ring felt more like a set of handcuffs than a promise to love and to cherish. A solitary tear rolled down his cheek and Charlie shot across to console him.

'Chin up, mate; think of all the tax benefits.' He put his arm around his shoulder and gave him a 'friend-in-need' hug. 'This will teach you for gardening in every bush you come across.' Charlie faced the Minister. 'You know about bushes, don't you, sir?'

'I beg your pardon,' the Minister replied, then realized what Charlie had meant. 'Oh, you mean the burning bush from the Book of Moses?'

'Yeah, that's the one. I doubt if Aaron would have gone gardening in her bush if it was on fire, hey?'

All three girls glanced at Aaron and his laughing friends with contempt and disgust. It was little wonder that the next words the Minister said were,

'Get out, the lot of you. You bring shame and disrespect to this ceremony. Please go!'

The wedding was followed by a scrumptious meal at Tuxedos restaurant washed down with a copious amount of booze. Although, the seven of them had nearly been thrown out of the posh establishment when Charlie had asked the *maître d'*, as he always asked when eating out, if he would be so kind as to warm through his home-prepared chicken and pasta meal, which he'd brought with him, in their microwave oven as he was suspicious of being poisoned by 'the enemy'. It was only after the others had explained that Charlie was an ex-Gulf War soldier that the reluctant *maître d'* took the Tupperware container and sent it to the kitchen for nuking. Nuking wasn't the best word that a paranoid, GWS-suffering war veteran wished to hear. But with the support of the table, Charlie had coped. It hadn't even occurred to Charlie that the *maître d'* could easily have poisoned his pasta while taking it to the kitchen. As it was, he only put a spoonful of French mustard in it instead. ('To give it some taste,' said the head chef after sampling it, 'God the English are so bland').

A food place that served booze, was followed by a booze place that served food. A pub called the Pig 'n' Truffle was a famous retreat for after wedding parties with its live music and oldie atmosphere. Jeena, Aaron and the gang sat around a thick oak table as huge tankards of cold, frothy beer were served up. It wasn't until after ten p.m. that the live music arrived in the form of a little old man and his violin. Most people were too pissed by now to realize that he was in fact the granddad of the landlord and had only stood in at the last minute when Hamish McDoodle and his bagpipes of peace couldn't make it. They were too pissed to realize who he was and too pissed to realize he couldn't play a single note either.

Aaron, who, like his new wife, had been taking his alcohol at a slow pace and therefore was relatively sober, nudged Jeena. 'Look at those two; they make me want to puke.'

He was referring to Kitty's shameless flirting with Tyler. Half her sari was already unravelled, exposing some of Scotland's highest silicon mountains. And boy did she have a great command of the English language when she was discussing her favourite twin assets, her breast implants. She could talk the ears off a donkey with how she'd endured two painful operations, how she was lucky in the little amount of scars she was left with, how most men couldn't tell the difference, 'Go on have a feel, they almost feel like real breasts . . . NO, not you, Charlie, I was talking to Tyler.' No wonder Aaron felt sick.

What the landlord's granddad lacked in musical talent, he more than made up for in effort, working that bow like his life depended on it. Suddenly, with an appalling screech, as if a cat had been strangled, his bow snapped and the live music for the evening, thankfully, came to an abrupt end. Rapturous applause and a standing ovation was Aaron's key to grab Jeena's hand and make a hasty getaway. Just in case grandma turned up with her tambourine.

Like criminals fleeing the scene of a crime, Aaron and Jeena half-walked, half-jogged until they arrived back at the Golden Arch Hotel. The large, stately-looking building beckoned them in. Yet another couple to cross its threshold and enter into the world of honest sanctity. A plump middle-aged concierge, clad in a black suit, bid them a good-evening, the undertone of his voice meaning, 'I hope you have a great shag', and asked if they would care for pre-wedding-night cocktails. They declined and took the winding stairs to their honeymoon suite. Honeymoon suite Number Three.

For once, the reality was better than the brochure,

thought Aaron, impressed. A gigantic four-poster bed draped with expensive linen. An antique table with matching chairs topped with a dozen red roses displayed in a crystal vase and a glass bowl filled with exotic fruit. A fully-stocked fridge with canapés, wine, chocolates and other splendid delights. Leading from the spacious bedroom was a luxurious bathroom, with a Jacuzzi, walk-in shower and a cast-iron bath. Scrummy, fragrant knick-knacks, like bath salts, oils and moisturizers were displayed in a wooden basket and a huge pile of fluffy-white towels and bathrobes were neatly stacked on the vanity table.

Jeena mused joyfully at how Aaron had spoiled her with this surprise. He'd been going out of his way up until this moment to prove that this wedding meant very little to him, without even bothering to wonder if the wedding meant anything to her. And now he had booked the most expensive room in the hotel. She wondered why. Kitty had often said that Aaron's kindness was only skin deep. Well, if that were the case then this evening Aaron must have the skin of a rhino. She watched him bouncing up and down on the bed, trying it out for size, possibly calculating if it could cope with his energetic antics. Forget having the skin of a rhino, this man had the horn of a rhino. And judging by the excited glaze in his eyes, he could charge at any minute.

Jeena edged her way towards the bathroom.

'Where are you going?' Aaron queried, jumping off the bed and removing his suit jacket. 'The fun is in this room not that one.'

'I need the loo.'

'Too much information, Jeena, way, way too much information.'

She stared in disbelief. 'But you asked.'

'Look, Jeena, just because we're married it doesn't mean that I need to know about all your dirty habits.'

She huffed and disappeared into the bathroom. What she needed right now was some thinking time. A moment's peace to collect her thoughts. All day she'd felt like she was on show, the centrepiece of a sham wedding. She'd lost count of the amount of people who'd walked up to her and Aaron wishing them good luck and congratulating them on their marriage and how they made a 'lovely' couple. She'd heard countless compliments about her sari dress and how original it was to wear one at Gretna Green.

Jeena checked her reflection in the oval-shaped mirror; the sari, her hair, her make-up, her . . . tears? Not again, she thought, as tears slithered down her cheeks; why couldn't she forget about her parents for just one night at least. Most people rush off to the honeymoon of their dreams the day after their wedding. Barbados, Sri Lanka, Australia, Hawaii. Not her. She and Aaron would be bombing it back down the motorway to enjoy the lecture of lectures from her parents as they broke the bad/good/devastating/heart-attack-inducing news. Most likely, if her imagination proved correct, Nanaji would have to be put on suicide watch after hearing that her granddaughter had married a white man. All sharp utensils and pots of paracetamol would have to be locked away until she could accept the inevitable. Bombshells in Indian families didn't get much bigger than this.

She could hear Aaron making martial arts noises next door. Slap, wallop, whack then the words, 'Oh, sorry, mate.'

A worried Jeena popped her head through to see Aaron pulling the room-service man to his feet, who, incidentally, was still clutching the complimentary champagne bottle given by the hotel.

Aaron shrugged towards her. 'It's not my fault. He asked me to demonstrate a few moves. I didn't know he would fall like that!' He patted the man on the back. 'You okay now?' And the room-service man bowed and legged it out of the honeymoon suite, trousering the hefty tip Aaron had forced upon him. Jeena returned to her seclusion in the bathroom.

She couldn't leave that man for five minutes without him getting into some sort of trouble. It begged her to wonder what he must have been like as a child. But, as she well knew by now, talk of his childhood was forbidden, out-of-bounds, KEEP OUT! Maybe, once they had been living together for a while, he might find it in himself to confide in her a little. It's so hard to get close to someone when they don't open up fully. And if she couldn't get Aaron to open up fully, what hope had she of getting him to fall in love with her?

She guessed that his childhood had been full of fun. Imagining him being extremely popular in school with both the boys and the girls (but obviously not the teachers). His outgoing personality would have her believe that where Aaron went others would follow. 'A bad example', the teachers would most likely have said. 'A great crack' would be the response from his countless mates. What about girlfriends? She guessed that

Aaron was two-timing them even back then. A girl for every day of the week. But what kind of parents would produce such a lad as an Aaron? Parents who spoilt their kid, parents who believed he could do no wrong, parents who encouraged him to set himself goals and see them through. She'd once asked him what had possessed him to begin martial arts as a hobby. His reply, 'I want to make sure that I'm supple for sex,' was the typical answer she might have expected.

Jeena had one last thought before she rejoined Aaron in the bedroom. This would be the first time in her life that she'd gone to bed with Aaron and woken up with him the next morning. Normally they would roll around in Aaron's apartment, swinging from the rafters, trailblazing their way to orgasmic paradise. And then it would be time for Jeena to go home and help her mum make *chapattis* and *dhal* for the family's evening meal. Never had they spent the whole night together. If only she'd planned ahead and brought her emergency staple gun then she would have been able to staple his eyelids shut before he had a chance to see what a state she looked in the morning without make-up and her hair frizzy. She wondered if she could order Superglue from room service as an alternative.

Back in the bedroom, Aaron was busy trying to piece together the crystal vase he'd smashed with one of his kicks. Another reason for that Superglue, concluded Jeena, not even bothering to ask how it had happened.

'Tell me, Jeena, if I was an Indian man, is there any wedding ceremony that I would have to perform before, we, you know, get down to business? I was thinking something like breaking a hairdryer or something like that.' His eyes remained fixed on the segments of broken glass.

'Tell me you haven't touched my hairdryer, Aaron, please.'

From underneath the pillow he produced Jeena's Remington Big Shot Glamour hairdryer. 'It's not my fault, I was trying to dry the water spilt on the carpet from the smashed vase and . . .'

'I don't want to know!'

Jeena lectured Aaron that traditionally the wedding night was about joining things together not breaking things apart. His clumsiness was partly excused because he wasn't used to drinking, but if he were to ruin anything else of hers, then so help him. It wasn't long before the lights had been dimmed, the champagne had been drunk and the two of them were lying together on the enormous four-poster bed. Kings and Queens didn't do it in better style than this.

Both were pretty good at knowing how to please the other and when Jeena began to remove her sari, she was quite taken back when Aaron told her to keep it on. Apparently, the thrill of fucking her in her traditional bridal outfit would be much more intense than if she wore sexy lingerie. She explained that this would be a grave insult to Indian men and the elders to which he replied, 'All the more reason to keep it on then'. It was no one's business what went on between two people between the sheets, he justified.

'As long as the animals aren't harmed,' he said, discarding his clothes on to the thick cream carpet.

She giggled and watched with complete excitement as his naked body appeared before her eyes. She'd never got used to how physically spectacular he was. As if his entire body was tuned for one purpose and one purpose only: to please a woman. And even though his exterior promised a right rough ride in the bedroom, sometimes his hands and other times his tongue would take her by surprise and wake up nerves that had lain asleep for what seemed like an eternity. She'd read plenty of articles about women who couldn't orgasm no matter what they had tried, well, here was the cure, thought Jeena, one night with this man and you'd wonder what the fuck you'd been prodding all these years. Jeena felt the warmth of his body through the sari fabric as he lay on top of her. Each kiss, each morsel of delight was wickedly teasing her. She wanted to rip off the sari and feel her skin against his, but he was having none of it.

He hitched up the silk material and rubbed his hands up and down her smooth thighs, dartingly between her legs, all the time edging her closer to the edge, each moment another second nearer the ultimate feeling of all. She closed her eyes and gave out a loud moan as he pushed his cock deep inside her. She loved how manly and rough he became when on top of her. She hated those men who brought manners to the bedroom. Leave 'em outside she thought, just fuck the woman senseless and leave her begging for more. Something Aaron did naturally.

After making love to Jeena in her sari, Aaron decided it was only right if he screwed her without it and, like a kid who couldn't wait for his next present, he began to unwrap the six metres of flimsy silk. Metre by metre he unravelled her, heartbeat by heartbeat his pulse rose, inch by inch her nakedness grew. All those women who pay a fortune for an all-over tan, when by birthright alone Asian people are born with it. Not a bra-strap mark or a panty line in sight. Just a perfectly naked body coated in the most perfect cinnamon brown. His mind was already working on the *Kama Sutra* volume II and before the lovemaking was finished volume III wouldn't be that far away either. Finally, after giving her his all (as best as a man can give while half-cut) he collapsed in a heap of contentment.

At last, for now at least, they were finished.

All worries, all problems, all fears and all nightmares disappeared. Just the pair of them exhausted from their passion. Two naked bodies lying next to one another with only the dim light of the table lamp to colour their skin. One white body and one brown body. Not a cheery sight for most Indian parents.

As Jeena lay snoozing with her head resting on Aaron's chest, he spoke, 'Do you love me, Jeena?'

As though someone had walked over the trip-wire in Jeena's brain, a small explosion woke her up immediately. Did she love him? Why the hell was he asking her *that* question? She collected her thoughts. The wrong answer now could ruin everything. The honest answer now would ruin everything.

'Do I love you? You must be joking, Aaron.' She laughed out extra loud. 'How could I love a man who sleeps around? It would mean I loved someone who didn't respect me and that is something I think you'll find most women can't abide. I'm fond of you but nothing more than that. I love our sex and that's about it really.'

Aaron closed his eyes. 'Good, keep it that way! I don't want you falling in love with me when there is a divorce to start planning.'

She shook her head. 'I'll try my hardest not to.' And in her mind she added to herself, *You arrogant pig.*

Chapter Eleven

Jeena's father, Papaji, blamed his wife for Jeena's rebellious behaviour. In fact, he blamed the way she'd breastfed Jeena as an infant if one really wanted to know. Not happy with her mother's left breast, Jeena had been given the right one instead. From that moment on, Papaji was adamant that they had a spoilt child on their hands. And his wife never heard the end of it.

Then one day, when Jeena was about thirteen, she arrived back from school crying her eyes out. 'What's the matter, *beti*?' Maji had asked, cradling her daughter in her arms. Jeena had sobbed out her reply, 'The boys all say that I stink. They say they can tell when I'm coming from two miles away. Simon Thornton wears a peg on his nose when he walks past me. It's embarrassing. I refuse to eat garlic anymore.' From that moment on Maji was forced to make two different curries for her family. One with garlic and one without. Spoilt? The girl was positively mollycoddled.

Then one day, when Jeena was about fifteen, she

141

arrived back from school crying her eyes out. 'What's the matter, *beti*?' Maji had asked, wiping her daughter's tears away with a tissue. Jeena had replied, sniffing, 'All the girls in my class wear skirts at least five inches shorter than mine. I'm a laughing stock. Katrina Smith says that I look like someone from *Little House on the Prairie*. I need a mini skirt, Maji, I won't go to school without one. I hate being the odd one out.' That very afternoon Jeena was rushed to the shops to buy her a new wardrobe fit for modern day school. Mollycoddled? The teenager was positively pampered.

Then one day, when Jeena was about sixteen, she arrived back from school crying her eyes out. 'What's the matter, *beti*?' Maji had asked, massaging her daughter's shoulders. Jeena had replied, blubbering, 'My knickers are the butt of jokes in P.E; all the other girls wear G-strings. Diane Ashbrook said that I borrow my knickers from Nanaji. I hate undressing in front of them. I won't be able to study hard enough to pass my exams without a G-string.' A confused Maji had queried Jeena what exactly was a G-string and when Jeena described one to her using a piece of knitting wool for her prop, Maji dragged Jeena to the portrait of Guru Nanak hanging on the wall and told her to kneel and pray for forgiveness. 'Never mention a hooker's G-string in this house again, Jeena. I'm disgusted at you.' Spoilt? Mollycoddled? Pampered?

Not this time.

But overall Jeena's parents, compared with most Indian parents, had been extremely lenient with her over the years. As so many lenient parents realize when it's too late, their leniency is often repaid with betrayal.

Or, in old fashioned English, their leniency is often repaid with a kick in the teeth. So, next time one sees an Indian man or woman with missing teeth don't automatically assume that they're addicted to Cola Cubes or *gulab jamans*. It might be that they've been too lenient with their children over the years. And there's nothing sweet about that.

Nor, indeed, was there anything sweet about their daughter right now. After searching for her all Monday and Tuesday, Jeena's parents thought they'd hit gold when they'd spotted her car parked outside Kitty's flat. A whole day of waiting and knocking led them to the conclusion that Kitty's place was just a drop off point for her Clio and maybe a meeting up point for her comrades. Jeena was nowhere to be seen. Using the spare key for Jeena's car, Papaji had driven it back to his house. Why he did this, he didn't really know, but anger had something to do with it.

Now it was Thursday afternoon; Jeena had promised that she would be home on the Thursday. It was for this reason that four Indian faces had been looking out of the living-room window since daylight broke through in the early hours of the morning. The milkman, Ronnie, had nearly let go of his crate in surprise when Papaji had knocked on the glass and wished him a 'good morning'. But it was important, in Papaji's head, to see who dropped off his daughter. It would be nice to know who was responsible for feeding Jeena's mind with poison and false promises. Something inside his suspicious brain was telling him that that white man Aaron would be involved somehow. The waiting continued . . .

JJ, who didn't seem to be taking this as seriously as everyone else, was under instructions to keep his mouth shut after his last joke when, in a moment of extreme boredom, he'd shouted out, 'Oh, my, God, Maji, Papaji, turn away from the window immediately as I think I can see Jeena in the distance walking with a Muslim. She's converted to Islam. She now listens only to Allah – may peace be upon him.'

Papaji's eyes had glared with fury. He didn't know what was wrong with his children sometimes, he really didn't. Hadn't they listened to his eight-hour stories of India and Pakistan? Hadn't they learnt a thing from his sixteen-hour lectures on Kashmir? It was a historical fact that Sikhs/Hindus and Muslims didn't get on. For a Sikh girl to hitch up with a Muslim boy, well, she may as well just pack her bags and get ready to be thrown out of the house. It was as simple as that! One certainly didn't joke about such things under a Sikh roof.

By the time Aaron's red BMW finally pulled up in the driveway, Papaji, who in a state of tedium had been counting the bricks on the opposite houses, was now in a position to tell Mr Sadhu that he had four more bricks on the front of his house than his neighbour, Mr Fisher. In the current climate of house price rises, it would mean Mr Sadhu's property was worth about four grand more than Mr Fisher's. A grand a brick.

And talking of bricks, JJ was bricking himself a wall. Amazingly, he'd come up with a plan (incidentally, he was only joking at the time) which his parents had approved. The idea was, when Jeena arrived she was to be ushered into the kitchen, where, while Papaji was holding her, JJ would handcuff her to the cooker with her own, pink, fluffy, sexy handcuffs, which they'd stumbled upon while searching her bedroom. Only when she was secure would she be told the news of her new life in India and the husband they had managed to find for her. Without the handcuffs, the chances were that she would run away for good this time.

As with all of JJ's plans, it was foolproof as long as nothing went wrong. And wrong was already walking up their path in the shape of an 8th-dan jujitsu expert. No wonder JJ was bricking it. He didn't want to die – he hadn't even been to the Glastonbury Festival yet or more importantly, he hadn't even touched a woman's breast yet.

Papaji, Maji, JJ and Nanaji all waited in the hall while Jeena unlocked the front door. JJ, in all his panic, was holding the pink handcuffs in full view.

'Hide them, you idiot,' Papaji ordered his son. 'Surreptitiously.'

'Eh?'

'Sneaky like a snake,' Papaji hissed, just as the door swung open.

For one long, gaping second, Jeena's eyes connected with her father's. Then, just as they had planned, she pushed Aaron in front of her and whispered, 'Remember, lay it on thick.'

Some homes have warm climates, thought Aaron, but this one was icy cold. It might have had something to do with the Arctic stares coming from within. On the journey from Gretna Green to Primpton, Jeena had been trying her best to teach Aaron the required techniques he might need to get into her father's good books. His *sensei* had always promoted the idea that forewarned is forearmed. But now, as Aaron stood at the doorway to Jeena's home, as the clock ticked past five p.m., he felt like an intruder of the worst kind. Someone who had no right being there in the first place. A hard nudge in his back from Jeena reminded him what they were here for.

Aaron spoke, 'God, it must be great living next door to you; it smells just like an Indian restaurant here. And I can tell you, Mr Gill, nothing, and I mean, *nothing* beats the smell of a well-cooked . . .'

'Aaron! Tell them!' Jeena hollered from behind him.

'I married your daughter yesterday,' he stated. 'I married the woman I love with all my heart. I couldn't let you steal her away from me.' He noted their dumbfounded expressions. 'It would have been wrong for our love to have been ripped apart by a tradition. I couldn't have stood back and let our wonderful relationship be savaged by the pressures of family loyalty. I know that we will be happy together and that no man will treat her better than me. I also know that if you had forced her on a plane to go and live with a man in India, a man of whom she knows nothing, she would not have been happy. In fact, I expect that she would have blamed you for her unhappiness. Is this what you would have wanted?' He paused. 'And I'm sorry if I upset you by wearing your turban but . . .'

'Aaron, leave it,' Jeena said. 'Honestly.'

A speechless Papaji beckoned everyone into the living room. Maji, Nanaji, JJ and Papaji squeezed onto the sofa, with Aaron and Jeena taking up the other two sofa chairs. It was an Us against Them situation. Papaji asked all those with mobiles phones to please turn them

146

off; he hated being interrupted by modern technology. Zee TV, which played almost constantly in the background, was, like Nanaji's mouth, put on mute.

'It would be so easy to sit here and shout,' Papaji began, sadness creeping into his voice, 'but, what good will it do? What has gone on between you two is *not* acknowledged by us. As far as we are concerned you never got married. But, as the law stands in this country, your piece of paper still stands.' He aimed his attention to Jeena, speaking in English so that Aaron could understand all that was being said. 'I want you to get this marriage annulled. I want you to spare this family any more embarrassment. Under no circumstances are we having him, a white man, as a part of our family. Not now, not ever.'

Maji shook her head sagely. Her only daughter had stabbed her in the back. A fifteen-hour labour, without painkillers, all for what? So that the young girl she had spoilt would grow up to be the young woman who thought nothing of breaking her own mother's heart. Tears cascaded down her face and dropped onto her lap. She'd been warned of daughters straying by other relatives, but she'd paid them little heed. If only the hands of time could be worked backwards, she would never have given Jeena the freedom she so enjoyed. It was the biggest mistake of her life and she was paying for it now with her heartache.

'Could I be so bold as to offer my congratulations,' said JJ, who rose up, walked across to take Aaron's hand, shook it and then bowed. 'You'll make a fine brother-in-law.' He returned to his seat grinning.

Papaji was beyond caring what came out of JJ's

mouth right now, he had bigger fish to fry. None bigger than the great white shark sitting opposite holding his daughter's hand. And if his anger was fire then the room was ablaze with it. Incensed and disgusted at their sparkling gold wedding rings mocking him with their shine, he reflected that this was the worst day in living memory.

'If you refuse to annul this hash of a marriage then, Jeena, you will be disowned. With immediate effect.' Papaji kept his gaze upon her. 'You chose this path and you knew where it would lead. You know how Indian households work, it's no secret; if you go against the Indian system, then you are told to leave. In your case, you have had more freedom than most Indian girls and still you disrespected us, your parents. You may want to think very carefully at the decision you make, for there will be no going back after that.' Papaji rose from his seat, a huge shadow of a man, and walked to the window where he looked out on the street. This was hurting him as much as it was hurting Jeena.

Any hopes that their marriage might persuade her parents that she and Aaron were serious about each other were fading fast. They were not even asking her why she got married, but just how it could be undone. Sometimes she believed her parents had been raised by robots. Either that or the damp English weather had rinsed out all their humanity. Whatever the reason, it was painful to know that her happiness meant so little to them. They, like their possible robot parents, just wanted to control her. Any major decisions would be made by their circuit-board brains and any moral dilemmas would be solved by their silicon-chip hearts.

There comes a time in every child's life when he or she has to call the parents' bluff. Unfortunately for JJ he called his mum's bluff, at the age of thirteen, when she said that if he continued to leave his bedroom in a state then she would lock all his toys in the garage. Sadly, his toys happened to include a stash of hardcore-porn mags his mum had found under the carpet. Trying to blame them on his father wasn't the wisest of moves. But, as far as bluff-calling went, Jeena had always believed her parents meant what they said.

'I've decided that there is no decision to make, Papaji, I will stay married to Aaron, because he is the man I want to be with.' Her tears began to fall in frustration. 'I wish sometimes you could just forget all this traditional stuff and concentrate more on what really matters. How many Indian families do you know who have disowned a daughter for falling in love with the wrong colour or the wrong caste? Loads. Well, you're going to have to do the same with me because there is no way I'm splitting up with Aaron. I love him.'

Aaron promised himself there and then that he would never *ever* shag an Indian woman again. Too much trouble, way, way too much trouble. One might have thought he'd learnt his lesson from the Japanese women. Or, rather, from the Japanese fathers who found out that their daughters were being sushied by a Westerner. For when a Japanese woman's father threatened to kill you, you bloody well knew he meant it too. God they could swing those machetes viciously. It was a simple motto to live by really: just stay clear of any woman who is Asian.

Maji decided it was about time she called upon the

services of the 'Mother's Bond'. Or, in other words, blackmail. She aimed her glare at Jeena and began to talk in Punjabi.

'If you refuse to follow our wishes, Jeena, then I may as well go up to the bathroom cabinet right now and swallow a hundred sleeping tablets. My life would not be worth living anyway.' Her crying turned to wails. 'How could you . . . how could you have married him behind our backs? What sort of daughter does this to her parents? Have you no *izzat* (honour)? I may as well walk upstairs and swallow those tablets right now. Were we so bad that we needed to be punished in this way? Do you hate us that much? Is this the . . .'

In Punjabi, Jeena interrupted, 'And what sort of parents send their daughter off to a foreign land to marry a . . .'

'FOREIGN BLOODY LAND?' Papaji roared across the room in English. 'INDIA? FOREIGN? HAVE YOU GONE COMPLETELY MAD?' He thrust out his arm and pointed to the door. 'GET OUT . . . THE PAIR OF YOU. YOU ARE NO LONGER MY DAUGHTER.'

Before Jeena and Aaron had a chance to move a muscle a glossy piece of paper shot across the room and landed by Jeena's trainers. Maji, the culprit thrower, watched her daughter's face with contempt as she picked up the photograph.

'That is the Sikh man you should be marrying,' Maji stated, referring to the picture in Jeena's shaking hand. 'That is the man we have arranged your marriage to. In India. This foreign land you speak of.'

JJ giggled. He'd already seen it. His poor, *poor* sister, the bloke was way too old for her.

Jeena, however, did not giggle. Far from it in fact. Staring back at her was a man in his early forties, pretty dapper in a suit, not bad looking, nice smile, quirky, greasy hairstyle, and to top him off, Jeena noticed a pocket watch on a gold chain hanging from his breast pocket. That was all well and good, but, from Jeena's point of view, there was no way of telling the man's personality from the photograph. Looks were definitely not everything. She'd learnt that from Aaron (looked great on the outside but was a bit of a bastard on the inside). And without further ado she handed him the photo.

Aaron was not impressed.

'The point is,' he began, eyeing Jeena's family with a certain amount of hostility, 'she doesn't love this man. This man doesn't love Jeena. I DO.' He turned to Jeena and in a low voice said, 'Come on, let's bag up some of your stuff and go. Until your parents understand that your happiness must come before their traditions, then it's pointless talking to them.' They both stood up and Aaron directed his next comment to Papaji. 'While Jeena is packing upstairs, I would like to have a private chat with you, if I may.' He paused. 'In the polythene room if possible?'

Hoping that Aaron didn't say anything regrettable, Jeena took a last glance towards her mother, who was now staring into space, and made her way to her bedroom to pack up her things. JJ switched the volume back on and continued to watch Zee TV with Nanaji. The atmosphere in the room had become lifeless. As though a murder had been committed here. And in some ways this room was the scene of a crime. The crime of Jeena's disownment.

Papaji refused to take Aaron to the 'best' living room (the polythene room) and settled on having this 'chat' in the front garden.

'I'll be quick,' Aaron started, 'I'm just letting you know that I'm quite aware of how Indian families operate when things don't go their way with their daughters and their arranged marriages. I've heard the stories of the gangs of thugs who threaten the white boyfriends with violence and I've witnessed it too, with you and your cronies when you turned up at my place trying to intimidate me with man power. I've heard a tonne of tales about girls being drugged and then forced on planes to India and Pakistan.' Aaron watched Papaji's face as it remained blank. 'Now, I don't normally go throwing my weight around threatening people unless I believe it necessary. My wife, your daughter, means the world to me. If anything should happen to her then I will hold you totally responsible. I think you know what I'm talking about here. The best thing you could possibly do is forget all this arranged marriage malarkey, accept our marriage and then everything will be okey-dokey.'

'Never!' was the only word Papaji said before walking back into his house. Gnarling and gnawing at Papaji's insides was the contemptuous attitude of this white Englishman who, like it or not, accept it or don't, was still his son-in-law (or to him, his sin-in-law). It was enough to make him gag. What would his Indian forefathers think?

While Jeena folded and stacked, Aaron stuffed and shoved Jeena's belongings into various cases, bags and bin liners. The packing was done at such a furious pace that Jeena didn't have time to brood and ponder. She didn't have time to reminisce and regret. All that remained was the feeling that her entire childhood, her teenage years and twenties were being jammed into containers so tightly that when it came to opening them, they would explode with the same intensity as her tears. If a woman's bedroom could be used as a metaphor to her brain then no wonder Jeena's mind was messed up most of the time – the amount of junk that Jeena had uncovered was enough to keep *Steptoe & Son* happy for a year.

At one point in the proceedings, JJ had knocked on the door, waltzed in as if he owned the place and, while both Aaron and Jeena watched in shock, he stood on Jeena's bed and retrieved a pile of pornographic magazines from on top of her wardrobe. His words in parting were, 'Thanks, Sis, for being my porn keeper all these years. You did a spanking good job. And don't worry; I'll still speak to you even though everyone else hates your guts.' He departed, no doubt, looking for another place to hide his filth. Possibly under Nanaji's mattress (as long as she agreed not to wet it).

'Unless we hire a HGV you're going to have to leave some of this behind. At least for today,' Aaron remarked, holding up sandal pair number fifteen. 'Your shoes alone will fill my boot.'

'Nice pun,' Jeena replied.

But he was right: some things would have to be left behind. Along with her family.

Just before departing, Jeena popped her head round the living-room door to tell them that she was off and would call soon, but this was all dismissed with a stubborn brush of her mother's hand. There are no quicker brick-layers than when an Indian builds a stubborn wall and before Jeena had even reached the front door, the cement was already set. She was now officially dis-owned and blocked out of the family.

Jeena jumped into her Clio and Aaron into his BMW. The convoy of two would drive the fifteen minute journey from her old house to her new. Yet, even though the journey would be a short one, the changes to her life would be major. Life with her husband was going to be the hardest challenge of her existence. Living with a man she loved but didn't love her in return. Living with a man who might bring back another woman to his apartment and screw her sense-less while she lay in the room next door. Living with a man who . . . oh, God, this was going to be a trial and a half. And if she had one piece of advice to Indian women across the globe it was this: never fall in love with a white man. They're too much trouble.

Way, way too much trouble.

As she waited at the traffic lights behind Aaron, a text message came through. There was just enough time to read it before the lights changed.

Wife! Wot R U cooking me 4 din dins tonight?
Your hubby Aaron.

At the next set of lights she texted him back.

Your testicles!

Chapter Twelve

The car park to the Paper Lantern Martial Arts Centre was nearly full. A St Johns ambulance stood on stand-by for that 'just in case' moment. Thursday nights, now dubbed Blood Fest, renowned for when over-keen pupils attempted one brick too many with their heads. It was almost a rite of passage, to smash the magic nine. Whether it was a coincidence or not, those pupils under the age of sixteen who could do the magic nine bricks were failing miserably in their school work. Aaron hoped that he wasn't encouraging brain damage within his club.

The sound of torture and discipline could be vaguely heard emanating through the walls of the centre, as Aaron helped Jeena take her bags up the metal stairs to his (their) apartment. It was too late to carry her over the threshold, but, he was sure he'd made up for it with the weight of her bloody clothes. God, how much crap did she pack? He wiggled the key in the lock, trying desperately not to drop her Mr Piggles two-foot high pink teddy-pig again. She still hadn't forgiven him for losing his grip on Mr Piggles in the car park when she'd shouted, 'Stop kicking him across the tarmac, Aaron, he's got feelings you know?' He agreed to stop kicking him but whispered in Mr Piggles' furry ear, 'When she's not looking, I'm going to beat the living crap out of you, you worthless piece of pork.' He punched in the number code to the burglar alarm, then closed the door behind them. Three days' worth of post lay scattered by the floor mat, which he picked up immediately; afraid of the bad Feng Shui that unopened post, otherwise known as 'clutter', gave off. From where he was standing he could see the answerphone flashing. To be dealt with later.

For now, it was about making Jeena feel welcome and comfortable in her new home. He was more than aware that right this second her mind was an emotional war zone and it was up to him not to set off any mines.

'Take which room you want,' Aaron remarked, referring to the two spare bedrooms. 'My suggestion: take the one with the river view. It's the biggest anyway.' He followed her through to said room and watched as she bounced on the double-bed. 'I think you'll find it up to standard. It's never even been used.'

The platform bed was obviously meant for someone scared of heights as it stood only inches from the ground. Aaron explained that it was based on the Japanese bedrooms and if she looked closely at the décor she might see a hint of Japanese influence. A HINT! The whole room looked as if it had been lifted from Tokyo itself. Bamboo shutters, bamboo wardrobe, bamboo side table, a *shoji* screen. The colours, black, red and white throughout. Even the walls had Japanese writing trailing downwards, which, Aaron informed Jeena proudly, dictated proverbs of life, love and soul. Slightly out-of-place and even partly crude was a framed film poster of *The Karate Kid* on one of the walls. The bedroom was big enough and grand enough for a Japanese princess, the question was: was it too good for an Indian peasant?

Which was just how she felt right now, leaving her family behind and saying goodbye to her traditions. They say that today is the first day of the rest of your life, well today felt like the worst day of the last of her old life. She smiled up at Aaron as she tried to pull herself together. She'd cried enough over the last two weeks to make three cups of tea and a Cup a Soup, and to be honest she was getting sick of it. Crying made her feel weak and useless. It also gave her puffy eyes, and every girl can well do without those. Unless, of course, she has high hopes of winning Miss Puffy Eyes competitions.

After giving Jeena and Mr Piggles a moment or two to become acquainted with their room, Aaron and his new wife collected the rest of the bags from their cars and then it was time for the 'anal retentive' tour. Or, as it is more commonly known, showing a lodger where all the emergency switches, taps and plugs are fixed. How one operated the fire extinguisher. What to do if there was a flood and Aaron was out. Which was exactly the same as: what to do if there is a flood and Aaron is *in* but he is meditating. (Never interrupt his meditation.) There were even instructions of what to do if she found Aaron dead. First rule, check to see that his underpants were clean and if not, make sure he is fitted with a clean pair before the emergency services arrive. Aaron added, 'Not that you'd ever find me with dirty underpants, but it's better to be safe than sorry, eh?' Jeena was already feeling sorry. Sorry for herself. He went on to explain how to turn off the gas, electrics. The whole shebang.

'And don't feed the fish,' Aaron said, plopping the water with the small green net. 'They die if fed too much.' He tapped the aquarium glass. 'They also die if they aren't fed at all. Come on, Tysee, where are you?' Before Aaron had time to dive in and find him, Tyson, the black fish, appeared from beneath a small bunch of plastic seaweed. 'Ah, thank God, Tysee, I thought you'd copped it.'

An amazed Jeena watched as Aaron attempted to stroke his fish through the glass. At one point it appeared that he'd forgotten she was standing there as he began to speak to his fish as if they were newly-born babies. It was all rather odd, but as long as he didn't hang a Beatrix Potter mobile above the tank, then Jeena wouldn't worry about his sanity too much. She coughed politely, breaking him from his deep discussion of plankton.

'They're far more intelligent than plants you know,' Aaron pointed out, full of pride.

'Since when were plants intelligent, Aaron? I can't remember one winning *Mastermind*.'

'Oh, sarky. What I meant was, people talk to their plants to help them grow, so I talk to my fish to help them float better. It also helps keep the harmony of the apartment. It gets rid of the negative vibes. It . . .' Aaron stood up and stared, confused, at the TV. 'You haven't touched the telly since we've been here, have you?'

Jeena explained that she'd been with him since the moment they entered.

'Strange,' Aaron said to himself. 'Very strange.' He was positive that he'd switched off the standby button before he'd left for Gretna Green.

Not one to dwell on mundane matters for too long, Aaron sipped a cup of Gunpowder tea, as he turned his attention to the answerphone messages while Jeena took a seat by the window in the office area and admired the River Wes shimmy on by in the evening sun. A small boat chugged past, chased by a barking collie on the bank. So sweet, thought Jeena, taking a dog for a walk in your boat; until the collie raced back down the river, wagging its tail madly, and began to bark viciously at another passing boat, petrifying yet another skipper. While Jeena viewed the scenery, she listened in to Aaron's messages. Yet another example of a woman performing two things at once. Three things, if Aaron had any more messages from sexed-up women. She'd throw the answerphone in the river. Woman after woman, was punctuated with the odd business call. Amongst the callers, a female voice spoke in a foreign dialect; Jeena guessed Japanese. The woman, whose name she gathered was something like Sakiko, laughed at intervals, to which Aaron also laughed in return. And even though Jeena's Japanese language skills was limited to ordering Sushi, hidden underneath Sakiko's mother tongue was the subtle language of 'Flirting'. A language which every woman, no matter what their origin, can understand. Especially when she kept saying,

'*Suki suki cock cock*,' or something like that, followed by a yard-long giggle.

'Finished,' Aaron announced finally, slightly embarrassed, pretty sure that Jeena had heard every word, making a mental note to listen to his messages in private from now on – like most people did. 'Would you believe it, Jeena, fifty wrong numbers.'

'Amazing how they all knew your name, hey?'

'Lucky guesses, I suppose.' He stood up. 'Anyway, I'm going to fix us something to eat. How does "burnt" sound?'

A few minutes later and he was chopping up fresh Italian herbs to add to the thick, tomato pasta sauce. The chrome kitchen, with its neatly displayed cooking utensils, pots, pans and gadgets, made a very clear statement: NO EXCUSES FOR BAD FOOD. Jeena was just overawed that he could cook at all. A very sexist notion, but, hell, women were allowed to be sexist now and again for all the sexist crap they'd put up with over the years. She watched him pop the pasta shells into the bubbling saucepan and breathed in the scrumptious smell of garlicky food. It was as if Aaron's feet were clad in ballet shoes, so gracefully did he move around his kitchen. It had her thinking: how long must a man live alone before he's in total control of four pans at once? Pasta sauce, pasta, chicken pieces and even a cheese dip for the garlic bread. Her own brother, JJ, went into Gordon Ramsay meltdown whenever he had to cook toast, normally needing half a loaf of cremated slices to produce *the* one perfect piece. But here, in Aaron's kitchen, it was cooking like clockwork.

'So, how long have you been living alone?' Jeena

asked, realizing yet again just how little she knew about Aaron's life. Wondering if the best time to delve into his personal territory was when he was holding a carving knife. Shikes, she didn't even know if he was left- or right-handed. She thought back to when he was fingering her. Right. Definitely right.

'Years!' he replied. 'Do you want it a little chilli hot? Or not?'

'A little, thanks.' She handed him a tea towel for the scolding saucepan handle. 'I'm not being nosy, but, I need to know what to say if your parents ring, or turn up out of the blue. What about the rest of your family? Your brothers or sisters? I mean, who do I say I am? A lodger?'

Aaron tipped the cooked pasta into the saucepan filled with sauce. It seemed for one long moment that he wasn't going to answer Jeena at all. Then he turned around and looked out of the window. 'My parents died when I was a kid. I'm pretty sure they won't turn up. Sorry, I don't mean to be sarcastic.' He swung back round and faced her. 'It's just me. I'm all that's left of my family. No brothers. No sisters.'

And in Jeena's eyes: no more conversation. The sense of hurt in Aaron's face was telling her that this was a No Go Area.

'I'm sorry,' she said, feeling terrible. 'Do you want me to lay the table?'

About to answer, Aaron noticed a few grains of spilt sugar beside the espresso/cappuccino maker. He didn't even take sugar; so how the flaming fructose did it get there? His forehead creased and his memory banks gave up all they knew. He remembered thoroughly cleaning the kitchen surfaces just before he set off for Gretna Green. Weird.

They sat down at the glass dining-room table with only candles for light. It was lucky Aaron already knew what Jeena sounded like in the sack as the noises coming from her mouth when she ate the delicious pasta would have given him a very good idea anyway. Orgasmic. Each mouthful was hitting her B-spot perfectly. B as in belly.

It was almost romantic until Aaron said, 'Don't expect this every night. Let's face it, there are going to be days when we can't stand the sight of each other and the last thing I'm going to want to do is to feed your mouth.' He touched her hand. 'I was sort of joking. But this living together business is all new to me. And if we're honest with each other, we're a long way off from how a married couple should be. In fact, in many ways we're total strangers to each other.'

The point had been made. This day/night, this whole experience was teaching Jeena a major lesson. It proved that when it came down to it, even though they'd been to bed a hundred times and they'd eaten out another hundred times, when it came down to it, Jeena didn't really know Aaron at all. In fact, in some ways she knew him less than she would have known the Indian guy her parents had picked for her. They would have grilled that man until his ears bled. They would have dug deep into his past until he couldn't hide anything. She would have known everything about his family, his job, his . . . dog. But, and here was where the difference between the two ways of marriage became clear, with the Indian guy she wouldn't have known about his personality, his hidden depths, his understanding.

Whilst with Aaron, these were the things about him which attracted her in the first place. It was now up to her, if she really wanted to become closer, if she had any hope that Aaron might fall in love with her, to get him to trust her enough to open up and talk about his past. Only then could she hope that he might begin to love her. And only then could she get to the bottom of why he couldn't commit.

She finished her last orgasmic mouthful with a low moan. 'That . . . was . . . the best,' she said and leant back on the chair, praying her stomach might jostle some space for the ice cream dessert.

Jeena knew how she wanted to thank Aaron for his kindness and selflessness and it involved plenty of time between the sheets. But, sometimes, words are better than actions. Underneath the flickering lights of the candles, Jeena went on to explain to Aaron how much she appreciated what he was doing for her. He tried to wave it away and shrug off her compliments, but she knew how much he was changing his lifestyle to help her and she needed him to know how deeply grateful she was.

She followed him across the room, explaining how she would repay him one day.

She followed him into the bathroom explaining how highly she regarded him.

She watched him undress explaining to him how she owed her life to his actions.

And she drooled as he stepped in the walk-in shower wishing she was the sponge that would wash down his dream body, swishing the foam in and out of his muscular six-pack.

Before Aaron switched on the jet spray, he noticed a few long, brown hairs clogged up in the plughole. Aaron thought back to the last time he'd used the shower. It was on the morning he left for Gretna Green. There was no way on God's earth that he wouldn't have noticed the hairs in the plughole back then. It was almost a standard check before showering. Make sure clothes are off, make sure front door is closed and make sure plughole is clear. Something was definitely amiss in his apartment. First, the TV light had been left on standby. Then sugar granules had been spilt in the kitchen and now this, long brown hairs in his plughole. What next?

Next, he dragged the fully clothed still-babbling and praising Jeena into the shower, ripped off her clothes and ravaged her senseless as the water cascaded down their bodies. Between kisses and mouthfuls of water, Aaron gurgled out a few words: 'Don't expect this every night, Jeena. Let's face it, there are going to be days when we can't stand the sight of each other and . . .' Jeena knelt down on the slip-free tiles. 'Oh, happy birthday to me.'

Amazing, thought Jeena, opening her mouth wide, amazing how suddenly a man can forget what's important in life as soon as there is a hint of a blow job. Pathetic!

The lot of 'em!

Chapter Thirteen

It would be so easy to be confused by Aaron's behaviour, thought Jeena on her way to work on Monday morning. And yet, she wasn't. After their lovemaking extravaganza on Thursday evening, she'd awoken to an empty bed, and a note on the dining-room table:

Consider the sex we had last night as your honeymoon.

All day Friday, except for the odd visit for food and his protein shakes, Aaron had been working downstairs in his martial arts centre while she was unpacking her belongings with only his fish for company. Saturday was no better, with Aaron downstairs in the centre, as she pottered around like a bored housewife, her highlight being watching *Bridget Jones's Diary* on DVD. By Sunday afternoon, when Kitty turned up with the wedding photos, and Aaron shot out the door for a 200-mile jog, the message was coming through loud and clear: she might live with Aaron but in reality they lived apart. To be fair to Aaron, he'd always told her that it would be this way. His life wasn't going to be put on hold for anyone.

To add lime to an already bitter pill to swallow, Jeena had noticed that just before leaving the apartment on Sunday evening, along with sprucing himself up, Aaron had removed his wedding ring. It didn't take a scientist to work out that Aaron was out with a lady. The honeymoon was *definitely* over. And her husband was out having sex with other women.

With all the manners of a true gentleman, Aaron had crept through the front door at approximately three a.m., and tip-toed to his room. With all the manners of a complete arsehole, he had woken Jeena up at five a.m. with his meditation. This time the tape playing at over one-hundred decibels was the revving of a Formula One car's engine with Eminem live at Milton Keynes Bowl. How anyone could meditate through this, thought Jeena, was beyond her, because . . .

'I can't fucking well sleep through this,' she'd shouted through the wall, covering her head with her duvet, wishing death and damnation on him. 'I'm going to work in a few hours!'

So here she was, travelling to work. And Aaron? Bless his little cotton socks, well, he was back in bed enjoying an interruption-free sleep. The one time she did manage to catch him for a small chat at the weekend, they'd agreed that the best approach with her parents right now was to leave things as they were, wait until the dust settled and after a short while see how the land lay. They say time is a great healer, which was all well and good, but time was also a great ager.

And Jeena didn't want this splinter she'd caused in her family to fester away the years.

STAFF PARKING. Jeena parked her Clio in the only remaining space and clippity clopped up the short path in her high heels straight into the entrance of *Asian Delight*. It didn't matter what she wore for work, a sleek designer suit or casual jeans and trainers, because Mrs Kapoor, the secretary sitting at Reception, was a stickler for Indian traditions and would always sneer for a second or two as Jeena passed by her desk. Today, Jeena, with her hair down and hooped earrings, was wearing a tight, white, low-topped shirt with a short black skirt. Mrs Kapoor sneered for five seconds. Two seconds because Jeena was late and three seconds because she looked like a slag. Possibly the biggest slag in the whole of *Asian Delight*. (It hadn't escaped Mrs Kapoor's notice the amount of times Jeena had returned from lunch 'adjusting' clothes that had obviously been ripped off in the throes of passion). But who was she to interfere? She only worked here.

Here at *Asian Delight*, the thriving weekly newspaper dealing with all issues Asian. What had begun as a hobby in a back room seven years ago had now turned into the most successful paper for British Asians this side of Mumbai. Mr Akhtar, the middle-aged boss and owner could often be seen walking around his 5000-foot office with a proud glint in his eye. From the outset his intentions had been to employ only Asians. From writers, editors, photographers all the way down to cleaners. His plan, one day, was to run Rupert Murdoch into the ground. 'Think big, achieve big,' was his favourite saying. Apart from when it came to dishing out wages, where his motto was, 'Give small and I stay rich.' All three of his sons worked there, buzzing around their father, barking orders at the menials. Jeena knew, after being employed here for four years, that to get on the wrong side of the Akhtar sons was like signing your own P45. But she kept her head down and tried her best, hoping that one day her hard work and journalistic skills would post her through the front door of a national newspaper. Until then, she would remain *Asian Delight's* Agony Auntiji and columnist.

Jeena walked into the main, open-plan office which was filled with computers, VDUs, printers and photocopiers and decorated with framed copies of *Asian Delight* back issues. Her desk was stationed near the end of the room, quite handily opposite the small kitchen. It was a great feeling knowing that when the chips were down, you were only a few steps away from a shot of caffeine. By-passing the glares from her colleagues, the tuttings and obvious looking to their watches, Jeena arrived at her desk, kicked her handbag under it and slumped in her swivel chair. She quickly typed in her password INSANITY and the screen came up with:

Jeena Kaur Gill
Ref JKG 369
Time of arrival 9.27 a.m.
YOU ARE TWENTY SEVEN MINUTES LATE!
Expect a visit from Mr Akhtar today.

'Shit,' Jeena mumbled to herself. 'Aaron and his stupid meditation. What do you expect when I can't get any flipping sleep?'

After sifting through some of her e-mails, Jeena popped into the kitchen where she helped herself to a couple of cold vegetable samosas (supplied by the employer each morning as a perk of the job). On top of samosas, a vast selection of pickles and chutneys were on hand to add to any meal which might be brought back at lunch. An office favourite at the moment was fish 'n' chip shop chips sprinkled with garam masala powder, a few slices of hot green chillies with mango and lime pickle on the side. Some cruder men in the office called this snack, 'The Ring Buster' or 'Griddled Bum'; Jeena liked to think of it as the Indian ploughman's.

Popping a teaspoon of spicy aubergine pickle beside the samosas, Jeena became aware of watching eyes, staring from the doorway. Nina, Jeena's best work friend, and also one of the office copyeditors, smiled the knowing smile. Eyes which were used to spotting the slightest typo or misspelled word, had no trouble at all in noticing the extra bling on Jeena's finger.

'Oh, my, God,' Nina announced, running across the carpet and grabbing Jeena's wrist. 'I thought you'd be the last of us to have an arranged marriage. Now look at you.' She stroked the ring as if it were a small, fluffy mammal. 'Why wasn't I invited? Why didn't you tell me? WHO IS HE?'

Jeena jammed a samosa in Nina's gob. 'Ssssh. I'll tell you later, I'm already in trouble with Akhtar.'

But Nina's mouth was running downhill and it didn't have a handbrake. It wasn't long before the small kitchen was filled with other women, desperate to know the story behind Jeena's new ring. Questions which began on the mantle, like what did her bridal sari look like? soon burrowed their way down to the core, where the questions became less subtle: when will you be starting a family? How rich is he? Did she know him well before she married him? Why is the ring *not* twenty-two carat Indian gold? Until Jeena held up her hennaed hand and quietened the excitable women down.

'Look, this may be hard for some of you to understand, but I did not have an arranged marriage.' She stared at the many sets of tonsils now on display. 'It was a love marriage. He is a white man. We got hitched at Gretna Green.' If the tonsils had been bell hammers they would have played the Death March. Instead, there was silence.

And silence did not get any quieter than this. Even the sound of blinking eyelids would have been heard if anyone had been blinking. They all stood, open-eyed, open-mouthed, but, unfortunately, with closed minds.

Nina, who was at her best when she wasn't speaking, decided to try and help Jeena out. 'Well, she had to get married. Didn't you, Jeena?' Nina declared. 'You were pregnant with his child.'

Gasps and groans of disgust ricocheted off all walls. Jeena knew only too well that the people of this establishment liked to overact when it came to bad news. She remembered the day when a certain Indian lady called Neema who worked here gave birth to a baby girl for the fourth time. It was only a matter of minutes since the news was announced and three quarters of the women in the workplace were wearing black armbands. Even the office seat where Neema had sat was taken to a skip and trashed, just in case any of them accidentally sat on it themselves. One never knew: the seat could have been the reason for the female births. Jeena used to think that this place, which was supposed to report news stories, produced more headlines within its own walls than what was on offer in the real world. Today, hold the front page, Jeena had married a white man.

Back at her desk, Jeena glowed with satisfaction. In order for her reputation to be tarnished amongst the Indian community, it was deadly important that the information of her marrying a white man was let loose. Her plan all along had been to tell the Indian people whom she worked with about her wedding to Aaron. As if the weight of this information was crushing them beyond endurance, her colleagues would then inform their relatives. Before five p.m. today, the whole of the Asian community in the Midlands would be aware that Jeena, the daughter of Mr Preetjeet Singh Gill, 56 Monroe Avenue, Primpton, West Midlands, had married out of her caste and religion. Yet another bird had left the flock of Sikhgulls. By lunchtime tomorrow the news would have spread to New Delhi. If things went well, then within six months the only way Jeena would be able to have an arranged marriage would be if she changed her identity.

As if news of Jeena's outrageous marriage were not bad enough, the fact that she and her white husband hadn't taken it upon themselves, out of respect and decency, to have a Sikh-style wedding, was a huge slap in the face. Especially as a marriage performed under the British rules wasn't even recognized by the Sikhs as authentic. One had to take the oaths under the sacred book, the *Guru Granth Sahib*, for it to be legitimate. In not so many words: under the rules of Sikhism, Jeena was living in sin with Aaron. Hardly the finest attribute to have yourself labelled with when one is trying to marry you off. 'Our daughter is a great cook, highly fertile, robust and in good health. Oh yeah, one other thing: she once married a white man (under the British rules) and then divorced him. Any chance she's the perfect partner for your son? No? Is that a gun you're pointing at me? Everybody RUN!'

No, no one would want Jeena once news of her marriage became common knowledge. It would be nigh on impossible for her parents to marry her off, after divorcing Aaron – no matter how vile the potential man. No wonder Jeena was glowing happily.

The pile of un-answered post on Jeena's desk looked as daunting as ever. The last time she'd taken a week's leave, she'd returned to her work on the 1st May and found amongst her post an envelope, dated 24th April, addressed to Agony Auntiji, labelled URGENT. Inside the poor woman had mentioned that she needed advice quickly, like in the next day or so, or she would kill herself. For the following few weeks, with a feeling that blood was on her hands, Jeena had frantically searched through the obituaries to see if the woman had indeed ended her life. Finally, in an act of desperation, she wrote back to the lady in her column: *To the woman who contacted me saying that she was going to kill herself. If you are still alive, then please don't do it.*

To this day, Jeena never knew if the woman was alive or dead. But she made a point thereafter to request that her urgent post should be dealt with by someone when she was on leave.

Jeena ripped open an envelope and threw the condom to one side. 'Nina, another Durex.' She laughed. Ever since Jeena had written a small article on safe sex, people had been sending her condoms. She often wished she'd written an article on diamond rings instead.

Next up, a simple: How do I get turmeric stains out of my silk sari?

Next up, a simple: My parents want me to be a doctor, but I want to be a nurse, how do I break the news to them?

Next up, a simple . . . Jeena read through the letter trying not to laugh. No, a not so simple problem:

Dear Auntiji Jeena,
I'm in a bit of a mango pickle. In order to hide
his cash from the taxman my dad placed 30,000
quid in my savings account. Now my dad wants
his money back. What shall I do?
Name withheld.

It was amazing, thought Jeena, how open some people are with their problems.

And others are so closed.

Inside the Paper Lantern, on a long, wooden bench against a wall, Aaron sat brooding. The huge training arena, known as the *dojo*, smelt of rubber matting and varnish. He remembered his architect viewing the place as an empty shell, and fixing Aaron with a stern look, 'And you're sure that you can fill this thing to capacity?' Sure? He'd never been surer. Once the wooden flooring, toilets and showers, low ceiling, potted plants, reception area and relaxing lounge had been installed, along with the specially imported Japanese stone statues of dragons, deities and Buddha's standing guard in corners and doorways, his architect did an 'about turn' with his belief in Aaron and even said, 'How much for me to join?' He was impressed with Aaron's vision and was never in any doubt after that of the place becoming a thriving success. As with most good businesses, reputation cannot be bought, it has to be earned. And the Paper Lantern was fast becoming *the* place in the Midlands for expert tuition and advice, although scraping together the money to fund the project would have been most people's idea of Hell.

Not having an expensive heirloom or rich relatives to call upon, Aaron had literally bought every brick of the place with his fists. In Japan, the gambling capital of the world, Aaron would enter open martial arts competitions and bet on himself. The odds of a white outsider beating an accomplished Japanese schooled fighter were very low. So low in fact that after twelve months of fighting and betting all his previous wins on each following fight, Aaron's wealth took on preposterous amounts. Just as people were catching on to the super fast white fighter from England, it was too late: Aaron was rich enough to return to the UK and set up his dream business, the Paper Lantern. The ease at which Aaron beat his competition would sometimes have his opponents, after the bout, checking very closely to see if Aaron had slitty eyes. Surely a man who fought with the passion he did must have had some Japanese blood in him somewhere. As it stood though, Aaron *only* had Japanese blood *on* him. Normally his fists and feet.

It was 5.30 p.m. on Monday and just half an hour until his first lesson of the week, the expert class (black belt and above), was due to commence. Dripping through the door in ones and twos were the early arrivals, who checked in with Mary at Reception, bowed respectfully to Aaron and then began to warm up quietly down the far end of the floor. Tonight, Aaron was worried that someone might get hurt. That someone being himself. If your mind wasn't on the job, then it was best to bail out. He often told his pupils that if they found that their concentration was slipping, then they should take a break, or risk taking a break.

'Evening, *Sensei*,' a man, clad in motorbike leather and a helmet, bowed.

'Evening, Billy,' Aaron replied.

Billy squeaked away towards the changing room. *I'm going to have to snap out of this*, thought Aaron. His brain had been stewing all afternoon. He was putting on a brave face to outsiders but inside his mind was a wreck. He felt how those people on the English Olympic committee must have felt, who kept pretending that London was 'IDEAL' for the games, when deep down they knew that it was a shit hole and it never stopped raining. What athlete wants to have to catch a red no. 99 bus to the stadium, only to find that their race has been called off due to bad weather? Who wants to tell the rowers that the Regatta has been rescheduled due to the amount of turds floating in from the River Thames? And who wants to have to say to the medal winners that, 'Sorry, you know what our kids are like, all on ASBOS and curfews, well, they've nicked them. Will a cup of Earl Grey tea and a cream scone make up for it?' Only Seb Coe knows what shameful lies he had to tell to secure the games for England; for his face looked just as shocked as everyone else's (including the French), when the decision came that London would play host in 2012.

And Aaron knew why he felt like he did, the answer was simple: Jeena, his new bloody wife. The luxury of living alone was gone, swapped with the feeling of claustrophobia. He'd assumed, with an apartment the size of his, that freedom of space would never be an issue. But that was before he'd added people like Big Mouth Kitty into the equation. All Sunday afternoon Jeena and Kitty had screamed and giggled their way through the wedding photographs. Tick, tock, tick . . . tock . . . . tick, time seemed to slow down and unless he wanted a double homicide on his hands, he thought it was best to go for his 200 mile jog. 'Bring us back a smile when you return, Bruce Lee,' Kitty had taunted him as he was about to leave. 'Go, fuck yourself,' was his reply as he slammed the door behind him. 'I'd rather fuck myself than be fucked by you,' he'd heard her yell out, as he slipped on his iPod and descended the stairs.

As if that wasn't enough to make a grown man weep, Aaron also had this problem with women's nosiness. It was nobody's business but his own regarding his family, or rather, lack of. He didn't want the likes of Jeena, or anyone else for that matter, opening up old wounds. He hated the person he used to be, the feeble, bullied, boy. He didn't want to talk about a period in his life which filled him with shame and disgust. If only he had a time machine and could transport himself back to those hateful years, then he'd stand up for himself, *then* those bullies would see the *real* Aaron. He hated knowing that he was once a wimp. A wimp who used to cry like a girl.

Before returning to the UK from Japan, Aaron had made a promise with himself that he would only open himself up completely to a woman if he was sure that he loved her and that she loved him in return. Only *that* woman would ever get to know his inner fears and regrets. Up until now, *that* woman hadn't crossed his path yet.

He was sure he would know her when she did.

As the clock struck six p.m., Aaron rose from his bench, adjusted his blue *gi* suit, and in bare feet, made his way to the lined-up students. All thirty or so bowed in unison as a further mark of respect. Aaron returned the bow and pointed to one of his finest fighters.

'You, kill me,' Aaron directed.

The guy, dressed in his pristine white *gi* suit, with his black belt attached, nervously walked towards Aaron, bowed again and then set himself into an attacking stance. He knew it was just a matter of time before he was yelling and screaming in pain as Aaron proved why he was the best.

Eyeing his attacker with venom, Aaron focused all his negative energy, and waited for the kicks to begin. Tonight, this pupil was going to pay for what Jeena had put him through all weekend. A roundhouse kick, perhaps, for having to put up with *Bridget Jones's Diary* on DVD three blasted times. A neck lock for putting up with Kitty and Jeena droning on and on about how perfect Tyler and Kitty were for each other. And a double-armed full Nelson because Jeena joked she thought the Liverpudlian accent was sexy. You don't joke about things like that; people will think you're mental.

'Bring it on,' Aaron demanded to his pupil, getting angrier by the second.

From out of the blue, the guy's foot came smashing through and kicked Aaron to the ground. A further knee in his chest, knocking the wind from him, meant that the attack was over. For the first time in living memory, Aaron had lost a simple fight to a far inferior fighter. No one cheered. The place remained in stunned silence as Aaron was helped to his feet. Humiliated, Aaron bowed to his victorious opponent.

'What have you got to say for yourself, *Sensei*?' asked an amazed pupil, breaking the silence.

'Apart from, "don't be so fucking cheeky, Patrick", well, I've got this to say.' Aaron ushered everyone around. 'Listen up; what you all just witnessed there was a "one off". It has never happened before and it will NEVER happen again. And I will explain why it happened.' Aaron tapped his head a few times. 'I lost concentration. My thoughts were somewhere else. In fact, my thoughts were with a woman.' A few wolf whistles were emitted. 'Not like that. More like, how to get a woman out of my life.' He noticed a few smirks amongst his class. People who knew Aaron well would have warned them against smirking when he was being frank. He clapped his hands together. 'Okay, I want one hundred press-ups from each of you. Next time you might think twice before smirking in front of me. Now move!'

After the lesson, Aaron was back to where he was before. Brooding and reflecting. Barely a week with Jeena and he was losing concentration in the gym already. How bad would things get after a couple of months?

Would he be begging his doctor to prescribe him Seroxat for his depression? He shook his head despondently: Aaron was not a happy bunny right now.

Chapter Fourteen

It was the last Friday in June: blue skies, bright sun, not a rain cloud in sight. The perfect beginning to any morning. Yet, inside 56 Monroe Avenue, the house was full of gloom. It had been a week and one day since Maji and Papaji had disowned Jeena and nearly a month since Nanaji had spoken. Attempts to jolt Nanaji's vocal cords into action had ranged from popping party balloons in her ear while she slept (JJ's idea, of course) to slipping half a box of Pro Plus tablets in her Horlicks. Her doctor had explained that some people's brains go into a sort of loop (hence the word 'loopy' suggested JJ, who was told to shut up) when they have been shocked (and nobody doubted that Nanaji had indeed been shocked by bearing witness to Jeena and Aaron's lovemaking session upstairs), it was quite common, and normally disappeared after a while.

But vocal cords were one thing, tear ducts were something else entirely. Daily, both Maji and Nanaji had been weeping and sobbing so much anyone would think that there was a hose pipe ban. So dense was the foggy gloom in the house that JJ decided to get himself a summer job just to get out. His second job interview proved a success when he told the Tesco supermarket recruitment officer that he'd always dreamed of being a Tesco shelf filler so that he could meet people and it would be a stepping stone for that corner shop he'd always wanted so much. As opposed to his first job interview with the Sainsbury's recruitment officer where he told him that he'd always wanted to be a shelf filler for Sainsbury's so that he could get a Sainsbury's discount. 'If I started work tomorrow,' JJ had asked the totally unimpressed interviewer, 'would I be able to use my discount card straight away? I've got my eye on a few CDs I want. And would the rest of my family be allowed to use the discount card?' Just before he left the interview he turned and said, 'Oh, by the way, how much exactly is the discount I would get?'

Papaji, Maji and Nanaji sat in the living room drinking cardamom tea. Rumours had been filtering through over the last few days about Jeena's circumstances. How she had shamed the whole Indian community. Like an out-of-control fire the flames of backstabbing had flickered and burned their way from one county to the next. Caller after caller had phoned the Gills' household asking if the news was true. Asking if another Indian girl had turned stray. Taunting with their questions, venomous with their intent. If an Indian daughter had shamed the Indian way, then it stood to reason that her parents had shamed the way too. Fault had to be laid somewhere and inevitably, when it came to runaways, the pointy stick was often aimed in the parents' direction; and the words which followed were always the same, 'You obviously had no control over her. You should have been stricter.'

Now, sitting huddled over their hot teas like a committee, they did question themselves: had they been too lenient? Had they let Jeena run too wild? Was it too much to expect a young girl to fit in with two cultures? It's hard enough sometimes just to fit in with the one. Papaji rubbed his wife's back, trying to soothe, trying to console. It was as though he was dealing with a bereavement. The heart-wrenching loss of life. And yet, in both their hearts, they knew they could resurrect Jeena at any time. They could bring her back from the dead as certainly as ice would melt in the midday sun. No miracles, no prayers, no shenanigans. Just a phone call, a few rings, then one sentence: 'Jeena, if he makes you happy, then we give you our blessing; we want you back in this family, where you belong.' Both parents were within reaching distance of that phone right now. Yet, for the shame she had thrust upon their family, to call her now would turn them into hypocrites of their culture. And being a hypocrite is certainly not in the Indian's version of the book, *How to Win Friends and Influence People*.

For such a huge man, Papaji often felt tiny. His massive shoulders were intended to bear the weight of the family and his strong personality was supposed to buffer them against any knocks and bruises. But sometimes the responsibility of keeping home, home sweet home, was too much. And this inability to cope was something his older brother, Gurjinder, would sneer at.

Gurjinder was a man who prided himself on his national identity. Born in India, he lived in India and thought like an Indian. He judged that moving to England was commendable, risky, brave. But not for him. A true Indian stays at home. And home has to be India. Born to die there. If God wanted him anywhere else then God would surely have put him there. For God was Almighty and we were just his flock.

And Papaji was praying to God Almighty right now. In a few moments he would have to pick up the phone and dial up his brother's house in New Delhi. After a few exchanges of tittle-tattle he would have to explain the bad news. How Jeena had run off and married a white man, bringing humiliation to the family. How the wedding planned in India between Jeena and the man Gurjinder had fixed her up with would have to be cancelled. How the family would not be coming to India after all.

'How in God's name am I going to tell him?' Papaji asked his wife. 'You know what he's like. He'll lay the blame at my feet; he'll accuse me of being weak.'

Nanaji looked to Papaji, her son, and sneered. Something in the way she stared seemed to agree: he *was* weak. Thank Guru Nanak for the likes of her other son, Gurjinder, the backbone of India, for if her great nation had had to rely on Preetjeet, the cowardly son sitting before her now, then surely India wouldn't have gained independence from the British in 1947. Oh, how she remembered those confusing times. White men with sticks and rifles ordering her countrymen around like dogs. Fearful of stepping out of line in case one received a whipping. Stepping out of line? How dare those hoity-toity Englishmen with their funny trousers and stupid hats lay down to another country what construed 'stepping out of line'. Who did the English think they were back in those dark days?

Then, as if they hadn't had enough of the English, that stupid son of hers, Preetjeet, decided to move to England in the seventies, dragging her along with him and his wife. His promises of a better life, with excellent health care and fantastic schools was just one of the many carrots he dangled in front of her before she agreed to leave her motherland behind. 'Watch your future grandchildren grow up into doctors and lawyers,' he'd boasted. 'See the smiles on their faces when they collect their diplomas'. It all sounded so perfect. And in the beginning it was. Preetjeet found himself a job with an accountancy firm which led to him opening his own firm, Gills & Bills, a few years later. Her daughter-in-law worked piece-work at a bra factory until she became pregnant with Jeena. Even Nanaji seemed to be enjoying her adopted country, meeting up with other immigrants, talking about India, watching Bollywood films at her local cinema, turning up at Indian weddings most weekends. Everything was going swell until that fateful day with Jeena and Aaron. A nightmare right before her eyes. Something she knew would never have happened in India.

Eleven a.m. in England meant it was 4.30 p.m. in New Delhi. JJ liked to say that Delhi was five and a half hours ahead of us but two centuries behind. Much to the disgust of his elders. A worrying development for some Indian parents is when their children begin to slag off their ancestral land before they've even been there. Papaji drummed up the courage and dialled his brother's number.

As soon as Gurjinder picked up the receiver, a vision of New Delhi flowed through the phone-line and into Papaji's heart. A bustling, frantic, growing city that buzzes with the noise of blood and sweat. Gurjinder lived only a short way from Connaught Place, the centre of the mad Delhi galaxy, the hub of shops and markets. He liked to live 'where it's at' among crowds of people and the smell of rupees. His sari shop, Gills Fashion Wonderland, kept up with the ever-changing style trends and made a small fortune with its high quality designs.

The two brothers spoke in Punjabi, cutting out unnecessary words as a matter of habit dating back to the time when phoning abroad used to cost them an arm and a leg. The Punjabi equivalent of 'Okay?' could mean, 'How are you, your wife, your kids, business, house, health, pets, anyone died lately, have you solved the Rubik's Cube yet, been to any weddings lately?' and '*Sat sri akal ji*'. But when the topic came round to Jeena's arranged marriage in India, no words were cut out. A heavy silence waited at the other end of the phone as Papaji explained what Jeena had done. With a quiver in his voice, he told his brother how they had had to disown her.

'You sound to me, like you feel guilty about disowning her, brother,' Gurjinder said. 'Get that thought out of your head immediately. You did the right thing on that part.'

'It's not easy living over here with English ways and English customs. I . . .'

'I don't want to hear it! Your daughter has shamed our family and for that she must be held accountable.

She must be punished, brother, for without punishment she will never learn true respect.' Gurjinder was cold and direct. 'It's very simple what you must do. You must drag your daughter back and keep her locked up. You must teach this white husband of hers a lesson. And then we will make plans to have her divorced and sent out to India where she will be forced into a marriage. You must put a stop to this crime before she has a chance to become pregnant. For even I would have trouble forgiving you, my young brother, if she were to have our blood diluted by the white man's. I suggest you see to this quickly. Our father would not tolerate this behaviour if he were alive today.'

Feebly, Papaji tried to explain that England had rules about kidnapping your own daughter. It was different to India. But Gurjinder brushed these comments aside with one statement: 'Please don't make me come out there and sort this shameful mess out myself. For that, Preetjeet, I would not be at all happy.'

As the phone was replaced in its cradle, Papaji dropped next to his wife on the sofa and held his head in his hands. It was so easy for Gurjinder to order him around. Go here, do that, see to this. Yet, he hadn't seen the look in Aaron's eyes when he'd threatened him: 'My wife, your daughter, means the world to me. If anything should happen to her then I will hold you totally responsible. I think you know what I'm talking about here.' Something in that threat told him that, when Aaron had said he'd hold him 'responsible', he wasn't talking about a stiff telling off. More like turning him into a stiff.

Who knew what some men were capable of?

*

Or some women for that matter.

Stacy was back. This time with a pink suitcase; ready to stay the night once again. On her last visit, nine days prior to this one, she'd copied down a month's worth of days from Aaron's schedule in his diary. According to the diary, this Friday, Saturday and Sunday, he was away in Northampton. As far as she was concerned, the plan to disrupt the romantic *chi* in his apartment with the matchsticks above the Romance Corner had failed. This had been made pretty clear by Aaron's refusal to meet up with her when she'd phoned him, repeatedly, last Sunday. It was time to try something else. Aaron was the best fish in the sea and she wasn't having him slip through her net – not again. Love like this only came along once in a lifetime and if she couldn't have Aaron in this life, then it wasn't worth living.

Her friends, manicurist, hairdresser, masseur, the gasman, paperboy and mother all said, 'How can you love someone like him? He only wants you for sex. Don't be so gullible to believe that there is a deeper man to the one you know.' But they didn't know the Aaron she knew. They weren't there when he made love to her (although the thrill of being watched did turn her on) so they wouldn't have heard his gentle whispers in her ear, or the way he tenderly caressed her body. It was completely obvious to her that Aaron only performed so fantastically in bed when he was with a woman he secretly loved. How many men out there would make sure the woman had at least three orgasms before he'd even considered having one himself? How many men would volunteer to hand whip the cream so that the woman didn't have a wrist ache? And how many men would offer to change the batteries when they were running low?

He was a true gentleman.

A gentleman and lover who Stacy missed immensely. Just the thought of staying in his bed for another night was bringing goose bumps to the surface of her smooth, moisturized skin. Just the idea of hosing herself down in the same shower as he did was making her knickers wet. Just the fact that she could sniff his XS aftershave-scented pillow was sending her heartbeat soaring.

So, with goose bumps, wet knickers and a heartbeat on the dangerous side, Stacy walked up the stairs and knocked on the front door. When there was no answer, she jiggled the key in the lock, punched in the alarm number and let herself in. Once again she was standing in her dream man's living quarters.

For the first few seconds, she stood there, hand on hip, suitcase on the floor, smile on face. 'I'm back.' Then, as if someone had stuffed poo under her surgery-reduced nose, her face turned to a grimace. The smell of women's perfume was obvious in the air. Obvious and, in this case, threatening. Like The Child Catcher in *Chitty Chitty Bang Bang*, Stacy stalked through the open-plan room, searching for hidden clues; her brown eyes peeled back on full exposure. On the coffee table, lay a stack of women's glossy magazines, by the DVD player were a pile of DVDs, *Bridget Jones's Diary, Clueless, Mean Girls, Bride & Prejudice, 13 Going on 30*, and if that wasn't proof enough that a woman was staying here, a box of half-eaten Milk Tray lay on the sofa. Aaron didn't eat chocolate; he was too much into his strict diet for that. He certainly never mentioned he liked Chick Flicks.

'I hate her, I hate her,' Stacy squawked, as she sped through the apartment into Aaron's bedroom. She threw back the fitted-wardrobe doors expecting to see women's clothes. But just men's. Only men's . . . and, she knelt down and peered at the steel casing of the enormous safe. Well, well, well, she thought to herself, standing up and brushing down her designer jeans, what secrets would a man like Aaron be holding in a safe like that? Or, was it just boring files and documents? Concluding the latter, she rushed out of the room and made for the two spare bedrooms. She pushed open the door to the room nearest Aaron's and was hit by the same smell of perfume, this time stronger. If she didn't have heart problems before, then she surely did now. Her dream day was turning into a bad dream.

Sure enough, the bamboo wardrobe was filled with women's clothes. Worse than that though was the minuscule size of the short skirts and skimpy tops. It was clear that this woman, this bitch, whoever she was, had a great figure and wasn't afraid to show it. Her only hope that Aaron had a sister lodging here was dashed when her eyes were drawn to a pile of photographs on the bedside table. Stacy sat on Jeena's bed preparing herself for the worst: that Jeena was prettier than her.

'I HATE HER!' Stacy screamed as she grabbed the wedding pictures and frantically looked through them one-by-one. 'I REALLY DO HATE HER!'

There was no getting away from it. Aaron the-complete-and-utter-bastard Myles, had got himself married to a beautiful Asian woman. Photo after photo of the pair of them smiling beside the Gretna Green sign. Him, looking handsome and her, looking stunning. Photos of them eating wedding cake, cutting the cake, swapping the rings, drinking champagne. Enjoyment written over their faces, happiness shining from their eyes. It was sickening.

It was also extremely upsetting. There was no point in trying to put a brave face on it as the only other entity in the room was a furry pink teddy-pig lying trotter-side up on the bed. Surely the pig wouldn't mind if she shed a few tears. And it didn't, not letting out so much as a small 'oink'. She sobbed quietly into her hands, making a mental note to fill in her diary later, expressing her emotions; where she would melodramatically write: *My heart seemed like it was fractured, my dreams lay broken and my future is in intensive care*. There was nothing left to do but get up and go. Just before leaving she pulled from the wedding photos a dashing picture of Aaron caught off guard, dressed in his suit, on his own by a small lake. So sexy did he appear in this snap that women could risk getting pregnant just by looking at it (for a nanosecond). She tucked it into her handbag and took one last glance around the room. Something was occurring to her now which should have occurred to her before. Something mighty strange.

Why did Aaron and his new wife sleep in separate beds?

Chapter Fifteen

Karen, the shop assistant at Occasional Occasions Florist in Northampton, had made up some lavish bouquets in her time, but today, on this ordinary Friday afternoon, was the first time she'd been asked to make up a bouquet worth 300 quid. If this was what the gentleman gave a lady for flowers she wondered what he gave her in the bedroom. And if her own boyfriend was anything to go by, if he had ever bought her flowers, which he didn't (because she worked in 'a bloody florist') then his bunch, if one was judging by his bedroom performance, would have been two droopy daffodils.

'She's a lucky lady,' Karen said, writing out the invoice in her best handwriting.

'I'm a lucky man,' Aaron replied, handing her his credit card. 'To be honest, I don't know what I'd do without her.'

Karen made a note to start a row with her boyfriend this evening. She was getting sick of men coming in and saying lovely things about their women only for

her to go home to her other half with his most romantic of gestures, 'What's for tea?' or 'Get your kit off,
woman, I'm horny as hell.' Sick of it!

With the gigantic bunch of flowers just about fitting
in the boot, Aaron drove away, passing many of his
childhood haunts on route. The green playing area near
the forest, where perverts threw away their porn magazines – and even more perverted teenagers found
them. The leisure centre where he'd taken his first martial arts lesson and heard for the first time the crack of
a nose breaking – unfortunately it was his own. The
stagnant pond with its homemade pirate's plank which
pissed adolescent boys would bet each other to cross.
The school. Collingsworth Comprehensive. The school
field where every seedling grew into a huge tree of
worry. Where the home-time bell meant being spat at
on the bus, or being kicked at as he was forced to run
through The Tunnel of Death. His school that nurtured
bullies and weakened confidence. His school that
taught him one lesson and one lesson only: never rely
on others to take care of you. You're on your own.

Onwards Aaron drove, excited about today, passed
the numerous shoe factories, passed the Carlsberg
brewery, looking forward to the weekend stay over. He
parked the car half on the kerb half on the road as was
per norm in this neck of the woods, leaving enough
room for the drunk drivers of the late evening to nego-
tiate a safe passage through. Rough neighbourhood?
Even the cats were on Anti Social Behaviour Orders
and, in the middle of the night, one could read a book
by the flashing blue lights of the police cars constantly
speeding by.

Aaron rapped on the door with one hand while in the other he held the mighty bouquet of flowers. He was wearing an Extreme Fighting T-shirt, shorts and trainers. The perfect wear in case he had to lay chase if someone tried to steal his BMW; even if the T-shirt logo was a bit cheesy: PREPARE TO MEET THY MAKER. With what sounded like a frustrated Houdini on the other side of the door, a dozen or so chains were undone and various locks and bolts were pulled to. Great exercise for her arthritis, thought Aaron, as his seventy-five year old gran appeared before him. He smiled as he moved in for a hug. Careful not to squeeze her too hard, careful not to break her. The smell of home-cooked cakes and biscuits scuppered as usual any notion that this weekend was going to be a healthy one. He would have felt too guilty not to eat the lovely treats that she always cooked for him when he came around every month. And this weekend was going to be emotional enough without throwing an extra dollop of guilt into the mixture. Tomorrow happened to be the twentieth anniversary of his parents' death. A day which both Gran and he celebrated (together if possible but sometimes, like when he was living in Japan, on their own). It was a celebration of the life before their death. An honouring of their spirits when others may well have forgotten all about them. A simple day of remembrance.

Inside was like walking into a time capsule. The place was adorned with artefacts and pictures of yesteryear, of family and of herself, clippings taken from the local newspaper featuring Gran, all kept in pristine condition as if the clock had ceased to tick. Worth nothing to an antique dealer but priceless to her. After finding various pots and vases for the flowers, they sat down.

Over tea and cake Gran asked her opening question: 'So, met anyone who takes your fancy?' She nibbled on her ginger and apricot slice. 'It would mean a lot to me if you could meet someone before I die.'

Aaron nodded. 'It's your fault, Gran, you've set my expectations too high. I assume all women to be as wonderful as you and yet . . . most are just dogs and tarts.'

She smiled. 'Oh, you silver-tongued smoothy. Still the same Aaron after all these years. Who's that woman who died a few years back? She was perfect for you.'

He scratched his head. 'You're going to have to be a little bit more specific, Gran.'

'Oh, you know the one? The Queen hated her.' She stared in a puzzled way into space for about ten seconds, until she remembered. 'Lady Diana, that's her name. She would have been perfect for you.'

'Shame.'

'Died the same way your parents did.' Her face took on a sad look. 'Your father, Michael, he was my only child. What a waste. God should have taken my life instead of his. What a waste.' She instinctively peered above the gas fire at the photograph of her son. 'Do you really believe that we get to meet our loved ones again when we die, Aaron? Father Karras seems ever so sure. He told me the other day after service, he said, "Margaret, between you and me, and this is entirely off the record, but I myself have experienced proof that the afterlife exists. I hear the voice of my deceased mother every morning as I boil the kettle for tea".'

Aaron picked up an old copy of *People's Friend* and flicked through the pages with an air of resignation. Father Karras, the friendliest pastor in the world, would say anything for a slice of Gran's walnut and almond cake. 'When you sadly pass away, Margaret, you must leave the church the recipe in your will. I'd hate to think that the only chance to taste this wonderful cake again would be in Heaven,' he'd once told her. From that moment on the cake was called Heavenly Cake and Margaret always kept a couple of them frozen in case death took her off guard. To be defrosted and eaten at her funeral, along with a cup of PG Tips.

'If Father Karras says that the afterlife exists, then you can be sure it does, Gran. Father Karras is a man who knows exactly what he's talking about. He's not one to make mistakes,' Aaron explained, trying to uphold the polished holy image of the local pastor. 'He's a good man.'

'He is,' Gran agreed. 'And he's awfully worried about you at the moment. He nearly knocked me for six when he told me that there was a good chance that you might be a homosexual. I thought to myself, "Well, I've never seen you with a girl". Maybe Father Karras was right. He showed me this article about children brought up without their parents. Apparently, many of them turned out to be homosexuals.'

Aaron was motionless and in shock, like a stuffed animal who'd caught one too many shotgun pellets. You could have mounted his head amongst the deer and buffalos with the caption KILLED BY THE SUGGESTION THAT HE MIGHT BE GAY. Father Karras *didn't* know what the hell he was talking about.

'I'm not fucking gay, Gran, Jesus H Christ.' Aaron was rather perturbed. 'I've had more women than he's given sermons.' He shook his head. 'Gran, don't believe everything Father Karras says, *please*.'

Despite her age, there was still enough elastic in Margaret's skin to give her grandson the 'I'm not amused' face. 'Since when have I allowed swearing before the watershed, Aaron? You know perfectly well how I hate to hear such profanities before nine p.m. If your parents were alive today, I wouldn't want them thinking I brought you up wrong.'

If my parents had been alive today, thought Aaron, you wouldn't have brought me up at all. But he knew when he'd over-stepped the mark and decided to retreat to his old bedroom to calm down. GAY? HOW DARE HE!

The room was a time warp. Everything was exactly how he'd left it all those moons ago as a teenager. Bruce Lee dominated most of the wall space (and not in a gay way either, he'd have people know) with scenes from his various movies carefully cut-out, mounted on cardboard and Blu-Tacked to the wall. A chest-of-drawers covered in stickers and a wardrobe covered in graffiti. Aaron lay back on the single bed and focused, as he had always done, on the small crack in the ceiling's plaster. The amount of times he'd plotted his revenge on the bullies from this very spot, he'd lost count. Dreaming of the day when he could walk the streets of Northampton without worrying about bumping into anyone from the Fletcher Gang. Imagining a future when he could sleep the whole night through without waking up in a pool of panicky sweat. Those fucking bullies really had stitched him up – they'd stolen his childhood completely. Even now, as the squeaks of his mattress springs complained at the extra weight from Aaron's mature body, his mind was awash with images worthy of a Quentin Tarantino film. What he would give right now to come across one of the bullies who had tormented him. What he would pay to have five minutes in their company again. Five minutes in their company used to seem to last for hours, these days, he was sure it would fly by as he watched them beg for forgiveness.

He thought of his gran downstairs. Since returning from Japan – a place that she wasn't too keen on him going to – Aaron had been trying, in vain, to get her to move nearer to him in Primpton which was over an hour's drive away. He'd offered to pay for everything. The move and the house. But he couldn't pay for the hassle. Or the memories she'd miss when she was gone; or the friends she'd made over the years. She'd totally understood why Aaron had had to leave Northampton, a man has to make the break someday, and even though it broke her heart, she was pleased that she'd brought her grandson up to be an independent young man. If only she'd known the real reason why he couldn't face Northampton anymore. The very same reason that Aaron used to wet his bed. Maybe if Gran had looked real hard at Aaron's Christmas cards from his school friends, she might have noticed that he'd written nearly all of them to himself. No one wanted to be friends with Aaron, for no one wanted to cross the Fletcher Gang. It was a far cry from the popular lad his gran had envisioned Aaron to be.

His bedroom window overlooked the street, a never-ending row of terraced houses that curled and twisted far into the distance. There were so many nicer places to live than this. Places which didn't need eight locks and four bolts just to keep Gran feeling safe. His thoughts turned to what she'd mentioned earlier about never having seen him with a girl. Well, it was true, she'd not. From his schooldays where no girl could risk going out with him through fear of retribution from the Fletcher Gang to his three-year period in Japan, up until now, where he'd promised himself that he wouldn't divulge anything about his family tree until he was sure he was with the right woman. The woman who loved him as he loved her. What was the point of taxiing his one-night, two-night, three-week stands to Northampton, introducing them to his gran, only to turn up four weeks later with a different woman? As soon as he'd introduced Gran to a girlfriend then the floodgates would open and everything about his upbringing and his parents' death would be exposed. It would have to be one hell of a special woman for Aaron to reveal his past. For in his eyes, his past was an expensive commodity and could only be bought by total, one-hundred per cent trust. He'd already reluctantly explained to Jeena, on the day she moved in, that his parents were dead and he was the soul survivor of his family. That information would stand. She didn't need to know about his gran. It would only lead to more questions.

Questions he didn't want to answer.

Jeena had a question right now: where the hell had Aaron disappeared to? A text from him at work today had read:

Away 4 wkend
Bk Sun – Don't
trash place. Aa

Jeena was going to have to remind Aaron that the cost
of a text wasn't per letter. He could, in fact, use up the
whole allocation before he had to pay a further 10
pence. Stingy git.

Returning home after another day of being blanked
in the office by the older colleagues over her marriage
to Aaron, Jeena felt the need for some company, other
than fish – even though the fish did speak more sense
than most men (in Morse Bubble language). Friday
evenings were normally a celebration, the beginning of
the weekend, the finish of the working week. That's all
fine and dandy if you've got someone to share it with,
but when you're on your own, weekends stink.

What's more, it was beginning to dawn on her that
Kitty's plan of seeing to Aaron's every need, the cooking, cleaning, washing and blow-jobbing so that he
became dependent on having her around, was pie in the
sky. Not happening. As if! He washed his own clothes,
he cooked his own food, he kept the place spotless, so
all she was left with was blow-jobs, and even then he
had other women kneeling for him. The overriding fact
was that their paths rarely crossed and she was lucky if
she saw Aaron for more than fifteen minutes in any one
day. Their timetables were so mismatched that when
she was returning from work he was just leaving for
work. By the time he entered the apartment later, she
was washed out and asleep.

Her mother used to joke, 'Loneliness is only horrible

if you're on your own.' Jokes aside, Maji was wrong. Loneliness was also horrible when you were living with someone. Especially if that someone was making it totally clear that he didn't want you to be any part of his life. It was almost as if their friendship (if one could call it that) had disappeared the moment they became married. Jeena considered the saying: *marriage was just a piece of paper*; well, in her case it was true. A piece of paper watermarked with the words: For One Year Only. And in this year what exactly was her role supposed to be in the partnership? To keep out of Aaron's way? To sit down, shut up and wait for the year to be up? Or was it simply to be his whore on tap? A woman kept on the simmer for those days when he couldn't be bothered to go hunting for a dame himself.

But she wanted more than that, so much more. She wanted to know the *real* Aaron, the man she sometimes saw peeping through this false persona. She wanted to delve into his past and learn more about him, to find out where the Aaron she unfortunately loved came from. What made him tick, what made him tock, what he feared the most, what he dreamt about. She wanted to find out about his upbringing; was he adopted after his parents' death? Was he fostered? Was he ... anything. SHE JUST WANTED HIM TO BLOODY WELL TALK TO HER!!! It amazed her: sometimes the men with the biggest testicles have the smallest balls when it came to opening up.

Jeena kicked off her shoes and lounged back on the sofa. A half-eaten box of Milk Tray was within grasping distance. The TV remote was balanced on the arm rest. The temperature in the apartment was cool and uplifting. Perfect was as good a word as any to describe this moment. Yet, one of the ills of getting what you wanted was that sometimes it didn't live up to your expectations. Hundreds of times Jeena had dreamt of moments just like this. Living away from her parents in a posh home with the freedom to come and go as she pleased without the parents constantly nagging: where are you going? Who will you be seeing tonight? Why are you wearing that short skirt? Are we that boring a family that you have to go out every night? Now the dream was real; her freedom was limitless and no one, not even the fish, cared whether she turned up drunk in only her bra and knickers at four a.m., or at any other time for that matter. Anyone who has fought for freedom would tell you that freedom costs, but Jeena would never have assumed that it would come at the cost of her family.

In many ways she missed them already. The never-ending questions which proved they cared. The serious chats from Papaji about investing her money wisely. The cookery tips from Maji. Even the tiring three-hour Bollywood movie-watching sessions she would endure with Nanaji just to keep her happy. In fact, she even missed the bickering and fighting with her brother JJ. Just the memory of his cheeky face made her smile. And as if God was tuned into her thoughts today, there was a loud knock at the door.

JJ was here.

'For you,' JJ said, holding up a Tesco carrier bag. 'Maji's mango pickle. If she finds out it's missing then I'm cheese on toast.' He strolled in, the bag leaking a trail of mango oil on the wooden floor. 'Wicked place.'

He continued his self-guided tour, dripping oil en route, obliviously swinging the bag as he went, right the way up to and on to the white sofa.

As soon as Jeena had realized the bag was dripping it was too late. Turmeric infused vegetable oil was now making pretty patterns on Aaron's expensive couch. Man had put men on the moon, but never had they come up with a product to remove Maji's mango pickle stains from suede. JJ's suggestion 'Tippex' didn't go down too well, although not quite as badly as his 'blame it on Aaron's skid marks' solution. But JJ was right about one thing, and that was the word 'blame'. As soon as Aaron set eyes on his wrecked sofa, he was going to be looking to blame someone. Having a piece of furniture which looked like it had eaten a curry (and smelt like it had too) would surely upset him. Suddenly the divorce seemed a lot nearer.

'Has Nanaji spoken yet?' Jeena asked, mopping up the oil on the floor.

'Just the odd belch and fart, apart from that, nothing.' JJ stopped checking through the satellite channels for a second. 'I don't think she's clever enough to be using her wind as some sort of code.' He shook his head. 'No, they're definitely random noises.' He continued with his search on the TV. 'What's a kid have to do to get some hardcore porn these days?'

'I don't think Aaron's got a porn channel, JJ. Weird hey?' she said, sarcastically.

'Dead weird,' he replied, non-sarcastically. 'What a waste of a cinema-sized telly. Imagine how great *Virgins Give it up For Lent* would look. A-mazing.'

Ignoring him, she picked up the mop and bucket

and headed to the kitchen where she made coffee and sandwiches. By the time Jeena was back, JJ was engrossed in a martial arts fighting DVD. It might as well have been porn, judging by the noises coming from the screen. She handed him the coffee and plate of chicken and salad sandwiches, and sat back waiting for him to become polite.

She waited.

She waited.

Twenty minutes later, Jeena finally exploded, snatched the remote from his hand and switched off the grunting half-naked fighting men. 'What are you here for, JJ? What do you want?'

'I came to see if you were alright.' He squirmed in his seat, clearly embarrassed at this sudden show of affection. 'I think what you did was right. I don't care what anybody else says. Our relatives, neighbours, Maji and Papaji, they're all the same, spreading the gossip, dragging your name through the dirty path. Our parents have always lectured us on how they were racially abused by the white people of this country. But you should hear what they say about Aaron, it's quite unacceptable. They say he's a fraud and a trickster. They say that they're never going to forgive you, sis.' And JJ lowered his eyes in shame. 'They say you're no longer their daughter. They say that as far as they are concerned you are dead.'

It was final then. Her ties to her parents were officially severed. Jeena had been preparing for this punch since she'd returned married from Gretna Green, but she hadn't realized quite how hard it was going to hit her until now. But also, like the condemned to die, she'd been waiting for that eleventh-hour phone call; a reprieve from her family, forgiveness for her actions. A skinny amount of hope based on family love. To console herself at night she'd told herself that her family would relent in their ways and make peace. They would do this reluctantly, but they would do it because they loved her.

But now, in their hearts, she was dead.

Chapter Sixteen

Aaron used to morbidly call cemeteries Calcium Dumps. Initially, after his parents had died, Aaron had lived in semi-denial of their departure from this world. Telling himself that they were on a long holiday and would be back soon. His referrals to Calcium Dumps and Marrowbone Fields was his way of humorously coping with death; and the moment he accepted that he was never going to see his parents again was the moment humour disappeared.

Today was a warm, sunny Sunday afternoon, a traditional day for people visiting their lost ones in the graveyard; and it was the second time Aaron had been here in two days. Yesterday, the anniversary of his parents' death, both he and Gran had paid their respects, placing flowers and cleaning up the joint headstone. After a traditional roast beef dinner fit for a king cooked by his lovely Gran, he'd waved her farewell, and come back to the cemetery.

And judging by the extra vase of flowers, so too had the mystery visitor. Aaron instinctively glanced up and down the rows of graves, as if a suspicious-looking person would appear and solve the riddle. For it was definitely a riddle. A five-year riddle. On his mother's birthday and the anniversary of his parents' death, a small bunch of flowers would be laid on their grave. Once Aaron had sat in the cemetery for the whole day in the hope of finding out who was placing these flowers. But the person never showed. And the mystery was never solved. There was a very slim chance that the flowers could have been placed by someone from his mother's family, but as far as Aaron was aware, she'd fallen out with all of them years and years ago and they'd all emigrated to Australia anyway; losing contact completely. Gran was as perplexed by the mystery grave stalker as Aaron. Racking her brains to think of anyone who had turned up at the funeral who might, just possibly be the culprit, alas, she could think of no one.

Oddly, as Aaron stared up and down the graveyard, it was he who felt like he was being watched. That tingle at the back of his neck, that shadow walking across his heart. Maybe next year on the anniversary of his mum's birthday he would leave a note with his flowers – for he was sure the mystery person would read a note if it was there to be read – and ask him/her to contact him. He'd love to know who this other person was who cared about his mother so much.

The quiet sobbing of an elderly man troubled Aaron as the sound of sadness always did in these places. Loss was never easy to understand. It had him thinking of his own loss, and the obligation that had come with it.

When his mother had left him that package in her will, surely she'd left it with the idea that Aaron would open it. Twenty years had now passed and still the package remained sealed in his safe. Somewhere in his conscience an alarm bell was ringing. What he was doing was wrong. Hiding from reality was wrong. Denying a dying woman's wishes was definitely wrong. Especially when it was his own mother. About to kneel down and have a private word with his mother, he started in shock when from behind him, a gruff male voice spoke his name.

'Aaron Myles? It's you, isn't it?'

Yet another heart in the graveyard ceased to beat. The voice in Aaron's ear brought with it many chilling memories. A feeling that had lain dormant for so many years, resurfaced. As if someone had flicked the fear switch back on. Aaron turned to face the owner of the voice and for reasons unknown to him right then, he froze.

The tall man with his shaved head, earrings, tattoo of a snake curled around his neck and a few gold teeth, stood in his clean, ironed jeans and perfectly white shirt. He put out his tattooed hand, pretty much aware that Aaron was kacking his pants. It had been twelve years since these two had crossed paths.

'Please tell me you didn't grow up to be a sissy, Aaron. Go on shake my hand, I ain't gonna bite yer.' Darryl Fletcher smirked as if he'd discovered a new toy (or in this case found an old one). 'Still living with granny or has she kicked the bucket?'

Aaron had been through this scenario a thousand

times in his mind. The day he confronted the head of the Fletcher Gang. He'd assumed that when that day did come, he'd have no trouble repaying Darryl some of the hurt he was owed. Yet, as old fears swam with new, all confidence left Aaron's being and all thoughts of retribution fluttered away. Once again, it seemed that Aaron was at the mercy of his bully. Martial arts meant zilch if you couldn't move your limbs.

Darryl continued, 'Nothing to say to me after all these years?' He eyeballed Aaron's jujitsu T-shirt. The slogan read I DON'T DO SCARED. Darryl cracked up laughing, pointing to it. 'Convince yourself, Aaron, you muppet.' He stepped right up to Aaron's trembling body like a sergeant to one of his platoon and whispered in his ear, 'The only reason I laid off you at school that time was because my old man said he would batter me if I got in trouble with the filth again. It had naff all to do with your martial arts like you'd like everyone to think. But that was then, this is now. Makes you wonder what tomorrow will . . .'

A female voice announced itself across the grave-yard. 'Darryl, would you 'urry up, the twins need feeding. Unless you want me to get my tits out here. Darryl? . . . Darryl? . . . DARRYL!'

Darryl shoved Aaron hard to the ground, leaving him with a sneer, wallowing in a pool of humiliation. As he walked away, Darryl's eyes said one thing 'That was just as much fun as it ever was' then he disappeared from view, pushing the baby buggy in front of him with his scantily-dressed girlfriend in tow.

Aaron felt defeated and drained. If ever there was a time to face his demons and cast away their spell on him, then it was now, in front of his parents. Except, their son was a coward, a deserter, a man who goes AWOL in his own wars. Hardly a son to be proud of.

Hardly a man at all.

Tomorrow he was supposed to be teaching his students how to defend themselves against aggressive attackers. In awe they would listen as he explained how to dispose of fear. In fact, make fear your ally, he would often say. HA! What a joke. How could he continue with his club, now that he knew his teachings were based on a lie? What would his mates say when he told them of what had happened? They would never understand, they would laugh in his face. 'You, Aaron, the toughest, 8th-dan, cage fighter, no-holds-barred expert on a multitude of martial arts, couldn't cope with Mr Joe Average?' Darryl was right: what a muppet.

The hour's drive back to Primpton was driven in a daze. It was as if he'd just come back from the hospital with terrible results. 'Mr Myles, I'm sorry to say but cowardice is still showing up on the X-ray. Unfortunately the Fletcher Gang virus has now spread to your heart and soul. We've tried all we can, but there are no more treatments we can recommend. Except: PULL YOUR THUMB OUT OF YOUR ARSE AND DEAL WITH IT YOU MORON.'

Climbing up the stairs to his apartment, dragging his feet, bag and battered confidence behind him,

Aaron had one last thought before entering inside: I wish I was a girl.

Slouched on the sofa, which bizarrely was covered in a tartan blanket, Jeena in a light-blue tracksuit watched *Bridget Jones's Diary* on DVD. Actually, decided Aaron, take that back, thank God I'm not a girl – he threw his bag on the floor and huddled up next to her on the couch – or this would look like an act of lesbianism. He went to kiss Jeena on the mouth.

'Off!' Jeena pushed him away. 'Get off me.'

Mates of Aaron said he had a skeleton tongue because he could unlock most women's mouths (and more besides). It was a rare day indeed to be faced with lips so tightly shut he'd need a crowbar to prise them open. And if his self-esteem was already low, now it hit rock-bottom. He moved to the other side of the sofa and sat there twiddling with a thought: what was wrong with his wife?

'Before you say it, it's not my time of the month,' Jeena stated, pausing the movie. 'From now on, I want no more physical contact with you. You may think that you can act like a dog on heat around me but I'm no bitch. I'm not your little wife on the side who you come home to and click your fingers at when you want a bit of sex.' She huffed. 'What did you think I was going to do when you went to kiss me? Was I supposed to go all gooey and melt and then drop my knickers on the floor? "Oh Aaron, oh Aaron". Is that what you believed I was going to do after you've more than likely been out all weekend fucking other women? You've barely spoken seven sentences to me all week and the longest one was, "Don't forget to set the burglar alarm on the way out".' She leered at him. 'Set the burglar alarm? YOU TELL ME EVERY FUCKING DAY!'

Aaron ogled at the paused picture of Bridget Jones's voluptuous arse in the midst of sliding down the fireman's pole.

'The cheek of it,' Aaron said tearing his eyes away from the round bottom. '*You* virtually force me into marrying you; move all your junk into *my* apartment.' He tugged at the corner of the tartan blanket, looking disdainfully at its pattern. 'You cover my favourite piece of furniture with this shit. Then *you* have the gall to hurl abuse at me when I kiss you hello. *As if* I want sex with a miserable cow like you.' He turned back to the TV. 'The fucking cheek of it.'

'Sex? Is that what you call it? With you, I call it a fucking chore. In fact I was so bored last time with you humping away I was thinking of bringing in a jigsaw puzzle to complete while you were trying your hardest to get me to orgasm.'

He glared at her. 'How many pieces?'

'At least a thousand,' she spat back.

'You'll never solve it; you can't even solve the puzzle of how to do a blow job properly. And that, my dear, is only one piece.'

'A very small piece.'

'You'll find most blokes' cocks will shrink when in the vicinity of ice.'

'Well, I must be an iceberg then, your cock is *that* small.'

'Well, it seemed to fill up your massive mouth the last time you gave it a blow. If I remember rightly you were gagging it was so big.'

'Not quite. I was gagging at the thought of having to suck you off.'

'Maybe you should stick to jigsaws then, at least that way I won't get blamed for messing up your hair.'

'You are disgusting.'

'Thanks, you're quite disgusting yourself.'

And so went the insults for an hour or more. Slowly his frustrations over Darryl Fletcher began to disappear as did her frustrations regarding her parents who now considered her dead. The slanging match, their first real corker, was like a thirst-quenching storm on a searing-hot day. Mellowing out the atmosphere, cooling down the surroundings.

As with any argument, however, it left them both feeling somewhat drained and wounded by the other's attack. Up until now Jeena hadn't realized that she clogged up the bathtub with her hair. Just as Aaron hadn't realized that he sometimes left the bathroom door open after doing a number two (and occasionally sometimes during). Big issues which were addressed and hopefully now sorted out.

Their conversation took them into the kitchen where Aaron began to mix up a strawberry protein shake essential for his diet. Jeena continued with a point she'd been labouring with for a while. 'Seriously, Aaron, it's impossible to sleep through your meditation tapes. Every morning at five a.m., I awake to the sound of planes taking off, the noise of humpback whales apparently talking to each other, rush hour on the M25 and God knows what else. Those ear plugs you gave me don't work and my job is suffering because of my lack of sleep. Can't you meditate after I've gone to work?'

'I'll go one better than that,' Aaron said, adding a few wild strawberries to the blender. 'I'll listen to the tapes through my headphones.'

Jeena was dumbstruck: Aaron had given way on something. A sure sign that he could change if need be. A flashing insight intruded on her thinking. Blimey, if he could change his headphones for her today, then who knows, tomorrow he might open up to her about his past, and then before she knew it, he would be in love with her. It was a slim fantasy worth clinging onto. One which had only come about by her refusing to sleep with him. Maybe, it was dawning on her, maybe that was the way to his heart. Let him window shop but never let him hold the goods. Besides, it was high time that Aaron looked upon her as an expensive luxury commodity, rather than a cheap bit of bedroom muff. It was high time she adhered to the decent morals on which she had been nurtured. Even today, while they were in the middle of their squabble, a woman had left her cheap-slag number on his answerphone, hoping for Aaron to call back. Jeena had gone beyond the point of being sick of hearing these women on the phone, and was now at the stage where she saw it as ridiculous. How many women did a man have to sleep with until his ego was full? A million?

No more sex with Aaron. It was the simple solution; and in this case, if she still wanted to keep a little self-respect, the only solution. It wasn't so long ago that she had been one of those women, leaving sexy messages on his answerphone, praying that he would call back just for the chance of a roll in the hay with him. And some women would have said, surely he wasn't *that* good in bed. WANNA BET! He had you hooked the moment he touched you and after that you were his. God, no more sex with Aaron was going to be hell.

She peered across; his face had now acquired a strawberry moustache. Normally she would have licked it off herself, but rules were rules and she threw him a tea towel instead.

Aaron did a huge, huge burp. 'So, do you want to sleep in my bed tonight?'

She looked at him amazed. Now what on earth had made Aaron assume that his five-second long belch was *so* sexy as to make Jeena want to jump into the sack with him?

'Erm, I don't think that would be such a great idea. You sleep in your bed and I'll sleep in mine and never the twain shall meet. Kipling, I think.' She ignored his puppy-dog eyes. 'Sex tends to complicate everything. Let's keep this marriage simple from now on.' Just to make sure he understood. 'That means no sex, no cuddling, no hanky panky of any sort.'

'No . . .'

'No blow jobs either.'

'Oh. Fine. You're right, I think having sex with me would confuse you loads,' he said sarcastically, and walked away with his pint of protein shake, skidded on the waxy-mango-pickle-oiled floor and landed half sprawled on the sofa; protein shake pooled onto the tartan blanket.

He shouted back, 'I'm okay, I'm okay. Thank God this shitty thing was here or the sofa would be wrecked.' He quickly folded the blanket in from all four corners and lifted up the soiled material.

Only to be faced with a manky, yellow, turmeric mess covering three quarters of his suede couch. The sofa *was* wrecked.

Jeena stood sheepishly beside him. 'Is this goodbye, Aaron? Should I pack my things and apply for a divorce?'

He slowly shook his head. 'It's only a bit of furniture. No harm done. I'm sure the stains will come out. Along with the bloodstains.'

'What bloodstains?' she asked quietly.

'Yours!' he said, tossing the ruined blanket in the bin. 'You've heard of "couch potato" well, I'm going to go one better with you, Jeena, when I make you my couch corpse. You have three seconds to get a weapon of your choice to defend yourself with. RUN!'

A death threat was always a great way to end the evening, but as Jeena turned to head for her bedroom, she noticed the 'I was only joking I want to kill you' smile on Aaron's face sink. Only to be replaced with a look of unease. A look she'd already spotted on his face a few times this evening. Oh what she would give to know what was going through that man's mind sometimes. She walked back to him and lightly touched his arm.

'You are okay, aren't you?' she started, easing the words out carefully, desperate not to upset his male ego. 'I mean, if there was anything you wanted to talk about or get off your chest, you know I'm only a wall away.'

Aaron's eyes seemed to bore into her. 'You'd never understand. I don't quite understand it myself. But thanks.' He pulled her towards him and cuddled her. 'It's like you dream about something all your life and then the chance comes along for you to grab it and do that thing you dreamed about and for some reason, you fuck it up. It's like I can't even trust myself anymore. The one person who I am supposed to rely on, me, turns out to be the biggest coward of them all.'

Jeena shook her head. 'You a coward? That's the last thing you are. I don't know anyone with more guts than you. Even on our first date together you saved that young lad from those thugs. I don't think a coward would have done that, do you?'

'A brave man confronts his fears and deals with them, a coward runs away.' He gently pulled away from the embrace. 'Anyway, it's my problem. 'Night.'

Typical, thought Jeena watching him disappear into his bedroom, the first time she manages to get Aaron to open up and he talks in code. Where was Bletchley Park when you needed it? All those years wasted trying to help win WWII, trying to solve the Enigma code when they should have been trying to crack the enigma of man instead. 'Coward?' God, she'd hate to know how far someone would have to go before Aaron would consider them brave.

'Coward?' Aaron said to himself as he held his hand over the naked candle flame. Wincing in agony he continued to let the heat burn his skin until he could bear it no longer. Back in Japan, his *sensei* would expect his pupils to take The Burning Oath whenever they showed signs of weakness.

Feeling slightly better after his punishment, Aaron lay on his duvet and tried to cheer himself up with a chapter or so from Jeena's dirty novel *Naked Rider*. Ironically the book that got him into this marriage mess in the first place.

It's been a month since I joined Billy Trapps Circus, hiding from Jimmy The Jammer. I've slept with the whole circus crew except the dwarf clown who I hear has the biggest cock in the tent. If only he would stop clowning around for one minute (his roly-polys are driving me nuts) and then I could gorge myself on his big top. What he lacks in height he certainly makes up for in length. Nikita needs her daily supply of juice.

After a couple of chapters, Aaron, now cramped with laughter, flopped off the bed and made his way to Jeena's – the Man Booker Prize winner – room. He knocked and entered. Jeena, in her pyjamas, was sitting in bed with Mr Piggles reading a magazine. Aaron held up the *Naked Rider* novel.

'I noticed that at the front of the book it says that it is entirely fictitious. But it seems *so* realistic, Jeena. Are you sure it isn't autobiographical? And the dwarf scene,' Aaron played a finger across his eye removing a fake tear, 'it was so moving. It was so touching how Nikita smuggled him out of the circus in a rucksack.' He paused dramatically. 'Only to lose him later down a wishing well filled with rabid Jewish crocodiles eating Passover chocolate-nut tart. The best line was when Nikita says, "Have an erection quickly, Dwarf, then I can pull you out of this dangerous well". Classic.'

A red-faced Jeena pretended not to hear and hummed her way through a few magazine pages. Eventually she looked up. 'Oh, sorry, Aaron, did you want something?'

He raised his eyebrows. 'I could pretend to be a dwarf.'

'And I suppose you want me to be Snow White?'

He eyed her as though she was daft. 'No, stupid, Snow Brown.'

They both laughed.

'And I suppose you have to be home by midnight in case your chariot changes back into a pumpkin?' he guessed, tossing the book on the floor.

'That's Cinderella, stupid.'

'Cinderella, Snow White, even Cruella De Vil. Disney pussy is all the same to me.'

She pointed to the door, holding back her giggles. 'Well, you're not my Prince Charming, so get out and take your crude mouth with you. Disney pussy? Whatever next?'

He kicked off his trainers, crawled across her platform bed and lay next to her. 'I was really referring to Disney's *Aristocats*, thank you very much. Nothing crude about that.'

And there was nothing crude about what happened that night either as they both fell chastely asleep next to each other with Mr Piggles in the middle acting as contraception – in case Aaron awoke in the early hours with any funny ideas.

By Monday morning, the threesome was a lonesome with both Aaron and Mr Piggles gone. Aaron was out jogging along the River Wes. While Mr Piggles . . .

Jeena screamed as she stood in the open-plan dining area staring up at the ceiling.

... Mr Piggles was dangling from the chandelier with a noose around his neck. A note was stapled to his left trotter.

Make us a bacon sarni, wife.

Chapter Seventeen

If Jeena had to describe the next few days with the title of a TV programme it would be *Happy Days*. Aaron had stuck to his deal of meditating with headphones, he'd made an extra effort to socialize with her when possible, and he'd even cooked her a healthy chicken and rice meal – leaving it on the side for her when she returned from work. Last night he'd sat with her until the wee hours discussing her parents and what JJ had said about them believing her to be dead now. His words were a great comfort but best of all was his listening ear. To know that he was in her corner was somehow much more meaningful than having her friends behind her. Why that should be she hadn't gathered yet, but she guessed it might be because she was in love with him. More importantly, she believed that it might be because she was getting a little bit closer to him.

If the first half of the week was *Happy Days*, then the second half was *Sink or Swim*. After returning from lunch on Thursday afternoon, Jeena's boss, Mr Akhtar had called her in for a 'chat'. A roomful of brown eyes watched her walk across the carpet towards his office, their faces seeming to spell the words: You're about to be fired!

Waiting in the small, dimly-lit corridor outside his door, Jeena thought of the worst that could happen. Jobless, penniless, honourless. What had she done which deserved being sacked? She was timely, organized, responsible, efficient, a team player, enthusiastic, confident, ambitious. Bloody hell, she concluded, I'm just too damn good. Periodically one of the Akhtar sons would pass by, give her a look of disdain, then continue wherever they were heading. It was obvious that Mr Akhtar was trying to give her the willies before she'd even entered his office. Cheap trick. Old trick. But it worked: she had more willies than a porn channel right now.

Finally, Mr Akhtar opened his door and beckoned her inside. The large room smelt of strong coffee and cigars. Stacks of old *Asian Delight* newspapers stood waiting to become yellow, proud pictures of his three sons and his five precious grandchildren donned the walls. Boxes, folders, computer disks and any other office junk was strewn all over the place. ORGANIZED CHAOS was written on a wooden placard that hung directly over a three dimensional map of the building which was nailed just behind his head. Disorganized Arsehole was the more common phrase used to describe Mr Akhtar behind his back.

'Sit, Mrs Myles,' Mr Akhtar barked, pointing to a chair. 'I haven't got all day.'

Mr Akhtar was a short, weasel-type Indian man,

balding with glasses. The kind of man who couldn't wait to get his first set of cufflinks but who always rolled his sleeves up – exposing extremely hairy fore-arms (possibly explaining the mystery of what might have happened to the hair missing from his head). He loved authority, especially when he was dishing it out. And, being from the old school, hc had little time for the weaker sex. In his eyes . . . women.

Jeena noticed an old article of hers splayed out on his desk. There was no way she was going to forget writing it, as it was the very same martial arts article in which she'd interviewed Aaron at his Paper Lantern centre, nearly nine months ago. Why Mr Akhtar had fished it out now was beyond her, but soon, no doubt, to be revealed.

He continued, 'Do you sleep with everyone you interview, Mrs Myles?' He prodded the colour picture of Aaron in the newspaper. 'In the tabloid industry, business and pleasure are a very volatile mix. One should always bear that in mind when thinking about sleeping with a subject. Whenever you leave this build-ing as a journalist you become a representative of my firm. A mascot, so to speak. It does my business no good when an employee of mine uses sex to get an inside story. It's neither here nor there that you later married this white man – something which I will be dealing with shortly – and you should be ashamed of yourself.'

Too shocked to speak, Jeena just sat there waiting for the next bombshell to hit. Like the innocent civil-ians in Iraq she didn't have to wait long.

Mr Akhtar stood up and walked over to a large,

green notice board on which was pinned a computer graph titled: SALES GROWTH FOR 2006. A red line denoted an upward trend.

'It's taken me many years to reach this position, Mrs Myles. A hard slog.' He looked up at the graph with admiration. 'I'm not going to let my sales slide because of the actions of one employee.' He glared at her menacingly. 'I'm referring to you. As far as many people are concerned, I should have sacked you the moment I found out about your shameful marriage. But unfortunately I can't do that or I'll have the Employment Tribunal/Race Relations board down on me like a ton of bricks. I've lost count of the times your colleagues have complained about working with a sinner. The last thing I want is a mutiny on my hands, Mrs Myles. So I have decided to – how shall I put this? – to relieve you of certain responsibilities.' His harsh look hounded out any fight Jeena might have put up, and she continued to listen in silence as Mr Akhtar explained what he meant.

To begin with Jeena's hours were to be cut from full-time to part-time. Mornings from now on only. Which in real terms meant she'd struggle to survive on the pittance that a part-time salary would afford her. Her car parking space would be given to a more worthy employee. Which in real terms meant she'd have to park a mile away from the office and walk in, and yet lose more money to the Pay & Display ticket machine. And, the biggest bombshell of them all: Mr Akhtar had decided to remove her from her agony aunt position – leaving her with just her articles to write – on the grounds that she wasn't fit to hand out quality advice when the whole Asian community knew that her parents had disowned her. How could she give advice to anyone when on the surface it appeared that she'd messed up her own life? Which in real terms meant: it was pretty obvious that Mr Akhtar was pushing for her to resign.

'Not crying yet?' Mr Akhtar questioned, a sly smirk upon his face. 'Normally girls like you turn on the waterworks as soon as things don't go your way.'

Jeena refused to fall for his goading, it would take more than a few weasely remarks to open her tear ducts. But she was amazed at the predictability of the Indian race sometimes. It was almost a foregone conclusion that when an Indian/Asian girl/woman goes against the Indian way, she would be punished, sometimes heavily, by the whole Asian community. Individualism is discouraged, thinking out of the context of the Indian traditions is frowned upon. In fact, by and large, if one truly turned the microscope on an Indian community one would find that on the Petri dish lay a mass of bleating sheep, with the odd black sheep being chastised for trying to be different. Being different can get you into a lot of trouble if you're Indian.

'I can't survive on part-time wages, Mr Akhtar,' Jeena said, nervously.

'I can't afford to pay full-time wages to someone who has such little respect for this company. Besides, you're married now, I'm sure that your new husband will be able to share this burden. Or don't white husbands share with their wives? I expect he spends most of it down the pub.' He sat back down and tidied up a

227

few loose pieces of paper. 'Have you thought of the consequences of bringing a half-caste baby into this world? The ridicule it would receive for being a mixture of brown skin and white skin! I suppose if you have children, if God allows it, then they will be as confused about their identities as any kid could possibly be. It's one of the main reasons that mixed relationships are discouraged, Mrs Myles, you must know that.'

He could sense that tears were close now and continued to push. 'Imagine the bullying and teasing. Kids are so cruel, your poor child won't stand a chance. Then, if that wasn't bad enough, when it came to its grandparents, half would be missing. Your half. Your parents. What excuse would you give your child that he or she only had one set of grandparents when all the other children in their class have two? Selfish you are and so is that *gorrah* husband of yours.' He thinned his eyes, which matched his lips. 'Your marriage won't last, mark my words. You'll end up another statistic. But in your case you won't have a family to help pick up the pieces for you; and rightly so. You're a disgrace. Now get out of my office, and I suggest it would be a good idea if you don't come back until Monday next week. Unpaid leave of course. You're dismissed for the rest of today and all of tomorrow.'

Not being able to hold back her tears any more, Jeena let them fall quietly until finally she wiped them away with the back of her hand. She felt giddy with anger. How dare this cretinous man sum up her life and future like that. What was it with Indian elders and their lectures? What gave them the right to pass judgement on someone just because she was Indian? It seemed to be an unwritten rule that any Indian elder had the right to put their two pennies worth into a younger Indian's life. Well, Jeena knew where she wanted to tell Mr Akhtar to stick his two pennies, but she had to think about her job and the three pennies it would bring her a week.

As she rose to leave, he coughed to gain her attention.

'When you return on Monday morning, I will expect you to wear clothes that conform to the policy of this company. My company. No longer will I put up with your prostitute short skirts, high heels and your low, revealing tops. No longer will I tolerate having to see your bare stomach with your navel jewellery. You will wear less make-up and have your hair up in the more modest fashion of the more respectable ladies who work here. I want your hair back to its original colour which I assume was black and not red like you seem to think it is. In fact, Mrs Myles, from now on I expect you to wear trousers, flat shoes and fully sleeved tops with no cleavage showing. Now get out!'

Why not put me in a sack cloth and be done with it, Jeena thought miserably as she collected her handbag from her desk and switched off her computer. She looked down the office to see just one sympathetic face, Nina, amongst the other smirking colleagues, and she mimed to her that she would phone her later. Then, with her head held high, Jeena marched out of the room, gripping her dignity tight, totally blanking Mrs Kapoor on Reception, and out to her Clio in the car park. After a little screaming session in her car and a boxing match with her steering wheel, she drove back home, crunching the gears in anger, extremely upset at today's outcome. For some horrible reason she was having trouble putting the picture of Mr Akhtar's hairy forearms out of her mind. Maybe she had a hairy forearm prejudice – just as he appeared to have a mixed relationship prejudice. Or maybe it was because his forearms reminded her of her family's Welcome Home mat – and she didn't want to think about that right now.

In fact she didn't want to think about much really. Not her job, family, husband or even the money problems heading her way. Right now she needed what she and her friends called a 'honey' moment. Which, when translated, meant a hive of Bs. Bubble Bath, Booze, Bonking, Box (of choccies) and Bed. The perfect remedy for a day that was only fit for the bin. She stopped off at the local off licence and left with a bottle of white wine and box of Dairy Milk. 'Who's the lucky fella?' was answered with, 'me.'

But 'me' wasn't so lucky when, after letting herself into the apartment, Jeena spotted Aaron and dropped the bottle of wine on the floorboards, sending the stinking liquid and shattered glass in all directions. She had expected him to be downstairs working in the martial arts club. She had expected the apartment to be empty. She had expected to be alone.

She had not expected to walk in to find a naked Aaron groaning and grinding on top of a naked squealing, busty, blonde babe on the sofa. Certainly she had not expected to find that the expensive red Egyptian throw she had purchased to cover up the turmeric stain was being used as a love blanket. Doldrums was a place she tried not to enter that often, but right now, she was down in the murky depths of it. Her shocked eyes connected with Aaron's also shocked eyes for a second before Jeena burst out crying and scurried away into her bedroom. If this were the future then there would have been a robot on hand to provide tissues for her tears, as it was the present, she was left scrabbling around in her drawers for one to wipe them dry. On 'the worst days in Jeena's life' hit parade, this one was heading to the top of the charts. The top spot: 'The day she was disowned' had been there for two weeks but it was now threatening to be knocked off.

Outside Jeena's door a commotion was taking place, and even though Aaron was trying his best to whisper his voice was clear enough for Jeena to hear.

'Hide the fucking costumes, Michelle, she'll go mental if she finds out we've been having role-play sex.' Sounds of rustling. 'She thinks it's exclusive to her and me.'

'I can't find the Conan sword,' Michelle replied, just as loud as him.

'We were in combat by the aquarium, have a look there.'

A few more frantic moments and all parts of the discarded costumes, wigs, loin cloths, weapons, leather straps and boots had been stuffed into a bin bag leaving the naked Conan the Barbarian and the naked Xena Warrior Princess quite chuffed with their clean-up operation. If only Jeena would be as chuffed, thought Aaron, then everything would be A-okay.

'I'm going to take a shower,' Aaron said, kissing Michelle goodbye on the lips. 'Let yourself out when you're dressed.' Just before he headed towards the bathroom he turned. 'Oh yeah, and mind the broken glass by the front door.'

But what about the broken heart in Jeena's bedroom.

Michelle slipped back into her modern-day clothes and gently tapped on Jeena's bedroom door. She wanted to apologize for any embarrassment she and Aaron had caused. He had explained to her that his roommate, Jeena, (who he occasionally slept with out of a favour to her) would be at work all afternoon. Obviously that had turned out to be incorrect. And so the apology.

'It's open, Aaron,' Jeena said, through gritted teeth, then on seeing Michelle's head peeping round added, 'Oh, sorry, I er . . . hi.'

Introductions were swift. Aaron's lover meet Aaron's lover. Sounded more like mug meet mug. Both of the girls had that same 'used by Aaron' look on their faces, like a branding from days gone by. A connection which neither of them was particularly proud of. Yet, after trying hard to slag Aaron off, they both had to admit, it was a pain, but he was far too sexy to be slagged.

Before the two girls knew it, they were begrudgingly discussing what made him so damn attractive. What was it that made women go so weak at the knees that they were willing to share him with other women? And using words which would not be suitable around the Pope, they answered that question by describing his bedroom talents in alarmingly sordid detail.

Outside the closed door, standing in a wet towel with wet hair and wet body, Aaron listened in with his ear pressed to a glass against the wood. It wasn't long before his ego was matching the bulge in his towel. He could understand what Jeena and Michelle were saying though, he was *rather* addictive. With that last thought, he smiled, walked into his bedroom and began to get dressed for work.

'Addictive,' he said to himself, changing into his jujitsu suit. 'Yeah, that's me. No wonder some of the women I *haven't* slept with in a while turn into cold turkeys.' He laughed at his own joke.

In Jeena's room the conversation had moved to a different territory. The wilderness of love. Michelle explained that once feelings for Aaron had taken root it became almost impossible to prevent them from growing stronger. She admitted to falling for him, being obsessed with him, willing to die for him.

'I loved him with all my heart *once*, Jeena,' Michelle continued. 'And then, I learnt how he operated. One evening he got so drunk that he confessed all to me. I felt like killing myself.' Michelle's eyes glazed over with memories. 'He told me that never, ever would he fall in love with a woman who threw herself at him. Never would he allow himself to become deeply involved with any of the women he'd slept with. It's a long list of women, I can tell you. And not one of them stood a chance. Especially me. He only had to click his fingers and I'd drop my knickers. Which in his eyes made me a first-class slag.' She stared into Jeena's worried face. 'And a second-class woman.'

Jeena nearly had to pinch herself at the situation she found herself in. A strange woman she'd just witnessed having sex with her husband was giving her friendly advice on how Aaron's mind worked. But it was great to talk to someone who understood about Aaron's hold over women. How, in the blink of an eye, your heart was trapped like a fly in a web. And the more you struggled to free yourself, the more tightly bound you became. Both Kitty and Flora refused to admit that any man could possess such powers and, as such, any suggestion that Aaron was a heart thief was poo poohed out of town. Which was why Jeena's connection with Michelle was so instantaneous. They both knew what it was like to want someone you shouldn't.

Michelle went on to describe the reason Aaron could not fall in love with any of his bed accomplishments was because he had no respect for women who succumbed to his charm so easily. For women who were willing to share him with other women. For women who, as far as Mr No Morals himself was concerned, had no morals. They were, as Michelle explained, in Aaron's words, 'His bedroom playthings.' Or, after a few more pints, 'His slags.'

'So, he looks on me as a slag, then?' Jeena asked, fiddling with the corner of her duvet, not liking what she was hearing for one moment.

'Yep, and me and every other woman he sleeps with. All slags.'

As far as Jeena was concerned the word 'Slag' had a sharp edge that cut deep. She'd never, in her wildest dreams, classified herself as a slag. Surely that title was meant for other women. Christ, she hadn't even bought her first vibrator until she was seventeen. Which was fairly ancient going by Kitty's standard.

After chatting for a little longer, Michelle rose to leave. 'I'd forget all about him falling in love with you,

Jeena, it's never going to happen. You're wasting your time, it's a pipe dream. My suggestion,' she opened the door and then shouted it out for Aaron to hear, 'USE HIM FOR SEX LIKE I DO. Take care.' And she was gone, blowing a kiss to Aaron, who was busy clearing up the smashed wine bottle, on the way out.

Even though Aaron had overheard some great compliments when listening in to Jeena and Michelle discuss him, he couldn't help but feel as if he'd let Jeena down in some way earlier. Today was a first for him in regards to sex. He'd made many women cry before while having sex, but today was the first time he'd had sex with one woman while making an entirely different one cry. Most odd. And why the crying anyway? It's not as if Jeena wasn't aware that he had women over every now and then. It's not like he hadn't explained to her before they got married that sex was a major part of his life and he wasn't going to let anything as trivial as a new wife interfere with his lovemaking extravaganzas. So what gives?

He dropped the broken glass in the recycling container and set about mopping up the wine. He'd heard on many occasions that it was impossible for a man to solve a problem involving a woman with logic. To understand her, one had to become her. One had to become the very fabric of her mind. Aaron meditated on that thought, repeating the phrase, '*I am Jeena, I know what Jeena knows. I am Jeena, I know what Jeena knows.*' Suddenly, almost as if Aaron had actually grown breasts and ovaries, his mind was that of a woman and all was clear to him. It was totally apparent why Jeena had cried upon spotting him riding

Michelle. He could hit himself for not thinking of it earlier. The reason she was so upset was because she'd spotted Michelle's Brazilian and ... erm ... erm ... wished she had one??? Aaron slapped the mop on the floor and mopped. No, if Jeena was *that* envious then she'd get one herself so it couldn't be that. So, what was it? Why do women shed tears? Break-ups, make-ups, break-downs, black-and-white movies, puppies, boy bands, births, deaths, for fuck sake, they cry over everything. By the time he'd finished cleaning the floor, the solution was obvious: the reason Jeena had cried was because she was filled with jealousy ... and she was filled with jealousy because she had strong feelings for him.

Aaron whispered to himself, 'I am Aaron again, and I think as Aaron thinks. And Aaron thinks it's the right moment to translate some of his guilt to an apology.'

He made his way to Jeena's bedroom and knocked on her door. Once let in he joined her lying back on the bed. Time was short as his first evening class was due in an hour.

'I'm not making any excuses because I don't need to, but I try to do this sort of thing when you're at work, Jeena,' he said, referring to bringing women back to his pad and bonking them senseless. 'I honestly believed you were working the whole day today. Like you normally do on Thursday.' He stroked her hair. 'I don't go out of my way to upset you.' He paused. 'Because it did upset you, didn't it? And really I can't understand why it should. You know what I'm like, I'm a legend.'

'Maybe you should have a flag at half mast when you're shagging.'

He thought about that and nodded his head in approval. 'Not a bad idea. I could even have a set of cannons on the roof and do a twenty-one gun salute when I'm finished satisfying the lucky lady. Imagine it: people for miles around would know when I'm spent.' He twirled her hair around his finger. 'Seriously though, why did you burst into tears?'

'Because God decided it was good fun to pick on me today, that's why.'

She went on to explain about what had happened at work and how Mr Akhtar had verbally abused her. Jeena was especially aggrieved by what Mr Akhtar had said about bringing half-caste babies into this world and how unfair it was on them. How a marriage with a white man would never work. How he was punishing her for marrying Aaron. A *gorrah*.

'He calls me a what?'

'A *gorrah*. It can be a derogatory term for a white person if said in a certain way.'

'Well, he sounds like a wanker, and it doesn't matter how I say that.'

Jeena described how low she was feeling after returning home early from work and all she had needed was a little bit of peace and quiet to calm herself down. Walking in on sexual position no. 54 was the straw that broke her back and that's why she cried. It was as simple as that.

Aaron sat bolt upright on the bed, his body charged with anger. 'You have worked for that wanker for years and because you happen to marry a white man he treats you like something he found on his shoe. No way can I let this one go. If I was really your husband, then I'd be down there first thing in the morning to sort him out. And as I *really* am your husband that's where I'm going tomorrow. We'll soon see if he wants to bully you after that. For bullying is what it is, Jeena, and you know how much I hate bullies.'

Jeena imagined a scene in her mind. Aaron bursting through the door of Mr Akhtar's office and grabbing him around the throat. Mr Akhtar's eyes bulging. Aaron talking coldly into her boss's ear, 'This *gorrah* will fill your life with crimson blood if you don't give Jeena back her job! You hairy forearm freak.'

Maybe letting Aaron loose in her workplace wasn't the best of ideas.

She shook her head. 'No. I don't want you to do that. It will only lead to more trouble. You'll get me the sack. I'm just going to have to look for a new job and stick this one out in the meantime. Promise me you won't go and see him. *Please*, Aaron.'

Aaron sighed. 'Whatever.'

He looked down at Jeena with sympathy. Her life seemed to be a huge struggle right now. He remembered watching the film *Zulu* and how one hundred British soldiers stood and fought to the death against more than four thousand of the Zulu tribe. Such bravery. It seemed like Jeena was in a battle of equal proportions. Easily out-numbered by a huge family of angry relatives, then, riding up the rear, the bigger army of the Asian community, all baying for the blood of one innocent Indian woman. And her crime? To marry a white bloke.

Even the Zulu showed humanity in the end, maybe the Asian community might do the same. Aaron wondered if the time was right to approach Jeena's father and argue out some sort of compromise. He could see in Jeena's face sometimes the pain of losing her family. Odd moments when he'd catch her daydreaming, watery eyed, in her own silent torture. Even though she was sharing the same apartment with him, there were times when she seemed so lonely. He glanced around her room while she lay staring up at the ceiling. This was not the life for her. Married to a man who shagged anything in a skirt and having to put up with his *Karate Kid* poster on the wall. He decided right there and then, he would visit Jeena's father next week (without her knowledge) and see if he could improve this existence she was currently shackled to.

'I've got a great prescription for the blues, Jeena,' he said, tying his red and white jujitsu belt tight.

'I'm listening,' she replied.

'This weekend, grab your friends, get pissed and dance away the evening at a club. Dr Blues has spoken.'

'And are you coming?' she asked, a vague hope in her question mark.

'Uh uh, afraid not. Dr Blues is only a giver of advice not a taker. Anyway, I wouldn't be able to keep up with you lot when the drink gets flowing.' He opened the door. 'Oh, yeah, one other thing. I was wondering, have you ever thought about having a Brazilian?'

Something hard was thrown at the rapidly closing door. It was time for Aaron to leave the aggression of upstairs.

And join the aggression of downstairs. Aaron checked the kitchen clock 6.16 p.m. LATE. He shot out of the apartment and down the stairs, waving to the St John's ambulance driver, sitting on emergency standby, the blue light flashing as ever for Thursday's Blood Fest night. Inside the club a long line of students in white *gi* suits bowed in unison as Aaron entered the floor.

'That's two strikes, *Sensei*,' a cheeky pupil shouted out. 'Three strikes and you're out.'

A titter of laughter rose from the class until Aaron hushed them all down. He told them to stretch for five minutes while he had a quick chat with Mary. Forty-five-year old Mary, as ever, was stooped over the computer at Reception. She'd been a proud loyal employee of Aaron's since he had begun the enterprise over six years ago. Always ready to chip in and lend a hand with duties outside her job description. If the cleaner didn't turn up, Mary would don the Marigolds. On the rare occasion that Aaron was late, she would open the doors and greet his students with a smile. For four evenings a week, Mary would help run the business as if it were her own. Booking in classes, sending out leaflets, phoning up potential clients, accounts, and anything clerical. Aaron once described her as the Paper Lantern's heart.

Today the Paper Lantern's heart had missed a beat.

'I've got some bad news, Aaron,' Mary said, removing her glasses and sliding a bookings ledger across the desk to him. 'Something odd is going on, I can tell you.'

The book was opened to a page titled Fight to Unite – his Asian class dedicated to bringing Pakistani and Indian youths together, sometimes called the Mini Kashmir Crisis class. A long list of Indian and Pakistani names were marked neatly in a column alphabetically.

These were the current members. Next to that list was another list of names for lads waiting to join. Cancellation of club membership was done with a red pen. In the last year the red pen had only come out on five occasions. Today, as Aaron trawled his eyes down both lists, the red pen was everywhere. Pupil after pupil crossed out. Stars of the future: no longer members of his club. He counted twenty-seven red lines.

'Most have ceased their membership by phone, but a few have handed in letters.' From a drawer Mary pulled out a small wad of paper, passing it across. 'They all say roughly the same thing.'

Aaron folded out the top letter and read it

Dear Sensei,
Family pressure has forced me into leaving your
club. I don't want to leave, but my loyalty must
be with my family's wishes. You have been a
great role model and teacher and I only hope
that you do not look upon me as weak for
pulling out.
Good luck with the future.
Yours Tarik Khan.

Mary flipped through her notepad. 'I managed to get the gist of what was happening with the cancellations from a few slips of the tongue. But basically—'

'I'm a white man who married an Indian and the parents don't agree with it, am I right?' She nodded. 'And the parents don't want their Asian sons mixing with someone like me. A fucking *gorrah*.' He slammed his fist on the counter and stared angrily at tonight's pupils.

An air of terror washed over the students. Their *sensei* was in a foul mood. He normally took things out on them when he was in a foul mood. It looked like the St John's ambulance was going to be busy tonight.

The phone rang, Mary picked it up and the red pen came out again. Aaron shook his head sagely. Maybe he would have to cancel Tuesday's Fight to Unite class. Which was quite ironic seeing as it was the Fight to Unite class that had introduced Aaron to Jeena in the first place, when she'd come to interview him for her *Asian Delight* newspaper article.

It was becoming apparent to Aaron that the Asian community was a multi-headed beast. Its eyes and ears were everywhere and its tentacles searched far and wide. First there were problems with Jeena's parents and family. Next came problems at her work. Now, he himself could feel the whip of a loose tentacle with these cancellations.

The question was: what was next?

Chapter Eighteen

Saturday night is when most teenagers and twenty-somethings get involved in their favourite game: Binge Drinking. Without Saturday night the population of Great Britain would be far less than it is now, as it's also the most popular night for that other classic game: Unprotected Sex. People who admit to quiet Saturdays in are more or less thought of as witches. Burn them! It's sacrilege to the youngsters in the same way as missing Sunday church is for the elders. Which was why there was a huge sigh of relief from her friends when Jeena had called Kitty and Flora to arrange a night out on the town. As far as they were concerned, since Jeena had been married, she'd been a witch.

Tonight she would be one of them.

It was eight p.m., and Aaron was due to begin fighting his mates at 8.30 p.m. That's if he had enough energy left over from fighting back the erection he was having right now. God, he'd never seen Jeena so ravishing. His eyes ogled as she slid into the passenger seat of his car. He'd offered to give her a lift to the nightclub before heading off to Charlie's house. On this warm July evening she seemed to be wearing as little as possible. A tiny slip of a mauve-coloured dress; its plunging neckline threatening to overheat most men's corneas. Glittery high-heeled sandals. Her hair was up leaving a few wispy curls dangling. In Aaron's eyes she was just dripping with sexuality; even her Dior Addict perfume was driving him nuts. And his nuts . . . they were driving him wild.

'Where to, mam?' Aaron asked, switching on the engine, acting out his chauffeur role. 'May I suggest Northern Lights nightclub? It's full of pretty women.'

'And you think that interests me, do you? It's hunky men I'm after. I'd much rather you take me to The Wall. You know the one, just off the High Street.'

'I know the one, with the bed floating across the ceiling. Righty oh.' Aaron smirked to himself, remembering the night Charlie had been banned from the club.

As the BMW crawled out of the busy car park, neither Jeena nor Aaron noticed the lone woman with the baseball cap laying low in her car. She could have been anyone. A mother waiting for her kid to finish the karate class in progress. Or a girlfriend waiting for her boyfriend. Or even an ex-girlfriend called Stacy stalking Aaron, waiting for him to depart the premises so that she could enter his apartment once again.

Aaron's diary entry for today had read: *out until late*. When Stacy had seen this on her last visit she'd prayed that Aaron would be taking his wife with him on this night. Her prayers had been answered – well, some of them had anyway. Tonight she was going to put into action a plan which would make Aaron repulsive to most women. A plan which would make Aaron not want to sleep with his wife. *And*, ultimately, a plan which would bring Aaron and Stacy back together again.

A well-known speed camera lay hidden in the bushes up ahead and Aaron pointed it out to Jeena, as he floored the accelerator (just to shit her up), slamming hard on the brakes at the last second.

'Moron!' she shouted.

'I read somewhere that when a woman is scared she lets off pheromones which are highly attractive to men. That's why I'm going to KILL YOU.'

She laughed, guessing that the only pheromones a woman would release in the knowledge that she was about to be killed were of the messy knickers kind. She doubted that that would be highly attractive to men – no matter how low their standards were.

The road took them past Lake Charlotte and into the High Street with the CD player blasting out Keane's 'Hopes and Fears' all the way. A long queue of scantily-clad women and strutting men waited for the bouncers to grant them entry into The Wall nightclub. Kitty and Flora were the most scantily clad of all, with less than a metre of material between them. They waved from the back of the queue as Aaron pulled up and he gave them a hoot on his horn.

'If you hear sirens wailing and someone says there's been a bomb scare, it's only me and my mates having a bit of fun. Okay?' Aaron said deadpan.

Jeena's eyes grew wide. 'You are joking, aren't you?'

'Moron! Of course.'

She leant in for a kiss on the cheek. 'Thanks for the lift. Enjoy your fights.'

He was just about to say goodbye when Aaron noticed Jeena's wedding ring was absent from her finger. He grabbed her hand without thinking – it wasn't as if the ring was suddenly going to appear from beneath a fold of skin – and blinked hard at her fingers.

'What's this?' Aaron glared at her. 'Why have you taken it off?'

'I thought that was pretty obvious. I don't think I've got a good chance of a man asking me out with a bloody wedding ring on my finger, do you? And if he did, then he's only going to be another bastard like you. Moral-less man.'

'Stone the crows, Jeena, seventeen fucking days we've been married and already,' he scowled at her, 'ALREADY you are out hunting other men. You're a disgrace.'

'A disgrace? ME?' Jeena could feel a different sort of hormone coursing through her body and it had nothing to do with pheromones. Testosterone – she wanted to bash his face in. How dare he? 'Let me remind you, Bruce Lee, that our marriage, as you love to point out, is a fake one. So, a lecture from you about right and wrong is comical to say the least. I suggest you go and take a long hard look at yourself and maybe you might see what everyone else sees.'

'And what might that be, Mrs Myles?'

'AN ARSEHOLE.'

The windows were beginning to steam up by now from their bickering. So much so that if a scientist were present to measure the carbon dioxide given off from

Jeena and Aaron when their tempers were flared, he might well theorize that arguing is damaging to the ozone. But a scientist was not present, just a queue of clubbers with a much bigger worry in life than global warming: would the bouncer, named Scuzzball III, let them in the club tonight?

Aaron turned off the CD player. 'I'm only going to say this once, Jeena, so listen carefully. It is very important that you keep the wedding ring on at all times just in case you happen to bump into a member of your family, or someone from the Asian community who knows you. Without the ring on your finger, it brings our wedding under suspicion. I'm not going to sacrifice a whole year of my life only for you to fuck it up because you won't wear the ring. You told me yourself that your mum and dad only had to get a hint that this marriage wasn't for real and there would be no hope *ever* of them forgiving you. And if I have learnt anything about you, Jeena, in our time together, that is you are someone who needs hope in your life.' He rubbed the back of his hand down her cheek. 'You know I'm talking sense.'

She aimed her eyes straight ahead. 'I'll put it on then. You're right. But it's at home. I'll make sure that from tomorrow it never leaves this finger,' she lifted up her ring finger, 'until we divorce in exactly three hundred and sixty five days minus the seventeen we've already suffered together.'

He jumped in immediately. 'Divorce is in three hundred and forty eight days. I've been counting. I'm always counting.'

A few moments of silence then, before Jeena had a

chance to ask, Aaron explained why he himself didn't wear his wedding ring. How the chances of an Asian thinking there was something untoward going on with the absence of Aaron's ring was negligible. How there was nothing out of the ordinary for a man not to wear one anyway (loads of married men get away with it, no one bats an eyelid). Besides, most of his time was spent either teaching martial arts or practising martial arts and it was inappropriate to wear any sort of jewellery in case one hurt one's opponent.

'And, more importantly, I'd hate myself if I wore it on a date, then took it off for sex and left it round some woman's house,' he said, joking. 'It means *so* much to me. In fact Charlie thinks the ring is too much of a burden for me to carry and I should take it to Mount Doom to get it destroyed.'

'Why don't you throw yourself in with it,' Jeena said, picking up her tiny beaded handbag to leave. 'You won't be missed.'

'Charming. Well, enjoy yourself and I'll see you later tonight.'

'Actually, I think I'll stay round Kitty's tonight. So, if you want to bring a woman home, who's sporting a Brazilian, feel free.' She opened the door, looked back briefly, then shut it behind her.

Trying not to make it too obvious, Aaron kerb-crawled down the road next to the queue of clubbers, quite pleased to see that no good-looking men were in line. He sniggered to himself at the thought that what was on offer didn't exactly read stud material. Then he screeched away wondering why he gave a flying fuck whether there would be any good-looking men in the club or not. It's not like he and his wife were an item. Anyway, he had much more important things on his mind, such as, how he was going to come away as King of the Fighters tonight. He was going to obliterate his mates.

The destination was Charlie's two-bedroomed house set in the newer, more expensive end of Primpton. All three mates, Tyler, Sean and Aaron arrived within a few minutes of each other and walked up the path to be greeted by Charlie in his full combat army uniform.

'At ease, gentlemen,' Charlie said, as was his usual introduction to Fight Nights. 'Whatever happens within these four walls, let us say now that we shall always remain friends.'

General agreement from the other three.

They were ushered inside and directed to their seats in the huge, modern, tidy living room. A gigantic slab of finest marble embedded with a glass top stood proudly in the middle of the floor masquerading as a coffee table. Apparently the marble slab was stolen from one of Saddam Hussein's palaces when Charlie was serving in the first Gulf War. On Charlie's return to the UK he'd had the slab turned into a fantastic-looking table, much to the envy of most of his battalion. Various other memorabilia from the wars were scattered throughout the house. A set of crutches hung in the bathroom (from when he'd broken his leg in Bosnia). A knitted scarf given to him by a woman who took a fancy to him in Kosovo. A potato from his stint in Northern Ireland. A load of old rubbish to most visitors, but memory lane for Charlie.

Charlie served non-alcoholic drinks (in order to keep

their wits about them for fighting later on) and raised his glass in the air. 'I would like to raise a toast to our friendship together, which seems to have lasted forever.'

The chink of four glasses and the shout of 'hear! hear!'

Aaron sipped his pineapple smoothy, reliving the unforgettable day he first met Charlie. Charlie, dressed as a ninja, had walked right across the Paper Lantern hall where Aaron was taking a jujitsu class and pulled a knife on him. 'What are you going to do?' Charlie had asked, full of smugness, until he was thrown to the floor and his arm was nearly broken. Charlie had gone on to explain to Aaron, through gasps of pain, that he was already a black belt in jujitsu and was keen on finding a top tutor who could take him and his mate, Sean, to the next level. Pulling the knife on Aaron was just a test. Far better than the live hand grenade he was originally going to bring. Aaron had yanked him to his feet and their friendship had developed slowly ever since.

'Let's get the nasty business out of the way and then we can enjoy the evening,' Charlie said, sliding the tape into the video recorder. 'Remember this was filmed on a very low budget.'

The film began. A sign written in red marker pen was held up by two shaky hands. Finally it came into focus: AARON AND JEENA'S WEDDING. IT WON'T LAST. Then the film cut to a scene of a naked, hairy bottom being lit with a match. There was the sound of laughter in the background with the words, 'We spared no expense for fireworks, Aaron.' Onwards and into the Blacksmith's Shop in Gretna Green. The lens zooms in to Aaron's perspiring neck as he takes his marriage vows, sweat dripping onto his shirt, the constant, oh-so-constant sound of Charlie, Sean and Tyler's tittering and chuckling. At the critical moment when Aaron is allowed to kiss the bride, the camera swings round and focuses tight on Kitty's silicon breasts. The final scene is of Charlie stuffing three quarters of the wedding cake down his throat. Then a placard reading, C.A.T.S. PRODUCTION with Charlie's voice boasting, 'C is for Charlie, A is for Aaron, T is for Tyler and S is for Sean. CATS, get it?'

'The more times you see it the better it gets,' spluttered out Tyler, cackling his head off and removing the wedding tape from the player. 'You looked scared shitless, Aaron, when the bulbous-nose Minister asked you to take your vows.'

The room was contaminated with loud, obnoxious laughter. Charlie literally stood right in front of Aaron's face and just continued to laugh at him, pointing his finger, wagging it to and fro.

Getting sick of the sight of Charlie's tonsils, Aaron sternly pushed him away. 'Grow up.'

'Oh, take it out on the one who has Gulf War Syndrome, why don't you?' Charlie retaliated. 'Is this how my country repays me? It's a ruddy good job my gun hasn't arrived, I can tell you, Aaron.'

A huge, bored sigh swept through the room. Not this gun talk again. Apparently, Charlie had recently heard that many GWS sufferers keep a loaded gun in the house in case their paranoia gets so bad that they need to commit suicide at short notice. Not wanting to feel left out, Charlie had been making enquiries to purchase one on the Internet. *www.dieyoungstaypretty.com*. Knowing his luck, the gun would turn up after the urge to kill himself had worn off.

'Look, Charlie, I know it's your house and your rules, but could we have just one evening without mentioning GWS. You're getting on my fucking nerves.' Aaron's voice was coated with anger. 'You're safe now; you're not behind enemy lines anymore. For fuck's sake I can't even mention that we're enjoying a hot cup of tea without you saying, "It's not as hot as the napalm they dropped on Vietnam." Or take last week when you came crawling up to me and whispered in my ear, "Are you sure you can trust your wife? India *is* a nuclear power nowadays. Don't give her any secrets." Now, after telling me for years that you can't eat food that you haven't prepared yourself in case the enemy have contaminated it, I see a video of you scoffing down nearly a whole wedding cake. MY WEDDING CAKE! Without a care in the world. What happened to your GWS then, Charlie? Hey? What . . .'

'Oh, come on, Aaron,' interrupted Tyler, 'this ain't like you. Jesus, he's only acting like he normally acts. Why are you picking on him?'

A collective look of puzzlement from all three mates was aimed towards their oddly-behaving friend. Why was Aaron acting this way? What had got his goat so wrangled? As Tyler had stated: this wasn't like him at all.

Glancing from Tyler to Sean then to a sulky Charlie, Aaron wondered if he was strong enough to confess to his mates what was obviously bothering him. What was causing these vicious tremors in his personality. He had two choices: one, risk ridicule and tell them the nature of his worries, or two, keep it to himself and risk an internal quake that could reach nine on the Richter scale. They say you can't choose your family but you can choose your friends. Well, he'd chosen this shambolic bunch and they'd chosen him, so maybe it was about time he opened up to them about this particular concern.

After apologizing to Charlie for his outburst, Aaron began, 'I've got something that I need to get off my chest and would appreciate some advice. This is a big deal for me, so please, no laughing.'

The audience became hushed as Aaron nervously explained about the bullied childhood that he'd kept hidden from everyone. How, after his parents had died and he'd moved in with his gran, the children at his new school, especially the Fletcher Gang, made his life a misery with their fists and mouths. Without interruption Aaron gave a complete history of how he'd taken up martial arts then moved to Japan to become an expert. Never in his life did he expect to be at the receiving end of a bully again. The word 'bullied' had been filed away under the title of 'childhood'. Soon Aaron's explanation brought him to modern times. In fact his explanation brought him all the way up until last week when he'd visited his parents' graves.

'I was paying my respects when Darryl Fletcher's voice called out my name, chilling me to the bone. I'm not joking, but I literally froze with fear. Me, an 8th-dan fighter, was at the mercy of a yob-next door. I couldn't do anything and what's worse was that the fucker knew it. After all these years he still knew that he could scare me, just like old times. Before I was aware of what was happening, he'd pushed me to the floor and left me with his contempt. I felt like digging a grave for myself and jumping right in. Now, I've lost my guts.' Aaron's eyes glistened with frustration as he slammed his hand down on his thigh. 'All those years of training have been stolen by a chance meeting with my past. How the hell can I teach people martial arts when I can't even defend myself against a useless cretin like Darryl? What happens if I see him again? Will I just run away like I always used to?' Aaron put his face despairingly in his hands. 'I'm finding it difficult to get enthusiastic about teaching anymore, my heart just doesn't seem to be in it. And everyday, it's eating me up.'

Flabbergasted would describe how Aaron's mates reacted to his confession. They were as shocked, or more so, as when Delilah found out that Samson's strength came from having hair longer than a woman's. It meant that Aaron's words about every man having an Achilles heel were true. And in this case, Aaron's Achilles heel was in his past. Trying not to, but finding it impossible, Tyler, Sean and Charlie exchanged shocked looks. Their iron-tough friend, who feared no man, was just like them. Sponge soft with jellied limbs. A bit of a relief really; they'd thought Aaron was a robot sometimes.

Sean piped up, 'Your behaviour isn't that odd, considering you were at the graveside of your own mother and father. Maybe something inside you held you back out of respect for them. Maybe if he'd caught you in any other place you would have kicked the living shit out of him.'

'Nah,' Aaron said, shaking his head. 'It was the same fear that I used to get as a kid. This had nothing to do with respect. If anything, I would have gladly given him a hiding in front of my parents, just to let them know I'm not a coward of a son.'

After another hour of suggestions and unworkable solutions, Tyler finally struck the right nerve. 'What would your *sensei* in Japan advise you to do? What would he say that could bring you back on track?'

Aaron answered quickly, as if he'd been waiting for this question all along. 'He'd tell me that I must face my fears. I must go to every single individual who ever bullied me and I must confront them one by one. I must make them see the error of their ways. Only I can destroy the bad spirits that haunt me.'

'But will you?' asked Charlie, serving up more drinks and piri piri chicken drumsticks. 'Or, will you keep taking it out on GWS sufferers?'

They all laughed.

With much of tonight's energy already spent on helping Aaron with his mental problem, Charlie wondered if the fighting should still go ahead as planned.

'I still want to fight,' Aaron said, warming up his fists. 'What about you, Tyler, you still up for it?'

'Of course, it will be fun to see you beg for mercy. I'm guessing that Sean might pull out with an injury though.'

But Sean was perfectly fit. And within five minutes, after all had agreed to abide by the rules, Fight Night commenced on the PlayStation and the Xbox. *Tekken. Mortal Kombat. Dynasty Warriors. SmackDown vs. Raw American Wrestling. Fight Club* and *The King of Fighters*.

Fifteen minutes later, Charlie complained that his joy pad wasn't working as well as the others. He was sure that someone had tampered with it. Normally he was champion of the games.

'Don't be so paranoid!' they all shouted in harmony.

Chapter Nineteen

Stacy's plan had been sculpted with the sharpened instrument of jealousy. Jealousy of the woman who lived with her ex man. Once again she was in his apartment and once again chills of excitement vibrated up and down her spine. Success was the ultimate prize of winning her man back. And success depended on the items which were stored in the heavy holdall she'd dragged up the stairs and into Aaron's apartment. Now – her eyes searched around the open-plan room – where to begin?

SEX! She needed to know if Aaron and his wife were having sex in his bed. Last time she'd been here she'd been unsure as to whether they made love or not. Her question: how many newly married couples sleep in separate rooms? would normally be met with a raised eyebrow or two. And yet, by all accounts, this newly-married couple *seemed* to do just that: sleep in separate rooms. It was time to investigate further. As if she were the captain of this ship, Stacy strode into Aaron's bedroom, whipped back the king-sized duvet and bent down searching for sperm stains. NO STAINS! Next she lifted up the pillows and gave them a good sniff. NO PERFUME! It was pretty obvious from where she was standing that there was NO SEX! Even the bedside table was devoid of women's knick knacks. Just a *GQ* magazine, a bottle of XS after-shave, an electronic golf game and, oddly, a book titled *A Painless Divorce* by N.U. Rofen. But what about the bedside drawers, anything remotely femi-nine in there? Stacy opened the top drawer and after removing a packet of tissues, a pile of boxer shorts, two pairs of pristine white socks and an unopened box of condoms she was gratified to spot a wedding ring. Not proudly displayed on Aaron's wedding finger but tucked away with his condoms. A telling sign that there was something odd about this marriage if ever there was one.

'Winning you back is going to be easier than I thought,' Stacy said out loud to herself as she pulled back the wardrobe doors and rummaged through Aaron's clothes.

Her view quickly anchored itself on the metal safe. The hidden box of secrets. Idly she gave the safe door a tug, just in case he'd forgotten to lock it, just in case it was Stacy's lucky day. To no avail, though, as the door refused to budge. 'You'll keep,' she stated. 'Nothing stays hidden for ever, my darling.' She smiled slyly. 'And after you divorce your wife and marry me, your secrets will be my secrets.'

A purple shirt caught her eye, and set her memory ablaze with thoughts of their past together. Plucking the garment from the hanger, she held it close to her heart.

Aaron had worn this very shirt on a day that was surely blessed by Aphrodite. Even now she could remember popping open the buttons and filling up with pure lust as he removed her panties. Never had a man touched her in the way Aaron had; never had a man given her so much sexual satisfaction that she could think about nothing else until the next time. Not only did Aaron have magical fingers, tongue and cock, he also had a magical body . . . and Stacy couldn't wait until she'd wrecked it.

The sound of glass smashing outside the building removed Stacy from her red-light-district dream and had her rushing out to the window round the back to see what had happened. A couple of men in white karate suits were dumping rubbish in the skip. Nothing to worry about. But enough to keep her on guard from now on.

Why am I doing this? Stacy asked herself, as she lifted up the holdall and dumped it on the kitchen surface. WHY?

It was a question that popped into her mind constantly. Why couldn't she just let Aaron go? Mr Barrow, her local butcher (who made excellent Cumberland sausages), had advised her that there was no point in trying to go into partnership with fate because fate liked to work alone. In other words: what will be will be and no matter how much you interfere, if it ain't gonna happen then it ain't gonna happen. On the other side of the coin, Mrs Mathews, her next-door neighbour, was of the opinion that love is worth fighting for. It comes around only as often as Halley's Comet and if you don't catch the bright star then you will be left with the trailing tail. Which meant: grab him if you can or accept another man who you don't love.

Stacy was sure she loved Aaron; apart from his fantastic looks, charm, humour, his amazing prowess in the bedroom, his fit, hard body (with his perfect six-pack – soon to be a one pack) they had had some amazingly deep chats over the months they were together. They'd discussed why Bruce Lee was such a good dancer. Why Bruce Lee was so quick with his fists. Why Bruce Lee moved to America. Why Bruce Lee didn't like other people doing his stunts. Even why Brandon Lee, Bruce's son, was so perfect for the part in *The Crow*. Deep, *deep* meaningful chats. She doubted that Aaron had such thought-provoking discussions with the wife – the woman he didn't seem to sleep with. With 'seem' being the appropriate word. All clues pointed in the direction of a relationship without sex and yet, thinking back to earlier when she'd seen Aaron's eyes nearly fall out of their sockets when his wife, dressed in next to nothing, got into the passenger seat of his car, well, he was drooling so much he needed the windscreen wipers on. That was not the look of a man ready to turn down some hanky panky. It was all so very confusing.

And as Aaron, bristling with hormones, drove out of the car park, it was a wonder that he hadn't spotted Stacy lying low in her car, praying to the God of Decree Nisi that she wouldn't be seen. For, as most people might know, a baseball cap is hardly a disguise for the green-eyed monster.

The Green-Eyed Monster unzipped the holdall and, one by one, lifted out the three heavy buckets.

Strawberry, chocolate and vanilla. The labels on the front read MIGHTY MUSCLE. 3000 CALORIES PER SCOOP, and the bodybuilding guy she'd purchased them from at the gym had confidently told her, 'I guarantee that anyone who uses this stuff will blow up like a balloon.' Then, from a cupboard under the sink, she pulled out Aaron's three tubs of strawberry, chocolate and vanilla whey protein powder and emptied the contents into a bin bag. She knew that Aaron had at least four protein drinks a day. As Stacy filled up Aaron's old tubs with the new powder, she giggled to herself, wondering how Aaron's metabolism would react to a further 12,000 calories a day. The average person only ate between 2500 and 3400. Surely it wouldn't be long before his gorgeous face began to grow and his chin began to multiply. His eyes would sink back further into his podgy face, giving him that Chinese slit-eyed look, and when he laughed lots of him would jiggle about. His once tight bottom would drag behind him and he would grow 36DDD breasts. His belly button would widen and his famous six-pack would disappear to lard. Eat-all-you-like buffets would quickly close when he walked past and his heavy footsteps would keep the scientists wondering whether an earthquake was imminent.

The scenario had been well thought out by Stacy. Aaron would steadily gain weight up to sixteen stone (not knowing where the extra pounds were coming from). He would become depressed and convinced that no woman would want to sleep with a 'fatso'. Aaron, the sumo, would begin to take out his frustrations on his wife who would end up leaving him, feeling he wasn't the gorgeous man she'd once loved. At this point Stacy would re-enter Aaron's life when he was feeling rock bottom and explain to him that she loved him for his 'mind and personality' and not his 'looks'; it didn't matter that he was a 'fatso'. Aaron would realize that Stacy wasn't shallow like his wife but a perfect example of humanity in its best light. She *was* the woman for him. And they would begin to plan their own wedding. Suddenly, as if by magic, his weight would begin to peel away. Suddenly, as if by magic, his protein shakes would taste like they used to a few months before. Suddenly, as if by magic, she would have her man back. It was a perfect plan!

But, just to add a little bit of conflict between Aaron and his wife before the *real* fireworks began, Stacy had a childish idea which would annoy Aaron to the utmost. She quickly threw the protein-filled bin bag and empty buckets of Mighty Muscle powder into the holdall and scurried out to the living area. Aaron's movie collection was about to be reorganized. Stacy pulled out the martial arts DVDs and replaced them back in the wrong cases. With Aaron's penchant for Feng Shui, Stacy was confident that disorganized DVDs would have him blowing his top and blaming his wife. Nice one!

The condom landed just by Kitty's stilettos who kicked it away before it could be diagnosed as being used or not. Jeena, Flora and Kitty all instinctively looked up to the bed which dangled from the ceiling of The Wall nightclub.

The nightclub owner, Pink, who was always dressed

in a pink velvet suit, in a desperate attempt to increase the turnover of his club, had decided on having a double bed, attached by chains, hanging from the rafters in a tribute to the band Pink Floyd. Couples could book the bed for an hour at a time, taking fresh linen with them, and use it as they wish while the clubbers danced below them. Hence the condoms which landed from time to time on people's heads. Hence a new wave of babies who could lay claim to having been conceived at The Wall in 'The Bed'. Of course in a place like this one would expect that every now and then someone would spoil the elegance of the club by ejaculating over the clubbers. That was the day a very drunk Charlie was banned from The Wall for life. (His defence: he was too paranoid to wank at home in case he was being watched by the enemy).

After witnessing another condom fall nearby, Jeena and her friends decided to take a break from the dance floor and sit at a table near the bar where they could hear each other speak. Even though it was only just gone eleven p.m., the place was heaving with people out for a good time. A mix of bright, pulsing lights and dark corners, loud music and quiet cubby holes; it didn't take this nightclub long to zap any worries you'd dragged in with you.

The girls tucked into their Comfortably Numb cocktails, with Flora removing her cherry and giving it to Jeena – for fear she might blow her diet.

'Men are a funny species, don't you think?' Kitty said, to no one in particular. 'Take that guy sitting over there all on his own.' She pointed to a bloke in his mid-twenties, fairly good-looking, sipping on his lager. 'Now, if I were to go over there and say that all three of us girls want a foursome with him, I bet you one hundred quid that he'd say "I'm up for it". No shame, the lot of them. In fact I'd go so far as to say that he'd leave his wife for us. And that is *so* low.'

All three girls sneered at the man – what a zero!

Then Kitty thought she spotted a Platinum credit card as he opened up his wallet. 'Actually, we shouldn't just assume that he's a loser,' Kitty said, now a little bit keener to gain the man's attention. 'I mean, he could be a really decent bloke underneath that average-looking face. I'm going to give the guy a chance. He could be The One, you know.'

Jeena and Flora stared at Kitty in confusion. Jeena spoke, 'And Tyler? I was under the impression that *he* was The One.'

Kitty brushed the comment aside. 'Tyler is old news. He didn't return my calls. No, this guy seems to me like The One. I've got great vibes about him already.' And with that, Kitty adjusted her silicon breasts, lowered her dress to expose more cleavage (hardly possible) and sashayed over to his table holding her cocktail glass as elegantly as she knew how.

'I wish I could be as shallow as her sometimes,' Flora said, jealous at how quickly Kitty could move from one man to the other without being held back by emotional baggage. 'Here today gone tomorrow' was one of Kitty's mottos. Alternatively she sometimes said, 'Today's cock is tomorrow's old sausage'. But it all meant the same thing: she was young, free and willing to put it about as long as men found her attractive and as long as there was a chance of finding The One on her journey.

While Flora and Jeena sipped their drinks, trying hard to ignore the show-off barman tossing his cocktail shaker in the air, a text rang on Jeena's phone. It was from Aaron:

Would U B joining me 4 Sunday dinner tomorrow? Would B great 2 eat as husband & wife 4 once. Let me know.

'I can't understand him sometimes, I really can't,' Jeena said, showing Flora the message. 'He goes hot and cold.'

'And there lies the problem,' Flora replied, after reading the text and handing Jeena back her mobile. 'You don't understand him because you hardly know anything about him. You're hooked up with a man who, let's face it, could be a murderer. You just don't know.'

Flora explained while Jeena listened. How Aaron's past was a complete mystery. How, apparently (conveniently), he had no family. How he never discussed his life before he moved to Primpton. How the only thing he talked about openly was his spat in Japan. It all sounded extremely dodgy. Flipping heck, the man might have a criminal record as long as his arm. He could be wanted by Interpol. A fugitive on the run from the FBI. He could even be one of those guys who is married to five different women, a Mormon, and he might have fathered enough kids to open his own school. He could be anything.

'We worry about you, Jeena, both Kitty and I. Something about you being alone in that huge apartment with him fills us both with dread. What if one day he were to turn nasty?'

'He wouldn't. I feel totally safe around him.'

'But what if. That's all I'm saying. You married this man not knowing anything about his past. You owe it to yourself to find out about that past – especially as he's not willing to share it with you himself. From my experience, when a man doesn't want you to know something, he's normally got a very good reason why and normally that reason is immoral. With most men it's because they're already married, with Aaron, well, we can safely say it's not that, so the question is: what is he hiding from you, Jeena? What secrets does your husband hold?'

Flora told Jeena about Friends Reunited. A service on the Internet which enables old school friends to look each other up. It would be a great way to begin snooping around in Aaron's past. The simplest way would be to pretend she was Aaron and see what came up.

'I don't even know what school he went to, Flo.' Jeena sounded a little downhearted. *And* a little unsure whether she even wanted to do this. 'Maybe I should just wait out the year.'

'It's easy. Just rummage through his personal stuff when he's out. It'll be there somewhere; an old school report or something. The sooner the better. The last thing I want is to have to identify your body down the local morgue after he attacks you with a hammer.' Flora finished her drink and banged the glass down. 'Have you seen what damage a hammer can do?'

Jeena remembered Papaji trying to build a wardrobe – oh, she knew what damage a hammer could do all right. But she understood Flora's concerns and was already aware, more so by the day, that Aaron was indeed hiding something big. And when someone makes the effort to bury something big, then it's always worth the extra effort to try and dig it up. Jeena glanced over to Kitty who was already sitting astride one of Mr Platinum Credit Card's legs, playing with his hair, giggling into his ear. The only sentence which carried across the way was from Kitty's mouth and it went something like this, 'I just love diamonds'. Jeena laughed then stood up and walked to the bar. It was time for a refill.

'Two Dark Sides of the Moon cocktails, please,' ordered Jeena, parking her bottom on a stool, then removing her phone from her beaded handbag to answer Aaron's text.

What's 4 pudding?

She smiled and returned the phone to her bag only to be faced with a gorgeous-looking man pulling out a stool and sitting next to her. Phew!

'That's a nice perfume you're wearing; what is it?' he said, shamelessly.

'Garlic!' Jeena replied, acting nonchalant to his obvious charms. 'Garlic Eau De Parfum natural spray.'

'Lovely, is it made by the same company which makes my Underpants Eau De Aftershave?'

She laughed. Not only good-looking but funny too. The cocktails arrived and he offered to pay. So what have we got so far? Good-looking, funny and now, generous. Things just kept getting better.

'I'm Sam,' he put out his hand, 'and you are?'

The words 'a married woman' were about to come out of her mouth, but instead, just her name emerged, 'Jeena. And that's with a "J".'

And so began a chat with a man who, on the surface, seemed ideal. Within the space of fifteen minutes she knew more about Sam's past, career, youth and family than nine months with 007 Aaron. The openness of the chat was in total contrast to the closed, almost 'I've-got-to-be-careful-what-I-say-in-case-Aaron-bites-my-head-off' attitude she was used to with her husband. Not only was Sam open about himself, he seemed to genuinely take an interest in Jeena's life, her past, her family and her dreams.

Flora was left to get drunk alone and managed to keep an entire dance floor amused with her disjointed, paralytic, puppet-lost-its-string moves. Before Jeena knew it, the evening was nearly gone. A laughter-filled night of fun and flirting.

Pink liked to close up the nightclub with a slowy from his complete collection of Pink Floyd hits. Tonight he chose 'Wish You Were Here' and the floor quickly crammed with smooching couples. None faster than newly-formed Jeena and Sam.

Touching another man, feeling his body close and smelling his scent filled Jeena with a mixture of happiness and guilt. Half her heart ticking with the excitement of lust, the other half beating with betrayal. He leant in for a kiss and Jeena let him in. She owed Aaron nothing, she thought, enjoying Sam's hands as they played over her body. Her skin tingled dangerously and Jeena wondered how quickly they could get to the bed above their heads. Kiss by kiss, Aaron's hold on her was disappearing. Embrace by embrace, Jeena's mind was opening up to other possibilities. Like sex with Sam. Like being with a man who gave her what she needed. Like knowing her man wasn't going to sleep with other women. Like . . .

'Do you want to go back to my place?' Sam asked, peppering her neck with tiny kisses.

It wasn't about wanting to – blimey she'd jump in the sack in a blink – but she had to retain some self-respect here. If she'd learnt anything about giving her virginity away so easily it was this: a man will respect you if he is made to wait. Aaron didn't have to wait, she went to bed with him on their first date, and look where that got her. He didn't respect her any more than he did his other slags.

Jeena explained to Sam that she didn't feel right sleeping with someone so quickly. He understood and handed her his number telling her that most definitely he wanted this to go further. He had really enjoyed her company tonight and would love to spend some more time with her and get to know her a lot better.

After gathering up her two totally drunk friends, Jeena hailed a taxi and all three fell in to the back seat. On the return journey to Kitty's flat, Jeena checked her mobile to find that, yet again, Aaron had texted:

Pudding you say? How about a cheesecake
topped with BRAZILIAN nuts? Or just
a plain Brazilian topped with my nuts.

She switched off the phone and, for the first night in a
very long time, did not think about Aaron.
Instead she thought about Sam.

Chapter Twenty

MIND THE GAP

Aaron thought of that familiar cautionary phrase and hoped he had enough sense to heed the warning if it came today. For today was about meeting Jeena's father – and today was about gaps. Surely when he spoke to her father there would be an age gap. There would also be a culture gap. Perhaps an honour gap? Maybe even an intelligence gap – but hopefully not a moral gap.

God, Aaron was gapping himself. What if he totally fucked things up for Jeena?

After demolishing a seriously tasty strawberry protein shake and dressing in plain baggy black shorts and a tight white T-shirt, Aaron added the one item one should always wear when meeting the father-in-law: the wedding ring.

It had been twenty-one days since the marriage, exactly three Wednesdays ago, and the ring had hardly been worn in all that time. It had been twenty days since Jeena's parents had disowned her and her smile had hardly been worn in all that time. Aaron crossed his fingers that after today, if things went well with Jeena's father, if he could try and get him to see life from his daughter's perspective, close a few of those gaps, then maybe he could give Jeena some hope to hang her wishes on.

The searing summer sun cooked the air and seemed to suck the moisture from everything. Word had obviously got out in the insect kingdom that England was getting hotter as swarms of midges invaded from across the seas. Weather like this brought out the 'cool' people. Those born to wear shades (even at night) and drive around in open-topped cars – otherwise known as wankers.

The sun also provided those with decent bodies a perfect excuse to expose as much of their physique as was legal. Aaron was well aware of the effect that his well-honed, tight muscular body had on many women and he abused this knowledge to the fullest. Besides, he'd worked long and hard to build a sex-bomb physique capable of taking the punishment that the sport of martial arts sometimes dished out; eating the right foods, training for hours at a time, jogging, biking, meditating and disciplining himself. Life was a battle, he was a warrior and if he lost his six-pack he'd cry.

Just before jumping into his car, Aaron let out a huge belch and was amazed to find that even the after-shake protein burp tasted better than before. Weird! Last week the drinks tasted like cardboard and this week, all of a sudden, they tasted like melted ice cream. Maybe he'd not shaken the pot properly – whatever the reason, he wasn't complaining. Feeling a little bit greedy, he burped again, then got in the car.

The BMW computer blinked 95.1 degrees – as if Aaron needed any more convincing that he'd need the air conditioning on. He slipped in The Killers CD, listening to 'Everything Will Be Alright', and cruised out of the Paper Lantern car park. At this moment, he felt as if he could fix the world, solve all its problems. Starvation in Africa – easy: spend less on weapons and everyone eats a good meal. AIDS crisis – easy: spend less on weapons and use the money saved to give free medical aid. The hole in the ozone – easy: order J-Lo to float up to the atmosphere in a balloon and plug it with her arse. So why did Aaron have this confidence all of a sudden? This fearless resolve that anything was possible. One answer: his mates. After confessing his worries to them on Saturday evening regarding Darryl Fletcher and the bullies from his past, he'd felt free of a weight he'd been carrying around since the age of eight. These were the first people whom he'd ever discussed his fears with. The first people whom he'd split open his belly and exposed his guts to. And, after listening to them admit their own weaknesses to him in return – Tyler was afraid of dying young; Sean was afraid of firing blanks and not being able to father kids; Charlie was afraid of coming across his double – the whole group felt a lot closer. Anything felt possible after that.

Even solving the 4000-year-old arranged marriage system. Easy. EASY? Aaron hoped so.

Parking certainly wasn't easy, as Aaron had to wait a full ten minutes before a space in the short-stay car

park was free. Wednesday in Primpton was traditionally market day, adding chaos to an already narrow
High Street. Even though it was only 10.30 a.m., the
smell of fried onions and burgers wafted through the
warm air, making Aaron feel slightly queasy as he
sped along the street, sunglasses down, ego up. He
arrived at Make My Day gifts and cards shop. Jeena's
father's accountancy firm, Gills & Bills, was situated
directly above the shop; its entrance was downstairs in
a narrow side alley. Through the door, up a short
flight of stairs and Aaron was standing in a small
Reception with a few pot plants and a low-beamed
ceiling. The place was so cosy it was a wonder that the
huge, welcoming smile of the pretty receptionist fit
in it.

'How can I help you?' she enquired, closing the file
she'd been working on.

'Could you tell Mr Gill that his son-in-law is here to
see him.'

She looked over Aaron's shoulder half-expecting to
see an Indian man behind him but soon cottoned on
that it was the handsome, white gentleman in front of
her who was in fact *the* son-in-law. She couldn't wait to
gossip with her friends about today's occurrence. Not
only were Indians stealing our jobs but they were stealing our hunky Englishmen as well. It was so unfair.
Then, she had a change of heart after realizing that if it
wasn't for Mr Gill she would still be on Job Seekers.
Weren't Indians great! She phoned through, then
explained to Aaron that Mr Gill would be out shortly
and asked him to wait on the sofa in the meantime.

The meantime didn't last long, as Mr Gill, in his green

turban and suit, soon appeared with a concerned expression on his face.

'She's all right?' he asked, nervously. 'Jeena is okay, isn't she?'

'She's fine,' Aaron replied. 'In fact she's the reason I'm here.'

Aaron was taken through an open-plan office with about five stations and into Papaji's private office at the rear of the building. He admired the elegant interior with its leather seats, oak table and a gold and burgundy décor that must have cost a small fortune. Standing proud on Papaji's neat and tidy desk was a framed photograph of Jeena at her graduation. Aaron picked it up and looked over it thoughtfully.

'She still means a lot to you, doesn't she?' Aaron began, pulling up a chair and sitting down opposite Jeena's father. 'You must have felt like shouting from the rooftops when she graduated, I bet. After travelling all the way from India, isn't this what all those sacrifices were about? Your children? Giving them the life you believed they deserved. The life you've dreamt about.'

'The life you have now stolen from us!' Papaji snatched the picture and replaced it to its spot. 'When people sit in that seat I normally charge them two hundred pounds per hour. I do not think too kindly of someone patronizing me from the very same seat when I'm getting paid nothing. Now, why is it that you are here?'

Cool as a cucumber, Aaron reached into his pocket, opened his wallet and threw ten twenties on the desk. 'It shouldn't take longer than an hour.'

Papaji tried hard to hide his admiration for the cheek. 'Go on.'

So he did. With a flashing MIND THE GAP sign playing in his mind. Aaron explained first about what it was like to grow up without parents. How winning the sprint in the school sports day meant nothing without his parents to watch. How doing well in a maths exam left him empty without his mum or dad to say 'Well done, son'. In fact just to be called 'son' again was a craving he'd never lost since the passing of his parents. Aaron described how his poor gran had tried her best to bring him up on her meagre wage. How his gran would sometimes joke that one day they might qualify for the bread line; until that time it was just crusts. But it was no joke and Papaji was more than aware of the sadness that lay hidden behind Aaron's eyes. Although amongst that sadness there burned within Aaron a belief that good sometimes comes of bad and his crap childhood had given rise to a promise he'd made to himself: to achieve and excel and to get what you want. To use this one life we have for the purpose it was given to us: for happiness. Papaji listened as Aaron told him of his time in Japan, of his setting up of the Paper Lantern and turning it into a successful business, of taking his life from virtual poverty to a life without financial worry.

He went on, 'If I was given a choice between keeping Jeena and losing everything I've worked for over the years, I'd choose your daughter every time. I love your daughter, Mr Gill. Can you honestly say that the man you would have chosen for her would have loved her the way I do? I don't think you can. We really are meant to be together.' Aaron grabbed a fountain pen off the desk and doodled on a note pad. 'I can't bear to see her beaten up with sorrow because you won't accept this choice she has made for herself. A choice which has made her happy. I'm begging you, *not for me*, but for Jeena, to stop all this family feuding and come to a compromise. No one knows what the future will bring, and tomorrow Jeena could die in a car crash. Just like my parents did – have you seen her driving? Would you really be able to face your Indian gods knowing that you never reunited with your daughter?' And Aaron picked up the photo again. 'The daughter you are so very proud of. I know what it's like to be without parents, but my parents had no choice but to leave me. Don't let Jeena be without you. Please. You *have* a choice.'

The room became silent, like the silence that comes when a firing squad stops shooting. With Papaji the one in the firing line. Bullets of guilt shooting into him and smashing into his heart. The blood of his family line oozing away. And the shame of being lectured on how to keep a family together by, of all people, a white man.

The huge bulk of Papaji rose from his desk and walked to the window. He peered down on the busy High Street below. It had been twenty years since he'd admitted to anyone that he was in the wrong and he knew that his next words to Aaron were going to be very difficult to utter.

'You're right, Mr Myles,' Papaji said, still looking out of the window.

'Aaron will do.'

'You're right, Aaron. We've all got lost in family honour and tradition. We've forgotten what's important here. No one but you seems to care about Jeena's happiness. And I must admit, although it's very hard to do so, I admire you very much for this.' Finally Papaji faced Aaron. 'You proved to all of us how much you loved my daughter when you married her. It takes a lot of guts to go against the Indian way, Aaron, and as I have learnt, guts are something you're not lacking.'

The meeting soon became an informal chat with coffee and biscuits served up by Anna, the receptionist. Papaji told Aaron how much they'd all missed Jeena in the last three weeks. The house had been full of tears, arguments and blame. The parents regretted their heavy-handed response of threatening to marry Jeena off to a man in India where she would have spent the rest of her life. Papaji wasn't that much in orbit outside reality to realize that if Jeena had lived in India with a strange new family, she would have been living in prison. And she certainly didn't deserve to go to prison for just one mistake – even if that mistake was being caught in bed with a white man.

Aaron listened to Papaji talk of Jeena with such pride. How he'd doted on her like a princess when she was a young girl. Oh, the compliments Jeena's beauty had attracted as she grew from a princess to a queen had had certain female relatives cursing with jealousy.

'Not only that,' Papaji continued, 'but Jeena is full of talent as well. You should see some of the stories she wrote in her English classes. I believe she'll be a Booker Prize winner one day, I can assure you.'

Aaron remembered back to the last page he'd just

read of *Naked Riders*. Where the ever-willing naked Nikita, the heroine, was being team-shafted against a Harley Davidson by the Bad News Crew.

'She certainly has got talent, Mr Gill, I've read some of her work and it "lives". It really does. Some of the scenes are so vivid, I sometimes feel like I'm there.' He then thought to himself, *that's when I get the tissues out*.

The chat concluded with Aaron and Papaji arranging a reconciliation meal at the Gills' house this coming Saturday evening.

'I suppose it's a silly question, but I'll ask anyway,' began Papaji, 'but I take it that home-cooked Indian food appeals to you.'

Aaron nodded his head approvingly. 'I look forward to it. I've never had home-cooked Indian food before. Sounds lovely.'

Papaji stared at him quizzically. 'Never had home-cooked Indian? Well, what in god's name has my daughter been feeding you all this time?' Aaron's pause said enough. 'You mean to say she hasn't cooked you a meal? After all the training her mother has grilled in to her, all those endless hours of peeling, chopping and stirring and she can't even cook for her husband.' Papaji rolled his eyes in total humiliation. 'This, I can assure you, Aaron, was not how we raised her. She's been brought up to look after her husband, not to leave him to fend for himself. This will have to be discussed on Saturday. I am so let down by this unexpected news. You must put your foot down on Indian women or they will walk all over you. Next you'll be telling me she has banned you from the bedroom.'

Aaron was at a loss at what to say so he said this, 'Don't worry, if that ever happens I've got a great selection of porno movies.' But it was amazing how accurate Mr Gill was with his comment. Jeena and he were beginning to behave like most married couples. They weren't having sex (with each other).

After shaking Papaji's hand, Aaron disappeared out of the office. Papaji rung through to Anna and asked her to continue to hold his calls. If ever he needed a few moments to himself then this was that time.

A painting of Guru Nanak, the founder of Sikhism, hung inconspicuously on the wall behind his desk. Staring into the brown eyes of his revered guru, Papaji felt the calming influence of his vision. Never is there a straight road in life, there are turnings along the way. Some lead off dangerous cliffs while others take you to wondrous mountains. Today, for some reason, Papaji felt as if he had served the Sikh community well; he had done it proud. Guru Nanak believed that a man should always stand up for his principles and that everyone was equal no matter what the colour of their skin, their creed or their faith. A view Papaji was sure that his older brother, Gurjinder, in India, would argue against with bite.

Over the last few weeks, Gurjinder had phoned on a number of occasions offering his advice, determined to influence his brother – even from afar. Gurjinder had lectured Papaji on the family tree. How keeping it pure and free of the white man's blood was the only way. Gurjinder had asked, demanded even, that Jeena should be dragged home (kidnapped if necessary) and taken to India for a lesson in discipline and family morals. 'A snake has bitten poison into this family and it needs to be sucked out,' Gurjinder had said, in his old-fashioned way. 'Our elders have struggled enough under the rule of the white man, it would be an insult to invite one into our family today.' Gurjinder was adamant: sort this mess out soon or he would come to England himself and sort it out. Gurjinder did not make loose threats.

Which in some ways was the reason Papaji had loose bowels right now. Papaji had seen for himself today the side of a white man which no Indian elder believes to exist. The side of humility and love. He knew that his daughter, Jeena, was in the safest of hands with Aaron and it would now be up to him to convince his stubborn brother of the same.

In Papaji's heart he knew that he couldn't have found a better man for Jeena. A man who put his daughter first, who had ambition, who had dignity, who worked hard. Aaron was a survivor who had not been born with that silver spoon. He didn't wait for his parents to give him a head start in life, like many British-born Indian men did these days. He had soul and he had passion. What more could a father want for his precious, only daughter?

Besides, Papaji liked Aaron; in some ways he even reminded him of himself; so it didn't matter what the Indian community thought, or even what his older brother thought for that matter, what mattered was that Jeena was happy. It was as simple as that.

And every father wanted their daughter to be happy. Didn't they?

Chapter Twenty-one

Jeena felt like giving her new best friend, the deodorant can, a huge kiss. If it wasn't for the loyalty of Sure for women then it was questionable whether she would have smelt human anymore; and some pundits of aromas might have likened her smell to that of a pig.

Since her boss, Mr Akhtar, had imposed his new 'cover your body' rules, Jeena had been suffering from virtual heatstroke. The stifling office with just a few tiny windows and the odd desk fan for air-conditioning was unbearable at the best of times when one could dress accordingly. But in the middle of a heat wave, where Jeena was forced to wear trousers and long-sleeved tops with high necks, it was a wonder she didn't leave a trail of BO behind her like snail's slime.

Home time couldn't come quickly enough, and as soon as Jeena was through her front door, her clothes were off so quick anyone watching might have thought she was infested with fleas. A short sprint to the shower and the day's grime was washed away in a bubbling frenzy of soap and shampoo.

Although bending to Mr Akhtar's rules felt like giving in, Jeena was left with the one consolation that she'd won in the hair department. He'd wanted her red-streaked hair returned to its original black. But Jeena had opted for the 'sod you' hair style instead. Keeping her hair the same colour but tying it in a ponytail. She wasn't going to dye it back for anyone – having it streaked had been her first act of individuality (she'd fought her parents to keep it) and there were already enough people in this world with black hair, at last count about four billion. If it came down to it, she'd give up her job for her red streaks, but thus far Mr Akhtar hadn't commented on it.

After drying her body Jeena stood at her bedroom door with a towel around her. Her floor was covered in pages ripped from local newspapers; various job vacancies circled in pink pen. It was a simple mathematical problem: she spent more than she earned. With Mr Akhtar halving her hours, it didn't take a genius to work out the sums. She needed more money. Aaron had said that she could use his computer to put together a CV and covering letter, but she wouldn't be using Aaron's advice on what to write as to why she needed a new job. His advice: because my old job can't pay for my cocaine habit – which seems to be getting worse by the day. SNIFF SNIFF SNORT – was less than useless, as far as she was concerned.

The relief of walking around in floozy clothes was total. A short, flowing white skirt and a tight yellow vest top. Bare-footed. Bliss. For one dizzy moment everything was perfect. She was happily married to Aaron living in a luxury apartment with no money worries and a fantastic future to look forward to. Then her eyes were drawn to Aaron's latest purchase screwed to a southwest wall – in the marriage corner according to Feng Shui rules – an A4 sized wipe board. Today, written in ink, it read: ONLY 344 DAYS UNTIL D DAY. Tomorrow would read: ONLY 343 DAYS UNTIL D DAY. Dizziness never lasted too long in Aaron's apartment. Even when he wasn't here, he managed to wreck the moment. Sometimes she hated him and other times she loved him. It was like living with a seesaw in your head.

Jeena felt like angrily rubbing out the ink and replacing it with the words: WHO CARES ABOUT D DAY? I'VE GOT SAM NOW.

She repeated the words aloud, 'Who cares about D day. I've got Sam now.' And nearly had to pinch herself. Sam had become a regular visitor to her mind lately and there seemed to be nothing she could do about it. She knew she still loved Aaron and yet, another man was taking up some of her think space. Kitty and Flora were adamant, 'Get into Sam's boxers pronto.' 'Shag him and forget about Aaron. He's only your placebo husband anyway.' The recipe of Kitty's life, 'Shag him.' Unfortunately, Jeena acknowledged, her own life was filled with too many ingredients as it was, it was mayhem at the best of times. And add masala to an already mayhem-filled life and what do you get: masala mayhem? Possibly the worst curry in the world. The last thing she needed right now was an extra spice. The last thing she craved was another man touching her body and . . . Jeena could feel the draught of confusion shiver right up her spine. Maybe a date with Sam wouldn't be so bad. Maybe breaking out of this shell she'd encased herself in wasn't such a terrible idea. To live a little and forget all these mad-cap dreams about a happily ever after with Aaron. 'Cos, according to Michelle, Xena Warrior Princess, it ain't gonna happen. Aaron would never commit to any of the women he slept with because they were, to quote from Aaron, 'His bedroom playthings' or 'His slags'.

Well, this slag had something she needed to do. After thinking seriously about what Flora had said regarding her not knowing anything about Aaron, Jeena had decided to dig into his past. If there was a slim chance that love could ever blossom between them, then it was important to Jeena that Aaron was free of his secrets. Even though it was wrong to delve, it was right to know who she was married to. Her watch showed 1.09 p.m., which gave Jeena approximately an unknown amount of time to nosey through his things. Which basically meant he could return at any given moment. It was a risk, but what the hell, she'd already risked a lot when she'd danced provocatively with Sam at The Wall on Saturday night. If anyone from the Asian community had spotted her there, kissing him, caressing him, rubbing herself against him as they slow-danced, giving the Asian culture a bad name, frolicking with yet *another* white man, cheating on her new husband already, there was a distinct possibility that in the name of honour, some sort of punishment would be dished out. It could take the form of being kicked out of the Asian community for life, or being beaten by a handful of angry self-made-jurors, or even killed. An Indian woman who cheats on her husband, even if the husband is white, is considered impure and low. From an Asian standpoint, if a woman is unfaithful, then not only is she mocking her husband, but she is also mocking the Asian culture; sticking her two fingers up at everything they stand for. This type of woman is not a good role model; the last thing any parent wants is for their own daughters to see such acts go unpunished, to see that adultery is okay. And therefore the punishment is often severe.

Now, where to start snooping, thought Jeena, staring at the nine fish swimming in the tank. 'Where is your master hiding his personal stuff?' she asked Tyson, the fat, black fish. 'Where does an extremely tidy man hide his messy past? His junk?' The fish were loyal and said nothing. Jeena was sure if she had a doughnut or two she might have got Tysee to open up a little. Either that or show him a Ken Hom Hot Wok recipe for ginger-fried goldfish.

In her mind, Jeena listed three areas to look. His office area, bedroom area and the high kitchen cupboards. The drawers in the office area were filled with diet sheets, monthly class schedules, bills and invoices. The kitchen cupboards revealed nothing spectacular apart from a fossilized apple core and vitamin tubs. So, the pressure was on the bedroom to expose Aaron's past. The chest of drawers was the obvious place to begin. She began by pulling out his three drawers, leaving just a shell, and placing them on the bed. Men could be devious creatures at times; they learn their amazing stashing skills as youngsters when hiding porn from their mothers. Jeena checked the shell and found a few loose socks and a full box of Potassium Iodide

Anti-Radiation tablets (given to Aaron by Charlie as it happens – just in case a Nuclear Bomb was detonated in a nearby town).

Carefully Jeena began searching through the items in each drawer, feeling around for hidden letters in boxer shorts, hoping to find a little black book with everything written inside. Piling stuff on the pillows, she began to hunt in finer detail, shaking out each sock, emptying out each pocket. No luck. Next her attention switched to the fitted wardrobes. From one end of the wall to the other. She started on the far right, where she found a range of expensive shirts, T-shirts, casual wear and a heavy-looking safe at the bottom, to the left where there were various suits, suit jackets, trousers, martial arts clothes and shoes. She was just about to begin looking through the trouser pockets when her eyes were drawn to a small jacket hanging at the very far left of the rail. Her heart skipped a beat as she lifted out the hanger.

Lo and behold, staring right back at her was a navy blue school blazer with its own school emblem. Collingsworth Comprehensive. Just as she shouted, 'BINGO', she heard the front door slam shut. Aaron was back, and his bedroom was a complete state.

'Jeena, are you in your room?' Aaron shouted out.

She winced. 'Actually, Aaron, I'm in *your* room,' she replied, gobsmacked at how messy his bedroom had become. The entire contents of his drawers scattered over his bed. Jackets, trousers, jeans and trainers. Even the police left things neater than this when searching for heroin. Panic placed its hands around Jeena's windpipe and began to throttle her. She managed to croak out, 'Please don't come in your room, Aaron, I've got a surprise for you.'

'Oh, don't be so stupid,' Aaron said, his voice chillingly getting nearer – he couldn't wait to tell Jeena the good news about the meeting he'd had with her father earlier. 'I'm coming in.'

With nothing left to lose, Jeena cried out in desperation, 'Please, Aaron, don't come in, you'll spoil the surprise and it involves . . . SEX. It's a SEXY surprise, so wait just a few minutes, please. SEX, Aaron, it involves SEX.' She listened for his footsteps, ready to hit him over the head with an empty drawer if he came through the entrance.

'Calm down, I won't come in,' Aaron conceded. 'I'll be back in a minute; I'm just making myself a protein shake.' He put his mouth right up to the closed door. 'This had better be good, Jeena, because I'm not so sure that I want to be aroused today. I'm not feeling horny at all. So, if you can get it up, then you deserve the orgasms you'll be getting.'

'Just give me five minutes to set the romantic scene,' she said in her huskiest, sexiest voice. 'Grrrrr.'

His footsteps trailed away to the kitchen and Jeena glared at the mess she'd created. She remembered a game she used to play as a child called Frustration. The idea was to fit the different shaped plastic pieces into their mould before the timer ran out and you lost the game. Today, if Jeena couldn't return all of Aaron's items to their respective places within five minutes, then she might not lose the game, but she'd certainly lose his trust. For EVER. With a deep breath and the self-belief that she was an octopus Jeena set about a frenzied attempt, to return Aaron's bedroom to how she'd found it. Those two old bags who clean up houses on TV would have been well impressed, thought Jeena, as she closed the final drawer in a state of triumph. Her self-satisfied smile didn't last too long though, when Jeena realized that she still hadn't 'set the romantic scene'. Aaron was bound to appear any second expecting her to be exquisitely dressed in sexy lingerie, possibly lying back on a bed scattered with rose petals, as the delicate light of fragrant candles flickered across her virtually naked skin.

Time seemed to giggle at Jeena as she thrashed around in her mind for something sexy to do. She'd already ruled out the plan of ripping a hole in her knickers and palming them off as crotchless underwear. It might have worked if the underwear was still its original colour of pristine white, but crotchless grey? She didn't think so. In one of Aaron's jacket pockets she'd found a small pot of strawberry jam (obviously taken from a hotel or motorway service station) and wondered if she could have smeared it over her and asked Aaron to lick it off. But he might have already had lunch, so that was another 'no'. The only other viable solution was the razors she'd come across.

Knock, knock, knock. Aaron was at the door. 'Can I come in now, Jeena?'

'Two minutes. Can you hang on another two minutes? I promise you it will be worth it,' Jeena replied, stripping off her clothes.

From a packet, Jeena removed a new Ultra Grip Gillette razor and pulled off the safety cover, hoping that she wasn't about to suffer Ultra Pain. She closed her eyes and prayed to any God who was willing to listen, 'Please don't let me cut myself.' And then she set about shaving her nether regions into the shape of a heart.

Carefully, and ever so slowly, the heart began to take shape, until, after two minutes of pruning and dead-heading, it almost, sort of, if one was drunk, looked like something resembling a hairy heart. Delighted that there was no blood, Jeena brushed down her handi-work and jumped on the bed confident that Aaron would be impressed.

'Lover boy,' she shouted out, 'lover boy, entrée, your lady awaits you.'

Cautiously, Aaron pushed open the door and stared at the naked sight before his eyes. With some confu-sion, he walked into the room and suspiciously scanned around, expecting to find something, anything, which would explain why Jeena had taken so fucking long to get undressed. Fifteen minutes just to remove a few items of clothing – it didn't make sense. Was this a joke of some sort? More importantly, why did she want to sleep with him all of a sudden? What the hell was going on?

'Do you like it, lover boy?' Jeena said, smiling and pointing to her artwork below.

Aaron's eyes dropped to where she was pointing; unblinking, fixed and questioning. He wondered why she'd shaved two big ears into her privates. Not one to judge too quickly, Aaron sped around the bed and took a closer look, peering as near as he dared without seem-ing to be rude.

'Two ears, why?'

Jeena's forehead creased up. 'Ears? What are you talking about, moron? It's a bloody love heart. I did it for you.' She seemed put-out. 'Ears? Get your eyesight sorted out, Aaron. Anyway, you'll probably want to ask why I did it? Well, it's because I couldn't make it to your Sunday dinner on . . . Sunday. I felt bad after you said it would be nice to eat as husband and wife for a change. So, I give you my heart.' She paused. 'Not for sex though, this is just for you to view until it grows back.'

'Let me get this straight, I can have a look at it any time I want to?' Aaron said, sitting down on the bed, hiding his smirk.

Jeena shrunk in shame. 'Yeah, any time, just give me a few minutes notice.'

He collapsed into the duvet laughing. It was too much to hold back anymore. What drugs was this woman on?

'I couldn't afford to have it done professionally,' Jeena shouted above his laughter, trying to justify her mindset, 'as I'm watching my pennies at the mo. That's why I did a DIY job instead. Besides, it's more personal this way, don't you think?'

Aaron was having too much trouble getting the thought of 'ears' out of his head to hear properly what she was saying. Ears for Big Ears. Ears for Dumbo. Ears for Prince Charles. Even ears for Charles Clarke – the home secretary. But ears for a woman's bikini line, well, it was a new one on him.

It wasn't long before his laughter had stopped and he was staring into Jeena's embarrassed face. It didn't take an awful lot of brainpower to realize that he had a certain responsibility to upkeep here. For goodness sake, lying naked before his very eyes was a woman of extreme beauty. A stunner capable of filling a man's mind with pure filth. Cue Aaron. There was no getting away from it, no matter what self-hypnosis method he employed, when it came down to the crunch, Jeena turned him on BIG TIME. He remembered the very first time he'd seen her naked body, on their first date together, and felt his nerves burn with desire. 'If I suck you off, you won't think of me as a slut, will you?' Jeena had asked. It didn't take a scientist to work out that Aaron had said, 'No, of course not. If anything, I respect you more for it.' And as Jeena had sucked, it hadn't taken Aaron long to realize that 'the slut' had done this sort of thing before. But she did turn him on and it was always a treat having sex with her.

So, here she lay, naked on his bed, obviously expecting him to deliver; who was he to deny her her needs? He yanked off his clothes, then knelt up on the bed and jiggled himself across the mattress until he was straddling her hips. Immediately Jeena's breathing became laboured and erratic. Almost panicky. And her eyes became wider, her pupils dilated and more excited. He lowered his head to kiss her.

And she reciprocated. Deep in her consciousness she'd been longing to feel his body up against hers again. To give herself to him and say, 'Do with me what you will, lover boy', knowing that the next hour or so was going to be filled with thrills; an illegal amount of fun and a filthy amount of orgasms. Jeena moaned as she felt his hard cock dangerously close to her newly-carved love heart.

Aaron was trying not to think 'ears'.

The two became tangled with desire as they rolled about the bed, pushing each other's buttons, forgetting about life outside this room. At this moment it mattered not whether Aaron loved Jeena, or Jeena loved Aaron, whether Jeena was having doubts about her future or whether Aaron was screwed up about his past, all that mattered was the orgasm.

All that mattered was . . . Jeena moaned out, 'Deeper, Aaron, right there.' All that mattered was . . . Jeena yelled out, 'Keep going, keep going, don't stop.' All that mattered was . . . Suddenly Jeena pushed against Aaron's chest with her hands. 'STOP! Please, Aaron, stop. I can't do this, it's wrong.' The orgasm shattered into a thousand pieces.

Like a steam engine that's run out of coal, Aaron's boiler stopped and his piston ceased. If only the train had gone into the tunnel a little bit earlier, then it may have cum on time. As it was, Aaron's train had quite a few passengers who still needed to get off. About four million actually.

'I'm sorry, Aaron,' Jeena said, wrapping the duvet around her. 'I told you that I wouldn't share you with other women anymore and I meant it. I'm not your bit on the side. It makes me feel so dirty. While you were on top of me I kept asking myself the question, who else have you slept with this week?'

'Not this shit again, Jeena. You know what I'm like, it's no surprise to you. Christ, you don't get me telling you that I won't share you with other men, do you?'

Jeena shook her head, feeling reasonably pleased that Aaron had forced her into a corner which justified her next comment. 'No, I don't. So it won't bother you that I have got myself a new boyfriend then, will it? His name is Sam and I met him at The Wall on Saturday night. That's why I couldn't come to your Sunday dinner, because I was in bed with him instead. That's the real reason for today; I felt guilty for sleeping with him. I feel like I owe you something because you married me.' She unwrapped herself from the duvet and began to dress. 'Not anymore. *Not* anymore.'

The engine came off the tracks. Aaron's face seemed to fall about three floors. War had been declared on his ego. Not quite knowing why, Aaron felt for his wedding ring and began to twist it furiously around his finger. How dare his wife sleep with another man. What could this 'Sam' bloke have that he couldn't provide?

'I'm your husband!' Aaron shouted, pulling on his shorts. 'You've only been married twenty-one days and already you've committed adultery. It's a disgrace.' He threw on his T-shirt. 'It's a bloody good job we haven't got kids, Jeena, that's all I can say. It would have torn them apart.' Anger scurried over his body like a heat rash. 'Have you told him that you're married? That you already have a committed husband at home? Have you? HAVE YOU?'

Jeena thought he *should* be committed with the amount of crap coming out of his mouth right now. Okay, so she had lied a little back then about sleeping with Sam and about him being her boyfriend, no big deal, nothing to growl about. But what a response from Aaron, it was nothing like she would have expected. For the first time in their relationship, Aaron was plainly jealous.

And as far as Jeena was aware, a man would only show this kind of jealousy when he had strong feelings for the girl in question. Wow, thought Jeena, with the verbal display she'd just witnessed, there was a good chance those feelings he held for her were 'hot'.

'You're jealous, aren't you?' Jeena aimed a knowing stare his way. 'Jealous and incapable of hiding it.'

'JEALOUS?' Aaron spat. 'I don't do jealous. I'll tell you what I am though, and that is very let down.' He began to do some martial arts moves in the air. Possibly trying to bring his heart rate back down to normal-ish. 'If anyone from the Asian community catches you with him, then you can kiss any chance of reconciliation with your parents goodbye, and it means that this marriage has just been bullshit. What a waste of my fucking time.' He sneered at her. 'Jealous? It's hard to get jealous about someone I haven't even seen. And take it from me, if there is a slim chance that I can get shot of you with this Sam I'll take it. So you go and shag him as much as you want. You won't find any objection coming from me.'

He opened the bedroom door, pulled his wallet from his pocket, plucked out sixty pounds in twenties and handed them to Jeena. 'Here's some cash to sort out your bikini line; we don't want Sam running away at the sight of it now, do we?'

She hurled the notes to the floor. 'Fuck you, Aaron.' And stormed out of his bedroom.

He slammed the door shut behind her and leant with his back to the door. Women didn't come from Venus at all, he realized, no, they came from the fiery bowels of Hell. One minute they could be knee deep in the mushy talk of romance and the next they want to slice off your testicles with a Black & Decker Jigsaw. There was no in between. Minutes ago Jeena was lying back asking him for a fuck and the next she was asking him to go fuck himself. He didn't even get the opportunity to tell her the good news about her father.

He moved to the window and looked down upon the River Wes. A rotten log was being steered down the waters by the river flow, twisting with the currents, bobbing with the waves. Wouldn't it be great to be like that log, to go with the flow, to leave decisions up to something higher? Aaron pondered. For right now, his once-simple life had been turned inside out and upside down by this sham of a marriage he'd agreed to. It was affecting his sex life – nowadays he was almost afraid to bring a woman back home in case he upset Jeena. It was affecting his business – after the Asian community found out about his marriage to Jeena, the cancellations to his Fight to Unite class had skyrocketed. Now it was affecting his state of mind – arguing with Jeena for petty reasons. If things carried on at this rate it would be amazing if the marriage lasted another month, let alone another eleven. But if the marriage failed before the year was up then it would mean that he had failed.

And no one hated failure more than Aaron.

Chapter Twenty-two

It was 6.04 p.m. on Saturday evening and Jeena gazed thoughtfully at the mound of clothes she'd assembled on her bed. Somewhere amongst that lot, she had to pick the right outfit to impress the man she was meeting tonight. For the man in question was her father.

Jeena remembered watching a magician on the TV cutting and restoring a rope as part of his repertoire. The rope was cut with scissors and when he held the two severed ends together, magically they became one again. She doubted that dinner with her severed family this evening would be as simple as that.

After arguing with Aaron on Wednesday, he had knocked on her bedroom door waving a white pair of boxer shorts in surrender. 'This doesn't change anything about me wanting to see the back of you,' Aaron had begun, 'but I think it's important that you know where I've been today.' And he'd gone on to tell her about the secret meeting he'd had with her father. It was at this point that Jeena's emotions had hit critical mass. She loved Aaron for this kind act. She hated him for what he'd said in his bedroom: 'If there is a slim chance that I can get shot of you with this Sam then I'll take it. So you go shag him as much as you want. You won't find any objections coming from me.' She was worried about tonight's reconciliation with her family. And she was unsure of how to deal with these feelings she had for Sam.

Over the last three days she'd talked with Sam several times on the phone. Late night chats, exploring each other's personality, strengthening their foundations. For every minute of guilt she had about the situation, she had three minutes of excitement in return. At one point, so explicit had their phone conversation become, that she had thought about jumping into her car and driving all the way to his house; except Sam wasn't at his house but on some business trip in deepest Devon. So they had arranged a date for this time next week. Sam would be cooking a meal for her in his house – and hopefully, later, cooking up a frenzy in his bed. Maybe after they'd spent the night together any uncertainty about Sam and her would be gone. And any feelings she had left for Aaron would be well and truly buried.

Picking up a bright red *shalwar kameez* and holding it up to herself Jeena checked her reflection on the wardrobe's inside door mirror. It was important that she dressed with respect for her family today. Walking into their house with a sense of tradition would be the least she could do since she'd last walked out of it with the sense of betrayal. But bright red? It was too much like the colour of Indian weddings. What about cream?

No, too much like the colour of an Indian funeral. Erm, what about aubergine? Okay, so it was the colour of a phallic vegetable but apart from that, perfect! Jeena held it up to herself. Silk, embroidered with gold stitching. Now all she needed was matching sandals and handbag.

Jeena thought of her fashion guru, Kitty. Kitty had been known to wear an outfit to match the colour of the condoms she had in her handbag. She left nothing to chance in the fashion stakes. Her advice would have been more than welcome today, except that Kitty was on a dirty weekend with Mr Platinum Credit Card. 'Listen to this, Jeena,' Kitty had babbled on the phone, just before sauntering off to Amsterdam. 'He said that if I were to have a further increase in bust size then he would buy me a yellow Porsche with my own personalized number plate. Guess where I'm booked into next month. Only the Sally bloody Grayson clinic. Can you believe it? He's definitely The One.'

Oh, Jeena could believe her all right. Jeena had asked her what colour eyes he had and Kitty had said, 'I'll find out for you.' She'd also agreed to find out his age. But one thing she did know – his bank account number.

A sharp knock at her door snapped Jeena from her shoe crisis. 'Come in, Aaron,' she said, as coldly as possible.

He stood before her in a pair of smart black jeans and a tight short-sleeved black and white printed shirt showing off his ample biceps. If silence was golden then Tutankhamen's treasure had nothing on this. An awkward, uncomfortable, unfriendly silence. Not that this atmosphere had suddenly descended upon them out of the blue. Ever since their scene in Aaron's bedroom on Wednesday the two of them had been virtually avoiding each other; just holding onto the barest of niceties.

With her moody face Jeena stared at his moodier face and tried hard to intensify the moody look in her own. For some reason the menacing stare coming from Aaron only increased his sexiness. His brooding, simmering, anger had Jeena wondering what it would feel like to be underneath him while he had his wicked way with her. Underneath him as he was driven by the demons inside him. Then she metaphorically slapped herself around the face. She had no time for worthless fantasy, she had shoes to match.

'It's a pity the *Guinness Book of Records* people aren't here to record this, Jeena, I mean, four hours prancing around in your underwear must be some sort of record.' He tapped his watch. 'We're out of this apartment in twenty minutes. That's twenty minutes before we start to play "Happy Couples".'

As he walked out of her room he was sure that he could feel the distinct wind change of a middle finger being aimed in his direction. He stopped at the aquarium and clinked the glass with his wedding ring. 'Okay, some of you lot end up battered and fried, but at least you don't have to have,' and he shouted, 'A SHAM MARRIAGE.' Once again he tried to pull off his wedding ring and once again his finger didn't want to let him without a struggle. Surely his hands hadn't put on weight, he hoped, for there was nothing sexy in having saveloy fingers. He tried to recollect whether he'd bruised his hand over the last few days in his martial-arts classes, but no joy. Without another thought he dashed out to the bathroom and unbuttoned his shirt before the mirror.

'Oh, my, GOD,' Aaron declared. 'What the fuck has happened to my abs?' A light smearing of water-retention was now covering a six-pack which used to be sharp enough to cut paper with. He breathed out all of his air and squeezed his stomach muscles as tightly as he could. 'FUCK! FUCK! FUCK!'

Lying back on his sofa, stressed out and confused, Aaron mentally worked his way through the routine he'd followed over the previous weeks to see if anything stood out which would, he yelled, 'FUCK UP MY BODY.' His martial-arts training had been its usual steady pace. As had been his jogging and stomach exercises. His diet had been as strict as ever. So why had he put on this weight? Depression knocked rudely at the door to his ego. He'd read that when a man or woman gets older their body begins to slow down. Fitness becomes harder to attain. Fat stores fill up more easily. Muscle wastes quicker. But not at the age of twenty-eight, thought Aaron, surely not now. Trying to think positively he decided to increase his aerobics and see what happened. In the meantime, he'd keep everything else the same.

Which meant, he looked at his watch, time for another delicious protein shake. He trotted out to the kitchen, blended up a vanilla shake and poured it into a glass with ice then returned to the living area where he still had enough time, just, to watch a few bouts of a Ralph Gracie fight on DVD. He slid in the disc, reclined himself back into the huge sofa (still covered in a red-coloured Egyptian throw), sipped on his shake and watched . . .

. . . *Fist of Fury* with Bruce Lee? Aaron groaned. He hated nothing more than to find a DVD in the wrong case: it was bad Feng Shui and it was so bloody annoying. Soon Aaron found that there was something he hated more than finding a DVD in the wrong case: and that was when he found out that his entire martial arts collection was in the wrong cases. Why Jeena would stoop so low, was anybody's guess, but right now Aaron was livid. How his wife could be so childish and nasty was beyond him. One by one he returned the discs to their correct homes. All fifty-five of the buggers.

'I'm ready,' Jeena announced, clomping across the floor in her high heels. Even though they weren't on speaking terms she still, sort of, expected a compliment on how she looked.

Aaron slammed another DVD into the cabinet. 'Are you trying to wind me up? I suppose Kitty, Flora and you had a great laugh over this, didn't you?'

She giggled nervously. 'Over what?'

'Over these fucking things.' Angrily Aaron flung a handful of DVDs across the room. 'It's all a game to you, isn't it?'

Jeena was shocked at this sudden flare up by Aaron. She was about to comment on one of the DVDs that shot past her face with a joke, 'At least I've seen a ninja fly now,' when she was struck by the look of rage glazing his eyes. What on earth was this man talking about now? Maybe this underlined the very reason why Flora had suggested she delve into Aaron's past.

For judging by his current form, the man was a certified psycho.

On Wednesday evening, after discovering the name of his school embroidered on the blazer she'd found in his wardrobe, Jeena had phoned through to Flora and relayed the information. 'I don't expect that you'll make much headway,' Jeena had guessed. An hour later Flora had phoned her back with news: Flora had logged onto the Friends Reunited website registered under the pretence of being Aaron and was now waiting to hear from his old school buddies. If Aaron was hiding anything, then something was telling Jeena it was hidden in his youth. She just hoped that the 'anything' wasn't that he dressed in his dead mother's frock and underwear and was really called Norman Bates. If that was the case then she certainly wouldn't be taking a shower with him around anymore.

Jeena denied touching his precious DVD collection.

Aaron accused her of lying – it couldn't have been the fish.

Jeena remarked that he seemed to think the fish were clever enough to understand him babbling on, so why not the fish?

Aaron replied that it would have taken at least four of his fish to pick up one DVD and as far as he knew fish didn't work well as a team. So it was quite clearly NOT the fish.

'Maybe if we cooked the fish, then if this world-shattering crisis ever happened again we could rule out any fish involvement,' Jeena said, growing tired of this verbal charade. 'A dash of soy sauce would go down a treat.'

He glared at her. 'You stay away from my fish.'

'With pleasure,' she spat, picking up her dinky handbag.

'This marriage is becoming more of a burden every day.'

'Ha!' she retaliated. 'I'm beginning to wish I'd been sent to India now. Suddenly a toothless goat-breeder with one arm and no legs is looking more attractive by the day. And before you give me any of this, "He'll be crap in bed", let me tell you, Aaron Myles, that a man lacking in one or two limbs will make the extra effort in the bedroom, so I'm sure he'll more than match your skills. In fact, I'm sure he'll be better.'

'I'd love to see a legless man carry you over the threshold.'

'He'd use pulleys and things.'

'Well, bugger off to India and marry him then. And release me from this nightmare you've trapped me into. I'm even willing to pay a hefty dowry to him, to get rid of you.'

Ten minutes later and the two of them were travelling towards Jeena's parents' house, music at full volume, faces fully miserable, not a word between them all the way. At last, after an uncomfortable journey, filled with tension, they approached 56 Monroe Avenue. As ever the front room window of the Gills' house was filled with brown faces watching for Aaron's BMW to drive up. Then, as if no one had seen them, the faces disappeared from view.

Waiting for the doorbell to be answered, Aaron noticed that Jeena was extremely nervous. Adjusting her clothing and unable to keep still. He took hold of her hand and gently squeezed it.

'Everything will be fine, I'm here with you all the way,' he whispered. 'And, by the way, you look spectacular. If I hadn't already married you, I'd marry you now.'

They both laughed and it was at this moment the door opened.

Papaji shook his blue-turbaned head at his beautiful daughter as a few tears trailed down towards his beard. It had been over three weeks since they'd last set eyes on each other. Papaji stepped out on the porch and hugged Jeena tightly. It was important to let her know that this meeting was about making up and forgiveness. It was not, as Jeena had worried it might have been, about blaming and shaming. She'd heard many stories about Asian girls who'd run away from home. Sometimes those girls are conned into returning to their parents with false promises that everything is forgiven. Once the girl has taken the step of trusting her parents, of believing that they now understand her, the Indian system pounces. She is taken to India under the pretence that she will be visiting a dying relative, 'It will be your last time to see them, so you have to go', or she will be taken under the pretence that she is attending a family wedding.

As soon as her feet hit Indian soil, her freedom is snatched away. Her life from that moment on is in the hands of her elders. And those elders would like to teach her a severe lesson or two about running away from home.

In some ways there is a grain of truth hidden amongst

the lies she is told. The family wedding she is travelling to in India may well turn out to be her own wedding (with a man three times her age). Or the funeral of the dying relative that she is flying out for, may well turn out to be someone in the family – herself (once they have murdered her under the honour killing system).

No wonder Jeena was nervous.

Papaji shook Aaron's hand and gave him a knowing wink. They were then ushered inside to the living room where Maji was already halfway across the carpet with open arms. Jeena's nan soon attached herself to the cuddling bundle. And even JJ felt obliged to put his arms around his sister (although it wasn't the cool thing to do). Jeena was thrown back in time to the very first school trip she'd had with her primary school Martin's Wood. Nearly a hundred relatives had come to see Jeena off on the coach. All hugging her in much the same way as they were now. It was a goodbye worth remembering with affection. Saris, turbans, *shalwar kameezes* and suits. Each relative deemed it appropriate to bring a little food for Jeena to take with her on her three day excursion to York. Auntiji's wrapped *samosas*, uncleji's Tiffin boxes filled with *dhal*; there were trays of *pakoras*, carrier bags full of Bombay Mix, *naan* breads, *chapattis* and two large containers of *tandoori* chicken. Even though the trip was only three days, there was enough food there for a month. As the coach pulled away, anyone would have thought a funeral had just taken place with the amount of sobbing. But if anyone had looked to the children aboard the coach, anyone would think a stink bomb had just been let off (either that or someone had smuggled a pair of Bernard Manning's used underpants on board) – sixty children all holding their noses from the pungent smell of garlic and spices permeating through the baggage hold below.

'Nanaji still refuses to speak,' declared JJ, once everyone was sitting down with refreshments. 'Still in shock at what happened in your bedroom I suppose, Jeena. I've tried everything. I even experimented with some porn therapy, forcing her to look at page after page of women in compromising positions. And still no response. Not a sausage.' He smiled at Aaron, trying hard to get a laugh from him, hoping that these horrendous lies about his gran and porn were providing great entertainment for his new brother-in-law. 'I hope you two are proud of yourselves, your bedroom antics have spoilt six weeks of potential bonding I would have had with my dear grandmother.'

Papaji gave his son an eyeful. 'I'm getting a little tired of your immature behaviour, JJ. It wouldn't hurt a little if you treated your gran with some respect.'

'Sorry Nanaji,' muttered JJ. 'My enthusiasm gets the better of me sometimes.'

The wonderful smell of Indian food laid siege to the hungry bellies in the living room. As if to prolong the torture Maji kept disappearing to the kitchen then returning with the news, 'Just a few minutes longer.' JJ apologized for the wait and offered Aaron a packet of crisps to keep him going until the food arrived, which he declined. He was here for Jeena today and that meant being the perfect guest. Aaron stared down at his cup of Indian tea and winced. To his Western palate the taste of the pale beige liquid was putrid.

Cardamoms, sugar and god-knows-what-else had apparently been thrown into a bubbling pot of tea leaves, diluted down with gallons of boiled milk and sieved. He wondered if the perfect guest would be required to down the whole, disgusting cup. (PG Tips it was not). He remembered a saying his gran used to use, 'Never make someone feel a stranger in their own home.' Which meant, never boast that you have a bigger TV, never complain that their house is too cold, never notice that their wallpaper is half falling off and even, in this case, never realize that their tea tasted like rottweilers' testicles. Aaron gulped it down and tried not to gag.

'Mmm mmm,' he smiled appreciatively, placing his empty cup down on the coffee table. 'Lovely.'

Another brownie point chalked up.

The topic of conversation chopped and changed and the once fraught atmosphere mellowed. Jeena watched in amazement as Aaron effortlessly glided from one family member to the other, making each feel special, reassuring them all that he was 'good husband material' for their daughter. The way he joked and complimented her was in complete contrast to an hour ago where they'd been having their own version of 'shock and awe' in the arguing department. What a total shame, Jeena decided. Her parents and family had finally given her what she wanted – their blessing – yet, as soon as she and Aaron left this house, they would surely return to the bickering twosome that they had become. Repeat: what a shame.

A minuscule silence in the living room was all Papaji needed to begin his prepared speech.

'All we ever wanted was for you to be happy, Jeena,' he began, his attention aimed towards his daughter. 'When you were born, your mother and I promised that we would do whatever it took to give you a life of fulfilment. Something which would have been impossible in India. We were generous with the amount of freedom we gave you. We were extremely lenient with our rules. We just wanted you happy.' He paused. 'And we still do. This is why we accept your marriage to Aaron and this is why we want to make a suggestion. We want all of our relatives to accept your marriage also; we don't want any of the whispering or finger pointing that occurs at family gatherings. So what your mother and I propose is for you and Aaron to have a Sikh wedding and make it official in front of the *Guru Granth Sahib*. Everyone will be invited. And everyone will be forced to accept it.'

Under the Sikh rules marriages not taken in front of the sacred book of the *Guru Granth Sahib* are deemed illegitimate. It was a rule that was really pissing Aaron off at the moment. He wondered if he had enough time to run to the Gills' kitchen, grab hold of a carving knife, inscribe 666 on his skull, then say his devil worshipping priest wouldn't allow it. Probably not.

Jeena could feel Aaron's glare begging her to say NO. 'I think it's a fantastic idea,' said Jeena, feigning enthusiasm, not daring to look Aaron's way. 'It would really prove that we are serious about each other.'

Aaron placed his arm around Jeena's shoulder and gave it a squeeze. 'Serious? Dynamite wouldn't blow us two apart.' He smiled at Papaji. 'What a fabulous idea. Tell you what, why don't you leave the arrangements up to me. I'll book the temple, I'll get the camels in, and I'll sort out the curry. Leave it to me. How does next summer grab you for a wedding date? A full year from now.'

Jeena lodged her elbow in his ribs. 'I think it's better if my dad sorts it out, but thanks for offering, it was sooooo sweet of you.' Her elbow twisted hard.

'I guess you already know that you'll have to wear a bright red turban, Aaron,' JJ said, grinning. 'Then again, it's not like you haven't worn one before, is it?' He turned to Nanaji. 'Remember the yellow turban?'

The room seemed to shrink as an embarrassing silence overwhelmed it. Nanaji stared venomously at Aaron. Yellow used to be her favourite colour – and that wasn't because it matched her teeth.

Maji filled her lungs with a satisfied breath. At last she would see her pretty daughter get married. At last the gods had returned her calls – thank god. Tears of sadness were now tears of joy. A mother without a daughter's wedding to plan is like an oyster without its pearl. And now Jeena had returned to the family, it was time to give that pearl a shine, and more importantly, it was time to go SHOPPING!

'There's that lovely bridal shop in Hunterslea. Bindis & Brides. We'll take a trip down there and have a look at their wedding saris. Your cousin Ravinder used them for her wedding, remember?' Maji had already pushed Aaron off his seat and was sitting next to Jeena now, pen and paper at the ready, dinner all forgotten about. 'We're going to splash out on this wedding. We don't want anyone thinking we're ashamed because you're marrying a white man.'

Aaron excused himself and headed for the bathroom. Large, tidy, clean and pink. Sitting on the closed toilet lid, he began to feel sorry for himself. He knew that Jeena had been put on the spot when her parents had brought up the Sikh wedding. He knew that she had no choice but to go along with everything. But Christ, he couldn't marry her *again*. The only thing keeping him going was the divorce. He had to think quickly, there must be something he could say or do which would change this bad luck around. Apart from squirting shaving foam on his knob and running through their sitting room, naked, swinging his jewels and shouting, 'I'm the best son-in-law you'll ever get,' he couldn't think of anything.

He was stuck with a second wedding just as he was stuck in his first.

He opened the door and . . . and his heart stopped beating. Blocking his way was Nanaji dressed in her white *shalwar kameez*, expressionless and deathly quiet.

'Oh, I was only using the toilet,' Aaron said. 'Erm, I love the soap dish.'

He moved to the left to let her pass. She moved to the right covering his exit. He moved to the right to let her pass and she moved to the left to cover his exit. He was just about to give it one more go when she suddenly bent down, removed her *chappal* from her left foot and then smacked him around the head with it.

'You cock-a-roach,' she hissed, in broken English. 'Jeena beautiful, you a bad man.'

He stared with wide eyes. 'You *can* talk?'

She hit him again, this time in the testicles. 'Bad

man. If you tell them I spoke then I deny.' She locked herself in the bathroom.

And how are you going to deny it without speaking, my little old granny-in-law? he thought, grimacing at the pain in his balls, knowing that there was no point in grassing up the bored biddy to her family as she was obviously only after attention. Holding his nether regions, Aaron returned to the living room where a heavy discussion was in progress. From where Aaron was standing, it appeared that Jeena was being lectured on her wifely duties.

'Do you see how happy your mother and I are today, Jeena?' Papaji continued. 'It's because she looked after me with her good food. Who knows if we would have lasted this long if she never cooked for me or washed and ironed my clothes. Women are good at women jobs. If you want to keep hold of Aaron, then you must learn to act like a wife to him. I was ashamed when he told me that you've never cooked an Indian meal for him. Totally ashamed.'

'He eats a weird diet, Papaji.'

'No excuse, you must learn to cook his "weird" diet.'

Jeena wondered if she were to yank down Aaron's jeans and boxers whether her father would kiss his arse, because that's what things seemed like nowadays. Aaron couldn't do a thing wrong and suddenly the white man who had no morals was the best thing since sliced brown bread.

Chapter Twenty-three

For the next week the climate in Aaron's apartment could only be described as moderate. No wild argumentative storms, no lightning flashes of anger, no sweltering hot nights of passion. Just an uneventful week with possibly a drought of fun.

When Jeena had approached Aaron regarding the Sikh wedding, his reply had been, 'Can we put this subject on hold, please.' She'd asked him, as his wife, whether he would like her to cook him an Indian meal. And his reply had been, 'Could you find out the calorie content of what you might be cooking before I decide. Until then, we'll put the idea on hold.' She'd jokingly asked him if her two rampant lesbian friends could share his bed with him tonight. His reply had been, 'I'll change the sheets. Until then, I'll put my orgasm on hold.'

'I only hope when you've done a number two, Aaron, that you don't put the flush on hold, that's all,' Jeena said, before picking up her car keys. 'Well, I'm off now, and I'm not coming back tonight; I'll be staying at Kitty's.'

It was Saturday evening; Aaron was splayed out on the sofa watching the rugby; Jeena was just about to leave. He pulled his eyes away from the screen to give her a polite farewell and was once again amazed by her ability to alter her style so dramatically. Last week she was the perfect Indian daughter, dressed in traditional clothes and colours, this week she was the perfect party animal, hardly dressed at all in traditional 'fuck me' clothes. Strappy red high heels were the foundation to a wisp of a tight red lace dress, partially see-through, partially fantasy. Her make-up and hair were the result of two hours' work. Only a man of impeccable moral character wouldn't think bad things of her tonight.

'Have a great night,' Aaron said, returning his gaze to the rugby. 'Oh, by the way, don't bother coming back before one tomorrow as I'll have female company.'

Polythene manufacturers had a lot to worry about, thought Aaron as he watched Jeena wiggle towards the front door, because he'd found something more transparent than plastic: Jeena. 'I'm not coming back tonight,' she'd said, 'I'll be staying at Kitty's.' Hogwash. Rubbish. Lies. He remembered an evening spent with Tyler, Sean and Charlie where they'd calculated the minimum amount of material needed to protect the average woman's modesty. This included nipple coverage, bottom crack and bikini area. They came to a figure of twenty-two square inches. Judging by the twenty-six square inches that Jeena seemed to be wearing tonight, it was extremely doubtful that this outfit was meant for Kitty. Pull the other one: it was for a man she'd dressed to impress tonight.

As far as Aaron was aware, the only other man Jeena was involved with was that arsehole called Sam. He'd heard her giggles on the phone to him late at night, PATHETIC! She was welcome to him – in fact, let the arsehole marry her the Sikh way. Let the goon drink the disgusting Indian tea. Let freak face be attacked by Jeena's nan. Let critter head bring a family back together. Let . . .

'Bye, Aaron.' Jeena closed the door behind her.

The summer breeze was enough to goose the skin slightly. Take 1. Jeena jumped in her car and headed for the nearest petrol station to change into the more conservative clothes she'd placed in the boot yesterday. She'd only worn the red slutty dress to get a reaction from Aaron, but alas, there seemed only emptiness behind his eyes. More in keeping with a first date was the trusty black dress, tights and black heels she now stood in. And just for that touch of extra class, she had on a fake diamond necklace. Take 2. This time she really was off to Sam's house. He lived in the village of Hernly just on the outskirts of Primpton. Following the signposts and Sam's clear instructions, Jeena found herself driving deeper and deeper into the thick countryside. Finally, she entered Hernly with its one shop, two pubs, one church and countless cottages. Driving up the small track that led to Sam's place, she parked her Clio next to his swanky Merc. The converted farm house that was his home was huge and imposing. A building this size would seem awfully lonely for just one man.

She sat in her car and twisted off her wedding ring. Right now Jeena could hear the raised voice of her conscience. What was she doing getting mixed up with another man when her life was still such a shambles? If her parents were ever to find out about this, they would have no choice but to disown her for good this time. But there was definitely something she'd seen in Sam which was worth taking a risk. A spark when she'd first met him, a small fire when he talked on the phone, who knew, after tonight he might well have set her life ablaze.

From the enormous front door, the tall figure of Sam leapt down the stone steps and greeted Jeena before she even had a chance to open her car door.

'It's really great to see you again,' Sam said with obvious glee in his eyes. 'Come on, let me show you inside. I apologize in advance for the lack of inspiration in the house but I only moved in a couple of months ago and I haven't had a chance to decorate.'

Jeena had forgotten how handsome Sam was: beautiful dark brown eyes set off his gorgeous face. Medium-length black hair. An athletic body surely capable of many hours of extreme activity in the bed. In not so many words, Sam was a hunky beast that needed taming. Besides all that . . . yes, besides all that, he had a tip-top personality which seemed to be able to make her laugh whenever he wanted to. Besides all that . . . yes, besides all that, he had a sensitive side, believing that monogamy was the only way to maintain a lasting relationship. Jeena rarely liked to score a man with a perfect ten but if ever there was a man who deserved it, then it was Sam.

Inside Jeena was shown into the spacious country-style kitchen: a racing-car-green Aga, thick wooden cupboards, pots and pans hanging from hooks and a chunky oak table in the middle. In one corner, to add a homely flair, two sofas faced each other across a coffee table. All the place needed now was good food and good company. Judging by the wonderful aromas spilling from the oven, the food would be fabulous. Jeena only hoped that her company would match up.

'I love your kitchen,' she remarked, sitting down on one of the sofas. 'It's very friendly, very welcoming.'

Sam poured them both a glass of white wine and sat on the opposite sofa. They chinked glasses and made a toast to a nice evening. As this was their first official date, this would have been the perfect 'small talk' moment. Finding out about each other. Trying to read each other's mind. Marking up each other's score card. But they'd already finished with the small talk by way of the numerous phone calls they'd made to one another when Sam, the computer analyst, was away in Devon on business, debugging some obnoxious computer virus. In fact, small talk had given way to big talk, to filthy talk right the way up to, 'I've never told anyone about this before' kind of talk. Today, Jeena wondered what kind of chat would occur without the safety barrier of a phone line to hide one's embarrassment behind.

'Please don't be angry with me, Jeena but I have a confession to make,' Sam said, gulping down a mouthful of pricey plonk for courage. Her silence was permission to continue. 'Well, after you told me that you were a Sikh I decided to find out more about your religion. As far as I knew, in my ignorance, a Sikh could have meant anything – for all I knew there were certain times in the day when I mustn't phone you, because you would be in prayer.'

'You're mistaking prayer for *EastEnders*.'

He laughed. 'Anyway, I looked up Sikhs on the Internet; bloody good job really because I was going to cook you Beef Wellington tonight.' This time they both laughed. 'Followed by beef ice cream.'

Jeena listened amazed as Sam explained what he had learnt about her culture and religion. Crikey, the man knew more about Guru Nanak, Guru Gobind Singh and Guru Ram Das than she did. But her heart beat quicker with excitement at the prospect of getting to know this man even better. Compared to Aaron, who on finding out that Jeena was a Sikh, came out with his pathetic joke, 'If it happens again tomorrow morning, then you must be pregnant. You're suffering from morning Sikhness, that's all,' Sam was a real gentleman.

A real gentleman with a surplus of talents. Fine cooking being just one of them. Jeena was totally impressed with the food that Sam served up. A succulent duck in plum sauce with a bed of Chinese vegetables along with noodles in a soy, chilli and sesame-seed dressing. Strawberry cheesecake filled up any unused stomach space. It was taste bud rock 'n' roll.

After dinner they moved to the back garden and parked themselves on a cast iron bench facing the hilly countryside which surrounded the farm land. The sun was fading fast, taking with it its heat, inviting the bluey/black of night. Jeena exaggerated her shivering and Sam obliged without a second's thought by placing his arm around her.

The smell of the country fields, the quiet of the country air, it all felt so right and it all felt so romantic. They began to gently kiss, enjoying the excitement of this new relationship, feeling the power of lust burning below the surface. No matter what the outcome of tonight, Jeena knew that this was one of those moments you hung onto as long as you could. For tomorrow it would be gone and the day after you'd wonder if it really had been that special. Sam pulled her up to her feet.

'There is something you should know,' Jeena said, her breathing erratic and heavy. 'I don't want you to have any regrets so this is why I'm confessing to you.'

Sam took hold of both her hands and looked her in the eyes. 'You don't have to tell me anything.'

Oh but I do, thought Jeena. 'That's sweet, really, but I think you should . . .' He put his finger to her lips. '– I think you should know that I'm newly married. Only for the last month though. It's not like we've been married for years or anything.'

He let go of her hands and let his own flop (along with his cock). Sam almost laughed to himself. He had known she was too good to be true. Married. Of all the things. The Internet never mentioned that Sikhs were adulterers, in fact, by all accounts, they were quite the opposite. He saw the sadness behind her false smile. But why wouldn't this beautiful, intelligent woman with everything going for her not have had a thousand offers by now? Her stunning figure, her immaculate, preened appearance, her – he had to say it – amazing large breasts, her one-off personality, her . . . why wouldn't she be married to some lucky man? Surely the gnat-sized mole by her left eyebrow wasn't going to put potential men off?

His last long-term girlfriend, Katy, had had an affair; in her defence she'd said, 'Sam, you're just too nice. I need some bad in my men. Sorry.' It was the worst excuse ever for a woman who, he'd since found out, couldn't say no to cock. Now, here he was with a woman doing the dirty on her own husband. He didn't want to be a party to that – no matter how stiff she'd made him earlier.

A tear trickled down Jeena's cheek. 'I hate him,' she said. 'Why do you think I'm being so honest with you?'

A thought struck Sam squarely in the brain. 'Was it an arranged marriage? I read about those on the Internet. Sikhs have arranged marriages, don't you?'

'It's not an arranged marriage, Sam. It's a sham marriage.'

Sham marriage?

Sam listened as Jeena explained to him about the 'sham' marriage. How she'd been caught in bed with Aaron by her parents. How she'd been forced to make a choice: her way or their way. How Aaron had married her for one year only. The whole story, warts and all.

'I used to have feelings for him but now I realize what a fool I was. There I was sharing him with six or seven other women and all he had to do was click his fingers and I'd come running. I felt so dirty and used. Now not a day goes past without us arguing or bitching at one another.' Jeena took hold of Sam's hand again. 'So, to put it bluntly, if you want our relationship to continue, then you will have to put up with Aaron being in the picture for the next eleven months.'

'And after that?'

'I'm a divorcee. No more Aaron. Get out the celebration fireworks.'

'And has he got feelings for you?' Sam asked, topping up the wine glasses.

A lengthy pause, then, 'He just thinks about himself. Even tonight he's got a woman round for sex. I don't know if he knows how to care for any one woman.'

Women seemed to get more complicated, thought Sam. This one, Jeena, came with about fifty rules. She's married but only for the next eleven months. She can sleep with who she likes but mustn't be seen in public with him. Her parents and family must not know about Sam until the divorce. He was allowed to come to Aaron's/Jeena's apartment but must bear in mind that Aaron was a martial arts expert who must not, repeat, must not be upset. Of course, when in Aaron's/Jeena's apartment, Sam must not, repeat, must not touch anything in case he disturbs the finely balanced Feng Shui of the place.

Although touching Aaron's wife was okay.

After much deliberation on Sam's part, they both agreed to give this romantic partnership a go and sealed the deal with a snog on the bench. With nothing more to say they made their way to Sam's bedroom and rolled around on the bed. Jeena tried hard to shove a vision out of her head as Sam went about trying to light a few candles. If this had been Aaron he wouldn't have bothered with candles, he wouldn't have bothered with a bed, he wouldn't have bothered with taking her upstairs, in fact he would have fucked her senseless on the very bench that they had sat on. For sure, these were two very different men. She stared at Sam's Y fronts. Very, *very* different men.

'Are you positive you want to do this?' Sam said, grabbing a condom from a bedside drawer.

She thought about Aaron who prided himself on the fact that he'd given Jeena eight orgasms in one session. Something was telling her that Sam would be lucky to hit the one.

'Of course I want to do this,' she replied, 'I've been thinking about it all day.'

She felt his eyes glued to her bikini line. He was obviously too polite to mention what he was seeing.

'They're ears,' she said, matter-of-factly.

'Oh,' Sam came in closer, 'I could have sworn it was a love heart.'

Chapter Twenty-four

Unfortunately for Aaron, unlike flu, it was impossible to catch fat off someone. Otherwise the poor woman lying next to his clothed body in bed would have been the first to get the blame. 'I was fine until I met you, the next thing I know I've lost my six-pack. You must be a fat carrier.' But you can't catch fat and the woman lying next to him was a skinny stunner (hardly a fat carrier) and it was the first time that Aaron had made love to a woman in a bed while wearing a T-shirt.

Amy woke up on this fine Sunday morning with the familiar disorientation that all women who sleep around must get when waking up in a different bed virtually every weekend. She peered across her pillow to Aaron who was still fast asleep. Of all the times she'd slept with him, last night had been the only time he'd insisted on turning the lights off and keeping his body covered. For a man with such a fantastic physique, always in shape and normally in a rush to get his kit off, she thought it most odd behaviour. The only thing she could think of was that Aaron was concealing a new tattoo. And judging by the name he kept shouting out in his dreams last night, the tattoo was obviously of a woman called Sam. Maybe it was this Sam who had moved in with him. There was plenty of women's para-phernalia around the apartment. Maybe Sam was Aaron's new live-in totty. Well, as long as this Sam didn't interfere with these out-of-this-world one-night-stand sexathons with hunky Aaron, Amy couldn't care less. She huddled up close and kissed him good morning on the lips. It was time to cook Aaron his breakfast. Her hand shot under the duvet and tried to grab his sausage. To no avail though as Aaron sprung out of bed. His sausage felt like it needed a holiday – Frankfurter would be ideal. Besides, last night had been a real test of stam-ina. Keeping up with Amy's demands was more strenuous than a heavy-duty work-out. In his eyes, the extra ten pounds weight he had put on was definitely interfering with his ability to please a woman in bed. Although there had been no complaints coming from Amy last night. No, last night Amy was just coming.

But the extra ten pounds worried Aaron.

After pointing out his inexplicable weight gain to his doctor, Dr Niap, in the week that Barry White, another love machine like himself, had died because of his weight, Dr Niap reluctantly agreed to take a blood and urine sample to keep Aaron happy. Thyroid func-tions, the onset of diabetes, the state of his cholesterol. The tests came back showing Aaron to be in great health. The doctor had one more suggestion which didn't please Aaron at all. Maybe, said Dr Niap, you're suffering from greed.

The whole world was turning against him. Doctors, mirrors and calories. But why was he gaining weight? Aaron still hadn't a clue. He'd even tightened up his diet and increased his calorie output by way of more aerobics. In fact, he was virtually living off protein shakes and nothing else at the moment. Surely his martial arts destiny wasn't heading for Sumo. The thought of having to wear one of those monstrous nappies, known in the fat trade as *mawashi* sumo pants, repulsed him.

'Do you want to watch me take a shower?' Amy asked, sliding out of bed naked. 'Better still, why not join me.'

Two weeks ago wild horses wouldn't have kept Aaron from a twosome shower. But now, when he was sure that parts of his body 'wobbled', he took a rain check and quickly helped Amy out of the apartment – keen to avoid any more of her sexual innuendoes. As soon as he'd shut the door behind her, Aaron jogged across the room (burning up more calories) and, while jogging on the spot, he rubbed off ONLY 334 DAYS UNTIL D DAY from the wipe board, replacing it with: ONLY 333 DAYS UNTIL D DAY. He then jogged to the kitchen area to make himself a chocolate protein-shake breakfast.

'Thank god, for these,' he said out loud. 'Yummy, nutritious and best of all, hardly any calories.' He turned the pot over and smiled. 'Yep, just *seventy* calories per serving.'

He dropped to the floor and did fifty sit-ups.

Sipping on his shake, Aaron wandered over to the office area and checked out his e-mails. Usual spiel, adverts for Viagra, limited edition penis pumps, more adverts for Viagra and a few requests for information packs regarding the Paper Lantern. Mary, his assistant, was a star when it came to keeping the e-mails up-to-date. Her do or die attitude to getting the job done always left him with more time to concentrate on other aspects of the business i.e. one-on-one training sessions for advanced members and diet plans for advanced waistlines.

Aaron picked up a wad of diet sheets he still had to calculate for some of his overweight members and set about working out the details. In time his eyes caught sight of Medusa's Head chugging past on the River Wes and Aaron waved just as he always did on Sundays. And like he always did on Sundays, the skipper waved back; this time in the company of a young boy, who Aaron guessed to be his grandson. What an adventure that must be for a lad all of ten-years old. Would his granddad reel off tales of pirates, or bandits smuggling liquor and gold? Would the boy imagine himself as captain of the ship or even Nelson? Whatever the story, it had Aaron back in yesteryear wondering about all he had missed out on in his life without his own dad. How he wished he could have grown up with a father figure in his life. Not that his dear gran hadn't tried to be some sort of role model, but baking cakes and knitting scarves were not in the same league as fixing car engines or building go-carts.

Oh why didn't his parents decide to leave the house ten minutes later that awful day. Aaron could still see their faces clearly as they bid him farewell in the hallway when he left for school. 'Mind the roads,' Dad had warned, like he always had. Ironic, that. Just ten minutes later and they would have missed the lorry which took their lives. Ten minutes and maybe, just maybe, they might have been alive today.

Aaron shook his head in disbelief: sometimes he couldn't believe that he'd spent so much of his life without them in person. Yet in spirit they were with him all the time. Aaron could feel the ghostly presence of his conscience gently pushing him to open the package his mother had left him twenty years ago. But what if he read something which upset him? What if there was something which changed his opinion of his mother and father for the worse? What if his mother told him something he didn't want to know? What if . . .

After an hour spent pacing his bedroom, eyeing the parcel on his bed, weighing up the pros and cons, Aaron decided that he was not quite ready to peel back the years and stare into the past. With a sense of guilt as heavy as the safe, Aaron replaced the package and slammed the safe door shut in relief. At least he had no one to explain his actions to because he knew he wouldn't have been able to if given the chance. He turned his head to face the framed letter from his *sensei* which hung above his bed. The letter, written in Japanese, spoke of his pride in his pupil. Knowing that his *sensei* lived by the saying: strive for honesty and truth, Aaron reflected ruefully that his *sensei* would be downright disgusted at him now.

After a quick chat on the phone to Tyler, they arranged to meet at the snooker hall in town. Aaron felt like an afternoon of brainless ball potting after a night of something similar. Picking through his casual wear in his wardrobe, Aaron was drawn to his old school blazer which was oddly half falling off its hanger. He held the garment out in front of him and stared at the blood stains still visible on the jacket's collar. The only reason he'd kept hold of the darn thing was to remind him of the pain the bullies had once inflicted on him. *What fucking use is it now,* he thought bitterly, throwing it on the floor. *I don't need a jacket to remember that I was once a helpless victim of bullies.* He glared down at the rumpled blazer, just like the bullies had glared down at him all those years ago. Sticking out of the inside pocket, the corner of a piece of paper was easily visible. Knowing immediately what the paper was, Aaron bent down to inspect it. A short poem which he'd written to himself at the age of eleven, in a science lesson, when things had got especially bad at school. Aaron opened the folded sheet and scanned his eyes down the scruffy writing:

My Punishment
They punish me for having no mum
They punish me for having no dad
And I haven't got my parents to punish me
for the punishments I should never have had.

It was right here and now that Aaron decided that, despite what he'd discussed with his mates, there would be no point in confronting Darryl Fletcher or any of the other bullies again. It made no sense to waste time on a bunch of wasters. It made no sense to go hunting for a gang of imbeciles to teach them a physical lesson when the problem was a mental one inside his head. And it certainly made no sense to look back on his life and see himself as a coward, when no kid, no matter how tough, would have been able to stand up to a beating dished out by nine bullies.

Feeling slightly lethargic with melancholy, Aaron plodded out to the bathroom, stripped off and stood under the hot hose of the power shower using whatever was at hand to cover his body in bubbles: Jeena's Dior Addict perfumed shower gel. Unfortunately for Jeena, the gel cost a small fortune and she would only use a small dab of the stuff on very special occasions. Unfortunately for Aaron he'd squirted over three quarters of the bottle on himself and now smelt like a tart in a whorehouse. He was just about to squirt the remaining Dior Addict perfumed shower gel on his feet, when he had a terrifying thought: had he securely locked the safe door? As if the shower water had turned to burning acid, Aaron shot out of the cubicle and strode out towards his bedroom leaving puddles of water behind him.

Only to bump into Jeena who had just arrived back home from Sam's.

'Where's the fire?' Jeena asked, looking down at Aaron's hosepipe. 'Or is it Mr Wet T-shirt competition and you forgot to wear a T-shirt?' She laughed at her own joke. 'Seriously, why are you running around soaking wet? Isn't it bad Feng Shui?'

Aaron grabbed her handbag to cover his privates. 'If you must know, Amy just left; she always leaves me this soaking.'

Jeena studied Aaron's body. He was definitely putting on weight. His once sharp six-pack had lost much of its definition. His once perfectly tight body had more –

erm, how could she describe it – marshmallow? about it. Although, luckily for him, his face appeared untouched by this invasion of soft tissue. A smile crept over her face as she told herself not to mention his weight. NOT TO MENTION HIS WEIGHT. NOT TO . . .

'Have you put on weight, Aaron, you seem, a little tubbier?' She winced. 'Just a little bit.'

'That's right. I'm bulking up,' he replied. 'It's totally deliberate. Everything is under control. I won't be needing the number to Fat Club just yet, Jeena, but thanks for your concern.' He scrutinized her dishevelled appearance. 'So, wife, did you have sex last night?' *with that tosser* 'You've got that windswept-glazed-eyes-knickers-on-quick look about you.'

'Yes I did. And you, my husband, did you have sex last night? Only you've got that pleased-with-yourself-smug-I'm-the-best-in-the-world look about you.' She snatched her handbag away from his jewels. 'Only you're not the best in the world, are you, Aaron? Sam is.' She walked off, happy that she had managed to get one up on him for a change.

She thought back to the disappointingly fumbling half orgasm that Sam had given her last night. Not quite the best in the world, but, with lots of practice (and a few erogenous zone charts) he could only get better. Jeena looked forward to practising with Sam because, although he might not be so great under the sheets, everything else about him was grade A.

What a fantastic weekend it had been so far.

Quite the opposite, in fact, of Jeena's father's weekend. Throughout most of Saturday Papaji had been worried about how he was going to explain to his brother, Gurjinder, in India, that they'd accepted the white man, Aaron, into their family. Even at the temple this morning, his mind had been in spasm, stressed to the maximum about how this news would be received in his motherland. He could present the news on a nice plate, dress it up with fine salad and smother it in tempting sauce, but at the end of the day, the problem would remain. Would his old-fashioned brother be able to digest the bitter taste of white meat in his family? Papaji's blood ran cold just thinking about it.

He climbed the stairs to his office and switched off the burglar alarms. When the business Bills & Gills was in its infancy, many a lonely Sunday would Papaji work into the late hours, building up his client base, strengthening his mini-empire. Hard work translated easily to high success. High success brought with it inner-belief. And as his father used to say, give inner belief to an Indian man and he can do anything.

Sitting at his desk, Papaji knew he could put off the inevitable no longer. With a sweaty hand he dialled his brother's shop, Gill's Fashion Wonderland in New Delhi, and waited for the line to connect. Papaji prayed that business had been good lately at Gill's Fashion. His brother was always more amenable when his till rattled with rupees.

'*Sat sri akal ji*,' greeted Papaji in Punjabi.

'*Sat sri akal ji*,' greeted Gurjinder in response.

More than a billion conversations start this way in India every single day. Some are great conversations, better than poetry, others just tittle-tattle, gossip and time fillers. But some are dark and bristling with sin.

Like the father who discusses with his cousin the honour killing of his unmarried daughter (because she was spotted laughing with a man). Or the son who complains to his parents that his wife is too lazy and would it be possible to have her burnt alive so he could remarry. Or even the brother in India who advises his brother in England to kidnap his own daughter and teach her white husband a lesson or two.

'I am not kidnapping my own daughter, brother; this is not some backward village in the Punjab. They have police here and forensics and prison. Men are treated equally here, brother, we don't get special privileges.' Papaji sighed down the phone. 'Anyway, as I mentioned, things have changed dramatically since I last spoke to you. You'd be surprised how decent this husband of Jeena's is. Very surprised.'

But Gurjinder didn't care about any of that. Aaron was white, he was wrecking his family and something had to be done about it. How would their forefathers react if they were to find out that their blood was being diluted down by the very same bunch of scoundrels who had tried to steal India from them in the past? Now his brother, Preetjeet, was talking of a Sikh wedding where this white man would be invited into one of their temples, sit in front of the sacred book, the *Guru Granth Sahib*, and after marrying Jeena the Sikh way he would officially become part of the Sikh community. This was not going to happen. Not when there was still Indian air in his lungs.

'I warn you to tread very carefully, brother,' Gurjinder continued. 'You know my feelings on this and yet you still wish to ignore me. Is she pregnant yet?'

'No.'

'You do not have my blessing on this wedding.' And the line went dead.

Gill's Fashion was now the theatre to a man with wild anger in his eyes. Amongst the vibrant colours of silk saris and the sparkling of the beads, Gurjinder paced up and down the shop floor, muttering to himself. His brother, Preetjeet, had become weak, his strength stolen by a British Empire with no morals. His niece, Jeena had lost all respect for Indian values, running wild and mocking her traditional upbringing. It was time that something was done.

Gurjinder picked up the phone again and within seconds he was making arrangements for his elder son to look after his shop during the coming months. How long the trip to England was going to take, he didn't know, but one thing was for sure, he wasn't going to travel 10,000 miles to come back empty handed.

And as for this Aaron, this thief of Indian culture – well, let's see how brave he really was when faced with the inter-village wrestling champion of Vishakhapatnam.

Chapter Twenty-five

A hot August evaporated away to be replaced by an even hotter September. Primpton folk joked that if the climate continued as it was then the council would soon be adding Costa Del to the Primpton sign. Even the annual 'women against shaving' march was being put on hold through fear that some of the more hairy members might suffer heatstroke. Summer just didn't want to end.

Throughout August, as the wipe board continued to be wiped, as the countdown to the divorce continued to be monitored, a sense of rhythm had crept into Jeena's life. Over the past five weeks her relationship with Sam had gone through the gear changes. The more time she spent with him the less time she wanted apart. They'd taken a romantic trip to Paris where, under the spell of the city, she found herself wondering if this was how love was supposed to be. She'd even sent Aaron a postcard from Paris to tell him how her love for Sam had blossomed.

Of course, Aaron had ripped up the card and stuffed

it in the recycling container, hoping, ironically, that the postcard would be recycled as the piece of paper confirming that their divorce had been granted. It couldn't come soon enough. On one side of the coin he was pretending to Jeena's parents that everything was hunky dory, even having them over for a meal last week, moving Jeena's clothes into his bedroom to add authenticity to the sham marriage, playing happy families, ignoring the 'mute' Gran Monster's constant glares, acting like the biggest prick in the world. On the other side of the coin he was putting up with Jeena's relentless drooling over this spud of a man called Sam, who – and Aaron still couldn't believe Jeena's cheek – had stayed the night . . . in his own apartment mind . . . while he had had to lie in bed listening to them pretending they knew how to have sex. Pathetic! 'I think I'm cumming, Jeena.' *You're either cumming or you're not, there shouldn't be any thought about it.* SPUD! After bumping into Spud on the morning after the so-called sex extravaganza, Aaron eyed him sympathetically. 'Don't worry, she'll finish herself off with a vibrator when you've gone. Coffee?'

To which Sam replied, 'Don't be so crude, that's my girlfriend you're talking about.'

To which Aaron responded, 'And that's my wife you're fucking – or should I say, "trying" to.'

The wipe board said ONLY 297 DAYS UNTIL D DAY.

So used to reading the board each morning and using it like a calendar, when a woman at work asked Jeena what the date was, she automatically replied, 'Oh, it's 297 days until my . . . never mind.' By a quick calculation, that meant that Jeena had been married to Aaron for sixty-eight days. Enough time for the moon to go round the Earth twice and more than enough time for Jeena to go round the bend. Although in this establishment, because the boss presumed he was the centre of the universe, he thought everyone should revolve around him. An e-mail popped up on Jeena's computer screen demanding that she go through to Mr Akhtar's office immediately. Surely not another pay drop, worried Jeena, as she walked through in her long-sleeved T-shirt, trousers and flat shoes. Or in Kitty's words, 'Get-a-life-wear.' It was so demeaning.

'Sit down, Mrs Myles, and complete the form in front of you,' Mr Akhtar ordered, with spite still in his eye.

Jeena checked over the two-sided form. Another questionnaire for his security files no doubt. For the umpteenth time Jeena began to write down the details required. Next of kin, family names and addresses, friends' names and addresses, blood type and any medical conditions. She queried why he would need her friends' details.

'In case we can't contact your *gorrah* husband,' he replied. 'Just fill in the form and hand it back to me. Everyone is doing it, you're not so special, Mrs Myles.'

So she filled in the form and departed his office. Each day Jeena would ask herself why she still worked here at *Asian Delight* and each day her empty purse would provide the answer. But gloom and doom would soon be a thing of the past thanks to the string of job interviews she'd attended in the last few weeks, as in just two months time she would be starting a new full-time job working for the local newspaper as a journalist. Her first story, she hoped, would headline: HOW I GOT MR AKHTAR TO KISS MY ARSE GOODBYE.

Sitting back down at her desk, Jeena was about to continue with her task of looking looking for double words in the typescript typescript of her latest article: WHY ASIAN WOMEN ARE HITTING THE BOTTLE, when her only office friend, Nina, pulled up a chair and wheeled herself in next to her.

'Have you seen Akhtar's latest sign?' Nina pointed to the wall:

UNLESS YOU TAKE YOUR WORK HOME WITH YOU DON'T BRING YOUR HOME LIFE INTO WORK

'Bloody cheek,' fumed Jeena. 'He's the one who wants to know everything about our home life. I'm sure if he had his way he'd be asking us for details on our time of the month.'

Nina giggled. 'He'll type into his Menstrual Data Base and work out when we're not on PMT and then he'll ask us to do overtime without fear of a hormone-induced bashing.' She ignored the exaggerated coughing of a displeased colleague at the desk in front and continued chatting to Jeena. 'So, when do I get to meet Mr Aaron Myles? How about I come round one evening? Give your place the once over, and your hubby of course.'

Time for a good excuse, thought Jeena. He's got measles? No. He's too busy? No. He's too shy? No. What about the truth: we're not talking to each other any more unless it's to insult one another. In fact, things are so bad in the apartment right now that any communication is done by text message. Only last night, Sunday evening, while sitting next to Aaron on the couch (a concession which Jeena was proud of), he'd sent her a text which read: *U R making 2 much noise with your crisps. Quieten down I'm trying 2 watch TV.*

She replied: *U R making 2 much noise breathing. Plse STOP. P.S. Since when did U like* Songs of Praise?

He'd texted back with: *Since I started praying 2 God 2 give me a way out of this sham marriage quickly, wife!*

'I'll see when he's free and we'll arrange something,' Jeena said, fobbing her friend off. 'But he's so busy at the moment that he's hard to pin down.'

A bit like Jeena's feelings at this very second: hard to pin down. It was all about Sam and Aaron. She remembered getting roped into a game with JJ when she was younger called Top Trumps. A simple card game where one person beats another person by having a card with a higher specification, i.e., a Rolls Royce would beat a Cortina. Or the Hulk would beat Spiderman. If Sam and Aaron were Top Trumps, she wondered who would come out on top. On most of the specifications Sam and Aaron were equal. Great personalities, great ambitions, great lookers, great sense of humour. On kindness Sam came out on top. In the bedroom Aaron came out on top, and underneath and sometimes even upside down. On who made her feel special, Sam did. On who made her feel weak at the knees, Aaron did. On who would protect her, Sam would try, Aaron would succeed. On whom there was a future with, Sam. On whom she wanted a future with . . .

And this Aaron, this bloody, stubborn, arrogant

Aaron. The man who had made it clear he wanted nothing to do with her after the year was up, the man she couldn't help but think about as her countdown to D Day continued. Even in Paris, while Sam was trying his best to whisk her off her feet with snails and romance, she was sneaking into the en-suite bathroom and writing a postcard to Aaron. In bed Jeena couldn't help but compare Sam to Aaron. A doctor might have diagnosed that Jeena hadn't got Aaron out of her system yet. And most women who'd had sex with Aaron might respond, 'Once you've tried caviar then scampi just won't do.'

The question was: could Jeena put up with scampi in the bedroom, along with a life of sweet happiness? Or did she still hope for caviar, along with a life of uncertain broken dreams?

As if the waters weren't muddy enough, looming like a grey storm was this Sikh wedding, which Jeena's parents were so keen to organize. Jeena's request that she would prefer to have the wedding in the summer of next year rather than the dreary winter months as her parents were planning was treated with suspicion until Jeena explained, with all the literary skills she could muster, that she'd always dreamed of marrying in front of her loving parents while the heavenly yellow blaze of the sun shone down, while the angelic singing of the birds cast their acceptance of this marriage with a chorus of perfect notes, while the intoxicating smell of summer flowers weaved their magic amongst the happy guests. But beyond all that, imagine Aaron's face as he set his eyes upon the bride of his dreams, dressed in lavish red and gold splendour, as the sun blessed them with its shine and heartbeats became still. 'Imagine it, Maji, Papaji, just imagine.'

'Basically,' Aaron had said, snorting at her description, 'she doesn't want to look like a drowned rat. You know what the British winter weather is like, it's so unpredictable. So, next summer seems ideal.' *And by next summer*, Aaron told himself, *you'll have a divorcee daughter on your hands and I . . . will be free.*

Reluctantly Jeena's parents agreed to the summer wedding, but had made it clear that they would much rather have had the marriage arranged for this year. 'We've got nothing to hide from gossiping relatives anymore,' Papaji had said.

Oh but we have, thought Jeena and Aaron. *We bloody well have.*

Jeena returned to the *Asian Delight* article she was working on. It was hard to believe that there was a whole new booze culture amongst the young Asian women in Britain today. Once, alcohol had been the property of men within the Asian households. But nowadays it was because of the men that Asian women had resorted to taking to the bottle. Maybe looking forward to a tipple took away some of the boredom of slaving away for the whole day. Maybe tipping a four-pack down their throats before going to bed was enough to make the man (who their parents found so attractive) seem less like the hair-bear beast he was when sober. Jeena read through a line or two of the article, remembering how sad the Pakistani woman had appeared when she was being interviewed: *My drinking got so bad that I began to add vodka daily to my bowl of lentils with the vague hope that it would cushion me*

343

from the horrible verbal attacks my husband would launch upon me most nights. It helped, but not a lot.

It was here that Jeena decided once and for all that she should never take her journalism into the field of TV. Many journalists dream of being newsreaders, but Jeena was sure, if ever given the chance, a typical news item read by her might sound something like this: 'Good evening, welcome to the six o'clock news. A man has been arrested for assaulting his wife . . . *serves the bastard right. Boil his testicles in hot tar, I say.* Also tonight: serial rapist Damian Foster has been given early parole . . . *lock him up for ever, I say. Throw away the key* . . . And now to the weather.' Women always seemed to bear the brunt of men's anger. She wondered if women were physically stronger whether things would be different. Maybe it wouldn't hurt some of them to take up self-defence classes, like Aaron offered at the Paper Lantern.

Oh, here she was thinking of Aaron again.

Taking a sly look up and down the office, Jeena pulled from her handbag a copy of an e-mail which Flora had passed onto her a couple of days ago. It was a response to the Friends Reunited website:

Hi Aaron,
You probably don't remember me but I was
in your English class. How time has flown. It
only seems like yesterday when we were in that
wonderful uniform we all had to wear. Although,
if I am truthful, you did wear it well, the cutest
set of knees in the school any day. (And the
cutest face I might say). It may sound strange but
I often think about you. Your lovely gran, who I

bumped into in Sainsbury's a few months back, kindly filled me in on your successful business. Well done! I don't think many in our year have done that well for themselves. I'm so glad you made something of your life. If anyone deserves success than it's you. There were a few times in school where I saw things going on with you and that horrible Fletcher Gang which made me cry. I just wanted to be brave enough to walk across the school field and hug you. But brave was one thing I was not back then. Unlike you. You just took it day in and day out. No one should have to deal with that pain – especially after losing your parents at such a young age . . . do you know, Aaron, I must have been walking around with this for a long time as I feel so much better now I've told you. Anyway, it would be great to see you. I don't know if you've heard but there is a school reunion the week before Christmas. It would be great to hook up. I understand if you don't come, I doubt meeting the Fletcher Gang would be top of your list of to dos.

E-mail me if you get the chance. If not, take care of yourself, Aaron.

Love Annabel Parry (If you still haven't worked out who I am, I'm the one who asked Miss Wallis if she was wearing edible knickers as they smelt like fishcakes. I'm a lot less crude nowadays).

Hugs and kisses.

Jeena felt just as miserable reading it this time as she had the first time. There's an old saying: 'He that pries into every cloud, may be stricken with a thunderbolt.' And Jeena had now received her first whack of lightning. Whatever she had been expecting to find in Aaron's past was certainly not this. God no. More like a string of ex-girlfriends ripping shreds out of Aaron for breaking their hearts. More like some amazing tales from fellow male pupils beginning, 'Do you remember when we set fire to . . .' or, 'Do you remember getting totally wasted on cider on the school trip to France?' With tears in her eyes, Jeena stared at the line on the e-mail, 'You just took it day in and day out'. She certainly had not expected to dig up a life which was buried in pain. Flora and Jeena had discussed the e-mail at great length, both feeling positively awful for sniffing around in the backyard of Aaron's childhood. Both deciding that their snooping days were over – another thunderbolt might just give them one shock too many.

Now it was making sense to Jeena why Aaron refused to talk about his past and why he had taken up martial arts. There was no riddle, just a man with too much pride to open up and confess to a childhood steeped in bullying and pain. It was so frustrating. She so wanted him to confide in her, to trust her, to lay his life bare. Yet, it was never going to happen. She'd never get to know the real Aaron, the man she was sure she would love indiscriminately if she did.

Chapter Twenty-six

It was a well known fact that pandas don't have sex that often, Aaron was told by the doctor when he'd rung up the hospital enquiring about his lack of sex drive. It took the doctor a further twenty minutes to explain that no – unlike the earlobe when one has not put an earring in it for a while – the urethra tube will not seal itself up if unused by sperm for a while (besides, one uses it for urinating). The doctor also advised Aaron not to use the Viagra he'd ordered from the Internet. He was too young and if he was overweight he might stress out his heart.

Thanks a lot, doc.

Aaron was under the impression that the extra two stone of weight he'd gained would put women off him in the bedroom. And the thought that women would be put off was putting him off. He was even having trouble getting it up to masturbate these days. Admittedly, since cutting out his protein shakes and dairy products ten days ago and upping the aerobics the weight was coming back down; and at the current rate of fat loss he should have returned to his normal weight in just two weeks time.

It was a mystery why he'd put on the pounds in the first place. Even more mysterious was how people managed to enjoy the rabbit food he was forcing himself to eat to regain his six-pack. But in the name of sexual science he was prepared to do anything.

He bit into another mouthful of dried banana and dedicated it to a minute's worth of future foreplay. This morning he'd been busy working out a new class to introduce to the weekly schedule now that he'd dissolved Fight to Unite. It was pointless holding on to the slimmed down class when he had a huge waiting list of keen non-Asian students desperate to join. No doubt a few hot headed Pakistani guys would interpret the move as racist, but, in business, you can't please 'em all. Now, what to call this new class. A list of ideas came to mind: Block It Like Bruce. NO! Erm. Bish Bosh Bash. NO! Erm. The Harder They Come The Harder They Fall. Too long. Erm. Stay Alive (Or Die Trying). Hmm, maybe. Aaron was about to see how Stay Alive looked blown up on the computer screen when a loud knock at the front door interrupted him.

Even before Aaron got to the door he could smell who had arrived. He opened it to be greeted by a sweaty man clutching a huge bunch of flowers sniffing like he had hay fever.

'Jeena Myles?' the man queried.

'Am I wearing a dress? Do I look like a Jeena?' Aaron grabbed the cellophane-wrapped bouquet and signed for it. 'Sorry about my manners, it's just that some bastard is sending flowers to my wife again. It really pisses me off.' He slammed the door shut and threw the bouquet on the dining-room table. 'Spud Arsehole.'

But boy did Spud Arsehole have good taste. A beautiful display of flowers in many different shades of pinks. The kind of bouquet that someone would send to the Prime Minister if they wanted to creep. Something Peter Mandelson would probably choose. Aaron sat on the sofa staring at the flowers with contempt. He knew Jeena was going to love them and that really ticked him off.

Returning to his office work, he decided on the new name for his martial-arts class. He smiled as he wrote it down. It was so apt. He would call it, How To Kill The Flower Sender class. SpudArse!

What annoyed Aaron about Sam was that he did everything right. It was as though he was following the *Idiots Guide to Dating*. Aaron was pretty sure that Sam was so straight that he'd never even gone through a red light. But to get to a woman's soul, Aaron thought, you had to go through many red lights. It was no use playing safe and calculating the next move. Chocolates, Paris, then flowers. Where was the spontaneity in that? It was all so predictable. All clueless men did that sort of thing. Exciting romances thrived on impulse not on the dreary cogs of perfect timing. Sam was definitely not the man Jeena should be thinking of spending her future with. Because the Jeena Aaron knew liked to bathe in the waters of chaos. He doubted that this Sam would know that Jeena liked it rough sometimes – clothes ripped off, gutter language in full flow, filthy requests and even filthier positions. No, Sam would be a gentleman to a T. 'I beg your pardon, Jeena, but would you mind awfully if I were to become aroused when you undress in front of me?' Yeah, Sam would be the ultimate boring gentleman. SPUD.

He was about to hunt for a vase big enough for a small forest, when, yet again there was a knock at the door. 'Not more flowers,' grumbled Aaron, tossing the bouquet in the sink. He would really lose respect for this Sam if he'd sent her two bunches.

Alas, no more flowers, just an old flame.

Standing in the doorway, dressed in a tight, printed mini-skirt, almost see-through shirt and bare legs in crocodile boots was Stacy Carter. 'Please have sex with me' was written all over her sultry-looking face. Although Aaron assumed that all beautiful women had that written over their faces when standing near him. He kissed Stacy on her sweet-smelling cheek and beckoned her inside. Quite understandably, seeing as though it had been five weeks since his last bedroom adventure, he had a chisel of a hard-on.

'Surprised?' Stacy beamed. 'I've come to tell you that I am now *out* of love with you. So, if you want to pick up where we left off ten weeks and one day ago, then I'm more than willing.' She stepped towards him and wrapped her arms around him. 'Ooh, pleased to see me?' she said, gyrating her groin against his. 'You look great and you feel great.'

Women like Stacy were known as circuit breakers to Aaron. Their full-on power and pumped-up sex drive was enough to blow most men's wires. In fact, it wouldn't be too far off the mark to say that most men were scared of Stacy; the words, 'bunny boiler' often being used to describe her. Even after Aaron had dumped her (for falling in love with him) those ten weeks and one day ago he had been expecting retaliation of some sort. A late night death threat perhaps or 'I'm going to kill myself, Aaron, if you don't take me back' bribe. Or even a streak jumping over the Embassy World snooker table with MARRY ME AARON MYLES painted on her bare buttocks. But nothing. Not a sausage.

He pulled her by the hand into the living area and they sat down on the sofa. 'You can't just turn relationships back on with a flick of a switch, Stacy,' Aaron began, wondering how to cushion-wrap his sentences. 'If it was that easy no one would divorce.'

'I'm not talking about a relationship, Aaron, I'm just talking about us continuing where we left off. Having sex. Having fun. No strings attached. I've told you already that I don't love you, and I'm willing to share you with other women. Is that so bad?' She cast him a sympathetic eye. 'And I kind of like the new look. You seem more sexy this way.'

He sat bolt up right in his seat. 'WHAT NEW LOOK?'

When Aaron had opened the door to her, Stacy had been disappointed with the weight gain Aaron had attained in the fifty-one days since she'd swapped his protein powders around. She'd been expecting him to blow up big, like John Prescott; she'd been expecting to see a man with a triple chin and stomach to his ankles. In fact she was kind of hoping that Aaron had grown so fat that he couldn't leave the apartment – because he couldn't fit out of the apartment door. Lastly, she'd expected his shallow wife to have left him because he wasn't attractive anymore. Alas, the wife was still here (the magazines and chocolates on the coffee table were proof of that) and Aaron still looked pretty damn impressive (even with the bonus weight). What a flop of a plan.

'The American look.'

He glared at her scornfully. 'I'm not that fucking fat.' And lifted up his top to prove it. 'See, you can still see my six-pack.'

Stacy stared more at his purple face than at his six-pack as he squeezed for his life to push out something that used to be there all the time. Admittedly the six-pack hadn't completely packed up and gone. In fact, most men (and women) would have been pleased with the body he'd kept hidden away lately. But Stacy wasn't like most women and she could sense that this meeting was going terribly wrong. It was supposed to have ended up in the bedroom. Aaron was supposed to have been so desperate for sex that he jumped on her the moment she walked in. He was supposed to have whispered in her ear, 'Stacy, you're the only woman who likes me for what I am. All the other women think I'm too fat. I know we can make a go of this.'

Right now the only thing Stacy was making a go of was pissing Aaron off. She watched him, in his boxers now, angrily pulling all sorts of poses to prove that he was still in shape.

'What about this one, hey Stacy? Still think I'm fat?' Aaron said, jumping to the floor and doing the splits. He rolled over and leaped up in the air. 'How about this, Stacy, could a fat man do this?' He high kicked and spun around to face her, finishing off with a flurry of martial arts moves.

'Look, what I meant was . . .' Stacy began, tears welling up in her eyes.

But Aaron was still busy contorting his body into various painful-looking positions and declaring, 'I doubt a fat person could do that!' Things were not going well at all.

Finally the exhibition was over and Aaron stood sweating in front of her. By this time Stacy's tears were in full flow. Something told her that she'd never win Aaron back now. She got up to leave.

'I apologize for my behaviour,' Aaron said, humbly, chucking on his clothes. 'I think I might have got a bit carried away there, I'm just a little bit sensitive about my weight at the moment, that's all.' He walked across and hugged her. 'Look, I'm really flattered that you still think I'm worth bonking but, sometimes it's best to let sleeping dogs lie, if you know what I mean?'

Through glistening pupils she stared into his blue eyes. 'So, it's definitely over then?'

'Afraid so.'

Niagara Falls now had a worthy challenger. Stacy Falls. It took Aaron completely off-guard how upset she had become and he racked his brains to think of something to do or say which would stem her waterworks.

'Hang on, I've got a surprise that I want to give you,' Aaron said at last, unclasping her hands from his back. 'I was going to place them around the apartment for good Feng Shui, but, under the circumstances, I feel they would be better suited if you had them.'

Trotting out to the kitchen, he looked in the sink at the huge bouquet of flowers Sam had sent Jeena. The question was should he give Stacy a half or three quarters of them. It's not like Jeena would know any different. Aaron decided on about three quarters and shook off the excess water. He then held the stalks together with an elastic band and smiled to himself at the result. Stacy should love them.

And she did.

'They are the most gorgeous, pretty flowers I have ever received,' she cried, sniffing the fine perfume. 'This heals my pain totally.'

'Great,' said Aaron, pushing her gently towards the front door. 'Make sure you use the feed that comes with them or they'll die too quick.' He opened the door, pecked her on the cheek and said, 'Take care of yourself, Stacy. And always remember, it was fun while it lasted.' He nearly puked at his last comment as he shut the door behind her in relief.

If someone were to have followed Stacy out of the car park and about fifty yards up the road, they would have seen a bunch of pink flowers being lobbed out of the car window on to the tarmac below. If someone were to have been able to listen inside Stacy's mind, they would have heard her saying, 'If I can't have Aaron then nor can anyone else. It's time to have some fun with his wife. SOON.'

Back in the apartment Aaron was arranging the remaining flowers in a small vase. He hadn't realized quite how many flowers he'd given to Stacy. He counted them again and sure enough he'd only left eight for Jeena. It was hard to make eight look good no matter how tiny the vase was. In some ways it was like trying to cover a bald spot with just a few strands of hair. He wondered if he had enough time to pop down to the nearest florist and buy in some desperately needed replacements. At a guess, to bring the bouquet back to its original volume, he needed at least fifty more. He picked up his car keys and opened the front door.

Only to bump into Jeena. They both stood in the doorway texting each other.

The text from Jeena to Aaron arrived first: *U R only going out cos U knew I was due home from work. Toss Pot.*

The text from Aaron to Jeena said: *Oh great, it's U. Lucky me.*

Jeena gently thumped him on the arm, then barged through. She was nearly up to talking speed with her texting abilities and would soon be on a par with the teenagers. Although at least the teenagers had the sense to text people who were more than a few metres away. It was costing Jeena a small fortune just to communicate with her husband in the same frigging room.

She was about to head to her bedroom when her husband decided to speak to her. 'Someone has sent you some flowers.' He pointed to the pathetic-looking vase standing on the dining-room table. 'I put them in water for you.'

Jeena dropped her handbag and marched to the table. She remembered a documentary on TV about this crop of wheat that had been decimated by a swarm of locusts, leaving only a few spindly sticks standing. It wasn't so different from what was stuck in the vase. A small card lay beside it and Jeena opened the envelope to read the words inside:

Dear Jeena,
Just a little something to thank you for the
wonderful time we had in Paris. You are one hell
of a woman and I am one hell of a lucky guy to
have you.
Sam XXX

'Bit of a stingy bastard, isn't he?' Aaron said. 'I take it that the eight limp flowers are from Sam? Having money troubles, is he?'

'If you must know, Aaron, he gave me eight flowers because we had sex eight times in Paris.' Jeena felt both annoyed with Aaron and elated with Sam's message – even though the flowers were a little bit on the scarce side. 'I think it's romantic.'

'It's a fucking good job I don't have to give a flower for each orgasm I give a woman or we'd have to mow up half of Holland, wouldn't we?' He chuckled. 'I suppose though, that by giving you such a small bunch of flowers to begin with, he won't find it hard to top, will he?'

Enough was enough. Jeena was sick of the smarmy remarks and sly digs. It was time for a few home truths. She strode confidently right up to Aaron and looked him directly in the eye.

'And when was the last time you bought flowers for a woman? When was the last time you put a woman's feelings before your own? I doubt you've even sent a birthday card, or a Christmas card or even a Valentine card, because I certainly didn't receive one from you. You live in this selfish little world which you've concocted for yourself where you criticize everyone and everything and yet what do you do yourself? Nothing. In the world of romance you're a bum, a loser and a waste of women's time. To be honest, and this may sound like a cliché, but I wonder what I ever saw in you. Really, I sometimes think I must have been mad to get myself mixed up with a cretin like Aaron Bruce Lee Myles. To share you with other women. What was I thinking?' Her eyes were filled with rage. 'All you give to a woman is an orgasm and, believe it or not, that's not enough. Not nearly enough. We get those from vibrators. You've got no romance, no passion, you're like this empty shell of nothingness and I really wonder what must have happened in your childhood to have made you this cold and this manip . . .' Jeena sealed her out-of-control mouth. The last thing she wanted was to bring up his past. 'Go to Hell, Aaron, Sam and his eight flowers are worth a million of you.'

Watching her disappear into her bedroom carrying the small vase and note, he wondered if he could claim some sort of tax allowance for having to live with a witch. He'd have to ask Anne Robinson's husband, he was sure to know. But maybe he was being too flippant here, maybe Jeena was right about a lot of what she'd said. Although he did take objection to her saying he'd never sent a Valentine card, because he could clearly remember writing one to Olivia Newton John, in blue crayon, when he was ten.

Maybe it was time to dust off that little word 'sorry' and use it. He knew that women in a crisis always turned to the song 'I Will Survive' by Gloria Gaynor. With that in mind, Aaron located the CD from his collection, shoved it in his portable CD player, turned the volume on full blast and walked into Jeena's bedroom whistling along to it.

He shouted above Gloria's voice, 'It's my way of saying sorry.'

The iron let out a hiss as Jeena continued to press her skirt on the floor rug, totally ignoring Aaron's attempts at waving the white flag. Refusing to acknowledge his presence, she carried on with her ironing. It wasn't long before the music was muted.

'I've got a confession to make,' Aaron said, passing her a hanger. 'It's about the flowers.'

Finally, Jeena's attention was roused and she peered at him. 'Go on.'

'Well, Stacy, an ex of mine, came round and she got emotional, all teary eyed and I didn't know what to do, so I gave her most of your flowers.' Aaron couldn't look Jeena in the eyes any longer. 'It did the trick; Stacy stopped crying. She said they were the best flowers that she'd ever received. Honestly, Jeena, you should have seen her face, she was so happy. I never knew flowers could be so potent.'

'You lowlife.'

'All I'm trying to say is that your flowers didn't go to waste, that's all. And not to be upset with Spud, I mean Sam, because he really sent you a massive bunch. He must love you very much. And I'm deeply sorry I used the flowers but I was desperate and I was going to replace them before you came back. It's the truth.'

Why was everything so complicated with Aaron? thought Jeena. Even receiving flowers from her boyfriend was like Mission Impossible. She was just about to send Aaron away when he sat on her bed and let out a huge sigh of exasperation.

He spoke, 'You were extremely unfair with what you said earlier with that outburst of yours. About me not sending cards or making romantic gestures and having no passion. Right from the start I explained to you that I'm not that type of bloke. I told you I only wanted fun, not to get involved with sending flowers and stupid bloody trips to Paris. You knew that about me and you agreed that it wasn't important. If I remember rightly, you yourself said that you too were only after a bit of fun, no strings attached, certainly no expectations of finding a boyfriend. So why throw all that shit back in my face?'

'I'll tell you why, Aaron, it's because you have made me feel cheap, that's why. And I expect that this Stacy woman who was crying also felt cheap because of you. Am I right?' She shook her head contemptuously. 'You make it so obvious that sex is all you want us for. You can't even be bothered with the extra trimmings. And that is hurtful to even the most thick-skinned woman, Aaron.' Jeena switched off the iron and wrapped up the cord. 'You know what I really think? I think that when it comes down to it, you're too afraid to get close to a woman. I can't work out why, but I'm sure I'm right.'

Aaron got up from the bed and walked out of her room. He felt a lot fuller than before he'd walked in to Jeena's bedroom. For now he was full up on home truths. These were not random shots by Jeena, but sniper fire, perfectly aimed and perfectly targeted. 'You're too afraid to get close to a woman', how right she was. Bull's eye.

Chapter Twenty-seven

It was the last Saturday of September, nearly two weeks since Aaron had been given some home-truths by Jeena in her room, and the wipe board was showing ONLY 285 DAYS UNTIL D DAY. Or, in other words: shamefully married for eighty days. Just before leaving his apartment this evening, Aaron had texted Jeena, who was busy cooking Indian food, with some information:

> *Jeena. It's a pity we didn't live on planet*
> *Mercury whose year is only 88 days long, then*
> *U and I would b divorced in just 8 days time.*
> *Then again that would make U 111 years old,*
> *and U know how I never date women over 60.*
> *I'll b back at 11.30, hopefully Sam might have*
> *gone by then? HINT.*
> *Aaron.*

Aaron had agreed to make himself scarce this evening so that Jeena could cook a romantic meal for Sam. As if her entire body had been plumbed by some shoddy cowboy, her nerves had been leaking out everywhere. Were the candles right? Was the music to his taste? Had she chosen the right wine? And, more importantly, was the meal tasty? Flora and Kitty would have chastised Jeena all night for making so much effort for one man. But if the truth be known, Sam had been making just as much effort for her in the nine weeks since they'd met. Knights in shining armour don't come along that often, especially ones who send off for 'Teach yourself Punjabi in six weeks' courses, so it was important to grab them when they did. There was even talk of meeting his parents on the horizon. Maybe, thought Jeena, she should send off for a 'Teach yourself snobby English in six weeks' course and a 'How to curtsy without showing one's breasts' instruction video, because what she'd heard of his up-market parents so far was enough to worry Queen Lizzy to elocution classes. Ain't that right, geezer!

After the delicious meal, the fine wine, the intelligent chat and the loud laughter, Jeena and Sam lay stretched out on the sofa, while the candle flames tickled their eyes and the soft music massaged their ears.

The smooching couple were soon lost in their own timeless world as the evening began to tip-toe away. Eleven p.m., came and went, as did twelve; it was at around 12.17 that the front door opened, Aaron appeared in the entrance and was nearly knocked unconscious by the smell of Indian food. Obviously his hint hadn't been taken. Spud Sam was still here. Either that or he'd forgotten to take his car home with him.

Bless them, Aaron thought, as he set off the burglar alarm on purpose. Bless them, he thought, as he switched on all the lights and started banging the door with his fist. Bless them, he thought, as he watched them frantically grabbing their clothes, half-falling over each other, limbs everywhere, faces locked in confusion.

'Just pretend I'm not here,' Aaron said casually, strolling across the floor. He stood directly in front of them.

'Oh, believe me, Aaron, we *are* pretending you're not here,' Jeena responded curtly, then mumbled to herself, 'I especially used to pretend you weren't there when you were on top of me.'

Unfortunately, Jeena's mumbles weren't mumbly enough and Aaron picked up on every word, retaliating in the style he knew best: sexual. 'Well, you must know another Aaron then, because if I remember rightly "Aaron" was the name you kept yelling out at the top of your lungs. And I certainly don't remember you closing your eyes, which would lead me to the conclusion you knew very well who was on top of you when we fucked. ME!'

Aaron grabbed a glance at Sam who appeared a trifle uncomfortable standing in the middle of a mud-slinging contest. But who was to blame here really? Jeena had confirmed adamantly that Sam would be out by 11.30 p.m., and knowing from experience that romance very rarely adheres to timetables, Aaron had given them a further forty-five minutes just in case. To walk into his apartment to find them kerfuffling on his sofa after he'd given them ample leeway was bad enough. What was worse, what really pissed Aaron off, was that he had been going out of his way *not* to flaunt his love life in front of Jeena, and now he comes home to find her and her boyfriend enjoying a 'porn' moment together. She obviously wasn't playing by the same rules of respect as he was.

'It feels like I'm a guest in my own house,' Aaron declared. 'Actually, it feels like I'm the unwanted guest in my own house.' He directed the next comment at Sam. 'And you, thanks for warming up the wife, Samuel; I'll take it from here. You can go now. Let me and my wife continue with our charade of "Happy Families".'

Jeena aimed a filthy stare at Aaron.

Sam placed his arm round her shoulder. 'How you live with him is beyond me, you deserve some sort of medal.' He eyed Aaron with contempt. 'How you live with yourself is beyond me. You seem to be able to bring everything down to gutter level. And another point, and this one really does keep me up late some nights, I'm really struggling with this marriage business you and Jeena have become entwined in; why a man so wrapped up in himself would help out someone in such a big way. I must be missing something.'

Aaron and Jeena swapped a glance with each other, then just as quickly looked away.

'Well,' Aaron began, 'I wouldn't lose too much sleep over it, for the fact is, I'm a lovely guy. Anyway, I'm off to bed. And if you have any sense, Samuel, you won't drive home tonight.' Aaron nodded his head towards the two empty wine bottles on the coffee table. 'One other thing, keep the sex grunts down to the minimum, please. It's so tacky to hear when you think you might be coming, Samuel. Nighty night.'

It was another hour before the apartment was quiet. Three bodies asleep and tucked up warm against the fresh, late September air outside. At 2.34 a.m., the only adventurers brave enough to be on the streets were cats trying to kill as many mice as they could before confession on Sunday. 'Bless me, Father, for I have sinned, I have killed fourteen mice and peed on three carpets. Meow.' But this night would not remain quiet for too much longer.

A HUGE crash of glass awoke everyone in the apartment.

Like a greyhound on heat, Aaron shot out of his bedroom and into Jeena's checking that they were okay. 'Don't switch on the lights,' he half-whispered as he ran back out to the open-plan living area. His heartbeat was erratic and fast like Morse code and adrenalin was swimming through his veins like a mini shoal of piranha. Red Alert moments like this didn't come along often enough for Aaron, but when they did, he was determined to put all his self-defence knowledge into practice. First rule: stay alive. Second rule: don't get killed. Third rule: leave dying to others. Fourth rule: if you see Jonah Lomu coming at you with a rugby ball, run.

In bare feet, Aaron crept slowly towards the large smashed window overlooking the car park, hoping not to step on broken glass. Already it was fairly obvious that some sort of projectile had crashed through the pane. But, not taking any chances, in case the culprit was still outside, Aaron left the lights off. It was on occasions like this that Charlie's Night Vision goggles would have come in handy (he made a note to ask

Charlie to order him a pair). By the time Aaron had reached the window's edge, Jeena and Sam had entered the room.

Outside in the car park it was nothing but shadow. If one could measure bravery by how slowly the heart beat in a crisis, then Aaron had nine heroic fish in his aquarium, swimming along with not a care in the tank. On the other side of the coin he had three humans kakking their pants. Aaron called out for someone to switch on the lights, and as soon as the glare hit their eyes, the full extent of what had happened hit their brains. A brick wrapped in bright orange paper and tied with string lay amongst the shattered glass. Either a new home delivery pizza place had just opened or someone wanted to cause some panic. Aaron untied the string, flattened out the paper and read through the message.

'I think you'd better take a look at this,' he said, passing the paper to Jeena.

Shaking like a jelly going cold turkey on a waterbed, Jeena held the note in her hand, noticing first the Sikh sign stamped in the corner and then the typed words; with Sam reading them over her shoulder:

THIS BRICK IS NOT FROM YOUR NEIGHBOURHOOD
NOR IS YOUR WIFE.
MIX WHITE WITH BROWN AND WHAT DO YOU GET?
RED.

Jeena's complexion turned pale and her hands gripped the note so hard she nearly ripped it. If fear was the intention of this message, then fear was the result. A hopeless feeling of panic and distress bludgeoned into one. The scariest moment in Jeena's life. She remembered an Indian girl from uni who had been caught messing around with a white guy. The Asian community was in turmoil at what to do. But they soon found the solution all right, Jeena realized, when she saw the white guy hobbling down the road with a broken leg and stitches on his face. She couldn't believe her own people had done this to him. And what had happened to the Indian girl? No one seemed to know. Jeena certainly never saw her again. It seemed to be a common practice for the Asian community to take the law into their own hands when dealing with stray Asian women. Their threats were always followed up.

The hope had been that when Jeena's family accepted Aaron then everyone else in the Asian community would. A fool's hope perhaps? Jeena read the message through again, praying for a change of interpretation, praying the words might read differently this time. But a threat is a threat is a threat and, without thinking, a very scared Jeena found herself falling into Aaron's arms and crying on Aaron's shoulder. Just as easily as Jeena fell into Aaron, Aaron found himself comforting her and whispering in her ear that he would sort everything out. Not to worry. It was yet another hurdle they would get over together.

Together?

Together. A word which Sam had presumed belonged to Jeena and him.

Sam watched the pair embrace. And as he watched he knew that his dreams of being with Jeena were only dreams. There was no denying the love that Aaron must have for her, Sam thought, as he watched how softly he soothed and cuddled her. How Aaron gently stroked her hair, continually consoling her, as though they were the only two people in the room. Many things were making sense to Sam in these moments. Aaron's odd behaviour, his rudeness, his crudeness, his instant dislike for him. All these actions were those of a jealous man. And it was so easy for Sam to spot a jealous man now, because he himself was one. Jealous that his girlfriend had gone to the arms of another man when she needed comforting. With the words 'Cupid has just left the building' ringing in Sam's ears, he was left with only one itsy hope. Did Jeena love Aaron? And it wouldn't have taken the winner of *Mastermind* to work out that Jeena loved Aaron to bits and any man who hitched up with her would always be second best to Aaron. Never the best way to start a relationship to know that you're the sub. Never the best way to make love to a woman when you know she might be thinking of someone else. But why weren't they together?

'Can you please answer this one question I have for the pair of you?' Sam said, interrupting the moment.

Embarrassed in the extreme, Jeena pulled away from Aaron and quickly joined Sam. 'Sorry about that, Sam, erm . . .'

Indifferent, Sam continued, 'I was wondering why it is such a struggle for the pair of you to admit that you both love each other. Because from where I'm standing, it's completely obvious. So wrapped up in proving to the other that you don't love each other with your constant bickering that you end up hurting people like me.

I honestly believe that you two get a kick out of these petty squabbles of yours and these back-stabbing text messages. I even believe you get a kick out of your stinking rows. I, on the other hand, do not get a kick out of this. My feelings for you, Jeena, have always been honest and I have never pretended to be something I wasn't. You, on the other hand, have lied not only to me but to yourself.'

It was at this precise moment that Aaron noticed Sam was wearing a pair of Y fronts. Baggy, white and shapeless. Something most granddads would be proud of. He used all his willpower not to mention them.

'Pants. This is all pants,' Aaron said, walking towards his office area. 'I'm just performing my duty, that's all. She is my wife after all, Sam. Which part of this marriage don't you get?' Aaron returned with a *Yellow Pages* and began to rifle through the book for glazers. 'You can have her after the year is up. I haven't got a problem with that at all. My husbandly duties will be over. Now, does that sound like someone who loves her? I think not.'

Sam shook his head. 'Here you go again. Denial, denial, denial.' He turned to Jeena. 'Look, I think I'll just go. It's best we cut this episode in our life short, don't you think?'

Ten minutes later and Sam was gone.

Clearing up the glass, Jeena fought to control a mixed bag of emotions. Guilt for hurting Sam. Fear for the brick-throwing threat and a certain amount of hope concerning Aaron. Having Sam had been like winning the lottery without having anything she wanted to buy. All she needed was right here, in that fantastic specimen of a man called Aaron. Looking elsewhere for men was futile when right before her eyes was the only guy she really wanted. Sam was an exercise in trying to forget about Aaron; an exercise that went wrong. She so wanted it to have worked with Sam, the last thing she wanted to do was to hurt him. But, alas, in a moment of crisis, the truth ousted itself and her real feelings had revealed themselves when she instinctively went to Aaron for comfort. If anyone in this world professes to understand love then they are mistaken. Love is something without explanation and sometimes the actions one does when in love are without explanation too.

As the last shards of glass hit the bottom of the blue recycling box, Jeena clapped eyes on Aaron's thoughtful face and suddenly needed to know whether what Sam had said was true. The wine had worn off, taking her courage with it. But her need to know was gnawing deep.

'Aaron, do you love me?' she asked, avoiding his eyes.

'It's getting late, can't we talk in the morning,' Aaron replied. 'And I've got to get this window taped up.'

'It's a simple question. Yes or no?'

'Bloody hell, what is it with you women and this poxy word "love"? Do you know how many men say that to their women and the next day they're screwing their best-friend's wife? Love used to mean something, but these days it means nothing. It tears people apart.'

'Answer the question.' And this time she was looking him right in the eye. 'Do you love me?'

'Well, that's a "no", then. Happy now?'

Liar, thought Jeena. His eyes told me the truth while his mouth told me lies.

Without so much as a blink, Jeena walked out to the kitchen and opened up the microwave door. Inside was a meal she'd prepared for Aaron; the very same romantic Indian meal she'd cooked for Sam, only Aaron had a bigger portion. She heated it up and took the plate to Aaron who was now sitting on the sofa staring into space.

'There you go, enjoy,' she said, passing him his knife and fork 'I didn't want you to think that your wife neglected you, did I?'

Aaron kissed her on the cheek then tucked in. If this meal was anything to go by then the signs were as clear as a summer night sky. Jeena loved him.

And here was the bigger problem.

He loved her back.

Chapter Twenty-eight

NEWSFLASH
AARON BRUCE LEE MYLES, WHO HAD BEEN
SUFFERING FROM FAT DEPRESSION, IS BACK TO HIS
NORMAL WEIGHT. HIS FAMOUS SIX-PACK AND TIGHT
BODY IS NOW A CAUSE FOR CELEBRATION.

'Hit me,' Aaron shouted at Jeena.

She flung her arms down by her sides. 'I can't do it.'

'Just hit me in the face, as hard as you can.'

'But what if I break something?' she said.

Aaron chuckled. 'You're not going to hurt me, I promise.'

'No idiot, I mean me. What if I break a nail?'

Time for a five minute rest.

It had been eight days since the 'brick' incident and heartbeats were back to normal. Aaron had convinced Jeena that it would be pointless informing the police, and besides, he figured, it was most likely just a disgruntled Asian youth upset that the Fight to Unite class had been cancelled, nothing to worry about. To be on the safe side, however, he thought it would be a good idea for Jeena to learn some sort of self-defence – even if it were only the basics. One never knew what was around the corner these days. So, for the last week, in the afternoons, Aaron had been putting Jeena through her paces, trying to instil a perfunctory amount of aggression when it came to fighting back against men. Breaking one's nail didn't seem too big a price for saving your skin.

Along with the high amount of physical activity going on, there was also a proportionate amount of mental. Even though Sam had gone, vanished from Jeena's life just as swiftly as he'd entered, his last words still resonated in her mind. Was Aaron living in denial, denial, denial? The mood between Aaron and Jeena had changed for the better. The arguments had ceased. They communicated by mouth rather than by text. And last night they even went out for a Saturday evening together, clubbing like they used to when they were first 'dating'. There was also a moment of shock for Jeena when Aaron had grabbed her tight on the dance floor and whispered how sexy she was. For the rest of the night Jeena had been puzzling over what it all meant. Did he grab her as a statement to other men, i.e., KEEP OFF SHE'S MINE. Or was it a friendly gesture? Or, God forbid, was he being romantic? Whatever the reason, it had Jeena's mind in such a spin that when they'd arrived back at his apartment, both feeling horny from their sensual slow dancing together, she'd half-expected sex. Alas, he just pecked her on the cheek and said goodnight. Which wouldn't have been so bad had she not run out of vibrator batteries. Which was made even worse by the fact that she could clearly hear Aaron knocking one off himself in his own room. All that energy spent on self-satisfaction when they could have both joined up for the night and spent it together. What a cum down.

And what a way to spend your Sunday morning, thought Jeena, still suffering from her hangover. She looked around the echoing Paper Lantern studio, waiting for Aaron to tell her that the five-minute break was over, praying that she left the lesson bruise-free and with a full quota of nails. Even though she felt privileged that he was taking the time to teach her the fine art of smashing someone's face in, she would much rather have spent it tucked up in bed . . . with him.

With him? she asked herself.

Yes, with him with him with him. God, why couldn't he just admit he loved her and then they could move on? An engagement ring to die for. A Sikh wedding. A wonderful honeymoon. Kids. A beautiful house in the country. Two maids (two lesbians so that he couldn't shag them. Make that two ugly lesbians so that he couldn't even fantasize about them. In fact, two ugly lesbians with guns so if he dared to make a move on them, they would shoot his bollocks off) and of course the happy, loving Labrador with its always wagging tail. Oh, Jeena couldn't wait to move on.

The sound of Aaron yelling, 'I'm a murderer and I'm going to kill you!' broke Jeena's daydreaming. Obviously the five-minute break was over. Either that or Aaron didn't like Jeena as much as she thought he did and she *was* about to die.

Jeena, who was feeling quite hot in her Pineapple

tracksuit, walked across the matted floor to Aaron, put her hands up in a posturing position and stared at him menacingly, like he'd taught her to.

'Take a deep breath, then swing at me,' Aaron demanded. 'Concentrate.'

Keeping high on her toes, Jeena moved from side-to-side, trying to outsmart an 8th-dan smart Alec. Now, just like Aaron had taught her, she dropped her eyes to the ground, giving Aaron no clue as to where she would begin her attack.

'Good, good,' Aaron encouraged. 'This is great stuff; now when you're ready, let go with all your force.'

More side-to-side, a little bit of forward then back, a few low growls (just like Aaron had taught her), then the surprise assault. With one ferocious kick Jeena landed her bare foot full force on Aaron's lower abdomen, following it up with two light punches to his head. The pair of them crashed to the springy floor with Aaron cushioning the fall as Jeena landed on top of him. For a stunt which wasn't choreographed, it was quite spectacular.

So, what next? We have two people lying together, hot and sweaty, hearts racing, hormones flowing, something is bound to happen. Jeena stared deep into Aaron's eyes and, without putting too much thought into her next action, she kissed him on the lips, almost desperate for him to reciprocate, to let his guard down again. Expecting him to pull away at any second, Jeena's whole inner self lit-up and tingled as he hungrily kissed her back, rolling her over so that he was now pinning her down. Self-defence classes didn't get more intimate than this – although it is doubtful whether

Aaron's idol, Bruce Lee, would ever have resorted to snogging to win a fight – proving that sometimes the tongue can be a superb weapon.

Giving out more energy than the Hoover Dam with their kissing and cuddling, the two finally took a breather.

'I don't recommend you use this technique against would-be thugs, Jeena,' Aaron said, standing up and pulling her to her feet. 'You'd have a queue of villains parked outside waiting for you to attack them with your fondling.'

'Well, I'm sure you'd help me sort them out, we make a great team.'

'We're not a team, Jeena. Never will be. Anyway, that's today's lesson finished, let's lock up and go home.' All the way upstairs.

'God, what is your problem, Aaron? You can't even accept that we make a "great team" in a joke, can you? You really have got a hang-up with commitment, haven't you?' With that, Jeena stormed off.

He mumbled to himself, 'Go then, I couldn't give a shit what you do.'

But he did. He gave quite a lot of shit actually. Heaps.

Aaron wondered how many men have been left staring at doors after women have slammed them shut in anger. Must be billions. If all that energy could be amassed we would have another Krakatau on our hands. Maybe he'd call Jeena 'Krakatau' from now on; that should keep her happy. His own angry volcanic island. Aaron smiled at the thought then, after switching off the building lights and setting the alarm, he locked up the Paper Lantern and headed upstairs to his apartment to see if Krakatau had simmered down. Things had been quite civil between them lately and it would be a shame to have an eruption today. Slightly worrying to Aaron was the inescapable feeling that some of his defences were down. Throughout his life if ever a moment arose where he thought that his feelings for a woman were becoming too strong, he'd dump her, in the words of Tommy Cooper, 'Just like that.' And his reason for dumping her would be the same excuse someone might use when trying to pick up Dawn French. 'Too heavy'.

So, when Aaron realized that he had fallen in love with Jeena on the night the brick came through the window – the exact moment he wasn't too sure, but it was around the time they hugged in front of Sam – why couldn't he dump her? Because he was married to her. And things were getting worse. After returning home from the Northern Lights nightclub last night, it had taken all the willpower in the world to refrain from pulling her into his bedroom – instead he'd been reduced to pulling on something else. Today, whilst rolling around on the Paper Lantern's floor, it had taken yet more willpower to keep his hands to himself. The question was: how much more willpower did he have before he totally lost it?

Dithering at the front door, deep in thought, Aaron was totally unaware that his apartment was being watched. Out of sight in a thicket of bushes, two Asian men waited patiently, collecting data, writing down the comings and going of Mr and Mrs Myles, and filing the information under the title: CULTURE PAYBACK.

Heavy is the price for those who take their culture lightly.

Inside, Jeena was making a toasted cheese, tomato, onion and mango pickle sandwich. The secret was in the cheese – it had to be mature. Unlike the man who had just barged in through the front door. He was like a stale bit of Edam stuck to her shoe. After walking through a field full of cow dung. What was Aaron's problem? Well, Jeena was pretty sure she knew what his problem was and as their eyes connected when he strolled across the open-plan room, Jeena realized that now was the moment to take off her armbands and swim with the sharks. It was time to confront Aaron about his past and this time she was determined to come away with some answers. She stared at her sandwich. Normally when people are about to be executed they are given their last supper. Surely mango, tomato, onion and cheese, no matter how great a sandwich, didn't qualify as a meal worthy of her demise. For surely when she showed Aaron the e-mail from his school friend Annabel Parry at Friends Reunited, her execution would be imminent.

So, it would beg the question: why not let sleeping dogs lie? Why take the risk of interfering in something which by all accounts is coated in barbed wire? Why? Because, deep down, Jeena believed that Aaron did love her. And she didn't want to lose him because he was too stubborn or proud or whatever to open up about his past.

This surely was the ultimate act of self-defence. Fighting for someone who you know should be yours. She watched him crouched down by the aquarium, a confused expression attached to his face. A moment later and, after removing the lid, Aaron was leaning over the top and peering into the tank. Next he rolled up the long sleeves on his T-shirt and plunged his arm in to the water. Jeena looked away, sure that Aaron was about to fish out a dead fish.

'One of my fish is missing,' Aaron declared suddenly, removing his arm and wiping it on some kitchen roll. 'Tysee is gone!'

'Are you sure he's not hiding round the back of the castle ruin? I often see them hiding there.'

'He's too fat to fit in the ruin. No, he's definitely gone. Vanished from a sealed tank, Jeena.' Aaron stared at her with suspicion. 'A sealed tank?'

'Maybe the other fish got angry with his greedy habits and they ate him,' Jeena said, walking up to the aquarium and taking a look for herself. 'He was here yesterday, before we left for the club. You sang to him, remember? Here Tysee, come out wherever you are.'

Aaron's mind was made up. 'You found him dead this morning, didn't you? Before I got up. And then you flushed him down the toilet, didn't you? I promised my fish a proper funeral; never would I send them the same way I send my number twos. It's not right.' He sat on the sofa and placed his head in his hands. 'Tysee was my friend. I looked after him and he looked after me by getting rid of bad Feng Shui, by absorbing all the bad luck.' He glanced up at Jeena. 'I'll have to get him replaced as soon as possible, you know that? If I don't, then the Feng Shui is ruined and God knows how much bad luck will knock at the door.'

Jeena explained that she didn't find Tyson dead, she

didn't flush him away, and the first she'd heard of the disappearing fish was now. How, when or why the fish upped sticks and went had nothing to do with her and Aaron was just going to have to accept that. And if he was so intent on buying a lie detector testing kit and rigging her up to it, then bloody well do it. She wasn't lying.

'*Comprende*?' Jeena said. 'Can we drop it now?'

'Only if you will join me in a short prayer.'

'Go on then.'

'It won't take long. "Dear Cod, please forgive me for losing my fish, he was my rock, he will be sole y missed. Top tip, if you do find Tysee, make sure to use cold fizzy water with the batter as it makes it so much lighter and fluffier."'

They both burst out laughing. Something which was happening more often these days. It was almost a shame to spoil things, thought Jeena, knowing that her next topic of conversation would put an end to any laughter. But if she didn't go through with this conversation, then that would put an end to any great future. Unless she could get Aaron to open up about his past, then in her heart she knew that there could be no going forward. And without a forward you have no future. Jeena dug deep to appear calm as she sat next to him on the sofa. It was now or never.

'I've done something which will make you blow your top,' Jeena began, gazing towards the window. 'Quite shameful really.'

'So, you did kill Tysee. I knew it.'

'No, it has nothing to do with fish.' She paused. 'Actually, in a way it has, you see, I've been fishing around in your past. I was worried that I might have married a murderer or a psycho. You keep so much to yourself about your life before Japan is it any wonder that I might think you've got something hidden back then that you're ashamed of?' She coughed for the sake of coughing. 'From where I sit, and believe me I always try to look on the good side of people, someone only wipes away their past when they've got something to hide. For God's sake, Aaron, you don't even talk about your family. It's as though you've left a complete life of yours behind in Northampton. It doesn't make sense. YOU don't make sense.'

'You said you've been fishing. What did you find?' he asked coldly.

'I found out which school you went to, Collingsworth Comprehensive, and then I registered to the Friends Reunited website under ... erm, your name.' Jeena shuffled uneasily in her seat. 'Anyway, a few weeks later I got a reply from a girl called Annabel Parry and erm, she said that when you were at school, erm ... I think you'd best read it for yourself.' Just before heading to her room to collect the e-mail, Jeena took a last look at Aaron, whose jaw was clenching so tight anyone might have thought he was chewing concrete. Not a good sign!

She returned with the e-mail and dropped it on his lap.

After carefully reading the printout, Aaron placed it on the coffee table in front, reclined his head back on the sofa and closed his eyes. From where Jeena sat, it seemed like Aaron was mentally revisiting that awful time in his life again. She didn't know whether to feel sad or guilty for bringing him back there. A minute or so passed before Aaron opened his eyes and looked directly into Jeena's.

'So, what conclusions did you reach? What did you gather from this "Friends Reunited" bollocks?'

This is it, worried Jeena, the moment it all crumbles away. 'I can understand why you don't talk about your past; I can see why you don't wish to discuss your childhood. But I think it's important that you do. You can't walk around with baggage like this all your life, it's unhealthy. How do you think that you'll ever get close to a woman if you don't open up? No woman will put up with someone who doesn't trust them enough to . . .'

Aaron stood up. 'Listen to yourself. This agony aunt shit won't work on me, Dr Can't-Mind-Her-Own-Fucking-Business. Have you not thought for one minute that talking about the past totally fucks me up? Has it not occurred to you that the last thing I want to do is explain the shitty life I had as a kid? Do you honestly think that by sitting me down and having a heart-warming chat about those fuckers who bullied me is really going to sort me out? DO YOU? And as for no woman will want a man who doesn't talk about his past; does it look like I give a shit? Here's a word of advice, Jeena. When someone says they don't want to talk about it, guess what?'

She mumbled under her breath, 'They don't want to talk about it.'

'GOOD! We understand each other. Now, if it's all right with you, I'm fucking off out.'

He picked up the e-mail, his keys and mobile, threw

the mobile on the sofa (keen to let Jeena know he was incommunicado) then walked out of the apartment, slamming the door behind him. Without wishing to boast to herself too much, Jeena had guessed that this was going to happen. Storming off, running away, desperate to distance himself. The next part of her plan she wasn't so confident with. The idea being that, after calming down and seeing sense, Aaron would begin to open up to Jeena in the coming weeks. Slowly his trust for her would build and slowly their relationship would blossom.

And they would live happily ever after?

Or, alternatively, more realistically, and especially more painfully, Aaron would go away and come to the conclusion that Jeena had pulled one stunt too many this time. She'd broken the oath of oaths and snooped around in his dark world of childhood. Tears formed in Jeena's eyes; polished drops of regret. This time she'd gone too far, she was pretty sure of that, and this time she'd lost Aaron for good.

Some people are just born to lose, thought Jeena to herself as she sniffed into a tissue.

While others are born to gain, thought Stacy as she admired the new lodger in her house swimming around in his glass bowl. Tysee, the fat black goldfish, seemed to have acclimatized to his new setting already; helped along by the framed photo of Aaron (at Gretna Green) staring into the bowl. Stacy pinched a small amount of fish food and sprinkled it on the water, giggling to herself, enjoying the fruits of her well-thought-out plan.

Stealing Tysee had been easy. Just a matter of waiting patiently for the right time, that's all. Saturday night was a safe bet that Aaron's apartment would be empty for most of the evening, and yesterday had been no exception. Stacy had anxiously watched from her normal spot as Aaron and his wife left for an obvious night on the town. Obvious because his wife was dressed like a first-class slut. MEOW! As soon as Aaron's BMW was out of sight, Stacy was in the apartment, fish net and cellophane bag in hand; envious eyes and bitter grin on face. Of course if she were to explain to anyone, the postman, her hairdresser, her paperboy even, that she was breaking into someone's house for a fish they might have thought her nuts. But Stacy had her reasons. Without Aaron's full quota of nine fish, and especially without his favourite black fish, the Feng-Shui-Obsessive-Aaron would fall to pieces under the strain of having an apartment which didn't conform to the Feng Shui rules. It should be enough to cause some problems with his wife.

Just before catching Tysee, Stacy had found the time to plant a pair of her sexy Agent Provocateur underwear in the washing machine, pour the wife's J'adore expensive perfume down the sink and to check that the safe door hadn't been accidentally left open. Unfortunately the safe was tightly shut, but lo and behold, Sellotaped to the back of the metal casing was a piece of paper generously giving clues to the code which would open it. Quickly Stacy had scribbled down the details onto her Filofax and giggled to herself at Aaron's stupidity.

Her last job before leaving was to copy down Aaron's diary entries for the coming weeks in order for her to plan her next visit without the worry of getting caught. It was important that everything went without a hitch on *that* night; the night she planned on breaking into Aaron's safe.

Chapter Twenty-nine

With the car's handbrake sticking up Aaron's backside, he awoke from his dream of colonic irrigation and let out a huge yawn. He'd been avoiding people since Jeena showed him the e-mail yesterday. For most of the day he'd driven around the countryside that surrounded Primpton, channelling his thoughts, knowing that if he returned to his apartment he was likely to let loose a barrage of abuse at Jeena. A whole bag of rattlesnakes had been spilt the moment Jeena had given him the e-mail from Annabel Parry. He remembered Annabel well and could even remember how she would sometimes flinch when he was being struck by the odd boot or fist. Once, she had handed him a tissue from her Bomber jacket pocket for his bleeding nose. It was a yellow one and he recalled it smelt like sweets.

Last night was the first time Aaron had spent sleeping in a car – it was also the first time he'd slept in a KFC car park. He was amazed at how much noise the fuel in the petrol tank made at the slightest of moves.

More amazing was just how cold the interior of the car got at around three a.m., forcing him to switch on the engine and restlessly doze until his watch alarm awoke him at five a.m., in time for his Monday morning meditation. As Aaron was human, he was tempted to say, 'Sod it', and forget meditation for today. But the eyes of his *sensei* looked down upon him and reminded him of all he had been taught, 'Your meditation is for your heart, do not let it lose a beat.'

So, after driving back from KFC on this chilly October morning, Aaron cruised into the Paper Lantern's car park, killed the engine, then nearly fell out of his BMW half-asleep; too exhausted to even think about parking it in his garage. It probably wasn't the best time to worry about murder but knowing the way his luck had been going lately, some poor sod would have been murdered last night in the vicinity of KFC and Aaron would be the only person in the whole of Primpton without an alibi. With that morbid thought pressing on his mind he climbed the stairs to his apartment and let himself in.

He could hear the judge now, '*Aaron Bruce Lee Myles, on the charge of murder in the first, how do you plead?*'

'*Not guilty, your honour.*'

'*And to the charge of fucking up relationships, how do you plead on that score?*'

'*Guilty, your honour, on all three hundred and twenty-two counts.*'

It was becoming more obvious by the minute that he couldn't cope with even the slightest suggestion of commitment. The barest whiff of coupledom would have him searching for the nearest exit. Aaron was beginning to admit to himself that whatever way you spun the dial it always ended up pointing at him. He was the problem, not them. Woman after woman, year after year, excuse after excuse. Never once had he ever conceded that it was *he* who was afraid of moving forward in a relationship. Until now.

Keeping as quiet as possible Aaron set himself up for his meditation in front of the Buddha. With earphones on, he listened to the noise of WW2 tank fire and tried desperately to enter The Zone. Cannon fire shot from ear to ear in stereo, screams of English officers yelling orders to 'reload, reload'. Bomber planes overhead. The general chaos of death and destruction. Yet, even with all that going on, Aaron still couldn't open his mind and lower his heart rate. His mind was too busy at war elsewhere. Which, incidentally, was something that had only ever happened once before. And in a fit of anger he yanked the earphones from his head and lobbed them across the room.

The video clock showed 05.45. Time for his morning jog around the River Wes. Equipped with his shorts, trainers, T-shirt, iPod and the all important black Beanie hat, he made for the front door. Only to stop in his tracks as Jeena called his name.

'Aaron,' she said. 'I wanted to apologize for yesterday. I feel so bad.'

He stared at her, and judging by her appearance she seemed to have had about the same amount of sleep as he had. In other words: she looked rough. 'We'll talk later. Tonight.'

'But . . .'

But Aaron was gone.

Aaron found himself almost sprinting around the course egged on by his sprinting brain. So much so that he did the course twice. On his return, after his stomach workout and a cold shower, he decided he would take a trip to his gran's in Northampton. It would be great to see her and as long as he was back in time for his evening martial-arts classes, then why not? He wondered, now that he was back to his normal weight, whether it would be too cheeky to phone Gran in advance, giving her plenty of time to bake him one of her famous Heavenly Cakes. Mmm mmm. Or maybe he should just surprise her.

Spruced up neat and tidy in jeans, sweatshirt and trainers, Aaron plonked in a CD, 'Hot Fuss' by The Killers, and turned the car volume up loud. It was just gone 7.30 a.m., giving him a gentle ride to arrive at his gran's by 8.30 a.m. (providing the early-morning rush-hour traffic wasn't too heavy). Concentrating on the miles ahead, Aaron didn't even register the car behind. The black BMW with its two Asian occupants, and tinted windows, which had been following Aaron since he'd first pulled out of the Paper Lantern's car park.

'I just love these tinted windows,' remarked the driver of the black BMW. 'It gives us complete anorm-ality.'

'Anonymity you mean,' corrected the passenger. 'He hasn't got a clue.'

The two Asian men were keen not to slip up today for they might not get another chance. They resumed their silence as they continued trailing Aaron's car. It wasn't long before smiles lit up their faces.

'He's heading for the M1 motorway,' the driver said. 'Phone Pav and tell him that we're on for now.' He had an afterthought. 'Oh, and tell him that we'll keep following our white bastard target and if he suddenly does a U-turn then we'll let him know quick sharp.'

The call was made and with that call life was about to change dramatically for Mr and Mrs Aaron Myles.

After getting dressed for work, Jeena made herself a couple of slices of toast while listening to an Anastacia CD. Reflecting on last night, she was at a loss whether things were going well or not. When she'd phoned Flora and relayed the situation so far, her friend's advice had been to give Aaron some space. If Aaron still couldn't bring himself to open up, then maybe it was time the men in white coats paid him a visit. That's if they weren't too busy with their other pet project: 'Charlie', Aaron's Gulf-War-Syndrome-Mate. On a positive note, Flora had explained to Jeena, as Kitty had kept to her bargain of having her third breast implant operation (size triple coconut) Mr Platinum-Credit-Card had gifted her with a bright yellow top-of-the-range Porsche. The personalized number plate read: BIMBO.

Nibbling on a slice of toast, Jeena looked at the wipe board and noted that for the first time Aaron had neglected to erase a day. She wanted to believe that maybe this was a sign of some sort, but more than likely he'd just forgotten. She shook her head at the board. Some days she wanted to trash the damn thing and scream at Aaron how pathetic it was to have a sodding divorce reminder on the wall. Eighty-nine days they'd been married. And if one converted all eighty-nine days into hours you would come close to the total amount of time her parents spent discussing India in one year. Eighty-nine days was enough time for Ellen MacArthur to circumnavigate the world. Eighty-nine days of hoping Aaron would love Jeena back . . . and more importantly admit it.

But last night he hadn't even come home. Not that this was really a surprise, more like yet another confirmation of how Aaron could so easily sleep in another woman's bed without the batting of a moral eyelid. Only dogs behave worse than that. (Except guide dogs of course, for everyone knows they are well-behaved creatures). Jeena was just about to panic that she was late for work when there was a knock at the front door.

She opened it warily to be faced with three Indian men in their late twenties wearing expensive suits. One of them, Jeena was surprised to recognize as her second cousin Pav (her father's cousin's son) and the other two she vaguely remembered from family weddings she'd attended over the years. Here was the problem with the large extended Indian family – anyone with brown skin could be your relation. And often was. Before Jeena had a chance to say anything, the three men barged into the apartment, one of them grabbing her by the wrist and dragging her to the sofa.

'Sit down, Jeena!' the obvious leader of the threesome ordered. 'We want you to quickly pack a bag and then you're coming with us.'

'I think you'd better leave, my husband will be back any second.' Jeena's voice was quivering and her eyes were wide with fear.

All three laughed. The leader said, 'The very same husband who is happily driving down the M1 as we speak. I think not, Jeena. Nice try though.'

Nothing more was divulged as they watched over Jeena while she stuffed a small carry-case with clothes, make-up and toothbrush. Whether it was the knives that all three kept flashing or the coldness in their manner, Jeena was well aware that her best option right now was to oblige. As soon as she was packed she was directed back to the sofa and told to get out her mobile phone.

'Call this white husband of yours and explain to him that you are leaving him. Tell him the marriage is not working and it is over. Tell him that a mixed relationship is not what you want anymore.' The leader broke off for a second, deep in thought. 'Scrap that. This is what you tell him; say that you're going away for a few weeks to think things through. You need time and tell him not to try and contact you as you don't want to be contacted. If you say the wrong thing, Jeena, then we will burn him in his bed. Make no mistake, it was us who threw the brick through the window and if you fuck up it will be us who will kill your husband.' As if to underline his threat, he pulled out his knife and cut it through the air. 'Phone him now.' He placed the knife a few inches away from Jeena's throat. 'Don't let your neck end up matching the colour of your red hair!'

With no choice in the matter, Jeena dialled through to Aaron's mobile and he picked it up after a few rings.

'Look, Jeena,' Aaron began before she'd had a chance to speak, 'I've told you that we'll talk later.' He sat down opposite his gran and whispered 'sorry' for the interruption. He'd literally just walked in the door and already his gran was taking second place to his mobile.

'I'm ringing to let you know that I need some space apart from you. I need to,' Jeena's breathing became laboured and her stomach felt sick. 'I need a few weeks to myself, Aaron. I'm moving out for a while and I don't want you to contact me. And I'm sorry about yesterday; I did it because I love you.' The blade brushed delicately across her throat and she began to sob. 'If you love me like you say you do every day, then respect my wishes and give me my space.' She swallowed hard. 'Aaron, take care of yourself and remember I will always love you . . . bye.'

'Jeena, hold on . . .'

Her mobile was snatched from her hand and the line was disconnected. Next the leader pulled from his jacket pocket a piece of paper with two phone numbers on it. One was Kitty's and the other Flora's. He then set about texting the two friends under the pretence of Jeena. His message to them was simple: Jeena wanted time away from Aaron and had gone away for a while to clear her head. She would contact them in a few weeks' time and not to worry. When Jeena asked how they knew about her two friends, the response was as cold as it was simple: 'We know everything about you, Jeena.' Leaving nothing to chance, the leader switched off Jeena's mobile and hid it amongst a pile of clothes inside her wardrobe. He'd seen on *Crimewatch* how meticulous the police were with their enquiries these days with their satellite and computer data bases and the best thing would be if the mobile-phone trail led back to Jeena's apartment. You can serve up to fifteen years for kidnap these days and he wasn't about to give up his life on account of a poxy Sim Card.

Back in the living area, he grabbed Jeena by the wrist and pulled her to her feet.

'Right, get your passport and make it quick,' the leader demanded.

Hesitating, knowing that the passport meant planes, Jeena tried her hardest to stall things. 'Passport? I don't have it here. It's at my parents' house.'

The leader pointed to Pav. 'Search her room, she's lying.'

Jeena knew they'd find the passport in an instant. Top drawer by her bed. Hardly the hiding place of the century. It was time to come clean or face further consequences. 'Okay, I'll get it; I just remembered where it is.'

A minute later and the leader was slapping the burgundy passport in his hand. He barked out another order, 'Take off your wedding ring and give it to me.'

By now Jeena was in such a state that her compliance with orders was automatic and immediate. She twisted off the ring and placed it on the coffee table. Two seconds later she was being escorted out of the apartment and into a waiting van.

Weird, thought Aaron, as he tried over and over to call Jeena back on her mobile, she'd switched off her phone. That was some pretty heavy shit she'd just said down the line and to cut it off cold like that was plain unfair. Unfair and unlike her. If he didn't know her any better he would have sworn that she was under the influence of alcohol or drugs just then; talking about leaving, going away, giving herself some space, and what was all that crap about him saying he loved her every day, what was that all about? He'd try her again later; hopefully her freaky mood would have changed by then. In the meantime he had a gran that he had to be a grandson to.

'So, I can't talk you out of getting this cockatiel then, Gran?' Aaron said, dunking his biscuit into his tea and biting into it before it fell to pieces. 'You realize that they live for years and years, don't you?'

'Meaning?'

'Well, what about a bunny rabbit? Or a hamster? They don't live long, much better for the elderly.'

She stared at him knowingly. It was patently obvious from the gibberish coming from his mouth that Aaron had something on his mind – and she was pretty certain what that something might be. More to the point, maybe he wanted to talk about it now, that's why he'd turned up out of the blue. She smiled as he munched on a biscuit. Maybe it was time to telephone Father Karras and see if he had a spare moment to pop over. Get this grandson of hers sorted out once and for all.

Gran made an excuse to leave the room, leaving Aaron to mull over his thoughts some more. Jeena's phone call smelt funny. Kind of scripted. And not only that, like someone who had been given the wrong lines in a school play, her words didn't fit right, they didn't sound like the kind of sentence structure that . . . maybe he was reading too much into it. Maybe she just needed a break. Maybe she'd have changed her mind by this evening and wonder why the hell she'd been crying down the phone. He'd heard through the grapevine that there was this awful disease that women pick up once a month, PMT, maybe this was only a bout of that.

Aaron found himself staring above the fireplace at the photograph of his parents. More and more often lately he'd been waking up in the night positive that he could hear his mother's voice calling from inside his wardrobe. He was sure he could hear her begging him to listen to her last words. But the word 'last' was the problem. Aaron was too afraid to hear her 'last' words. Yet something was telling him that time was running out if he didn't open that package. Running out for what, he wasn't sure, but the sand in the egg timer was nearly gone.

Returning from the hall, Gran sat back in her armchair. 'Father Karras is popping over in five minutes. I mentioned you were here and he thought it would be a splendid idea if you two had a little chat.'

'About what?'

'Life, the church, he might even mention the birds and bees, who knows.' She took off her glasses and let them fall around her neck. 'Oh, before I forget, more flowers appeared at your parents' grave last week. Beautiful they were; it's such a shame we don't know who is placing them there. Someone must miss them awfully. It's such a mystery, it really is.'

A comforting mystery though, believed Aaron, knowing that when Gran did pass away and if he himself were to be taken out by a devil's swerve ball, then at least someone would still lay flowers at his parents' grave. There was nothing sadder than an unkempt grave.

And nothing brighter than a Father's smile.

'Good morning to you, Margaret,' Father Karras greeted Gran in the entrance, then walked into the living room and greeted Aaron. 'Good morning, Aaron, such a long time since our paths last crossed. Such a very long time.'

Aaron's boxer shorts were full of sins, as were his mind, body, mouth, and all about him. In fact, just like the Great Wall of China, if you could have a Father for each of Aaron's sins and line them up side-by-side, you would be able to see the line of Fathers from space. Each with their mouth open saying, 'You disgusting creature.' And in the confession box the Father would be advised to wear a crash helmet for when he fell to the floor, shocked at some of the lurid, sexual acts Aaron had been involved with over the years. Shocked and yet maybe, in some ways, impressed.

'I understand that you're coming out of the closet today, Aaron,' Father Karras assumed. 'Margaret informs me that you've made this brave decision and would like the full blessing of the Lord. Well,' he put his hand on Aaron's shoulder, 'this is something I cannot officially sanction, Aaron, homosexuality is a sin and in the Lord's eyes you are treating him with disrespect. I advise you to control your urges and to question your path. It is wrong for a man to lust over another man and I suggest that you snap out of this phase you are going through. Read your bible every day and ask for God's strength and he will give it. Jesus will help carry your burden which weighs you down, just like he carried the cross.' He pulled from his pocket a small crucifix and handed it to Aaron. 'Take this and wear it whenever you are feeling weak; whenever you are,' Father Karras thinned his eyes and his face seemed to turn grey, 'thinking about men in a sinful way.'

Aaron's face twisted like a gnarled piece of wood. His eyes grew to double their size and his mouth became dry. He glared at Father Karras. 'I AM NOT FUCKING GAY. JESUS MARY MOTHER OF CHRIST AND JOSEPH, GET A GRIP.'

'How dare you swear in front of a man of cloth, Aaron Myles, how dare you! Not to mention blaspheming in front of our Father. It's behaviour of the worst kind. You jolly well know the rules I have in my house about swearing before the watershed.' Gran turned to Father. 'Sorry about this inexcusable behaviour, he's obviously not ready to come out yet.'

Father whispered in Gran's ear, 'Pray for him, Margaret, pray for him every night.'

Aaron strode out of the room and out into the garden. He was tempted to shout out, 'Would you like me to make a daisy chain or something?' Then he saw his gran's frumpy bra swinging on the washing line. Maybe they'd prefer it if he stripped off and walked back in the house wearing that!

Chapter Thirty

October ate up nearly another week, and it was now Saturday, five days since Jeena left. All week Aaron had convinced himself that if she didn't turn up today then she would turn up tomorrow. By the time five tomorrows had passed, she still hadn't showed and Aaron was beginning to worry. He'd phoned her work on the Tuesday and was informed by her boss, Mr Akhtar, that Jeena had asked for a month's unpaid leave. He'd phoned Kitty who just threw abuse down the line at him: 'I'm surprised she lasted this long with a pig like you,' Kitty had shouted. 'If she's got any sense, Bruce Lee, she'll stay away from you for good.' And Flora explained that she and Kitty had both received a text message. Flora advised Aaron to contact Jeena's parents if he was that worried. But Aaron couldn't contact them, what would he say, 'Sorry, but I've lost your daughter; you haven't got a spare one have you?'

Aaron tossed Jeena's wedding ring up and down in the palm of his hand. As far as statements went, the discarded wedding ring was one of the strongest. It beat the smashing of crockery and ripping of suits every time. It really meant 'It's over'. Aaron pocketed the ring and began to pace the room. Maybe Jeena had finally got sick of him and his secretive past. Maybe she'd given up on him ever settling down. Maybe she was sick of his other women. Maybe she was ashamed of what she had done with Friends Reunited on his behalf and couldn't face him through guilt – God things must be bad, worried Aaron, as he was beginning to sound like a *real* married man.

And maybe he was missing her now. Actually, there was no maybe, it was *definitely*. Aaron was finally feeling the churning stomach pain that comes with love. The extra hot spicy chilli sauce that screws up your digestion and eats into your gut. The one that leaves you gasping for air. The uncontrollable sensation that . . . Aaron paced with frustration. Why was her phone still switched off? Why was her car still parked outside? Why hadn't she called? Why did she go? If she didn't take her car, who took her? A taxi firm?

Aaron pulled out the entire list of taxi firms' numbers and rang around asking for them to check their computers to see if any cabs had come to his address last Monday. Each taxi firm had the same answer, 'No.' The situation seemed to be getting bleaker the more Aaron questioned Jeena's whereabouts. There had to be an answer to all these questions somewhere. Aaron decided to take another look in Jeena's room to see if there was something, anything, untoward which might point him in the right direction. But everything was the same as far as he could tell; her bed was made, the curtains were open, her un-ironed clothes still waited to be ironed, magazines were strewn on the floor; she'd even left Mr Piggles in his normal spot sitting on the centre of the bed. It was hopeless. If only he'd done what Charlie had suggested and set up a spy camera in her bedroom then all would have been solved.

What now? The only place left to look really was Jeena's drawers. Reluctantly and with a sense of guilt and unease, Aaron opened her bedside drawer and was faced with the most futuristic-looking vibrator he'd ever seen with its glitter-coated purple plastic and tungsten-tipped bulbous end. Dials and buttons were everywhere. A G-spot tickler. There was even a warning sticker on the side: DO NOT LET YOUR PARTNER KNOW ABOUT THIS. HIS EGO WON'T TAKE IT.

Ha! thought Aaron, *as if* a vibrator could compete with a well-hung male stud like me. After replacing the dead batteries (God, Jeena was a dirty cow, how much did she use this contraption?), Aaron switched the machine on then pressed it against his crotch. 'JEEPERS CREEPERS.' His eyes nearly shot off their stalks as he let out a small yelp. This was some heavy-duty sex toy. Men had lost the battle. It was over. The machines won in the end. The fact that the sex object was battery operated was quite a relief to Aaron; otherwise, he reflected ruefully, there was a high chance that his quarterly electricity bill would have spiralled out of control. But, more importantly, why hadn't Jeena taken this amazing contraption with her? What mental state must she have been in to have forgotten something as powerful and fantastic as this? He gave himself a little more pleasure then stuffed it back in her drawer. And another thing, how come she'd left poor Mr Piggles behind? She had mentioned on numerous occasions that Mr Piggles went with her everywhere; he had even been a guest in their hotel room at their wedding in Gretna Green, so why hadn't she taken him with her now? Things were not looking good at all; in fact, they were looking positively shite.

It was 6.30 p.m., and instead of getting ready for a Saturday night out with his mates like he'd planned, Aaron decided to cancel, knowing that he wouldn't be the best company tonight with this business of Jeena's disappearance hanging over him. Besides, a gut-feeling was telling him that Kitty was bound to know something about Jeena's whereabouts and it would be worth paying her a visit this evening. Although Kitty was to be congratulated on her loyalty to Jeena for not shedding any light on her best friend's hideout, it had come to crunch time, and if she did know something then now was the time to own up.

After switching off the building lights and setting the burglar alarm, Aaron jumped in his car and headed for Kitty's flat. He hoped she was in.

Stacy couldn't control her giggles as she watched Aaron drive away. Yet again Aaron had followed the writings in his diary word for word. Tonight the diary entry had read: *7 p.m., meet round Tyler's then onto Broken Wagon nightclub until late*. That was Aaron out of the picture. But what about his wife? Well, the apartment lights were all off so Stacy could only assume that the wife was somewhere else this evening. Whatever, it meant that Stacy had the upper hand and, more importantly, as long as her calculations were correct (and she was sure they were) then she had broken the code to Aaron's safe. She stepped out of the car into the cold, dark night and took in a deep breath of air. Tonight was going to be special, she could feel it.

Parked up outside Kitty's flat, Aaron smiled at the BIMBO number plate on the yellow Porsche. It was amazing what plastic surgery could achieve sometimes. Gone was the time when man relied on nature to build him a beautiful woman, now is the time when he paid a good surgeon to build one for himself. Aaron climbed the stairs to the top floor and rang the doorbell. No answer. He was about to ring again when Kitty's voice shouted out.

'Okay, okay, I'm coming, just a second.'

After a few minutes the door bolt slid across and Aaron was facing Kitty, dressed in a short, black, almost see-through nightie thing, at the entrance. The first thought that came to Aaron's mind was if her breasts burst then I'm gonna need a surfboard to ride the silicon wave. They were soooooo enormous that he couldn't take his eyes off them; not in a sexual way, more in a 'why have you done this to yourself?' way. He was well aware that she might fall forward at any second. Gravity can be a bit of a bastard for implants. He was also aware that if he didn't start talking soon and continued to gawp at her cleavage then he would get a slap.

'Sorry to turn up out of the blue, Kitty, but I'm worried about Jeena. I was hoping that you might have an idea where she might be. Something doesn't feel right about this whole thing.'

Kitty beckoned Aaron inside and told him to chill on the sofa while she fetched her dressing gown. As Aaron waited for her return he was sure he could hear her talking to someone in the bedroom and his heart began to twitch. By the time Kitty had returned, wrapped up in a red, silk Japanese kimono, suspicion had joined him on the sofa. Could it be that Jeena had been here all along? Were some of his worries about to self-destruct?

Sitting next to Aaron on the sofa, Kitty spoke, 'I hate to be too personal, you know me, Bruce Lee, but I have to ask: did you and Jeena have an argument on the day she left? It's not unusual for women to run off after they've had a massive row, you know. I once took a holiday to Ibiza for two weeks when I caught an ex of mine mentioning he thought J Lo was sexy. *As if*. I've seen sexier curtains than her.' She paused. 'What about you, do you think she's sexy? J Lo?'

He gave her a distant 'I'm not even going to answer that' look, then replied, 'We did have a row the day before which, and this sounds really pathetic I know, which ended up with me sleeping in the car. Basically, I didn't come home that night. And . . . well . . . anyway, the next morning she tried to talk things through with me but I told her that it would have to wait until the evening. That was the last I saw of her.'

A shake of Kitty's head was followed by a sigh then a pitiful glance towards Aaron. 'Sounds to me as if

Jeena is just pissed off with you and has taken a time out. Try to give her the weeks she asks and I'm sure everything will come together in the end.'

A crashing noise came from somewhere in the flat and Aaron fixed a stern gaze Kitty's way. 'What was that?'

'What? I didn't hear anything,' Kitty answered feebly.

'You didn't hear *that*?' Aaron got to his feet and half ran across the floor to Kitty's bedroom. He was sure that Jeena was inside and without a further second's contemplation, ignoring Kitty's wails, he flung the door open and . . . suddenly wished he hadn't.

'Sorry, mate,' Aaron said to the naked man tied up on the bed. 'My mistake, I thought you were my . . . wife.' It wasn't the best time in the world to shake Mr Platinum-Credit-Card's hand but Aaron had been well brought up. 'I'll leave you to it then, enjoy your bondage session,' he said, as he closed the door behind him to face a hail of laughter from Kitty, followed quickly by laughter from himself.

After the pair had calmed down and the disappointment of not finding Jeena had resurfaced, Aaron made for the front door.

'I don't believe you're leaving me without having a feel of these,' Kitty said, undoing her kimono and presenting her new treasures for Aaron's inspection. She grabbed his hands and pressed them tight against her breasts. 'They feel real, don't they?' She smiled. 'Bloody hard to sleep on though.' Just before Aaron opened the front door and disappeared into the night, Kitty added something she thought she'd never say.

'Underneath this big show you put on for everyone, you're quite a sensitive bloke. It's obvious you care about Jeena. You know, I much prefer the Aaron I'm looking at now than the one I used to know. And, even though it's none of my business, and I hate to interfere in other people's personal stuff, you know me, well, I say this, Aaron Bruce Lee Myles, if you love Jeena like I think you do then you must tell her. You never know, she might just love you back.' And she kissed him on the cheek, gave his bollocks a quick fondle, then said goodbye.

As Aaron drove back to his apartment he made up his mind. Kitty was right, the best thing to do right now was to give Jeena all the time she needed. This paranoia that something terrible had happened to her would have to be knocked on the head. Jeena was taking a break; there was nothing sinister or cloak-and-dagger about that. If anyone were to consider what she'd been through recently, they would come to the conclusion that she might very well need this break. First, there was her fear of having an arranged marriage in India. Next, her parents disowned her. Following that, she had had to put up with a boss who bullied her for having a mixed relationship. None of that could have been easy. Then she had this doomed relationship with Spud Sam. Then the brick through the window. If that weren't enough to make someone trek to the other end of the world, she had had to put up with me, thought Aaron. The endless arguments, the constant bickering, the unnecessary battles. She couldn't even get a straight answer out of him. Does he love her or doesn't he? Forget giving the woman a holiday, she needed a fucking medal. And Aaron couldn't wait for the day she walked back through the front door – however long that might take.

Chapter Thirty-one

Stacy stared at the eleven digit code to Aaron's safe. She'd heard of office workers leaving their computer passwords stuck on their VDU, or pin numbers stuffed in with their credit cards, but what sort of imbecile leaves his key to the code Sellotaped to the back of his metal safe? Stacy read through Aaron's note:

A=1 B=2 Z=26

'Here goes,' she said out loud to herself. 'Let's see what you've been hiding from Stacy.' With a steady finger Stacy pressed in the numbers on the electronic pad. '2 ... 18 ... 21 ... 3 ... 5 ... 12 ... 5 ... 5 and ENTER.' Her guess was that Aaron had used the key-word BRUCELEE as his password. It had taken her one 'blonde' week to work this minor IQ problem out. With a slight delay the safe bleeped, Stacy's heart took a lap of her chest cavity and the heavy door was unlocked. What sort of imbecile leaves his key code taped to the back of his safe? Well, that would be AARON.

Now to empty the safe. First she pulled out a number of martial arts medals, some in boxes, some loose. Stacy put a few around her neck and checked herself out in the wardrobe's inside door mirror. Quite impressed with the 'bling', she set about removing more of the safe's contents. Boring files came next. A velvet jewellery box. A small wad of cash which went straight into her handbag. A briefcase filled with photos of Japan, family, friends and Bruce Lee. And a manky-looking package sealed with electrician tape and marked with the words, *Dear my beautiful boy, you must only open this when you are ready. Love Mummy x*. Stacy smiled. Who cared whether Aaron was ready or not, Stacy was ready, and that's what mattered. With a ruthless aggression she ripped open the package and spilt out the entire contents on Aaron's bed. She spread it all out on top of the duvet and sneered at the use-lessness of it all. His wife would have to take the blame for this. Bored and disappointed at the safe, Stacy yanked off the medals around her neck and flung them across the room. Maybe it was time to have some fun with his fish again.

Outside in the open-plan living area, Stacy viewed the aquarium. She noticed that Aaron had already replaced the black fish, its identical successor happily swimming amongst the other eight gold ones. Not unlike the way he treats his women, she thought bit-terly, replacing them at the drop of a hat. She walked out to the kitchen and returned with a snappy bag. She'd been promising Tysee a mate since fish-napping him a week ago. Using the small green fish net, Stacy set about catching her second fish.

'I'm becoming quite the expert at this,' she muttered, as she popped the black fish into the snappy bag. She giggled. 'I'd love to be a fly on the wall when the wife tries to talk her way out of this.'

By the time Aaron drove into the Paper Lantern car park, he'd put to rest most of his worries regarding Jeena. He remembered his *sensei* talking about relationships. How two people in a partnership are like two stonemasons working on a piece of rock. Sometimes, if they are lucky, they will sculpt something of beauty and their relationship will last, other times the two of them will hack away at the stone until it's nothing but rubble. Aaron suspected that if he and Jeena were ever to become a proper couple, then it wouldn't be too long before their rock was nothing but dust. And why? Because Aaron knew in his heart that he could never commit. And why not? Because . . . because . . . Aaron didn't know why not. He only knew that even after admitting to himself that he loved Jeena, he *would* never, *could* never, *won't* ever marry her for real. He'd heard a saying once which rang all the right notes in his mind: *If love was supposed to be a drug, then fucking up your life was definitely one of its side effects.* (Written by a bitter divorcee no doubt).

After parking the car in the garage and lowering the electronic garage door, Aaron realized that the lights to his apartment were on. ON as in someone was in there. ON as in that someone must be Jeena. ON as in thank God she was back. Keeping a cool head, Aaron casually took the metal stairs to his apartment, mentally warning himself not to get into another argument and especially not to let her know how worried he'd been. Once a woman knew which buttons to press she'd press them whenever she wanted a bit of fun or attention.

He let himself in and froze, for there, sitting amongst his DVD collection, with her back to the door, humming obliviously to herself was a woman who most certainly was not Jeena.

'And I think I'll put *Fight Night 2* into *Game of Death*,' the woman giggled. 'And *The Swordsman* into *Prodigal Son*.' She switched the required DVDs and picked up another two from the pile. 'Ah, what have we here? *The Big Boss* which I will swap with, erm, *Fist of Fury*. I'd love to see his wife talk her way out of this little mess.'

Just about to introduce himself to the intruder, Aaron spotted a cellophane bag filled with water and his new substitute black fish, Muhammad Ali. A split-second later and Aaron had recognized the voice of the woman in his apartment. STACY. And all of a sudden many things were making much more sense to him now. For instance: he now knew why Hell was invented, for people like Stacy Carter. He continued to watch her as she muttered and giggled to herself, lost in her own little world. The only thing missing from this scene was the witch's cauldron.

Aaron slammed the front door shut and Stacy dropped the DVD she was holding.

'I've got a gun,' she shouted, before turning round. 'Oh. It's you; I thought it might be a burglar or someone.' She stood up and opened her arms out. 'Surprise!'

Written on Stacy's T-shirt were the words: TELL ME IF MY NIPPLES ARE SHOWING. Which would have been just about passable if she hadn't cut out two holes for her nipples. What was he dealing with here?

'First, I want to know how you got in,' Aaron demanded, walking towards the fish, opening up the bag and plopping Muhammad Ali back into the aquarium. 'And secondly, why?'

Stacy explained how she'd secretly made a copy of his front-door key on Valentine's Day in case of an emergency. How she was head-over-heels in love with Aaron and she would not let anything get in the way of having him back. That included his new, Asian wife. Stacy boasted to Aaron that she was sure if she could get rid of the wife then he would be quick to have her back and just as quick to fall back in love with her.

'I was never in love with you, Stacy; you were just one of many women I had fun with.' Aaron sat down. 'I made it crystal-clear to you how I operated from the beginning.'

'I know. What I mean is: I know that now.' Stacy's eyes began to brim with tears. 'When I found out you were married only days after dumping me, I wanted to hurt you. That's why I had so much enjoyment in this place of yours. It was almost like a drug coming up here and wrecking your Feng Shui. I got such a thrill messing with your mind. Knowing that you would be blaming the wife. Knowing that there would be arguments. Honestly, Aaron, I think I was addicted to the buzz of it all.' Through her teary eyes, she glanced at him. 'I'm sorry, Aaron, but you always thought I was a dumb blonde without the blonde. And yet, here I was getting one over you every time.' She watched Aaron's face – it was a picture of torment. 'I made you put on weight, I messed up your DVDs, I took Tysee, I –'

'You made me put on weight?' Aaron interrupted. 'How?'

Stacy enlightened a very angry and miserable-looking Aaron with the hilarious story of how she mixed up his creamy smooth protein shakes.

But there was nothing creamy or smooth about Aaron's face right now. It was positively bursting with ill-feelings. Surely there was a law out there that said if a woman destroyed a man's six-pack then he could murder her. Surely.

'I'm not such a dim bimbo after all, am I, Aaron?' She smiled sweetly. 'And today I broke into your safe using your so obvious "Bruce Lee" password. What a joke! Not that it was worth breaking into. You really do keep some junk, don't you?'

Aaron shot off into his bedroom, quick as a distress flare. And by the look on his face when he arrived, no one was in greater need of rescuing. Momentarily confused by what lay before him, scattered crudely over his duvet, Aaron searched around, praying that Stacy had not done the unthinkable. Praying that . . . but his eyes spotted the ripped up packaging from his mother's parcel . . . it was too late, Stacy had given Aaron the body blow of body blows. He dropped to his knees and closed his eyes. There was no getting away from it now, he was going to have to look at what his mother had left him in her will all those twenty years ago. He was left with no choice.

Trying to pull himself together, Aaron stormed back into the open-plan living area and demanded that Stacy hand over his front-door key. Trembling, she slipped it off her key ring and dropped it in his palm. She'd never seen Aaron this angry before. In fact, she'd never seen anyone this angry before. Maybe it was her cue to leave.

'Get out before I fucking kill you, Stacy. And you make sure that you bring back Tysee. MOVE!' Like a sergeant chasing an army recruit Aaron marched her to the front door and virtually pushed her out. There was no doubt in his mind that if she didn't go now, he would murder her.

There was no doubt in Stacy's mind that if she didn't go now, she'd be dead.

Back inside Aaron found himself some candles, placed them on the dining-room table and lit them. It was time for him to take The Burning Oath. Without a second's thought he placed his hand over the tip of the flame and began to transfix his mind to another place. A place without pain. A safe light in a dark wilderness. Slowly the fire licked at his hand, trying to gnaw into Aaron's mind, only to be shut out by the force of self-belief. Second by second Aaron withstood the heat until the battle was won and he dropped his hand on the flame, snuffing its life out, giving himself the courage to face his nightmares.

After slapping a generous amount of Savlon on his burnt palm, Aaron took a deep breath and walked back into his bedroom. He looked down on the duvet. First to catch his eye were a few items of baby clothes. Tossed in the corner were two hospital tags bound together by an elastic band. There were two small teddy bears which didn't ring a bell to Aaron at all. A plastic bag containing two locks of hair. And two sealed envelopes. One addressed to someone called Tamzin. And one addressed to Aaron.

Overcome by an overwhelming sensation that his mother was watching him now, Aaron picked up his envelope and carefully opened it. He could tell by its thickness that there was a lengthy letter inside, but he hadn't expected it to be ten pages long. Feeling nervous, he began to read:

Dear Aaron,
If you are reading this, then I can only assume that I am already dead. You know very well that I believe strongly in God and therefore you must take it as a given that I am up there somewhere floating with the angels. Please do not cry that I am gone for really I am still with you in every breath you take . . .

The letter went on to say how much she and his father loved Aaron. She advised him to make something of his life, to be the best he could be, to treat women with respect. She told him that what she was to write next must be kept a secret from his father and Gran. No word of this must ever be passed on to them. It would break both of their hearts.

Basically, Aaron, you have an older sister. When I was fourteen I fell pregnant and was forced by my parents to give up my child for adoption. I expect this is a huge shock for you and believe

*me if there had been another way of breaking
this news to you I would have done it. Things
were very different in those days and as soon as
my baby was taken away from me I was
forbidden to ever speak of her again. It was
because of this attitude that I fell out with my
parents who decided to emigrate to Australia to
join the rest of our family. Years later I lost
contact with all of them. Maybe part of me
wanted it that way, because of what they had
forced me to do. Anyway, to cut a very long
story short, I moved to Northampton where I
met your father and years later you, my darling
son, were born. I never told your father about
this. I think I was too ashamed . . .*

With a lump in his throat, Aaron continued to read
the lengthy letter. Learning of his mother's terrible guilt
and her struggles to come to terms with losing her
daughter to a family she knew nothing of.

*It was a shock to receive a letter from my
seventeen-year-old daughter who I now know is
called Tamzin Preston. In this letter Tamzin
explained how she would like to meet up one
day and she left the address of her adopted
parents for me if I ever felt I could reply. It's
been a year now and I haven't felt strong enough
to meet her face to face or even respond to her
letter. How am I going to explain why I let her
go? How am I going to look her in the eye and
tell her that I didn't fight to keep her? I never*

stopped loving her, Aaron, and it is so important for me to let her know this. In case something ever happens to me, I have written her a letter explaining why I gave her up, who her natural father is and how I pray for her happiness. And, because you are reading this, I guess something awful has happened to me and it is here that I must rely on you to post this letter I have left for Tamzin. Maybe, if the time is right for the pair of you, you will one day be a brother and sister . . .

They say the pen is mightier than the sword, well, each word felt like a sledgehammer to Aaron as he read through the letter his mother had left him. He used to believe that marrying Jeena had been the biggest mistake of his life. Unfortunately he'd just found out about an even bigger one. The mistake of not opening the package his mother had left him when he should have twenty years ago. The thought of his sister writing a letter to their mother and then abandoning hope of a reply as the years passed was gut-wrenching.

A hundred different emotions were tripping over themselves to gain Aaron's attention. To think that he had a sister out there in the world, someone he could call family, his own flesh and blood, it was enough to make him dizzy. He remembered, many years ago, when he was about nine years old, visiting Santa's grotto in a department store. Santa had asked what he would like for Christmas and Aaron replied he would like a sister. 'Not a brother?' Santa questioned. 'No, he might bully me.' Instead Santa gave him a

Ladybird book on the fire service and a generous helping of his tobacco breath.

Picking up the envelope for Tamzin, Aaron looked at the address and was shocked to find that her adopted home was only a short way up the M1 motorway in Coventry. To think of the amount of people he'd sent to Coventry and all the time he had a sister who lived there. Or, a sister who he *hoped* still lived there. Who was to say that she hadn't moved away after all these years?

Only one way to find out, decided Aaron, already gearing himself up to take the plunge tomorrow. Twenty years was a long time and he owed it to his sister to track her down and he owed it to his mother to grant her her dying wish. He took another look at the open door of his safe and half-smiled. In some ways he was indebted to Stacy, for if she hadn't been such a bitch the chances were that the parcel would have remained sealed for years to come.

Chapter Thirty-two

Forget the Atkins Diet, if you really want to lose weight then what you need is the Kidnapped Diet. Not only will you lose weight with worry, but the food that your captor feeds you (if he feeds you at all) is normally worthless. Within just a week of captivity you could have that dream starved look that all modelling agencies crave these days. With the Kidnapped Diet, you'll be glad you were taken hostage after all.

Jeena pulled up her satin *kameez* and studied her dwindling waistline. If she looked carefully she was sure she could see her intestines as they worked to transport the digested Digestives she'd been given for breakfast, lunch and tea these last six days. Crikes, had it really been *only* six days since she'd been taken from Aaron's apartment? It felt more like six years. And only Digestive biscuits? Apparently, she overheard one of them saying, they didn't want to have her full of energy or she might try and escape. Jeena viewed her surroundings, who wouldn't want to escape?

The walls were plastered with McFly and Busted

posters, *get me outta 'ere now*! The small bedroom itself obviously belonged to some teenage girl, what with its single bed and single wardrobe. Everything else, it seemed, had been removed. The room's saving grace, which just about spared it from being too claustrophobic, was the little window which overlooked an open field. Taking nothing for granted, even though the frame was far too small to squeeze through, they had nailed it closed with six-inch nails.

Jeena stared out of the window into the dark morning. At the moment her captors held all the cards, she was trapped, no one knew where she was and most likely, because of the phone call she'd been forced to make to Aaron, no one was looking either. But, even though they held the cards now, she was keeping an ace up her sleeve just in case. At every opportunity on the two-hour journey here, Jeena had made notes in her head of where she was going. Of where she was being taken. Road followed road which turned into lanes. More lanes then a turn-off towards a village called Grovely. And once in Grovely down a rough track and into the grounds of this isolated, picturesque cottage named Vine Leaves. If the opportunity arose, at least she knew where she was being held.

And today, Jeena was hoping to make that opportunity arise.

The routine was always the same. 7.30 in the morning she was woken (not that she could really sleep) with a cup of coffee and the four Digestive biscuits which would be her breakfast. She was left alone to study the English translated version of the Sikh bible – *Guru Granth Sahib* – until one p.m., when she was given a glass of orange juice and four more Digestive biscuits. From one until 6.30 p.m., Jeena was forced to listen to tape recordings of Holy Teachings explaining in depth the Sikh religion. At seven p.m., she was given her final meal of the day, four more Digestives with a glass of milk. At nine, she was allowed to have a wash in the adjoining bathroom. Finally it was bed time. One other thing: if she needed to go to the loo then she had to use a green plastic bucket which was placed in the wardrobe. Not quite a luxury toilet and not quite a hole in the ground either, somewhere in between.

Noises from downstairs broke Jeena's concentration. Her breakfast was on its way up. And so would last night's dinner be if she let her nerves get the better of her. The sound of footsteps stomping along the corridor to her room. The slide of the bolt on the other side of the door, another bolt and finally the key. The door creaked open slowly and yet again, the same thing happened as yesterday morning when Kidnapper two, or K2, was on breakfast duty; yet again K2 was munching away on one of her sacred biscuits. Jeena knew not to complain as he'd only eat another one. As soon as he bent down to place the tray on the edge of the bed, well aware this was her chance, Jeena fired up all her aggression (just like Aaron had taught her) and with one monster kick, jammed her foot in the side of his ribcage. The coughing and spluttering that came from his mouth was a sure indication that she'd hit his kidneys. As he flopped forward and rolled over, clutching his side in agony, Jeena flew past him and out of the door. Her breathing was tight and her lungs were already burning, but her mind was clear and her intent was escape. At all costs escape. The top of the stairs came next and with a quick look she saw that her way was free and bounded down them, two-by-two, no sign of lacking in energy. The front door beckoned and she knew that this was it; she was getting out of this sick house for good.

She could hear someone shouting angrily behind her as she whipped off the door chain and opened the lock. The voice was so near she could almost feel it down her neck, but somehow she threw back the front door and darted into the darkness outside. Her legs were heavy and ponderous on the gravel, almost betraying her heart. She could hear the chasing footsteps behind. She forced herself to move quicker and . . .

'Jeena!' the voice of the leader, K1, called out. 'There is no escape.'

One second later, her hair was grabbed and she was thrown backwards to the ground. In a last attempt to stop this nightmare, Jeena picked up a handful of the gravel and threw it hard at K1's eyes. Blood shot from his forehead and in an angry retaliation he tightened his fist and punched her in the face. 'There *is* no escape, Jeena!'

Too scared to feel any pain, Jeena was manhandled back into the cottage by two of the guys. She'd heard many frightening stories of Indian and Pakistani girls being locked up because they had gone against traditions. It was not as uncommon as some people might imagine. Locked up, beaten up and messed up. But even worse than that, just like in the book *1984*, in Asian culture, women can even be charged with thought-crime. *Thinking* about running off with a man can be punished in just the same way as if she *had* run off with him. And Jeena's crime – marrying a white man – was top of the heap when it came to crimes against culture. Her worry right now was what they held for her in Room 101.

She was taken to a cosy-looking living room with low beams and an open fire place where she was shoved into a sofa chair. Sitting and standing before her were six Indian men. The two who had followed Aaron. The three who came to collect Jeena from Aaron's apartment, which included their leader, K1. And the master of this mob, her Uncle Gurjinder (Papaji's older brother from India).

'I warned you all not to harm her,' Gurjinder ranted, referring to Jeena's growing black eye. 'Physical violence is only to be used as a last resort. How can we remain inconspicuous at the airport when she's walking around with that on her face?'

Jeena's stomach sunk at the mention of the airport. It reconfirmed all her worst suspicions: they were planning on taking her to India. She needed a heart donor quickly as hers was about to pack up. INDIA!

Gurjinder continued, 'You've let everyone down, Jeena. You have slandered the good family name. But if you think that I'm going to sit back and watch while you piffle away our family blood, then you are mistaken. I won't allow this cross mixing in our family. I must honour our forefathers and put a halt to this embarrassment once and for all. Your own father is too weak to keep you in line, but he is my brother and I know that inside he is ashamed of you.' Gurjinder took off his large orange turban to scratch his head and then placed it back. 'You will be taken to India in five days time, on Friday morning. You will be kept under lock and key until that day arrives. I warn you, Jeena, if you try to escape again then I will personally see to it that your white husband suffers unnecessarily. I will take his last breath from his body with pleasure. I was the inter-village wrestling champion of Viahakhapatnam, his martial arts do not frighten me. It will be an easy matter for me to beat him to a pulp.' He paused. 'And if you don't know this already, I always keep my promises.'

Keeping quiet and still, Jeena listened to the plan, which seemed to have every base covered. On Thursday evening Aaron would be taken and held hostage in his own house until word was out that Jeena's feet had hit Indian soil. Meanwhile, she would be holed up in the cottage until Friday when her flight was due. She would be taken to Heathrow Airport and chaperoned onto the plane. WARNING if she dared to cause a scene or even a slight fuss at the air-port then instructions would go out to a group of Asian men to kill Aaron. If she behaved, he would be a free man.

'Now get her out of my sight,' Gurjinder ordered one of the men. 'It's time for her to study the *Guru Granth Sahib*.' Just before Jeena was ushered away, he called out, 'Oh, and give her some ice for that eye.'

Uncle Gurjinder was here on family business. He hated cold England and couldn't understand why so many of his countrymen set up shop here, pardon the pun. He'd been in this country for a few weeks now and the more he stayed the more he realized that this was no place to bring up an Indian girl. No wonder his niece Jeena had succumbed to temptation when it was everywhere. In the streets, in the parks, on the TV, in the newspapers. Little by little Great Britain had lost its great and little by little the people of Great Britain had lost the world's respect. Drugs were cheaper than chips nowadays and women were drinking as heavily as men. Fashion was more important than family. Dope was more important than self-respect. Who had the better car or who wore the Armani clothes. The gutters were filled with pushers and pimps and sex before marriage was almost a given.

Gurjinder was still suffering from a mild case of shock at seeing how little English women wore when the sun came out – even prostitutes in India wore more than these shameless women. At times he wanted to phone his brother, Preetjeet, and let rip with a lecture on how bad Britain had become, but he didn't want his brother to know he was here. He certainly didn't want his brother to know that he'd kidnapped his daughter.

And this kidnap, it was amazing how it had all come together really. There were many people to thank. First, he had to thank his cousin who had hired this cottage many weeks ago. He had to thank distant relatives who had agreed that Jeena's parents had been too soft and they really should have disowned her. He had to thank these same relatives for offering the services of their sons and their friends. He had to thank his brother for mentioning that Jeena's boss, Mr Akhtar, and Jeena had been having some altercations regarding her marriage. And, lastly, he had to thank Mr Akhtar, for providing him with certain information about Jeena's friends, their phone numbers and addresses. Mr Akhtar had been a credit to the Indian way, for as soon as he'd heard of Gurjinder's plight in redirecting his niece to the correct path, he was more than happy to oblige. It was proof once again that when the Indian community is having a problem, they will go out of their way to solve it. Sticking together like *ghee*. In fact, Gurjinder checked the time 8.08 a.m., it would soon be time to make his daily phone call to Mr Akhtar's office, whereupon he would ask him whether Jeena's husband, father or even the police had been asking questions about Jeena's disappearance. Then Gurjinder remembered that it was Sunday and Sunday for most Britons meant lie-ins and car boots. Mr Akhtar, no doubt, would be down his local *gurdwara*. He would contact him tomorrow.

Pulling his chair closer to the open fire, Gurjinder contemplated the near future. Obviously he wasn't going to take Aaron hostage, that would be a complete waste of time and an unnecessary risk. As long as Jeena thought that her husband would be killed if she screwed up, then that was enough. He thought of her studying upstairs and knew that he was doing the right thing. Once he had Jeena back in the arms of India then she would know what hardship and struggle was all about. These British-born Asian girls had things far too easy and it was about time they found out how hard their parents had to work to bring them this lush lifestyle they all took for granted. She'd soon know respect for her elders. How not to back-chat them. How not to get in their way. How not to undermine them. How to agree with everything they say. How to learn and understand her religion, what being a Sikh really means. And especially how not to upset and disgrace her own parents.

Oh, roll on Friday . . .

Chapter Thirty-three

Sitting in his BMW, Aaron stared across the road at the large, detached house that he presumed his sister had grown up in. A well-to-do house in a well-to-do area. The driveway, with its huge conifer trees on either side of the entrance, was empty of cars, and Aaron guessed that the occupants were either at Sunday church or a car boot sale. It mattered not, for he was still working out the best way to approach the situation and he couldn't afford to screw this up. He was already twenty years late as it was and God only knew what Tamzin had been thinking all these years about her mother not replying to her letter. It was as if she'd been dumped on twice.

Aaron felt like a cryptologist as he tried to decipher his feelings. Last night he'd tossed and turned, his pillow spiked with guilt and his duvet burning acid with regret. All these years he'd wanted, no, *craved* a family, and yet, just forty minutes up the motorway in Coventry, was his sister. Gran was great but somehow he always felt lonely with her as his only relative. What would his life have been like now if he'd opened the package when his conscience had prodded him to all those years ago? What memories would he have if he'd met his sister when he was a teenager? How was Tamzin going to react when she found out that she had a younger brother? That her mother had died? That she should have been given a letter from her many years before. That . . .

Slap! Aaron slapped his head and called himself a moron: the house he was staking-out had a double garage. It might have explained the missing cars. With a quick check in the rear-view mirror that his hair was okay, Aaron, in jeans, Nikes and a long-sleeved T-shirt, jogged across the road, up the drive and knocked on the pristine white front door. He'd contemplated making a good impression by arriving in a suit, but that would be false and not him. Then again he wasn't going to turn up in his martial arts outfit either. And that *was* him.

The door was opened by an elderly woman in a tracksuit. She spoke with a northern accent, 'How can I help you, dear?'

For a nanosecond Aaron's brain malfunctioned as he stood gazing at the woman wondering why she looked nothing like him. It was a moment before he realized that this shrivelled woman couldn't be his long lost thirty-eight-year-old sister. THANK GOD! He was only glad that he hadn't said, 'Hello, surprise, I'm your brother,' or it would be just a short trip to the nut house for him.

Pulling himself together, he replied, 'Oh, hello, I'm looking for Tamzin Preston. This is the last address I have for her. I'm an old friend.'

'It's Gary, isn't it?' the lady presumed. She shouted back into the hallway. 'It's Gary. You remember, he used to go out with our Tammy.'

A male voice shouted out, 'Hello Gary. Keeping well are you?'

'A lot of people think I look like Gary,' Aaron said, cringing at himself. 'But, I'm not him. He sounds like a good bloke though. No, I'm Aaron. That's like Ron with Alcoholics Anonymous at the beginning.' He told himself to shut up, before he made even more of a fool of himself. 'Erm, I was in the neighbourhood and I thought it would be grand to hook up with Tamzin again.' Aaron paused. 'Not in a sexual way. Or anything like that. Or—'

'She moved out about ten years ago, dear. Let me write down the address for you. It's only up the road really.' She then whispered, 'Tammy's married now, though, with twin girls. Lovely grandchildren. I'll write her phone number down as well then you can always call her if she's not in.'

Aaron thought that it was a good job he wasn't Bin Laden for she told him fucking everything. Didn't OAPs know about secrecy? He drove away from the sweet woman's house, following the map she'd neatly drawn on a sheet of paper. She'd even given him a ham roll with granary mustard for the ten-minute journey. Although Aaron had to say a firm 'No' to the striped pullover she wanted him to wear on account of the breezy weather which was brewing – but it was nice to know that his sister had been brought up by such caring people.

From one stake-out to another, Aaron pulled up

across the road from the semi-detached house and finished off his roll. From his vantage point he could see more or less everything. They had a new people carrier parked in the drive. A small front garden which was neat and tidy. Fancy net curtains. And a crazy pathway which led from the front gate to the front door. Who lived in a house like this? Aaron was quite pleased to say, his sister did. He didn't know what he had expected but it was a relief to find that she lived in a 'normal' residence and not some rundown block of flats she shared with the local heroin addict.

Once Aaron crossed the road and walked up the pathway to his sister's house, then there would be just a two-inch thick piece of wood standing between him and a life-changing moment. On the map of his life this one compass point, behind that door, could change his course for ever. Not too keen on waiting for his nerves to devour his entire stomach wall, Aaron got out of his car, crossed the road, walked up the pathway to his sister's house and knocked on the door. It felt like an eternity waiting, and it was only now, as the nippy weather began to bite, that Aaron wished he'd taken up the offer of the striped pullover.

Finally the door opened and standing right before Aaron's eyes was his mother. Not just someone who looked like her, she *was* her. Her slim build, her medium height, her watery-blue eyes, her long brown hair, her olive skin, even down to the very same expression that his mother used to have when she was shocked by something. Considering that there was only five years difference between the age his mother had been when she died to the age of Tamzin now, it was not all that remarkable that there should be some similarities; but Aaron had definitely not been prepared for this! The resurrection of his mum. He couldn't help feeling as if his mind was playing tricks on him and in some ways half-expected his father to appear behind her.

Aaron stood speechless, gazing into Tamzin's eyes. And there he was last night thinking that if Tamzin didn't believe that he was her brother he'd get a DNA test done for her. Just one picture of his mother (their mother) would prove it.

'I know who you are,' Tamzin began. 'You're Aaron, aren't you?' She stepped outside and hugged him warmly. 'My brother.'

Inside Aaron was briefly introduced to Tamzin's husband, Neil, and their twin two-year-old daughters, Jenny and Nicola. With a knowing look to his wife, Neil considerately took the twins out for a walk in the park, leaving the two of them alone. Tamzin seemed more than happy to take control of the situation, as if she'd been waiting for this for some time. They sat next to each other on the sofa with coffee and biscuits.

'Maybe I should start, if that's okay,' she said. 'I know that our mother died twenty years ago. I found this out . . .'

She went on to explain all she knew. How five years ago she'd turned up at her mother's house in Northampton, only to be told by the neighbours how Mrs Myles and her husband had tragically passed away in a road accident. She had been given the address of the cemetery and it was here that she discovered she had a brother by the flowers that Aaron always left on Mother's Day, the anniversary of her death and Mum's birthday. For five years she'd seen Aaron on every one of those days, watching him from afar as he left his flowers and cards. Even though she had wanted to approach him, in fact was desperate to approach him, out of respect to Aaron she had held back – for all she knew Aaron was totally unaware that he had a sister. It was not her place to tell him. But, God, had she waited for this day to happen. Praying that the yin and yang of this world would put them together. Hoping against hope that the one blood relative she knew existed would find a way to be in her life. Tamzin continued with her tale: how she'd also found out the whereabouts of her natural father and was disappointed to find that he was a complete waste of time. 'I never fucking wanted you then, and I don't fucking want you now. So, piss off,' he'd told her. Nice!

It was strange listening to his sister who had a similar pitch to her voice as Aaron remembered his mother to have had, yet Tamzin's voice was freckled with a northern accent. Stranger still was how easy it was to talk openly about his mother, a subject that, up until now, had been hidden deep within himself. Yet everything about this meeting felt natural, as though the two of them had known each other for a lifetime. They say that blood is thicker than water, surely this proved that blood was thicker than time.

'So, it was you who visited my parents' grave and placed flowers by their headstone,' Aaron realized, walking around the room, stretching his legs. 'I always wondered who the mystery person was. I even hung around the cemetery for a whole day once on the off-chance that I would catch them.'

Tamzin nodded. 'I remember that day well, you just wouldn't leave. I only wanted to lay the flowers and go but you were hiding behind another headstone. I wouldn't have minded but I was seven months pregnant with the twins at the time.'

They both laughed, and as they did so their eyes connected with warmth. This was something special and unexpected and right. While Tamzin disappeared into the kitchen to make some more coffee, Aaron found himself looking around the large, clean room. Children's toys scattered on the wooden floorboards. Throws on sofas (presumably to hide the children's puke stains). Wallpaper peeling from where the children had played their favourite game 'Let's wreck the joint'. Aaron could only describe it as lived in and loved. It was certainly not the home of someone who was hard up, which had been another one of Aaron's worries. The last thing he would have wanted to find was that he had a sister who had been struggling while he had been basking in luxury.

Tamzin returned with coffees and a joke, 'At least we've got someone to baby-sit our two rotters now. For some reason no one volunteers anymore.' She nodded her head towards a set of crayon markings on the wallpaper. 'It's not like they ruin things on purpose.' She sat down. 'So, are you married? Kids? I never saw you with anyone at the cemetery. Apart from the old woman.'

'My gran. That's my dad's mum.' He sighed heavily. 'Look, Tamzin, I have to tell you something. Actually

I've got to give you something. It's a letter to you from our mother. The reason I . . .'

As if the Arctic weather had just blown in, Tamzin began to shake. Up until now most of what she knew about her mother and her reasons for giving her up for adoption had been guesswork. From the gravestone she'd learnt her mother's age and worked out that she was pregnant with her at just fourteen years old. Having met her arsehole father, it was blatantly obvious that he wouldn't have cared if she was adopted, aborted or even miscarried. Taking into consideration the year when all this was happening, in the Sixties, it was no surprise that she had been given up for adoption. An unmarried fourteen-year-old mother without a partner to support her would have caused a huge scandal. Tamzin held no grudges towards her mother, but now, she was most likely about to find out the truth and she just prayed that in the letter, her mother didn't admit to having grudges against *her*.

' . . . And that's why I couldn't open the package, I hope this makes sense,' Aaron said.

Tamzin had been miles away. 'Sorry, what package?'

Aaron repeated the reasons why it had taken him so long, twenty years in fact, to open a package. He explained how he was just too afraid to finally say goodbye to his mother. Too afraid to hear her final words. Obviously, if he had known there was a letter in there for a SISTER, then he would have opened it years ago.

'But, come on, you were only eight when they died. I'm glad you took your time to open it; it might have been too much for an eight-year-old boy. First losing your parents and then finding out that you have a sister. You can't blame yourself, Aaron.'

'But I do. I'm twenty-eight now. Even Royal Mail are a little bit quicker than me when it comes to delivering packages.' They both laughed.

Tamzin took the envelope from him and placed it on the arm of the sofa. 'I think I'll read this later. I'm going to have to psyche myself up, if you know what I mean.' A calmer Tamzin composed herself. 'You haven't answered me, are you married? Or is there someone special in your life?'

Can I phone a friend, thought Aaron, or use a 50/50? How do I answer this cherry without choking on the pip? Or rather, how do I answer this cherry without looking like a complete retard who was caught in a girlfriend's bed with her father's turban on and ended up agreeing to marry her for one year only so that she wasn't forced into having an arranged marriage with a total stranger from India?

'I've been married for ninety-five days but there is no one special in my life,' Aaron said, rather pleased with his reply.

'Okay.' Tamzin nodded. 'And are you looking forward to day ninety-six?'

'Erm. The day I'm really looking forward to is day 365 because that is the day we divorce.'

'Okay.' Tamzin nodded again. 'Just a minor point, but do you love this woman?'

Aaron stood up and began to pace the room, suddenly feeling enclosed and uncomfortable. 'She's okay. She's a good wife when she's not got another bloke like Spud Sam in her bed. But it works both ways, as I have to admit my bed is often full of other women too.' He paused. 'This is coming out wrong. Our marriage is not like a normal marriage.'

'I can see that, Aaron.'

'Look, if you must know, she loves me and I love her, but I can't commit to her. I can't box myself in like that.'

Taking a sip on her now cold coffee, Tamzin tucked her feet under her legs and studied Aaron. He was desperately handsome, that was plainly obvious, and his personality shone bright. It would be a short-sighted woman who turned down her brother, Aaron. Which more or less completed her calculations: he was a womaniser. A womaniser with too much choice. Too much choice often makes a man picky. And picky men are notorious for not being able to commit.

'You don't want to box yourself in and yet you are married. How come?'

Aaron sat down and explained in detail how his marriage worked, or rather, how it didn't. How they didn't love each other when they agreed to marry but since that time how love had blossomed. Tamzin noticed how fondly and warmly Aaron spoke of his wife, Jeena. She listened as he told her how he was missing her since she'd disappeared to 'think things over'. How it was driving him nuts that he couldn't speak to her. How each day he went to bed disappointed that she hadn't returned home. How . . .

'It's totally obvious that you are head-over-heels in love with Jeena, Aaron. You can pretend all you like that you're looking forward to a divorce, but if I were to have a guess I believe that if that day came it would break your heart.'

The truth hurts and Aaron was covered in bruises. He knew his arguments sounded weak, but he persisted with them anyway. 'I do love her but I don't want to settle down with Jeena. Or any woman for that matter. I just can't do it and it drives me fucking insane that I'm this way, it really does.' Aaron's frustration was obvious. 'Life is just so much simpler for me if I haven't got to worry about . . .' He broke off. 'Let's say life is simple without them.'

Reading Aaron was easy. Maybe Tamzin could understand Aaron because in some ways she was part of him. She was pretty sure where the problem behind Aaron's fear of commitment lay and it had a lot to do with the death of his parents.

'Aaron, everyone feels what you feel. Fear. The fear that if you get too close to something you'll lose it. I'll play big sister here but I believe that you are afraid that if you get close to someone either you will die on them and leave them like your parents left you, or that they will die on you and you'll relive the same nightmares all over again. It's so much easier for you not to get too close. But, Aaron, when you love someone and they love you then it's too late, you're close whether you like it or not. Do you think that I don't worry about losing my husband or my children? I sometimes wake up in the night wondering what would happen to them if I were to die. Who would take care of my babies? But it's not healthy to think that way. It will drive you batty. Love is precious, Aaron, and you must take it when it comes. It may never pass your way again. Think about that. And one day, when you are getting on the bus aged ninety-five you might bump into Jeena and think, we could have lived such a great life and I messed it all up by worrying too much. Soppy but true.'

Before Aaron had a chance to respond his mobile rang. The display showed it was Jeena's father and it was a call that Aaron could not afford to miss. Shrugging to Tamzin, he walked out to the kitchen to take it.

After greeting each other, Papaji began, 'Could you put Jeena on the line, Aaron, only I can't get through to her on her phone. It's switched off.'

Aaron was about to ask Tamzin to pretend to be Jeena when he realized that no, it was doubtful that she could speak Punjabi. There was only one other way to deal with this, like a good poker player he would bluff. He had known it was only a matter of time before her parents called anyway.

'Jeena? You want to have a word? I'll just go and get her.' As soon as Aaron said it he regretted it, the chances of Jeena turning up here were pretty slim. Erm. He put the receiver back to his mouth. 'Oh, what a stroke of bad luck, she literally just popped out about a second ago to get the ingredients from the supermarket. She left me a note on the side to say that she would be cooking Mango Tikka Hot Pot tonight. Have you ever tasted her Mango Tikka Hot Pot? It's amazing. Anyway, I'll tell you she called. I mean, I'll call her and tell her that I called. Hang on, I mean, you called to tell me I'll call so I'll just wait for you to call her and I'll talk to her then. That's if she hasn't already called you before . . .'

'Are you on drugs, Aaron?'

'Look, Papaji, I'm ashamed to say that we have had a bit of an argument and she's gone off in a huff for a few days with Kitty. That's why her phone is off; she doesn't want anyone to contact her. I'll let you know the minute she comes back.'

'Okay, Aaron, but you make sure that you don't let Indian women walk over you. You never back down to them. They are as stubborn as camels. Remember you are the man and she is your slave. She can't go gallivanting off like that. How can she see to your bedroom needs if she's not there? This is not how we brought her up, I can assure you, Aaron. I am so embarrassed. When she returns, I will give her a good talking to.'

Just as Aaron switched off his mobile, he saw Tamzin's husband pushing the children in their double buggy down the garden path. It was probably a good time to make an exit. There was much thinking to do. After leaving his number and address, he bid Tamzin, Neil and the twins goodbye and promised that he would be in touch soon.

'I'm so pleased that you looked me up, Aaron,' Tamzin said as she kissed him goodbye at the door. 'I hope you feel the same way.' Aaron's hug confirmed that he did.

Five minutes later and Aaron was driving back to Primpton with a head full of home truths. Pulling into a side road, he parked up next to a row of thick bushes. He needed time to think. Tamzin's idea that he was scared of committing to someone because he was afraid of dying on them, or them dying on him, was a hole in one. And par for the course was Aaron's self-denial up until now. Maybe it was time he took his head out of the bunker and grabbed hold of Jeena before his life reached the eighteenth hole.

Banging his hands down in frustration on the steering wheel, Aaron shouted, 'Where the fuck is my wife? Where the fuck are you, Jeena?'

Chapter Thirty-four

Kidnapping is so common in India and Pakistan it's a wonder it isn't on the school curriculum. Yet, if a family has to resort to this ghastly deed to force through an arranged marriage, something must be decidedly rotten at the core of Asian values. And now this lowly practice has spilt over to the West.

Jeena knew that at this very moment she wasn't the only British-born Asian being held against her will in Britain in the name of family honour. Chances were that she was one of many. Like caged monkeys they wait to be set free, although, ironically, that very freedom is a misnomer for something far worse: a life sentence with a man you've never met before, your new husband. A man who you must obey. A man who, let's face it, owns you.

Like a caged animal, Jeena paced the small room. Nine days she'd been stuck here. She was well aware that her time was running out, it was already Wednesday evening, just two days before she was due to fly out to India and just one day before her captors were planning on taking Aaron hostage. The thought of him being manhandled by this bunch of crooks was making her heart bleed with guilt. She only hoped that Aaron didn't try anything stupid when they arrived as he might end up with a knife in his stomach. Or worse, a knife across his testicles. Jeena stood still for a moment and looked out of her pokey window. The night itself was an added wall to her prison. 'There is no escape, Jeena' still echoed in her mind from the other morning's attempt at fleeing. First there was Colditz. Then there was Devil's Island and now it was Vine Leaves Cottage. Papillon would have laughed.

She lay back on the bed and closed her eyes. She had three choices. One, to think about Aaron, which would end up with her crying. Two, to think about her family, which would end up with her crying also. Or three, to think about escaping, which might end up with her being killed. Over the nine days that she'd been here, it was hard not to be impressed with the military-style discipline instilled by the head honcho Uncle Gurjinder. His five soldiers were making a great effort to please their orange-turbaned commander. This could have been any one of their sisters, as far as they were concerned, and to crush these ideas of love marriages from Indian girls one had to cut the roots wherever they showed. Amongst the five soldiers, there was just one, K3, who seemed to show Jeena some pity. He always asked how she was feeling and when it was his turn to bring her biscuits there was always an extra one on the plate. Last night he'd sneaked her in a chocolate bar, making sure that he took away the wrapper when she'd finished eating it. K3 definitely had a heart, and maybe, just maybe, she could use him to escape.

But how? And if she did, how far would she get? She was getting weaker by the day on the Kidnap Diet. She metaphorically hit herself, giving herself a metaphorical black eye to match her real one, leaving her resembling a metaphorical panda. This was no time for negativity. She had to be positive all the way from now on. Aaron's life might depend on it. At the very least his testicles might.

Another minute dragged along, and another and . . . another. Time flowed slowly like it was stuck in syrup. It seemed an eternity before Jeena heard the seven p.m. footsteps stomping across the floorboards and along the corridor to her room. The slide of the bolt on the other side of the door, another bolt and finally the key. The door creaked open and K3 stood there with a plate of five Digestive biscuits and a glass of cold milk. With his bottom he closed the door behind him and then handed Jeena the tray.

'Thanks,' Jeena said, placing the tray on the floor beside her. 'I just want to say that I don't hold a grudge against you. You have been kind to me and I will always remember you for that.' Jeena tried her best to smile sexily, but with a swollen black eye it was a pretty impossible task.

K3 smiled back. 'We are only doing what we think is right. One day you will thank us.'

Jeena couldn't help but notice that K3 had not been talking to her but to her breasts. She'd never seen eyes dribble before and, at a guess, Jeena would say that K3 was weighed down with hormones all bursting to get a slice of anything on offer. Jeena asked herself: what was on offer? Or, rather, was there anything she could offer him. And if there was, what could he give her in exchange? She worked her vision over his body and spotted that he had a mobile phone clipped to his trouser belt. There was no way he was ever going to let her use the phone, no matter what she offered to do to him, but if there was some way she could get him to remove his trousers, then who knows, she might be able to steal the phone without his knowledge. Now, the only trouble was, what on earth would she have to do to make him remove his trousers?

She passed her eyes over him again. He seemed clean and good looking. There was no wedding ring. And, more importantly, she wasn't related to him, like she was to K2, K4 and K5. She'd written about this sort of thing as her alter-ego heroine, Nikita, in her book *Naked Riders*, how she was willing to sleep with anyone to get herself out of a tight spot; now it was a matter of doing it for real. It was Jeena's only hope and she prayed that he wasn't gay – but judging by the way he'd been ogling her breasts he was as straight as the next man. Above all else, she had to convince him why a woman such as she would suddenly want to do things with a man such as he. Claiming that she had suddenly fallen in love with him might smell like a bit of bullpoop. So what? Play to his ego, that's what, no matter how ridiculous it came out.

'You are a very attractive man,' Jeena said, internally cringing. 'Quite edible in fact.'

K3 nodded in agreement. He suspected most women thought as much but were too afraid to tell him. 'Thanks.'

'Pure eye candy.' Jeena fiddled with her hair, twirling it around her fingers. 'I should have gone for a man like you. I doubt that you would leave me wanting in bed, would you?'

He grinned. 'What did you expect from marrying a white man? Maybe if they had concentrated more on writing something like the *Kama Sutra* rather than that poxy *Domesday Book*, then you wouldn't be left "wanting" like you say.'

Jeena slowly trailed her hand down her collarbone and towards her breasts. 'Not only sexy but educated too, no wonder I'm getting hot.' His pupils widened dramatically and Jeena took her chance. 'Why don't we have a little bit of fun while the rest of the guys are busy?' She removed her *kameez* top, leaving her bra in full view.

K3 didn't need another invitation. Jeena was so tantalizingly beautiful, he thought, as he half jumped on the bed and began to kiss her on the lips. Sparing no thought for his bride-to-be in India, K3 unhooked Jeena's bra straps and moved his face to her breasts. With his face busy upstairs, he tried for some action downstairs by thrusting one hand between her legs. All the time Jeena was moaning quietly, pretending to enjoy his attempts at turning her on. But her plan was moving in the wrong direction. It wasn't her clothes she wanted removing, but his.

'Let me give you a blow job,' Jeena whispered, as sexily as possible. 'Lie on your back.'

Doing as he was told, K3 lay back with a grin on his face as Jeena began to undo the buckle on his trouser belt. To the right of her hand the mobile phone hung by its holster; Jeena prayed that the battery was charged and the credit was topped up. Slowly she slid his trousers down to his ankles, continuously complimenting him on the size of his bulge, totally ignoring his knobbly knees. Deftly and almost elegantly, Jeena unclipped the phone with one hand while removing his boxer shorts with the other. Just as she took the end of his cock in her mouth, she slipped the mobile under the duvet, hoping against hope that she wasn't sucking on a man's cock for nothing here, and hoping against hope that she hadn't bitten off more than she could chew!

And why am I sucking on this man's cock? thought Jeena, as she gave him what he wanted. What sort of person does this kind of thing with any old stranger? Well, the answer to that one is most Indian girls. Almost every Asian woman who has taken the route of the arranged marriage will have to perform sexually for a virtual stranger on their wedding night. She may never even have seen the guy before, and yet, come wedding night, she's expected to lie back and be screwed. This guy Jeena was sucking on could so easily have been the guy her parents had arranged her marriage with. She would have had to perform then. There would have been no choice in the matter. And no one would have batted an eyelid. Yet, in this case there was some dignity involved. Jeena was giving K3 a blow job to save Aaron and herself. In some ways it made Jeena feel less sick about what she was doing. But in other ways it didn't.

Each time K3 moaned, Jeena felt her stomach churn. Giving pleasure in this way was supposed to be saved for someone special. He wasn't special and it felt dirty;

in fact his cock almost felt diseased. Not much longer, she kept telling herself, as his thrusts became more vicious, not much longer. By now his eyes were at the back of his head, his body in ecstasy and his feet doing a little Morris dance on the bed. She just hoped that at the grand finale he didn't let out a humungous scream with the words, 'I'M COMING'. The last thing Jeena needed right now was for Uncle Gurjinder to walk in on this scene. His turban would most likely self-combust with his anger.

It helped to be experienced in these matters, as, right at the final moment, Jeena removed his cock from her mouth and let his gusher explode somewhere else. For the next five minutes K3 just lay back with a smile stamped on his satisfied face and half a cup of sperm stuck to his goatee beard.

'What was that?' Jeena pretended to have heard something. 'Sounds like someone's coming up the stairs. You'd better go.'

In a mad rush K3 threw on his trousers and just before he opened the door, Jeena called out. 'Bring more biscuits tomorrow and I'll reward you with more of this . . . BIG BOY. And lock the door on the way out. *And* make sure you wash your beard.'

Instantly, Jeena swished her mouth out with milk ten times (probably not the best drink to try and forget about sperm, but what the hell) and spat it in the urine bucket. Next, she grabbed the Motorola mobile and immediately put it on mute. A feeling inside was telling her that it couldn't be this easy, something was bound to go wrong. Yet the phone battery was full and when she checked the credit there was twenty three pounds available; more than enough to call Aaron. She knew it was pointless contacting the police as when it came to matters between Asian families they liked to stay out of it. Just explaining to them that she had been kidnapped by her uncle would use up the whole credit. There was also the risk that the police might think it was a hoax call and not even bother turning up. With Aaron she was sure he would come through for her.

The phone clock read 19.24 p.m. Aaron would be taking a martial-arts class right now. Quickly Jeena dialled the Paper Lantern and within seconds Mary, the receptionist, had picked up.

'Mary, it's Jeena, I need to speak to Aaron. It's very, very important.'

'I can't possibly disturb him in the middle of a class, Jeena, you know what he's like. Leave me a message and at the first opp—'

'Now, Mary, I need to speak to him right now. Tell him it's life or death. Please, Mary, just get him for me. Please. I beg you.'

Mary rested the receiver on the desk and took a deep breath. She walked down the edge of the centre and waited for Aaron to spot her.

'What?' Aaron said. 'This had better be good, Mary, I was just about to break this one's leg.' The man being held in an arm-lock seemed relieved at the interruption.

'It's your wife on the phone; she sounds distressed, almost hysterical.'

Immediately, Aaron let the guy drop to the floor and sprinted down the hall. His face became stony-white as he listened to what Jeena had to say. Five minutes later, after jotting down the address of where she was being held captive, Aaron stood before his class of thirty and pulled aside his top fighters.

'I need as much muscle as possible,' he said, pacing up and down the line of men. 'If anyone doesn't want to get involved after I've explained, then I won't hold it against them.'

'Count me in, mate,' Charlie shouted out. 'Unless it means going back to the Gulf, I don't know if I could handle that again. Has anyone here heard about the time I . . .'

'Shut the fuck up, Charlie!'

Aaron explained that his wife was being held by a mob of six Indian men, two hours away in the village of Grovely. It was up to them to rescue her. Simple as that! Twenty minutes later, fifteen of them were changed and ready to take a convoy of cars into the country-side. Charlie, as he was an expert at wartime strategy, had been given the job of operation leader – or rather, he'd presumed that the job had been given to him.

Just before jumping into his jeep, Charlie called out to his soldiers. 'I name this operation, "Mission Samosa". People, follow me, we've got a civvy in trouble here. Roger and out!'

Casting a doubtful look in Charlie's direction, Aaron hopped in the passenger seat and clipped on the seat-belt. The jeep lurched forward and the convoy of four cars followed them all the way to the petrol station (Charlie's vehicle was running low on fuel). Aaron watched with frustration as one by one, his students left the garage with sweets, fizzy drinks, chocolates and crisps. What the fuck did they think this was? A school trip? Besides, hadn't they learnt anything about dieting from him over all these years? He jumped out of the jeep in anger.

'Right you lot, on the ground. Fifty sit-ups,' he growled. A few dropped to the petrol-stained concrete and began to count out the sit-ups. 'Feel the burn.'

He was just about to reprimand a student for not doing full movements when it occurred to Aaron that his mind wasn't functioning correctly. In fact, he feared he might be losing it. What the hell was he doing wasting precious time when Jeena was relying on him? Sit-ups? On a sodding garage forecourt? With an audience from pump one and pump twelve? He ordered his pupils to get back in their cars and to follow the jeep. There was no time to waste.

Onwards as the convoy snaked out of Primpton and onto the M1 motorway. Aaron couldn't help but notice the gadgets lighting up the dashboard on Charlie's motor. A police scanner. A satellite navigation system. A speed camera scanner and a tiny tape recorder in case he was stopped by the police and they happened to lie about what was said between them if the matter was ever brought up in court. Oh, and a fluffy air freshener. The irony was that the gadgets probably weighed so much that it was doubtful that the jeep could speed anyway. But if it kept Charlie happy, then it was all right by Aaron. For a happy Charlie was a helpful Charlie and boy did he need Charlie's help tonight – as long as he didn't mention GWS.

The speedy motorway finally came to an end and the convoy was soon to be found driving down the dark country roads which would eventually lead them to the village of Grovely. Twice, a very paranoid Charlie had to be warned not to try and lose the following cars – they were *meant* to be following him. They were *not* the enemy.

'Did I ever tell you about the time I was on a reconnaissance mission in Baghdad dressed as a local woman? I had the complete head to toe thingamajig on. You know . . . the berky . . .'

'The burka,' Aaron corrected.

'Yeah, that's the one. So, there I was mingling in with the crowd when this little Asian lad comes up to me and points to –'

'They're not Asian, they're Iraqis.'

'Whatever. Anyway, this IRAQI lad comes up to me and points to my broad shoulders and then, the little shit points to my feet. Guess what?'

'What?'

'I forgot to take off my size twelve desert boots, didn't I? Next thing I know the lad is screaming his head off in Arabic and before I know it the square is full of armed Saddam guards, you know those Special Republican Guards and their sidekicks, the all in black Fedayeen Militia, and I'm running for my life with a fucking dress on.' Charlie took a quick swerve down yet another country lane, following the directions on his navigation system. 'My point, Aaron, is this: I'm experienced with Muslim people. I've lived amongst them and I know how they think. So when we get to the cottage, I want you to leave everything to me. We don't want to upset these Muslims anymore than we have to. Okay?' He peered through the gloom at Aaron. 'They are very fundamental. Get it, funda . . . *mental*.'

'Jeena's a Sikh, not a Muslim, Charlie,' Aaron said with despair. 'They're all Sikhs.'

And a pretty poor showing for Sikhs they have been so far, decided Aaron as he tumbled off into deeper thought. Kidnapping and violence just because one of their flock doesn't think within the same boundaries as them. How would this world be if everyone was punished for speaking out, for taking the less-trodden path, for expressing oneself, for living life freely, for falling in love? Does the Sikh religion really advocate locking someone up, denying them their rights, and forcing a frightened woman on a plane to India? Does the Sikh religion say that fear can be brandished in order to get a woman to obey?

Cursing himself over and over, Aaron watched the miles dwindle past. He should have known that there was something wrong the moment Jeena disappeared. The phone call he had received from Jeena when he was visiting his gran was weird enough, and it was only now that he knew that she had undertaken that call with a knife at her throat. In the short conversation he'd had back at the Paper Lantern, Aaron had asked Jeena whether she had been hurt in any way. Or, God forbid, sexually abused. 'Just a black eye', was her reply.

Just a black eye, Aaron had thought to himself. He'd kill the person who gave her 'Just a black eye'. Although first he must take care of rescuing her. He checked the jeep's clock: 9.10 p.m. He'd promised Jeena that he would inform her father of the situation. But, as far as Aaron was concerned, if this rescue was to go smoothly, then it was important that there were no unnecessary personnel who might interfere. He wanted to do things

458

his way. He picked up his mobile and dialled Jeena's father explaining to him the crux of what had happened, telling him not to phone the police as this involved members of his own family, his own brother in fact. Aaron had an hour's head start before her father could arrive and that, he hoped, was more than enough time for pay back.

Finally the small sign of Grovely loomed in view. An innocent-looking road headed down a fairly steep slope. The light of an isolated residence could be seen about one hundred yards further down the lane and Aaron agreed with Charlie that one, this was most likely the place and two, they should park here, out of sight and then creep up to Vine Leaves Cottage on foot. It would be an awful mistake to get caught out by the sound of their own car engines.

Aaron stared down the track. It was now or never.

Chapter Thirty-five

Sixteen shadows tip-toed across the gravel under the disguise of night. They rested up by an ancient flint-stone wall, using its height for cover. Charlie ordered five of the eager soldiers to make their way round to the back garden and, once in position, to text him. No one was escaping from this place without Charlie's say-so. Aaron repeated what Jeena had told him. That normally at this time of night the six men would congregate in the living room watching TV. The living room was the second door on the right after the entrance. She was being held upstairs, down the hall, the last door. He would know it from all the bolts on the outside.

'Remember, they will have knives. They may have guns. We don't know. So, don't risk anything stupid,' Aaron said. He was amazed to see how excited his students were. They were always complaining that they had a ton of martial-arts expertise but never got into a situation that warranted its use. Well, that would all change today. If ever there was a time when you needed to be an expert in martial arts then it was now! 'And try not to break too many bones.'

The text message bleeped on Charlie's phone and his smile said it all. Mission Samosa was underway.

'Storm the building,' Charlie croaked. 'Let's kick that fucking door down.'

The group surged forward and four of the best kickers, including Aaron, counted to three. One, two and three, the door shot down the hall and smashed against a shoe rack. Charlie's instructions had been clear: as soon as they were in the building to make as much noise as possible. This would disorientate the kidnappers and scare them senseless.

It was mayhem downstairs as nine heavily muscled martial-arts experts surrounded the six petrified Indian guys in the living room, rudely interrupting their Bollywood film, *Mere Jeevan Saathi*. Meanwhile Aaron had sprinted up the stairs and was busy unlocking the bolts. Five seconds later and Aaron and Jeena were in each other's arms. It wasn't long before the tears began to fall from a totally worn-out but relieved Jeena. If this was a Hollywood film the credits would have been rolling up Aaron's back as he cuddled her. And if this was a Bollywood movie, Aaron would have yanked off his mask to reveal brown skin and he would have said in Hindi, 'Hi, I'm Aaronjinder Gorrahinder, your long lost first cousin's wife's brother's second cousin's half-sister's brother-in-law's next-door neighbour. We marry tonight.'

But this was neither and there was no magic editing machine which Aaron could use to cut out the bad that had happened to Jeena over the last nine days; and to see Jeena so beaten down and weak felt like his heart had been given a hundred lashes. If he had ever been in any doubt about his feelings for her, then any last uncertainties had been banished the moment he'd heard her frightened voice down the phone. He loved her completely and he only hoped that this horrible episode in her life (their lives) didn't wreck things between them.

He moved away from their embrace and held her hands, staring into her eyes. 'I've been going out of my mind with worry, Jeena. It's just as well I hadn't known you had been kidnapped or my imagination would have had you cut up into a thousand little pieces and spread over the farm land. Or even visions of you being put in this sort of vessel and the water was pouring in and you couldn't breathe and . . .'

'Aaron, get some help.'

'Sorry. It's so good to see you're alive.' He glanced with disdain at the posters of Busted and McFly on the wall. The poor girl really had been through hell. He continued, 'I would have had this horrible thought of having to stand over your coffin and declare that I never got to tell you how much I loved you.' Aaron kissed her on the lips. 'Because I do.'

Her mouth quivered. 'You love me?'

''Fraid so.' He sighed. 'I've been such an idiot, I really have. And I've got a million things I want to tell you. Stuff that you want to know. Things that I've kept locked away all this time without telling a soul. I really want this sham marriage to work now. I've even ripped off the wipe board.' Aaron sat on the bed, pulling her beside him. 'Anyway, now is not the time to talk about this.'

Yes it bloody well is, thought Jeena, wondering why she hadn't come up with the plan of being kidnapped herself. Blimey, if it made a man declare his love then 'Hostage takers here I come.' She closed her eyes and rested against his shoulder. God, was she tired.

Aaron looked upon his wife, noting how thin she'd become and his blood felt thick with hate. Right at this very second he was willing to go to prison to make those men pay for what they had done to her. Willing to tear into their bodies with his punishment. He studied her eye which was obviously very sore; her face was gaunt and her whole body was gently shaking. Those fuckers would pay the price and, Aaron promised, it would be steep.

'I'm going to get you home soon, but I need to know who gave you that black eye.'

Jeena stared at her feet, feeling Aaron's anger wafting over her. There was no way she could tell him, however much she hated the man who did this to her, the leader, K1. No way. There was something in Aaron's eyes which hinted that if she told him, blood would be spilt tonight.

'I can't remember,' she responded. 'It was all so quick and it doesn't matter now. You're here. Where's my father?'

Aaron explained that her father and family would be here shortly and he'd have to find out who gave her the black eye another way. He was just about to take Jeena downstairs when she feebly tugged on his arm, halting Aaron in his tracks.

'I've got something awful that I must tell you, but first you have to promise me that you won't go mad.'

With a cagey look of suspicion, Aaron agreed.

Here goes, thought Jeena, knowing that if she didn't tell Aaron then there was always the risk that K3 might tell him as a final insult. She spoke quietly, 'The mobile phone I used to contact you was one of theirs.' Jeena paused. 'I stole it from him when I was . . . Promise me you won't go mad, I had no choice in this, Aaron, I really didn't.' Aaron motioned for her to continue. 'So, I stole his phone while giving him a blow job!'

Silence.

Aaron racked his brain to see if he could think of another meaning for the words, 'while giving him a blow job'. But to no avail. Now the obvious question.

'Did you swallow?'

'NO!'

'Well, let's just forget it then.'

Except Jeena knew that was easier said than done. She wondered what he might have said if she *had* swallowed: 'Go and Listerine your teeth! I'm not in the habit of tasting another man's DNA.'

Downstairs Charlie had tied all the kidnappers' feet together with Uncle Gurjinder's orange turban, explaining as he did so that in the army one had to improvise. If there was no rope available then you get the next best thing, in this case, a six-metre long turban. Out in the kitchen, some of the hungrier men were helping themselves to the pot of chicken curry and basmati rice that was supposed to be the kidnappers' late supper. It was of the general opinion that for kidnappers they certainly could cook. And it was a race to eat the wonderful food before Aaron came back in and ordered them to burn off the extra calories by doing sit-ups.

Aaron entered the living room with Jeena behind him. The main light was intermittently switching on then off like a disco strobe. He noted that Charlie had lined up the six Indian men against a wall with their feet tied together. Not one of the kidnappers was smiling. The opposite of Charlie who had never stopped. Mission Samosa was already a success.

He beckoned Charlie over for a word in his ear. 'What are you doing?'

'Sensory deprivation, sir. Or, in other words, torture.' The lights on then off then on then off . . .

Aaron shook his head. 'Look, mate, I understand what you're trying to do and all that but if you want to torture the subjects by flashing lights, then wouldn't it be a good idea if the rest of us weren't suffering along with them? It's enough to drive me fucking spare.'

Charlie nodded. 'That's the point but I see your point, sir.' He clicked his fingers and shouted across the room, 'Leave it on.' And the guy who had been given the trusted job of switching the light on and off did as he was told.

'Right,' Aaron said, standing before the kidnappers. 'Which one of you fuck heads did this to my wife?'

One of the kidnappers' eyes dropped and Aaron knew it was him immediately. Like a giant snake's tongue, Aaron's arm flicked out and grabbed the culprit round his neck. A groaning sound came from K1's mouth as his windpipe was crushed. Jeena could see the potential problems if this was left to continue: death, police, prison. After getting Aaron to finally admit he loved her, only for him to throw it all away for a life sentence in prison was stupidity in the extreme. She shouted for

Aaron to leave him, begging him to let go. But Charlie took the initiative and grabbed Aaron from behind, twisting him into an arm-lock, forcing Aaron to release his hold on K1's neck.

Charlie clicked his fingers again and called four of the martial-arts experts over.

'You, you, you and you. Keep this man restrained,' Charlie said, referring to Aaron. 'He's a danger to himself and this mission. This is a court martial.' As Aaron was led away, Charlie added, 'I'm sorry, sir, it's for your own good.'

Aaron and Jeena waited in the garden, Jeena clinging to him tightly, Aaron's anger cooling down in the cold of the night. It wasn't much longer than twenty minutes before three cars turned up in the drive of Vine Leaves cottage. Jeena's immediate family and some of her extended family had taken the journey up here.

If justice was going to be served tonight then it would be done the Indian family way. Which to some is worse than the electric chair. Or, worse, giving granny a sponge bath after a garlic balti.

Chapter Thirty-six

A strong family is like a good boxer. It takes the odd hard punch, gets scarred with the odd cut or bruise and even takes the odd fall with a knockout. But always, always, always does it get back on its feet. Never does it throw in the towel.

Jeena's family had taken quite a battering over the period when Uncle Gurjinder had tried to kidnap Jeena. That was about seven weeks ago and the bruises were still raw. That awful night when the kidnappers had been caught out was like a new dawn in the age of the Gill family. A huge feud began, resulting in one half of the family agreeing never to talk to the other half of the family again in this life. But on the positive side Jeena's parents couldn't say enough kind words about Aaron and her father best summed it up when he told Aaron that he couldn't wish for a finer son-in-law than him. Even Nanaji had regained her voice all of a sudden, jumping on Aaron's lap and telling him 'what a good boy you are' every time he paid a visit. Obviously JJ was over-the-moon with Aaron's *total* acceptance in the family, knowing that the future of his porn stash looked bright. Lately it had been harder and harder to walk into a newsagents and buy a porno mag, because inevitably the shops were all owned by Asians; word would get round; JJ was a perv. Thankfully, Aaron had agreed to buy the porn for him. People just didn't get nicer than that! JJ had also decided that he would give Aaron a few more weeks, and if the time was right, he would ask Aaron if he would mind purchasing a blow-up doll for him. Oh happy days.

And as the weeks had passed, so, too, had the nightmares for Jeena. Every now and then she'd think to herself, what might have happened had Aaron not shown up? Where would she be now? Then a ripple of delight would cascade through her, telling her to forget about what if, and think about what is. Right now *what is* was her relationship with Aaron blossoming like flowers. From the moment he'd rescued her to the present, her life had been one huge bubble of enjoyment. He'd even surprised her with a holiday in Canada about a week after that night in Grovely. One log cabin up in the mountains with not a soul in sight. Open fires, snow on the ground and silence in every direction. It was here that Aaron proved how romantic he was, and it was here where Aaron bared his soul for her inspection. What an amazing ten days they were together and what fantastic nights. Did someone mention Paris was the place for love, well try a log cabin in Canada and see if that fits your criteria of intimate.

And coming back down to Earth, well, that hadn't happened yet, for right now, as Jeena awoke in Aaron's bed (their bed), there beside her was the man she'd always wanted. What's more, he was the complete man she'd always wanted. The man with a past he could share and a mind which was open for her. While tucked away in their log cabin in Canada, Aaron had described his childhood, the loss of his parents, the bullying, the fear of commitment, the loneliness. Each revelation was such a struggle to pass through Aaron's throat it was as though the very sentences were coated in broken glass. Jeena had listened, sometimes in tears, sometimes with her mouth open in shock as Aaron told of the nightmare that came to be known as his childhood. 'I got sick of the sound of myself crying,' Aaron had said. 'And I hated the kid that I was. I hated not being able to fight them.' And the 'them', the Fletcher Gang, were a boil that definitely needed lancing as far as Jeena was concerned. Even to this day she could tell they still haunted his life.

But listening to Aaron wasn't all doom and gloom. There were a thousand and one stories about his gran that had had her nearly cramping up with laughter. Most of them related to Gran's obsession of appearing in the local newspaper. Once she'd even baked a huge biscuit and carved the face of Jesus in it, making out to the newspapers that the vision had appeared in the oven. The headline had read: MARGARET MYLES BAKES TURIN COOKIE. Meeting her a few weeks ago hadn't been a disappointment for Jeena either. Innuendo after innuendo coming from Gran and aimed in Aaron's direction referring to his apparent 'gayness' had had Jeena in stitches. Even after Aaron had told her that Jeena and he were husband and wife, she had said, 'You can't

471

hide from what you are, Aaron. If you were born gay then you must accept that you *are* gay.' Initially Gran was very upset that her grandson had got himself married without her knowledge, but, after explaining to her that there would be a second wedding, a Sikh wedding next year, her happiness returned. 'You have my blessing, if that's what you want, Aaron, but do bear this in mind: somewhere, out there, there is a man with a broken heart. He would have been yours.'

Amazingly, if Jeena had been allowed to meet Aaron's family two months ago, then his gran would have been it. Since then, his family had doubled in size and he now had a sister to call his own. Just last weekend, Tamzin, Neil and the twins had visited Aaron and Jeena at their apartment for a meal, a chat and a laugh. Jeena was bowled over by the kindness bestowed upon her by Aaron's new-found sister, almost instantaneously becoming friends. At one point she'd watched Aaron playing with the twins and found herself calculating her next ovulation. At which point Aaron had spotted her staring at him with that far away look and later that night he'd said, 'Think about your career.' Career? Well, if landing a new job working for the local rag was a career, then whoopee!

Jeena yawned and glanced across to Aaron lying beside her. She noticed that there was a gap between their bodies and moved across to fill it. Throughout the night Aaron had been tossing and turning, his mind on a sprint with his heart catching up. It was important that today of all days Aaron knew he had the support of his wife. They were a team now and they had to pull together. She cuddled him from behind and could tell that he was awake.

'It's going to be fine,' Jeena whispered. 'I know you can do this.'

'What if I freeze up? What if the same thing happens again?'

She kissed him on the back of the neck. 'Then you must confront it. Like you said, Aaron, it's all in your mind, anyway. You're far stronger than them. Far, far stronger.'

Above the bed a few Christmas decorations danced in the air. The twenty-fifth was only nine days away now and Jeena couldn't think of a better present than for Aaron to have a totally clear mind after tonight. No more worries. His hard drive cleaned out completely.

After a quick kiss and cuddle, Aaron jumped out of the bed and stretched, his naked body better than any wake-up coffee Jeena had ever tasted. He stared at her with a massive grin on his face.

'The more I think about tonight, the more I'm beginning to look forward to it,' he stated. 'It's going to be fun.'

Her eyes zoomed in on his cock. 'Come back to bed, it's Saturday. Don't be a spoilsport.'

'Look,' he walked across the room, yanked open the drawer and pulled out her futuristic vibrator; tossing it on the duvet. 'Use that, I need all my testosterone for tonight.'

Disappointed, Jeena grabbed the machine, which Aaron described to his mates as something like a disco light show crossed with an industrial drill and a rugby team on heat, and slid it under the duvet. She turned it on, which in many ways turned Aaron on, and in a blink he had joined her – sod the hormones, he had a rampant wife to please. After twenty minutes Aaron had run out of batteries. Something, Jeena knew, her vibrator had not. Maybe Aaron's lack of form had something to do with tonight, she pondered, buzzing the machine down below. Whatever the reason, she'd try to be quick, as he was cooking her breakfast outside in the kitchen.

Aaron cracked an egg against the side of the frying pan and dropped it in the hot oil. That bloody vibrator, he thought to himself, it was spoiling her. It never said 'no'. But, he smiled to himself, she never said 'no' either. It was amazing how much his life had changed since meeting Jeena. From fooling around with her to being virtually forced into marrying her to falling in love with her. Now he was fearful of ever losing her. It was all well and good promising Jeena that he would never look at another woman or be tempted into her bed, but it was more important that he promised himself. To have so much now only to throw it all away on a sexual whim was the realm of losers. Jeena was the only one for him as he hoped he was the only one for her.

He cast his eye around. Slowly but surely, Jeena's personality was attaching itself to the place. Little vases of flowers here, pots of pot-pourri there, candles and candle holders, their Gretna Green wedding photos framed and adoringly placed on a side table, a few Indian antiques and a wipe board to remind him how many days until their wedding anniversary. His one rule had been not to upset the Feng Shui. Something a certain Stacy had been keen to do. It was a fine moment when he was reunited with Tysee, the black fish, and as soon as he was swimming back in his kingdom Aaron could feel the whole apartment lift up with energy. At the risk of disturbing the *chi* of the place, Aaron had kept Muhammad Ali, the replacement black fish, guessing that it was worse Feng Shui to get rid of him than to keep him. As for Stacy, upon returning Tysee to Aaron, she'd boasted she had become firm pen pals with a notorious killer imprisoned in Woodhill maximum-security prison in Milton Keynes. Apparently, Stacy was thinking about helping the convict escape. And then she would write a book about it and sell the rights for a Hollywood movie. Aaron had asked if she was feeling well. 'Of course,' she'd replied. 'So why are you wearing slippers then?' But she was gone.

Immediately the locks were changed, as was the alarm number, and even the safe which now had a new code word, in Japanese, *chotto okii desu*, chosen because it was the first thing giggling Japanese women used to say to Aaron when he dropped his boxer shorts. It had taken him a while to find out what it meant. He'd said it to a few Japanese men first to see if they might know its meaning. Oh, they knew what it meant all right as they chased Aaron up the side roads with their meat cleavers and hot woks. Finally he'd overheard a young boy say it to his father when they were standing in front of this huge statue. Aaron had asked the father if he knew what *chotto okii desu* translated into and the man said, 'It means "it's rather large".' Which was about the size of Aaron's grin after he'd found out.

Just as the baked beans were being scooped onto the plates, Jeena traipsed in, in her pyjamas, red in the face, twinkle in the eye. A full English breakfast waited for Jeena to Easternize with her mango pickle. She kissed Aaron on the cheek and sat on a kitchen stool.

'So.' Aaron passed her a glass of fresh orange juice. 'Satisfied now?'

'Oh, it's so much better with you, but hey, the vibrator does the job okay. Can't complain.'

'But can it mend a fence? Can it cook you breakfast? Can it buy you an engagement ring?' His gaze was aimed at her new, diamond encrusted engagement ring which she'd more or less forced him to buy her for being 'kidnapped'. 'Can it whisper sweet nothings in your ear?'

'No. Christ don't you think that if I had a vibrator that could fix a fence it might be on the news?'

They laughed and at a snail's pace worked their way through this Saturday morning. It was only a matter of hours before the pair of them were to drive to Northampton. It was only a matter of hours before Aaron was due to face his last nightmare. Before today it had been called off, then it was back on, then Aaron would call it off again. It took a fair amount of convincing from Jeena that if he didn't sort out this mess once and for all it would be left to fester like an infected wound. Today it was time for Aaron to meet up with the nine bullies from the Fletcher Gang.

Today it was time to attend the school reunion that Annabel Parry had mentioned on her e-mail all those months ago.

*

The main assembly hall of Collingsworth Comprehensive was covered with Christmas decorations. A bar serving drinks was set up in one corner. A DJ's deck and sound system was set up on the main stage. And a scattering of tables and chairs were fitted around the edge of the dance floor. A few of the teachers mingled with some of the early arrivals with the inevitable sentence always popping up, 'Oh, no, he died years ago.' Which might be what happened to this reunion if the DJ kept playing Peters & Lee.

Jeena and Aaron waited in the warmth of the BMW, watching others drive into the school car park. This place did not hold many happy memories for Aaron and he wanted to make sure his stomach was settled before entering. A couple of cars later and the two of them stepped out into the cold, dark December night, and walked hand-in-hand across the tarmac and into the main entrance. An elderly woman was just inside ready to take their coats and issue stickers. Tonight was a black tie event making Aaron's choice of wear, black dinner jacket and trousers, a cinch. Jeena looked like she'd dressed to impress. A short, off-the-shoulder, shimmering black dress, high-heeled sandals and the perfect body to pull it off.

'Aaron Myles,' Aaron said to the elderly lady. 'And wife.'

The lady traced her finger down the list of people in Aaron's school year and crossed him off with a pen. She then wrote out two stickers one with AARON MYLES the other with GUEST and instructed them to wear them on the shoulder. They were just about to enter the hall when the elderly lady spoke again.

'Oh, one more thing. You haven't got a gun or a knife on you, have you? I have to ask for security reasons.'

'No, no guns or knives,' Aaron replied, laughing. 'It's good to know that these stringent checks are in place though. It makes me feel safe.'

Inside the hall was mostly full. The music not too loud for fear of overpowering the talk. For that was what this reunion was all about. Talk, catching up and third-degree boasting. If one listened carefully you could hear the words, Porsche, Mercedes and self-made millionaire over and over. And if you listened really, really carefully you could probably hear their partners thinking, 'Bullshit'. Aaron shimmied his way across the floor to the bar and brought back drinks for Jeena and himself. They set up fort on the furthest table from the DJ. Aaron's eyes scanning all the time for the Fletcher Gang or any of their accomplices.

'Aaron?' A woman heavily into make-up arrived. 'You don't even recognize me, do you?'

Jeena whispered, 'Tell her to wash off the make-up and you might be able to.'

Aaron kicked his wife under the table. 'Of course I recognize you.' He looked at her sticker. 'It's Clare Hooting, isn't it?'

'You remember,' she squealed happily, pulling up a chair. 'I was the fat one.'

Oh, boy, Aaron remembered her now. Christ had she lost some weight.

'So, what was it, the Atkins' Diet or the Banana Diet?' Aaron made a face to Jeena: DO NOT LAUGH. 'You look great. This is my wife by the way.'

Clare glanced at Jeena's sticker. 'Nice to meet you, Guest.'

The three of them soon became four as another woman joined the table. Then four became five. Story after story was relayed with the girls having the sense not to mention Aaron's bullying. The evening was going pretty well until there was the sound of a glass smashing. All eyes turned to where the sound had emanated from. Then all eyes turned to Aaron.

Staring at them from across the hall, locking eyes on Aaron, was Darryl Fletcher and his groupies. A deathly quiet filled the room like gas. Just the soft sound of the DJ's background music. Just the thud, thud, thud of Aaron's heart.

'Brave of you to turn up to my party,' Darryl stated loud and clear. 'I don't remember inviting you though, you little grub.'

Darryl smashed another glass on the table's edge and then rose from his seat. He swaggered his way across the floor with his gang just footsteps behind. Mr Askew, one of the P.E. teachers, tried to stand in Darryl's way but was shoved to one side as easily as a baby. Teachers weren't going to save the little grub this time. The entourage arrived at Aaron's table and all nine of them stood with their legs so wide apart anyone would think they had medicine balls for testicles.

'Mummy and Daddy still dead, are they?' Darryl said, setting off the tittering behind him. 'Couldn't be bothered to stay alive for you, could they?'

Appalled at the nastiness of this thug of a man, Jeena struggled to stand up. She wanted to punch the goof right in his smug-looking face. But Aaron pulled her back down. This was his problem and this was his fight.

Instantly, Darryl clocked on that the Asian bird was Aaron's partner. 'Does he still cry? It used to drive me crazy. Every time I hit the little shit he would begin crying like a little girl. Because that's what you are, Aaron, a little girl who cries.'

'He wet his pants once, do you remember? Now, that *was* funny,' spoke one of Darryl's side-kicks, through his missing front teeth. 'What sort of man wets his pants?'

No one dared to step in and put a stop to this saga unfolding before their eyes. Plain and simply everyone was too scared to get involved. It was the kind of situation that bullies felt right at home with. Even Mr Askew was having second thoughts about doing the teacherly thing. It was only five years to early retirement. The last thing he needed right now was a broken jaw.

Darryl stared in disgust at Aaron. 'Look at you, such a wimp, yet again you can't do anything because you're too frozen with fear. It's pathetic.' He turned to Jeena. 'With your looks, darling, you could have sex with any man you wanted so why you choose a wimp like him, I'm fucked if I know. If you want a real man then I can oblige.' Darryl moved in and stretched out his arm to stroke Jeena's face.

'Touch her and I'll kill you,' Aaron spat, standing up and squaring right up to Darryl. He thought of Darryl's words, 'frozen with fear' and up until now it may have looked that way. Sitting there while abuse was being hurled his way. Keeping quiet when he was the butt of the joke. But the truth of the matter was this: everyone deserved the benefit of the doubt. For all Aaron knew, tonight Darryl Fletcher and his mob might have been man enough to apologize for their past behaviour. Surely they hadn't *all* grown up into older bullies. Unfortunately, the mob appeared to have got worse. Standing there with their tattoos and shaved heads, swigging their beers, sounding off expletives like there was no tomorrow and generally being tit-arse wankers. Aaron had hoped that this night would be as advertised: a Night of Reunion, but it now looked like it would end up a Night of Retribution. He repeated his threat to a dithering Darryl. 'I mean it, touch her and I'll kill you.' It was plainly obvious to all that if Aaron had once been a man frozen by Darryl then those days were truly over.

A smirk appeared on Darryl's face. 'At last, there is a man in there somewhere. Well, Mr Tough Guy, maybe I want to touch this woman. Maybe I want to see what a Paki feels like to touch, maybe I . . .'

Faster than a cowboy's whip Aaron's hand grabbed Darryl's wrist and twisted it backwards in such a way that Darryl literally fell to the floor in agony. A further kick under Darryl's legs had him face down on the ground with Aaron's knee in his back.

'Pardon, Darryl, I can't quite make out what you're saying,' spitefully Aaron cried in his ear.

'My arm, my fucking arm, you're breaking it, for fuck sake's, I was only joking.'

One more push and sure enough Darryl's arm would snap like a stale chocolate Matchstick. It was so tempting but something in Jeena's expression prevented

Aaron taking that extra step. Maybe in her eyes it would seem like he was the bully if he took things too far. Let's face it, there really was no contest here. He was an 8th-dan expert and Darryl was a first-class joke.

Aaron looked to Darryl's retreating side-kicks. His eyes begged them to join the party; there were presents enough for everyone. But, as expected, at the first sign of trouble, the bullies, now in fear of being hurt themselves, suddenly didn't want to play anymore. Their faces blended into the crowd and quickly disappeared from view.

'Loyal bunch of wankers, aren't they, Darryl?' Aaron dug his knee in harder. 'It makes you wonder whether they'll even bother turning up at your funeral, doesn't it? But not to worry, you know how much I like grave-yards, I'll make it a priority to pay your grave a visit every time I'm in the area and when I'm there I'll piss all over it.' He pulled Darryl's head up, watching his eyes dart from side to side, seeing the panic and fear that was once an everyday part of Aaron's school life. 'Next time you see me I suggest you walk the other way. No one likes a bully, Darryl, everyone here knows you are one and everyone here used to be scared of you. I bet that if I were to put a knife to your throat and ask if anyone here were to object if I cut it, I wouldn't get one person.'

'Yes you would,' Jeena said. 'Me. I wouldn't let you go to prison for a waste of space like him.'

The wrestling match was over and Aaron stepped away from Darryl's shamed face. He looked pitiful lying there in a heap. Even the snake tattoo that curled around his neck (the one that made his two children cry) seemed like it wanted to slide away and leave him alone. Aaron cast his gaze around the crowd of people raising his eyebrows as if to apologize for 'maybe' wrecking their evening. There was nothing left to do now. The reunion had been a success. He grabbed Jeena's hand and they made their way to the entrance.

After collecting their coats the elderly lady said, 'Oh, before you dash away, neither of you two have stolen anything, have you? Only I have to ask for security reasons.'

'Now you mention it, I did accidentally swipe the headmaster's secret stash of ganga plants,' Aaron replied. 'Don't tell him. It will be our secret.'

Outside in the car park, Aaron took a last look at his school. Some people had left that place with enough qualifications to wallpaper a small room. He, however, had left it with a nightmare, one which he'd confronted today. Finally, finally Aaron could finally put this behind him and move forward. FINALLY.

Already Jeena could feel a marked change in Aaron. His mood on the journey back from Northampton to Primpton could only be described as joyous. It was as if he'd been living in pain for years and finally FINALLY the doctor had cured it. Oh thank thee Doctor Violence for ridding Aaron of his fears and boyhood troubles. Oh thank thee Doctor Violence for giving Aaron the courage he needed today to finally, FINALLY see that he is not the boy he used to be and all this worry was in his mind after all.

After parking the car in the garage, Aaron and Jeena stood under the dark black sky in the Paper Lantern's car park and savoured the moment, enjoying a warm cuddle. Happiness comes in many varieties. Today it came as a couple madly in love with each other, knowing that from now on things could only get easier. Without thinking, almost a habit now, Jeena rubbed Aaron's wedding-ring finger to feel for his ring. It was the best feeling in the world knowing that he was hers (even though the ring was from Elizabeth Duke at Argos, although he'd promised to replace it at their Sikh wedding with a classy one).

'I'm dead proud of you, Aaron,' Jeena said, hugging him, looking over his shoulder. 'So much so that I think now would be the perfect time to extend our family. It would make our bond so much stronger if we could—'

Aaron snatched himself away. 'I'm not hearing this. First you force me into marrying you. Next you force me into falling in love with you. Then you force me into buying you an engagement ring, which, I might add, even the Queen couldn't fucking afford. And now you want to force me into becoming a father. There are limits, Jeena, and this is one of them. I am not interested in wasting my sperm on one of your eggs so that we can breed an offspring which will grow into a nappy-filling baby who will one day say, "I didn't ask to be born". NO WAY!'

Jeena pointed to where she was looking over his shoulder. There, balancing on a wall, was the cutest dark grey tabby cat she had ever seen. 'I was talking about getting a kitten, you moron.'

'What? And let it eat my fish, are you mad?' He noticed her face drop, then turned and stared to where she was pointing. There, balancing on the wall, was the cutest dark grey tabby cat he had ever seen, but now it was licking its arse. 'Okay, okay, we'll have a baby.'

'But, Aaron, I didn't even ask for a baby.'

'You'd rather a bum-licking moggy?'

She smiled at him. 'Can we just drop this, please?'

'I'd rather you drop something else,' he said, eyeing her dress. 'I've got a ton of testostcronc to use up.'

'How romantic!'